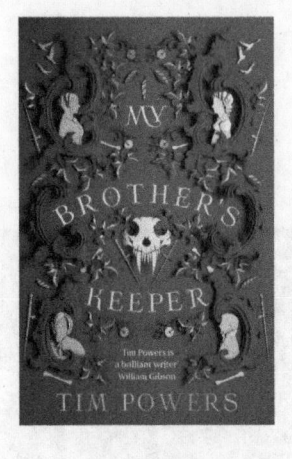

12 October 2023

229x148mm • 320 pages

HB • 9781035903900 • £20
XTPB • 9781035903917 • £15.99
E • 9781035903870

Publicity • Polly Grice
polly@headofzeus.com
+44 (0)20 3089 0379

Sales • sales@headofzeus.com

Howarth, 1846. The edge of the Yorkshire moors.

Here, in solitude, live a widowed parish priest and his family: three daughters and their single brother.

Though the future will celebrate the three daughters, right now they are unknown, their genius concealed. In just a few short years, they will all be dead.

And it will be middle daughter Emily's chance encounter with a grievously wounded man on the moor that sets them on the path to their doom.

My Brother's Keeper introduces an ancient secret haunting the moors, a dark inheritance in the family bloodline and something terrible buried under an ogham-inscribed slab in the church...

An atmospheric, claustrophobic gothic novel from a revered fantasy author... featuring... have you not guessed yet?

TIM POWERS is the author of seventeen science fiction and fantasy novels, including *The Anubis Gates*, *Declare*, and *On Stranger Tides*, which was the basis of the fourth 'Pirates of the Caribbean' movie. His work has won the World Fantasy Award, the Philip K. Dick Memorial award, and the Locus Poll award, and has been translated into more than a dozen languages. Along with K. W. Jeter and James Blaylock, Powers is considered one of the founders of Steampunk. He lives in San Bernardino with his wife of more than forty years, Serena.

'Tim Powers is a brilliant writer'
WILLIAM GIBSON

'Truly original'
FORBES

'Powers orchestrates reality and
fantasy so artfully that the reader
is not allowed a moment's doubt'
NEW YORKER

'Tim Powers is a master'
WIRED

'No one writes historical fantasy
quite like Tim Powers'
WASHINGTON POST

'One of the field's truly
distinctive voices'
LOCUS

MY BROTHER'S KEEPER

Tim Powers

An Ad Astra Book

First published in the US in 2023 by Baen Books
First published in the UK in 2023 by Head of Zeus,
part of Bloomsbury Publishing Plc

9 7 5 3 1 2 4 6 8

A catalogue record for this book is available from the British Library.

ISBN (HB): 9781035903900
ISBN (XTPB): 9781035903917
ISBN (E): 9781035903870

Printed and bound in Great Britain by
CPI Group (UK) Ltd, Croydon CR0 4YY

Head of Zeus
5–8 Hardwick Street
London EC1R 4RG

WWW.HEADOFZEUS.COM

MY BROTHER'S KEEPER

Books by
TIM POWERS

My Brother's Keeper

The Skies Discrowned
An Epitaph in Rust
The Drawing of the Dark
The Anubis Gates
Dinner at Deviant's Palace
On Stranger Tides
The Stress of Her Regard

Fault Lines Series
Last Call
Expiration Date
Earthquake Weather

Declare
Three Days to Never
Hide Me Among the Graves
Medusa's Web

Vickery and Castine Series
Alternate Routes
Forced Perspectives
Stolen Skies

Short Story Collections
Night Moves and Other Stories • *Strange Itineraries*
The Bible Repairman and Other Stories
Down and Out in Purgatory: The Collected Stories of Tim Powers

To my wife, Serena

And with thanks to Fr. Aloysius Aeschliman,
John Berlyne, Dave Butler, Joy Freeman, Russell Galen, Steve Malk,
Fr. Jerome Molokie, Eleanor Bourg Nicholson, Serena Powers,
Steve Roman, Joe Stefko, and Toni Weisskopf

What winter floods, what showers of spring
Have drenched the grass by night and day;
And yet, beneath, that spectre ring,
Unmoved and undiscovered lay

A mute remembrancer of crime,
Long lost, concealed, forgot for years,
It comes at last to cancel time,
And waken unavailing tears.

—Emily Brontë

PROLOGUE–1830

Come walk with me, come walk with me;
We were not once so few
But Death has stolen our company
As sunshine steals the dew . . .

—Emily Brontë

Halfway up the steep grassy slope, the three children sat down to rest. It was only midafternoon and the sky was clear, but their breaths were steam on the cold spring wind, and the two girls pulled their woolen coats more closely around their shoulders.

They were in shade now, for thirty feet farther up the slope stood the imposing stone edifice known as Ponden Kirk, its weathered, striated blocks looking like nothing so much as two stacks of gargantuan petrified books. Its top was level with the western plateau, and a few bare tree branches could be seen up there against the empty blue sky.

The boy tipped back his cap. "This is exactly how it was in my dream," he assured his sisters.

It had been a tiring three-mile hike from home across the low hills. They had followed sheep tracks and clambered over dry-stone walls and waded through broad fields of flowering heather and foxglove, and hopped from one flat stone to another across the rushing water of Dean Beck; and this rectangular crag had been a punctuation mark in the otherwise featureless horizon for the last mile.

The taller of the two girls took off her straw hat and pushed back her disordered dark hair. She squinted up at the twenty-foot stone monument.

"Do we climb it? We could have got round to the top from the north path, by the old foundations." Though only twelve years old, she had many times walked much farther than this across the moors, often alone.

Her brother Branwell, a year older, blinked at her. "Foundations?" His hair was carroty red, and random curls poked out from under his tweed cap. "You mean that old ruined farmhouse?"

"Closer than that—flat stones. They're broken up, hard to see among the grass unless you're right on top of them."

The younger sister giggled. "Emily imagines a Pictish temple out there."

Emily gave Anne a wry smile and shook her head. "They might be Roman foundations. Did the boy in your dream look like a Roman?"

"Maybe," said Branwell. "Like a gypsy, really. No, we won't climb it." He pointed at the base of the edifice on the north side. "Our destination is the fairy cave, in the bottom corner."

"I don't want to get married," Emily told him. According to local folklore, any girl who crawled out of the little cave through a narrow gap between the stones would marry within the year.

Anne just tugged the hem of her skirt over her boots and looked on, her eyes wide under her knitted wool tam.

"That doesn't work with children," said Branwell impatiently. "I doubt it works at all. No, that's—" He hesitated. "That's not what the dark boy was talking about."

For several seconds the wind whistling between the stones of Ponden Kirk was the only sound.

"In a dream," Emily said finally.

"What *he* said only happens in our stories," piped up Anne.

The three children, along with their older sister Charlotte, had for the last several years been making up stories about an imaginary country they called Glass Town, and frequently the plots required that one character or another be restored to life after being killed in an earlier adventure.

This afternoon's hike had had the flavor of an enacted scene from their stories; it was only now that they were here, under the shadow of this primordial monument, that Emily seriously considered the supposed purpose of their journey.

Two of their older sisters, Maria and Elizabeth, had died of tuberculosis five years earlier—Maria, who would have been the oldest of them all, at the age of eleven. Their mother had died three years before that, and their aunt had moved in to help their father with the feeding and clothing and instruction of the children ... but it had been Maria who became almost a second mother to the others, inventing games and cooking treats for them when they were sick and telling them stories when it was time for them all to go to bed. The surviving children had mourned Elizabeth, but it was Maria whose absence they still felt every day.

Emily carefully shifted around on the slope to look away from Ponden Kirk, down the wide valley that stretched away for miles between moorland hills streaked with green grass and purple heather. Distance and intervening hills made it impossible to see Haworth church, of which their father was the perpetual curate, and the adjoining parsonage, where Charlotte was no doubt reading to him from *Pilgrim's Progress* or *Paradise Lost*, since he was nearly blind with cataracts.

This morning the three girls been peeling apples at the parsonage kitchen table when Branwell had come clattering downstairs to tell his sisters that he had dreamt of meeting Maria at Ponden Kirk, and that Emily and Anne must accompany him there directly after their midday dinner.

Anne had glanced apprehensively at Charlotte, now the eldest, who had frowned at the heathen fantasy. *That's an unwholesome place*, she had said, *and Maria is a saint with God now.*

But Emily and Anne had finished their chores, and Branwell didn't have any to do, and Charlotte had of course known that even young Anne missed Maria as much as she did herself.

Very well, she had said finally. *You three go and have your game.*

And after their noon dinner of boiled beef and turnips and apple pudding, the three children had set off. It was only when they had walked over the first hill that Branwell told his two younger sisters the details of his dream. *There was a dark little boy*, he had said, *younger than you, Anne—he was at Ponden Kirk, and he said we might bring Maria back to life there.*

Emily stood up now and brushed off her dress. "What do we do?"

The children often enacted fanciful plays, though generally in the

parsonage parlor, and often got very carried away with the characters and the plots; and Emily was nearly certain that this was another of the same, performed outdoors for once. Certainly she didn't really expect some ritual here to let them see Maria again. She was pretty sure Anne looked at it in the same way.

She was undecided about Branwell.

He had already resumed climbing toward the foot of the monument, leaning forward to grip firmly seated stones while his scrabbling boots found purchase against woody clumps of old gorse. He looked back over his shoulder and gave a jerky nod. "In the dream," he called, "the three of us—"

"You saw us here?"

Anne got to her feet. "Not Charlotte?"

Branwell took a deep breath, then said loudly, "She wasn't in the dream. The dark boy showed me where..."

Emily quickly glanced along the plateau edge that loomed above them, from south to north, giving particular attention to the broad black topmost stones of Ponden Kirk; then she looked at the slope on either side, and back at the sunlit valley behind them, and she exhaled. Of course no *dark boy* from Branwell's dream would actually be here.

Anne hadn't moved. "Didn't he want her to come along?"

"She couldn't, she wasn't *there*." Branwell was now standing beside the bottom blocks of stone, panting. He waved impatiently to his sisters. "Shift yourselves!"

The two girls looked at each other, then simultaneously shrugged, spread their hands, and began carefully climbing up the slope to where their brother stood.

"Round the corner here," he said, and stepped out of sight behind a moss-streaked block, taller than he was, that made a crude pillar under a long horizontal lintel slab.

When the girls had got up to the base of the structure, they saw that Branwell had already crawled into the roughly square waist-high opening on that side; it led into a narrow cave perhaps six feet long, with gaps between the sharply angular stones of the floor and an opening onto daylight at the far end. He was sitting against a projecting shelf, his cap brushing the low overhead stone, and he shifted to make room for his sisters.

"Come on, then," he said, his voice sounding metallic in the constricted space. "Here's where we do it."

Emily tossed her hat aside and hiked herself in, and edged forward on her hands and knees. The rough stone surfaces under her palms were damp and cold, and the breeze from the valley below sluiced the tiny cave with the smells of earth and heather.

Branwell contorted to get his hand into his trouser pocket, and pulled out his penknife and opened the short blade.

"That won't incise stone," Emily said.

"It's to incise us," he said. He made a fist with his left hand and carefully drew the edge of the blade across an old scar on his wrist. "There," he said, pointing with the knife at a smooth surface of stone in front of him; and he slid the back of his hand across it, leaving a streak of blood.

He swayed, then held the knife out to Emily. He cleared his throat. "Right next to mine," he told her.

She was looking at his now blood-streaked hand and recalling that the scar was from the bite of a strangely malformed dog that they had all supposed to be mad, though the bite had healed quickly and with no aftereffects.

Emily slowly reached across and took the knife.

She looked at the damp rock with Branwell's blood on it—then shook her head. "And you should pray you don't catch a pestilential distemper." She had borrowed a copy of Richard Bradley's *The Plague at Marseilles Consider'd* from their neighbors at Ponden House, and had been impressed with the notion that microscopic poisonous insects transmit diseases.

Branwell shrugged. "Just as you please. My hand will heal. And Maria can recede again into oblivion."

"She's in Heaven," said Anne, who had crawled into the cave beside Emily.

"And might have visited with us," said Branwell.

Emily exhaled through pursed lips, then quickly cut the tip of her left forefinger. She rubbed it across the stone beside the faint streak of Branwell's blood—and leaned against the rock at her back, momentarily dizzy.

Branwell said, "That's two," and Anne took the knife from Emily's hand.

"No, Anne, wait—" began Emily, but Anne had already cut her finger. Emily caught her wrist and said, "Don't touch the stone."

"You did." Anne brushed the tip of the cut finger with the thumb of her other hand and pressed it against the stone.

A cloud might have passed overhead, for the light dimmed briefly.

"Ah!" said Anne softly. Emily squeezed her wrist and shook it before she let go.

"And that's three," said Branwell.

Anne sat back, sucking her finger, and after several seconds she said, "This wasn't all a game, was it? And it never had anything to do with Maria." She looked past Emily at Branwell. "Did you know? Or did that dark boy in your dream lie to you about it? That," she went on in a wondering tone, "is why Charlotte wasn't in your dream—why she isn't here. She wasn't *there*."

Emily felt as though all the warmth had drained from her body, leaving her as cold as this cave. Until Anne spoke, she had thought that the memory, which had surfaced when she touched the stone, had been a stray association of her own.

"Yes," she said, "it was the three of us then." Turning to Anne, she added, "I'm surprised you remember. You were only four."

Six years ago, just a few months before Maria's death, Branwell and Emily and Anne had gone for an afternoon walk on the moors with the parsonage housekeeper, Tabby. A mile northwest of where they now sat, a sudden gusty rainstorm had sent the four of them running for the nearest shelter from the wind, an abandoned and roofless stone farmhouse. From the doorway they had watched the curtains of rain sweep heavily across the suddenly shadowed moors...and then the hill from which they had descended only minutes before had exploded.

With a boom that shook the dirt floor under them, the side of Crow Hill had erupted in a spray of flying chunks of earth and even spinning boulders, and half the hillside had broken up and slid away in a torrential flood down into the valley; the earth had rumbled for a full minute as water continued to cascade through the new channel.

✴ ✴ ✴

Branwell took the knife back from Anne and closed it. None of them stirred to see if Maria might have appeared outside, on the slope or the plateau.

Branwell was blinking in the streaks of daylight as if disoriented. "So it was just a dream," he said gruffly. "A fantasy—we all miss her."

"No," said Emily. She stared at her brother. "You knew this would be some kind of... continuation of that afternoon in the storm, the eruption on Crow Hill. On the climb up here, when Anne asked you why Charlotte didn't come with us today, you said she couldn't, she wasn't *there.*" She cocked her head, and her eyes were narrowed as she smiled at him. "Do we have some pestilential distemper now? Who was your dark boy?"

"Out," said Branwell. "It was a game, an adventure in Glass Town."

Anne slid her legs out of the opening and then carefully lowered herself onto the steep slope. Emily followed and retrieved her hat, and when Branwell joined them they began picking their way down toward the path at the bottom of the valley.

"Best not to bother Papa with any of this," said Anne breathlessly.

Previous curates at Haworth church had warned the congregation of devils that still roamed these remote northern hills, and the children's father often emphasized the same spiritual peril in his sermons. Too, he was more superstitious than seemed quite right in a clergyman, and took all sorts of eccentric precautions at the parsonage.

"No," agreed Emily. "Why worry him—" She couldn't, with any conviction, add the word *needlessly.*

When the three children had hiked back across the moors and marshes in the waning daylight to the parsonage, they told their older sister Charlotte about crawling into the fairy cave in Ponden Kirk, and the knife, and the blood on the stone. Branwell did his best to dismiss it all as a game inspired by a meaningless dream, but Charlotte seemed uneasy at having given them permission to go, and emphasized Anne's advice that they not trouble their ailing father with it.

Oddly, for the four children were closely united in their losses and their shared stories and their preferred isolation from most of the people in their small Yorkshire village, it was to be many years before any of them would speak again of that day.

PART ONE: MARCH 1846

"But where did he come from, the little dark thing,
harbored by a good man to his bane?"
—Emily Brontë, *Wuthering Heights*,
chapter XXXIV

CHAPTER ONE

On the spring morning when she found the wounded man below Ponden Kirk, Emily Brontë was thinking of that afternoon, long ago now, when she and Branwell and Anne had climbed up there and left blood in the narrow fairy cave.

In the ensuing years the four Brontë siblings had sometimes been separated, when one or another of them was at school or employed, but those periods had been brief, and now they were all again living at the parsonage with their elderly near-blind father. Four years ago Emily had spent ten months with Charlotte at a school for young ladies in Brussels, but she had come home when their aunt died, and now at the age of twenty-seven Emily had no intention of ever again leaving the village of Haworth and the parsonage and her lonely, beloved Yorkshire moors.

Anne and Charlotte had both held positions as governesses of children in affluent families, but had eventually been dismissed— little Anne because she had tied her unruly charges to a table leg so that she could get her work done.

For a long time they had all hoped that Branwell would achieve success as a portrait painter, but those hopes had proved vain.

He had always shown some innate skill at drawing and painting— among other projects, he had done a portrait in oils of himself and his three sisters that had effectively caught their likenesses, though his own face in it wasn't recognizable—and it had been decided that he would apply for professional instruction at the Royal Academy of Arts in London.

And so in the early autumn of his eighteenth year he had set off on the first part of the two-day, two-hundred-mile journey, carrying cash and letters of introduction . . . but a week later he had come back home to Haworth, penniless and claiming to have been robbed by "sharpers" before he had even got to the metropolis. He had been evasive about details, and Emily had come to suspect that he *had* got to London, and done something there that he was ashamed of, though she knew better than to try asking him about it.

He had tried various employments to support himself after that. He had been a tutor briefly six years ago, but had been let go because of drunkenness, and then he had worked at the new railway station in Halifax, but lost the job when the entries in his account books proved to consist mostly of poetry and drawings.

Branwell and Charlotte had always been close, even through these temporary separations. They had for a while collaborated on stories set in their fictional land of Angria, and they had signed their work UT or WT, for *Us Two* or *We Two*.

But last year he had been abruptly dismissed from a position in Thorpe Green, twenty miles northeast of Haworth, and had come home in disgrace. He had been employed by a Mr. and Mrs. Robinson as tutor to their young son, but had, he claimed, fallen in love with his employer's wife, and been driven from the house by Mr. Robinson. In the nine months since then, he had simply devoted himself to strong drink, and these days Charlotte could hardly bear the sight of him.

Privately, Emily wondered about the exact circumstances of his termination—Mr. Robinson's angry dismissal letter had threatened to "expose" some unspecified action of Branwell's, implying something more heinous, much more ungodly, than simply making advances to a married woman.

Casting about for some way to make money without the ordeal of leaving home, the three sisters had spent thirty-one pounds to have a thousand copies of a book of their poetry printed, pseudonymously, as *Poems by Currer, Ellis, and Acton Bell*. The book was scheduled to be published two months from now. And though as a boy Branwell had joined them in writing their verses and stories, they had kept him ignorant of this new literary effort—which was not difficult, since lately he slept till noon and spent his evenings at the Black Bull,

an inn that sat a hundred yards downhill from the parsonage front door, just past the Haworth churchyard. It was a short walk, but he often needed help getting back home.

On most days, in any weather, Emily left the parsonage to go for sometimes daylong walks, always with her dog, a big bullmastiff named Keeper; but she nearly never ventured down to the village. She walked west, away from the church and the parsonage and the churchyard, out across the moors; and today she had followed familiar ways along paths and across wind-scoured hills to Ponden Kirk.

She had often wondered what she and Anne and Branwell had actually done on that day sixteen years ago when they had left streaks of their blood there. Twice in the years since then, both times just at sunset when she'd been hurrying home to the parsonage, she had glimpsed what appeared to be a little boy standing at the top of Ponden Kirk; both times she had paused to peer more closely, and both times the shape had proved to be a momentary illusion, for it had fragmented and dispersed as a flock of crows.

Shortly after dawn on this bright, sunny day, she had as usual been awakened by the pistol shot that her father fired over the churchyard every morning. A glance at the window had shown her that it was a day to be outdoors, and she had put on a long wool dress and hurried downstairs.

She had put on her boots shortly after making oatmeal porridge for herself and her sisters, and promising Tabby that she would wash the pot and dishes when she got back. Sometimes the wind that shook the parsonage windows seemed to carry the strains of a wild, remote music—repetitive and atonal, as if older than humanity's ordered keys and scales—and as Emily hastily put on a coat and stepped outside she had felt that today she could almost dance to it. Keeper was trotting right beside her as she crossed the yard to the wall-bordered road, raising his great head and sniffing energetically, as if he too found something exciting in the wind.

The two of them had hurried along the road and soon left it to follow a curving sheep path. Only a few weeks ago these moors had been white with snow, and the black lines of stone walls had made broad geometric figures across the far-off hills, but this morning the path curled between acres of waving green grass. Emily's dress

billowed behind her and her loose chestnut hair was tossed back over her shoulders. She was the tallest of her family, with a rangy, athletic figure, her plain, strong face tanned by endless days spent outdoors.

They were soon out of sight of the parsonage, and from habit Emily watched the hilltops, and called cautions to hares bounding where hawks might see them beside the rushing waters of Sladen Beck, and walked wide around the ancient standing stone known, for no remembered reason, as Boggarts Green. When they had hiked a couple of miles across the hills, the wind had shifted to the north, and was colder. Keeper had paused on a wet stone halfway across the rushing water of a creek where the wind was turbulent between the hills, and cocked his head and snarled.

It was a sound he sometimes made when the two of them had stayed out past dark, and at those times Emily had thought of boggarts and gytrashes and barguests, the legendary devils that, according to local folklore, roamed the moorland hills and dales at night; though right now the rippling heather at the crests of the hills shone pale purple in morning sunlight.

But she trusted the dog, and when the path on the far side of the creek mounted to an elevation higher than most, she glanced around at the uneven horizon behind her and the long rising ground ahead, and she could make out a figure at the foot of the ascent to Ponden Kirk, apparently crawling on all fours in the bracken. It was too clumsy to be an animal.

She clicked her tongue to tell Keeper to stay by her and not go running ahead, and she carefully picked her way around projecting stones down to the valley floor. The figure wasn't visible now among the lowland marsh ferns, and it wasn't until she was only a dozen yards away that she got a good look at the wounded man.

He was slowly and laboriously crawling south, moving left across Emily's view. The visible sleeve of his broadcloth coat was torn free at the shoulder, and the left leg of his woolen trousers was dark with blotted blood. Any hat he might have had was gone, but his face was hidden down to the jawline by a mane of disordered black hair.

Keeper snarled again, and the man rocked over onto his right side, facing Emily and the dog. With his free left hand he pried a knife from his bloodstained right fist and raised it. Emily noticed that it had two narrow blades, in parallel.

Keeper tensed his massive shoulders and hindquarters for a lunge, but Emily had already clicked her tongue again to keep him still; he froze, quivering.

Emily frowned and bit her lip, staring at the man. He was probably taller than she was, solidly built, and his now-visible face was swarthy—he might be Welsh, if not a Spaniard or a Portuguese. She guessed that a black cloth disk on a ribbon across his lined cheek was a displaced eyepatch, though in fact both of his brown eyes were glaring at her. There were streaks of bright blood on the blades of the knife.

Keeper stood rigid, the fur on his neck bristling.

Emily looked around again, but saw no sign of who or what might have attacked the man; there might be murderers up on the plateau, but she had Keeper.

"How badly are you hurt?" she asked. "You need a doctor."

"I need," the man said through gritted teeth, "to get out of view." His voice was a deep rumble, and his accent wasn't local; it sounded vaguely French to her. He dragged his left leg up and pressed his right palm against the dirt. "I can stand—I can walk."

Emily had often rescued injured birds that she found on the moors, even hawks; she certainly couldn't leave a man in this state.

"You can't walk," she said. "Put away the knife."

He exhaled. "Is there anyone visible on the Kirk?"

Emily quickly looked up at the massive black stone edifice, and left and right along the edge of the plateau. The empty blue sky made every detail of rock and tree branch along the edge starkly visible, and there was no spot of animation.

"No," she said; and she recalled, not for the first time, that the word *kirk* was commonly used in Scotland to mean *church*, and it had been used the same way here in northern England, long ago. The black monument did appear to be a construction, not a natural stone outcrop—a church to what sort of god?

"You were attacked?" she asked. She got no answer.

He raised himself back up on his straightened right arm and one knee, and was struggling to get his other leg under himself. Sweat gleamed on his knotted face.

His arm folded and he fell back onto his right shoulder.

Panting harshly, he extended his left hand to the side, palm up;

and after a few seconds Emily stepped forward and took the knife. Its leather-wrapped grip was sticky with blood, and she just dropped it on the ground.

To Emily's surprise, Keeper turned away from her and the wounded man to growl and bare his teeth at the knife.

The man had got up in a swaying crouch; Emily raised a restraining hand to Keeper, then crouched beside the man's left side and slid her right arm under his. "Get out of view how quickly?"

"Ah—quickly."

She gripped his side and draped his left arm over her shoulders; then she took a deep breath and straightened her legs. He was heavy, but she was able to stand, holding him up.

He pressed his boots against the ground, taking some of his weight off her, and the two of them began hitching their way forward. Keeper padded close beside the man, growling deep in his throat and, every few steps, turning his head to glance back.

"Assist with your feet," Emily said breathlessly, "all you can. There's a—" She tossed her head to get her windblown hair out of her eyes. "There's a beck among rocks down to our right."

He took a deep breath and pronounced, "A beck."

"A stream. Water. Place your feet and flex your legs! I can bathe your wounds—perhaps bandage them—and get help." The narrow stream lay a couple of hundred feet downhill, and she wished she could just roll him to it.

"I'll—have no help," he said.

"Obviously."

He was walking, slowly and haltingly, though it seemed that she still bore most of his considerable weight.

"Aside from yours," he conceded, "until we reach your beck." He inhaled sharply between his teeth and halted, his eyes clenched shut, then resolutely lurched forward another step. "And then you—go back to your sheep. I won't—" He blinked sweat out of his eyes and peered blearily ahead. "I won't be here if you come back."

Emily had the breath to say, "We shall see." She was sweating herself now, in her long wool dress and coat, in spite of the chilly wind that tossed her damp hair.

In a few minutes they reached the bank of the narrow creek bed. Several great granite stones stood up at angles among the luxuriant

reeds that grew along the edge, and Emily followed Keeper between two of them and carefully lowered herself and her burden until they were both sitting on the grassy bank. Only a few feet below them, clear water rushed over gravel and trailing weeds. The creek was narrow enough that Emily could have jumped over it.

She freed herself from under his arm, and stood up and stretched. Keeper nudged her thigh with his great jowly head, crowding her back as if to say that their task here was finished.

Emily patted the dog's head. To the wounded stranger, she said, "Can you slide down?"

He gripped the bank with both hands and pushed backward, and slid down until his boots were in the stream.

The abrupt movement made him arch his back and pound one fist into the mud; he relaxed slowly.

"There," he said, panting. "Now go home, girl."

She certainly didn't want to establish an acquaintance with him, but she wasn't going to leave him yet—and *girl* wouldn't do. Recalling that he had taken her for a rural shepherdess, she just gave him, "Emily."

She stepped down beside him on his left while Keeper scrambled down and stood watchfully at his right. For a moment she stood on tiptoe to scan the nearby sunlit hills and the rim of the plateau; no motion was visible, so she crouched beside the wounded man.

He seemed alarmed that she had not left him. He pulled the eyepatch back into place over his left eye, though he could obviously see well enough out of it, and said, "Right—Alcuin, yes? Be on your way now, will you?" When she cocked her head he added, "It's a name, my name."

"How do you do." She began unbuttoning his coat, and when he tried to prevent her she pushed his bloodstained hand away. "I know who Alcuin was. Advisor to Charlemagne."

The man was breathing more normally now, and he turned his head to see her with his right eye, looking closely at her for the first time.

"Yes." Reluctantly, for he clearly wished she would go away, he asked, "Are you Irish? Your vowels aren't all that far from County Down."

Emily had now begun unbuttoning his blood-sodden waistcoat,

and she could already see a broad gash in his side through the torn fabric. At least it wasn't bleeding energetically. "Top Withens is a mile south of here," she said. Seeing his baffled look, she explained, "That's a farmhouse. I'll get Mr. Sunderland and his sons to carry you there. You'll need a doctor to prevent this from mortifying, and to do some stitching up."

"I heal fast."

"Not from something like this." He really didn't seem to be in immediate danger of dying, and she gave him a curious frown. "Though I'd judge your eye, at least, is well enough that you could get rid of the patch."

"It's a—formality."

She had spread his unbuttoned coat to see if he had other wounds, and he caught her hand. Keeper's big front paws were instantly on his chest, and Emily could feel the vibration of the dog's growl through Alcuin's hand.

He released her hand and slowly lowered his own, blinking up at Keeper's teeth. When the dog stepped back, he turned his head toward Emily and said, "That scar on your hand—a burn?"

She nodded. "On an iron."

"As for ironing shirts?" He peered again at the irregular white scar on her knuckles. "You must have leaned on it."

"I must have."

His face and hands showed scratches, but the gash in his side seemed to be his only serious injury. She unfastened the last buttons of his waistcoat to get a better look at the wound, but the blood-soaked tatters of his shirt prevented a clear view. This time he didn't risk pushing her hand away but groaned, "Oh, let it be, damn you!"

She ignored the profanity; but clearly he would accept no help from her, and in any case his wound would need more expert attention than she could provide. She stood up and brushed dirt and fern fragments off her dress. "I'll be back with the Sunderlands."

He grimaced and shook his head. "I suppose I must beg your pardon . . . Miss Emily! But—" He sat up experimentally. "*Ah!* Save your trouble—I won't be here." He winced and grabbed his side, but didn't lie back down. "Irish?"

"My father is." She stepped up the bank, closely followed by Keeper. "He came over forty years ago."

"Forty . . . wait." Alcuin turned to look up at her, evidently careless of his wound. "The scar on your hand—would your father's name be Brunty?" In fact her family name was Brontë, and she was startled at the near-accuracy of his guess, but kept her face expressionless. He went on, "Is he aware of Welsh?" Still getting no response, he slumped back down. "No, never mind, child. You wouldn't be here. Run along to your sheep."

For a moment Emily was on the point of asking this Alcuin person whether he actually knew something about her family, and what he meant by *Is he aware of Welsh*—but that would lead to questions and answers: to some unpredictable and certainly unwelcome degree of intimacy with this stranger.

"We may be well over an hour," she said. "Press your hands on the wound to slow the bleeding."

His eyes were closed, but he waved at her. "It's stopped bleeding. Go *away*, for God's sake."

Emily stepped up onto the level ground and scanned the horizons. The bleak landscape still showed no motion except for the heather shaking in waves along the hillsides in the cold wind, and with Keeper at her heels she began walking south with a ground-covering stride.

For twenty minutes she and the dog hurried south, following a path along the east slope of the Middlemoor Clough, and when the path ascended to the highland and eventually to the base of the hill at the crest of which sat Top Withens farmhouse, she paused and looked back across the miles of tan-and-green hills. Ponden Kirk wasn't visible from here.

Keeper had loped on ahead, and now came trotting back and licked her hand encouragingly.

"A moment, boy," she told him. She raised her hand and looked at the scar on the back of it. Anyone could guess that it was from a burn—but were the old tooth punctures perceptible too?

One twilight seven years ago a strange dog had got into a fight with Keeper in the churchyard out in front of the parsonage; the animal had resembled *Dogues de Bordeau* she had later seen in Brussels—a muscular, short-snouted mahogany mastiff—but with a bigger head, and longer legs and toes. In fact it had resembled the dog that had bitten Branwell fourteen years before that.

She bared her teeth now, remembering how she had broken up that fight between Keeper and the other dog. Armed only with a hastily-snatched-up pepper pot, Emily had abandoned her ironing and run down the front steps of the parsonage and vaulted the low churchyard wall, and she had dashed the black powder into the strange mastiff's face. The creature had retreated, and galloped off across the moors, but not before clamping its jaws on the back of Emily's hand. She had hurried back to the kitchen, where she washed the wound; and then she had picked up the iron, filled with live coals, and pressed it against the wound for five agonizing seconds.

Remembering it now, she flexed her hand; then looked more closely. She spat on her thumb and bent to rub off a spot of Alcuin's dried blood on a clump of grass.

"Do you think he's dying?" she asked Keeper. "He didn't think he was."

She straightened and looked at both sides of her hand to be sure no spot of his blood remained; then started up the hill toward Top Withens.

When she led Mr. Sunderland and two of his sons to the beck below the standing stones, Alcuin was gone, as he had told her he would be—though traces of blood on the grass and the prints of his boots bore out Emily's story. Mr. Sunderland invited her to have midday dinner with his family, but they were all virtually strangers to her, and she dreaded the thought of sitting among them while they tried to engage her in social conversation. It had been a fair ordeal even to approach their gate.

She declined the invitation with reserved politeness, and declined too the subsequent offer that one of Sunderland's sons should escort her back home.

She and Keeper retraced their long route back to Ponden Kirk, and then across the well-known trails and fields and becks that would take them back at last to the parsonage—though on the way she did stop at the spot where she had first seen Alcuin, and, in spite of Keeper's evident disapproval, retrieved his peculiar knife.

CHAPTER TWO

Back at the parsonage, Emily found that Anne had saved a plate of mutton, mashed potatoes, and preserved cucumbers for her, and the mutton bone for Keeper.

Branwell had looked up from an issue of *Blackwood's Magazine* when Emily came into the kitchen after hanging up her coat, and the chaotic state of his red hair and skimpy chin-beard showed that he had got out of bed only recently.

It was a new issue of the magazine. *Blackwood's* editors consistently ignored Branwell's letters offering to write articles— which he assured them would far outshine the ones they published—but he still read every issue that the family borrowed from their father's sexton, and he probably still hoped to be featured in the magazine's pages one day as a great writer . . . or painter . . . or perhaps politician.

Charlotte stepped in from the hall holding a dress she'd been stitching.

"Papa was asking where you'd got to."

Branwell peered at Emily through his little round spectacles. "Are you in trouble? Have you been drying clothes on the gravestones again?"

Emily sat down across the table from him. He would doubtless spend the afternoon slouching around the house in an irritable daze, and at dusk walk down to the Black Bull. She gave her sisters a wide-eyed look that promised more later, and for now just said to Charlotte, "West and then east again."

Charlotte nodded, then snapped at Branwell, "We've found your coat out there on more than a few mornings."

Anne caught Emily's eye and touched her own wrist. Emily looked down and saw a spot of blood on her sleeve. Quickly she folded the cuff under.

Branwell blinked at Charlotte. "On these cold nights," he drawled, "I sometimes leave my coat there in case some poor ghost might need it."

Tabby the housekeeper had bustled in from the yard in time to hear him, and snorted derisively. "Careful they don't want your trousers too."

Emily made quick work of her late dinner and stood up; and Alcuin's knife tumbled out of the pocket of her dress and clinked on the stone floor.

Branwell leaned over and picked it up. The twin blades, at least, were clean, for Emily had plunged it into the ground several times to get the traces of blood off before pocketing it. The leather grip had already been dry when she had picked it up.

"I found that," she said.

"This hasn't been out in the weather," Branwell noted. His hand trembled as he brushed his thumb across the tips of the blades—but his shakiness wasn't unusual. He cleared his throat. "I think I saw one like it in London."

"In London?" said Emily, intrigued by this careless admission that he had, after all, traveled to London eleven years ago, and not been halted on the way by a robbery. "Where in London?"

Branwell glanced around quickly, then laid the knife down on the table. "I don't recall."

None of the others had apparently noticed his slip. Charlotte muttered something to the effect that most things eluded her brother's memory these days.

"It was just . . . lying on a path," Emily said. "Is Papa in his study?"

Anne nodded, her eyebrows raised in obvious anticipation of hearing how Emily had got blood on her blouse, and how she had actually come across the knife. Emily picked it up as she pushed her chair back and got to her feet.

Her father's study was down the entry hall, and she rapped on the door and then opened it and stepped in.

Old Patrick Brontë was seated at his desk with a bright oil lamp at his elbow, squinting and tilting his head as he peered through a magnifying glass at his sermons notebook. His chin was buried in the many layers of the yards-long silk cravat that he wrapped around and around his neck every morning—always clockwise from Christmas to midsummer, and then counterclockwise till Christmas Eve.

When he looked up over his nearly useless spectacles, she said, "I found a wounded man on the moors this morning, by Ponden Kirk."

"Oh?" Her father frowned and laid his notebook aside. "Badly wounded?"

"I thought so, at the time. There was a serious-looking gash in his side," she said; and added with a shrug, "which didn't stop him walking off while I was fetching the Sunderlands. I talked to him, a bit, and he seemed to know our name, though he pronounced it *Brunty*."

Her father's mouth opened, but he didn't speak; so Emily continued, "He asked—I don't know what he meant—if you were aware of Welsh." Still her father simply stared at her, in evident dawning alarm. Quickly she added, "Perhaps he simply wanted to know if you spoke the language. He *looked* Welsh, actually—dark."

Her father gripped the corners of his desk and scuffed his shoes on the carpet, as if to stand up—or, it occurred to Emily, as if to reassure himself of the solidity of his room, his house.

"He was rude," she said, to break the silence. "Abrupt, at least." She rocked her head. "Understandable, I suppose."

"By Ponden Kirk, you said."

"At the bottom of the slope below it."

"Close the door." She passed in front of the window, and he said, "You're carrying something."

The door's hinges were silent, but at the click of the latch he leaned back in his chair. Emily walked to the desk and laid the knife on the blotter. "He dropped this. It's a knife. There was blood on it."

He groped for it, and slowly slid his fingers along the length of it from the pommel to the paired blades, not touching the tips, and lifted his hand away. He stood up and walked across to the window, which overlooked the churchyard.

Facing the glass, he asked, "Did he—have both of his eyes?"

Emily was startled by the question. "Yes. But he wore an eyepatch anyway. He called it a formality. You know about this?"

"What else did he say?"

"He decided he was wrong in his guess at our name, because, he said, I wouldn't be here if he'd been right."

Old Patrick turned to face her, his white hair backlit in the afternoon sunlight. "I expect Branwell will be going to the Black Bull this evening. When he's gone, I will—it seems!—have some things to tell you and Charlotte and Anne. But for now," he said softly as he returned to his chair, "bide you girls in the parlor or the kitchen, and," he added with a sigh and an unhappy smile, "leave the world to darkness and to me."

Emily recognized the line from Thomas Gray's "Elegy in a Country Churchyard." The remembered view from the window was probably what had prompted it, but as she opened the door and stepped out into the entry hall, she was a good deal more apprehensive than she had been when she'd gone in.

As she walked back toward the kitchen, she took a deep breath and let it out, and she raised her eyebrows to smooth any furrow between them.

Branwell's eyes were still on the pages of *Blackwood's*, but in his mind was the image of that double-bladed knife.

It was in a church sacristy, he thought, ten years ago, that I saw a knife like that, Emily.

But why would one like it be found on these moors? And whose blood is that on your sleeve, Emily?

When she walked back into the kitchen, she wasn't carrying the knife, and in spite of her expressionless face Branwell recognized alarm in her tense, empty hands and the set of her shoulders. Of course Anne and Charlotte could see it too—but none of his sisters talked about important things with him anymore.

He stood up and stepped past Emily into the hall—embarrassed that he had to brace himself against the doorframe—and hurried past his father's study to the front door. When he pulled it open he flinched at the cold outside air that buffeted his face and found its way down his collar, but he couldn't go back now to get a coat. He tucked his hands in his trouser pockets and hurried down the steps

to the paved walk. He crossed Emily and Anne's sparse garden to the low churchyard wall and swung one leg and then the other over it.

The view of the churchyard made him aware of the almost constant sound of hammer on chisel from John Brown's stonecutting yard, where the sexton seemed always to be cutting letters and numbers into fresh gravestones.

Branwell let his melancholy gaze play over the old gravestones in front of him. Interspersed among the standing markers, many of the graves were covered with raised, rectangular slabs laid flat, and he kicked through drifts of last year's fallen leaves and sat down on one of the farthest of the cold, table-like markers.

He looked at the palm of his trembling right hand and thought, Can my perverse baptism have followed me here from London?

When he had set out on that two-day trip to London he had been eighteen, and his mind had been alight with fantasies: of astonishing the instructors at the Royal Academy of Arts with his portfolio of drawings, immediately getting commissions to paint portraits of lords and admirals, and very soon living as splendid a life as "Northangerland," his fictional alter ego in the stories he had then still been writing with Charlotte.

But by the time the coach had got as far as Bradford, the fantasies had begun to seem like mirages. Even the ordinary men waiting for the London coach at the White Swan Hotel had been too clearly engaged with the *real* world—purposeful and responsible and competent—for Branwell to imagine the contrived figure of Northangerland among them.

And, the next day, the gross reality of big London had dwarfed him: the immensity of St. Paul's Cathedral on Ludgate Hill; the imposing Neoclassical Somerset House, where in fact the Academy Schools were located; the endless broad boulevards crowded with noisy cabs and carriages and busy pedestrians.

He'd had letters of introduction to a number of influential painters and the secretary of the Royal Academy—and he had approached none of them. His father and aunt and several family friends had managed to come up with money for his first month of food and lodging and books—and in three days he had spent virtually all of it on rum and roast beef and cigars at the Castle Tavern in High Holborn.

The Castle Tavern had proven to be a warm, sociable refuge. It was licensed to a onetime champion pugilist, and its patrons were a mix of journalists, boxing enthusiasts, and visitors from the country like himself. And in this undemanding company he had been able to shine.

He was a charming and witty addition to any group of drinkers, always ready with a joke or an apposite literary quote, and from his wide reading he could talk intelligently about any subject, from history to sports to politics. Among several anecdotes on the wilds of Yorkshire, he told the story of how he had been bitten by a malformed and apparently rabid dog ten years earlier. He noted that he had suffered no ill effects from it; though he didn't mention the month of nightmares that had followed.

The story caught the attention of one well-dressed man who had been watching him from across the room, and who had hurried out when the story was finished.

Before closing time the man returned, in the company of a fair-haired, youthful-looking clergyman in a black cassock and clerical collar; and after pointing out Branwell, the man quickly left the premises.

The clergyman joined the group of Branwell's new friends, and asked him for more details about his life in Yorkshire; and he soon separated Branwell from the crowd beside the bar and led him to a corner table.

He introduced himself as Reverend Farfleece, and Branwell, drunkenly cautious, had used the name Northangerland.

Farfleece had wanted to know all about the peculiar dog that had bitten Branwell. He asked about aftereffects, infection ... disturbing dreams? ... and smiled at Branwell's awkward insistence that there hadn't been any.

You were marked, that day, Farfleece had told him, *by an inhuman power.*

Branwell had tried to shift the conversation to another topic, but Farfleece's next question was, *Have you seen the dark boy by Ponden Kirk?*

It had taken Branwell several seconds to answer: *In dreams.* Mentally he had added, And once in the churchyard, barefoot in the snow.

Farfleece had sat back. *You're a kinsman, Mr. Northangerland. Will you have power over men, be feared by them? Come with me and be baptized.*

I've been baptized.

Not to this lord. Come.

If the conversation had not so perfectly fitted in with his forlorn, melodramatic fantasies about Northangerland in the imaginary land of Angria—anger upon anger!—Branwell might have bidden the man good night.

Farfleece had a hired carriage waiting on the street, and Branwell had obediently followed him out and got into it. The cold night air somewhat dispelled the drink fumes in his head, and he assured himself that he had not yet committed himself to anything.

Their destination had been only ten minutes away—a narrow, apparently abandoned *faux* gothic church in St. Andrew Street. After dismissing the carriage, Farfleece had led Branwell through a broken wrought-iron gate and around the side of the building, in deep shadow, to the sacristy door. Branwell had been increasingly uneasy during the carriage ride, and had now been on the verge of running back out to the street in search of a cab—but after Farfleece knocked on the door, it had been opened by a dark-haired young woman wearing a white silk robe and carrying a lantern; she smiled at Branwell and stepped aside, and he found himself following the young clergyman into a high-ceilinged room. The scent of mimosa mingled with the smells of lamp oil and old wood.

The woman's lantern was the only light, and she set it down on a long table that stretched away into shadows. At least a dozen chairs stood alongside the table, and it took Branwell several seconds of peering to see that they were all unoccupied. Bookshelves lined one wall, and ornately framed, age-darkened paintings were hung edge-to-edge on the opposite wall. Altogether the room appeared to be in use, in spite of the church's neglected exterior, but he could still see the steam of his breath.

The woman drew a curious knife from within the folds of her robe, and Branwell took a step back toward the door, where Farfleece was standing; but she just laid it on the table beside a little unlidded glass jar. Branwell noted that the knife had two narrow, parallel blades, with an inch gap between them, and that the grip was just scored steel.

She sat down in one of the chairs and waved at the one next to it; and after a few seconds Branwell shuffled over and lowered himself into the indicated chair.

Farfleece moved to the other side of the table and spoke guardedly of his religious order, which he called the Obliques. He spoke of a "biune" god, which Branwell took to mean a god in two persons, as the Christian Trinity was described as "triune." Farfleece said that the two persons of this god were presently separated, and it was the long-standing goal of his order to reunite them and bring all of England under the restored god's power; though Branwell got the idea that this was not something Farfleece expected—or even wanted, really—to happen soon.

In the meantime the order's mission was to support certain "extra-natural saints" in northern England and parts of Europe, who together constituted something "comparable to the electrical battery of the American Benjamin Franklin." The "aggressive missionary activities" of these saints generated an influence, or field, or spiritual shadow, within which members of the Oblique order could extend their lifetimes and even perform certain sorts of miracles.

You have been chosen, Farfleece had told Branwell, *to be among those who conjure those ancient and powerful forces. Your years will be numberless, and even kings will fear you.*

Branwell understood that in spite of this church and the young man's cassock and circular collar, this enterprise had nothing to do with any recognizable religion. He knew the kind of things his sisters would say about it all—and his father!—but he had long since seen through the repressive Christian mythology of his youth, and this disappointing trip to London had shown him that he was not a man to waste his best years in subjection to wearisome practice and instruction and intermediate measures.

And—*your years will be numberless, and even kings will fear you.*

The words resonated in the part of him that was Northangerland.

Farfleece pulled some musty old books down from a shelf, and showed him a 1592 printing of the suppressed original text of Christopher Marlowe's *Tragical History of Doctor Faustus*, and a manuscript that he claimed was John Wesley's account of apparent demonic possessions in Yorkshire . . . then, catching a look from the

woman beside Branwell, he hastily put the books back and said that Branwell must be baptized before he could progress further.

The woman took Branwell's right hand and turned it palm-up on the table, and Reverend Farfleece picked up the double-bladed knife. Branwell flinched, but the woman's grip was unexpectedly strong, and Farfleece assured him that he would administer only the slightest of pinpricks: *A token wound, a spiritual scar, a sign to those who have eyes to see.* Branwell bit his lip to stop it from trembling, but relaxed—and the young clergyman tapped his palm with the twin blade points.

The light punctures had not stung, precisely; they had sent a tingling sensation all the way up his arm, and seemed to make him even more light-headed than he had been already.

Reverend Farfleece bowed and left the room through an inner door then, taking the knife with him.

Branwell turned a questioning look on the woman, and she dipped her forefinger into the little jar and began speaking to him, slowly. It was a language he didn't recognize, but every series of words ended on a rising note, as if it had been a question, and each time when Branwell shrugged or mumbled in baffled response, she poked his forehead with her finger. Her fingertip gleamed in the lamplight, and Branwell could feel a slickness of oil between his eyebrows.

Suddenly it occurred to him that this was very similar to the Catholic sacrament of Extreme Unction—the Anointing of the Sick, customarily administered to someone on the brink of death; and he shoved his chair back and leaped toward the door he'd come in through. As he yanked it open and blundered through the doorway into the cold night, he heard the woman laughing softly in the room behind him.

He ran through the midnight London streets all the way back to his room at the Chapter Coffee House in Paternoster Row, and the next morning he boarded the first of the coaches that would carry him back home to the Haworth parsonage.

Now he scraped his fingernails across the rough surface of the gravestone under him, closing his fists on nothing. Behind him was the parsonage, in which his sisters were engaged in some literary

compositions they imagined he didn't know about. In front of him, past the far churchyard wall and a few steps down the hill, was the Black Bull, where he could probably find someone to stand him to a glass or two of all-forgiving gin.

He knew that plain cowardice had prevented him from taking the opportunity to become a professional artist, and had also made him run away from a darkly glamorous chance—and he now believed it had been a chance, at least—at . . . power, dominance, respect!

He opened his right hand and looked closely at his palm. The twin pinpricks of Reverend Farfleece's knife had left no mark even at the time, but the clergyman had called them *A token wound, a spiritual scar, a sign to those who have eyes to see.* Perhaps his hand was not empty after all.

He held it up against the already fading sky.

A very short, dark figure moved against the trees on the other side of the churchyard, but when Branwell whipped his head around, he saw that it had only been several crows perched on one of the upright marble gravestones, and they had begun flapping away even as he'd turned.

He frowned. In any case it had been crows *after* he looked.

The crows—there must have been at least half a dozen, to so eerily resemble a short person or child standing over there—came arrowing this way, and flew closely around Branwell's head; he quickly threw his arms across his face to block them, but a moment later they went cawing away between the treetops.

Branwell's heart was still thumping in his narrow chest. When the crows had for a half-glimpsed moment appeared to be the dark little boy he had seen in his dreams—and once while awake, here in the churchyard!—had the apparition been beckoning?

The black birds had disappeared from sight now, fortuitously in the direction of the Black Bull.

Call it a summons, he thought with wry, self-conscious excitement.

Branwell hiked himself down from the flat gravestone.

One vigilant pair of eyes watched Branwell's hunched figure hobble away to the street.

Emily's big bullmastiff, Keeper, had padded outside through the kitchen door, and around by the peat room and the windowless south

side of the house, and he stood now sniffing the cold wind from out over the endless moors. He had seen the crows flying away, and Branwell following them.

Keeper knew the sounds that identified the members of his household, and that retreating figure was *Branwell*. In Keeper's mind Emily was a tall divinity, loved and worshipped; and Emily accepted and even loved Branwell, though Keeper sometimes caught a troubling non-family muskiness in the changing presentation of his smells. It was one of the many things for which no reason was evident.

And that elusive scent of Branwell's was related to the strong, threatening smell that had clung to the wounded stranger this morning. Keeper had soon understood that it was the blood on the weapon, and not the stranger himself, that had caused his nostrils to flare and his lips to curl back from his teeth in unreasoned urgency to attack. The stranger had only been wounded by whatever had left blood on the weapon, and Emily had indicated at least conditional approval of the man by helping him stand up and walk.

Out there by the plateau and the black stone tower, Keeper had sniffed the wind, and flexed his ears and swung his great head to look in all directions, then allowed himself to relax into his customary caution: whatever had attacked the man had been beyond the reach of his canine senses.

Emily had cleaned most of the affronting blood from the weapon, and the incident had happened far from the house—but the smell of it, and the syllable *Welsh*, uttered while the smell was fresh in the air, had awakened far-off memories in Keeper.

Try as he might, he wasn't able to place them—they were memories so remote that they seemed to belong to another dog altogether.

Emily's father worked a tool that made a sharp noise every morning at dawn, and Keeper understood that the effect of it was to intimidate something, to keep some bad thing away. And on most evenings at sunset Keeper had a self-imposed job too—he stood by the churchyard wall and barked ferociously at the frail things that looked something like humans but weren't. And his bark then had a particular depth and resonance, as if it roared out of more than one dog's throat. At the noise, the frail figures generally fled.

The daylight was still bright now—it wasn't time yet for those spiderwebby false humans to come drifting in from the moors or rise from the stones in the churchyard.

Keeper lay down in the short grass and rested his chin on his big front paws.

CHAPTER THREE

"I expect Emily has told you about her adventure today by Ponden Kirk."

Patrick had joined his daughters in the parlor, where the windows also faced the churchyard. Emily was reclining on the green leather couch against the far wall, and Charlotte and Anne sat in two of the chairs at the table. Old Patrick stood by the entrance hall doorway.

"You know I was born in Ireland," he said, "but you know little more than that. There has seemed no need to trouble you with the reasons why I left there."

He touched Anne's head as he walked past her, and stopped in front of the windows and took a deep breath. "Brontë is not an Irish name."

"It was Brunty," said Emily with sudden conviction, "before."

He smiled faintly in her direction. "Yes. When I arrived in Liverpool I was twenty-five, and I'd been admitted to St. John's College at Cambridge as a *sizar*: a student so poor that the college would cover his fees. Homespun clothes, thick Irish accent, I—" His blind gaze was directed over the heads of his daughters, as if seeing the unprepossessing young man he had been then. "And I . . . had reason to be frightened."

Charlotte and Anne shifted in their chairs.

"Brunty sounds like some Papist subsisting on nothing but beer and potatoes," said Charlotte. "I'm glad the Brontë name was in the papers at the time, to suggest it."

"And the umlaut is nice," put in Anne. "Otherwise everybody would pronounce it as *Brawnt*."

Patrick shook his head. "It really had nothing to do with Lord Nelson. It was the old *name*."

The old name? thought Emily. She recalled that Brontë was the town in Sicily of which Nelson had been made honorary Duke, but that didn't seem relevant.

Patrick went on, "When I landed in Liverpool I went directly to Chester, a few miles to the south. It's at the end of one of the old Roman roads, and—God help me!—there's an ancient shrine to Minerva there."

Anne looked at him sharply, though of course he couldn't see it; and it was Charlotte who cleared her throat and asked, with forced lightness, "What's Minerva to you, or you to Minerva?"

Emily felt only a liberating sort of excitement. Throughout her life, their father had displayed eccentricities, superstitions unique to him—like the long cravat that he had his daughters cut up and reassemble several times a year, and firing his pistol over the churchyard every morning at dawn!—and even as a child she had suspected them to be precautions against unearthly misfortunes.

"I was . . . *pursued*, from Ireland!" Patrick said. "I thought I had left it behind, but it . . . rode across the Irish Sea on me, *in* me, in my blood!"

Emily sat up. Her father might conceivably have been talking about a disease, but that wouldn't have sent him running to a pagan shrine.

"It?" said Anne.

Patrick raised his head and went on more quietly. "Our faith admits the existence of demons."

"And," Anne went on hesitantly, "Minerva?"

Patrick took a deep breath and let it out. "It was, in plain fact, an old pagan demon that I had inadvertently brought with me, and it—wanted revenge. On every Brunty son. So when I should have put my trust in our Lord, in my fright I sought armor from a pagan goddess. I was young, alone in a foreign land!" He waved a hand out in front of him. "Emily?"

Emily shifted on the couch. "Yes, Papa?"

"Do you remember who made Minerva's impregnable armor?"

Charlotte slapped the table. "What do you mean, an old pagan demon? Revenge? For what? What—do you *mean*?"

"Of course, forgive me." Patrick pulled out a chair and sat down. "In 1710," he said, "my great-grandfather, Hugh Brunty, was on a cattle-boat from Liverpool to Warrenpoint in County Down." It was clear that he was unburdening himself of a story he had long kept from them, and he raised a shaky, spotted hand to stave off inevitable impatience.

"Halfway across the Irish Sea," he went on, "a stowaway child was found aboard—a dark little boy in rags, and some of the passengers guessed he must be Welsh. The crew said it was a devil, and wanted to throw the child overboard—but my great-grandfather, in his perilous compassion, intervened, and, for lack of anything else to do with the boy, adopted him. Through general carelessness and procrastination, the boy's name became simply *Welsh*."

Emily shivered, remembering what wounded Alcuin had asked her this morning: *Is he aware of Welsh?*

"As Welsh grew up, he came to *control* old Hugh," Patrick went on, "and after Hugh's death he became legal owner of the Brunty farm. His foster brothers resented it and tried to kill him, and they were convicted of attempted murder and transported to the colonies. Then Welsh married Hugh's daughter, and, by nature unable to father children himself, adopted one of his now-fatherless nephews-in-law. That nephew was my father, also named Hugh Brunty."

Not far outside the window, Keeper voiced an uncharacteristic howel, and they all jumped. Emily stood up and hurried to the window; her great mastiff was standing in the walkway between the house and her garden, facing out over the churchyard. As she watched, Keeper turned around twice clockwise and sat down, though even through the window she could see that the fur was bristling on his back.

Emily stood for several more seconds by the window, but there were no sounds of commotion from down the street, and Keeper didn't stir.

She walked back to the couch, and when she sat down she shrugged. "Spirits abroad."

"My father had a dog named Keeper," said Patrick. "You recall I suggested the same name for yours. Welsh killed that one. Welsh had begun to . . . *take over* my father, as he had done—"

"Possess," corrected Charlotte, grudgingly.

"Yes. By this time Welsh's human body was old and had begun to fail, and my father was just sixteen—but he resisted *possession*. He and his Keeper managed to kill Welsh's body, though in the fight Keeper perished, valiantly. Young Hugh Brunty fled, and five years later married my mother."

For several seconds none of them spoke. Then Anne asked, "Did he fire a gun over a churchyard every morning?"

Patrick glanced toward her voice. "We lived in a one-room thatched cottage, and he could no more afford a gun than a . . . a gold watch. What he had was a kiln for drying corn; people there in Ballynaskeagh grew their own corn, and so many of them came to our cottage to have it dried that his kiln was roaring night and day. I'm certain he had consulted a local witch-woman, or even a priest, for devil-repelling herbs and incenses to add to the fire."

He lapsed into silence, staring at nothing.

"But you left Ireland," prompted Emily.

Her father nodded. "I was a teacher at a village school near our cottage. My students were poor—the fee was a penny a week, and a turf of peat every Monday for heating the schoolroom. I enjoyed it, I was doing the students good . . . but one morning there was a new face at the back of the room. A little dark boy, in rags. When I met his eye, he smiled and hurried outside . . . I followed him out, and he—"

"—Was an optical illusion," supplied Emily with a shiver. He fragmented and dispersed as a flock of crows, she thought.

Her father looked up at her. "Yes, I suppose that's what he was." He pushed his chair back and stood up, and went on more strongly, "I saw him several more times, standing outside our house at dusk, but the corn-kiln was reliably throwing its charmed smoke. And sometimes it was a big ungainly dog out there . . ."

"So you crossed the sea," said Charlotte, clearly more than half believing that her father was delusional, "here to England—but it came with you."

"Yes. It *returned* here—I inadvertently brought it back. The demonic child was found on the boat from Liverpool, remember. And, God help me, back to Liverpool I delivered it—I saw it, him, on the dock when I disembarked, and he met my eye and smiled." Patrick spread his hands. "And I knew there was an old Roman shrine

to Minerva nearby. I was terrified. It seemed foolish to hope that some Anglican priest could provide much protection, but a pagan goddess . . . !" He dropped his hands. "So, Emily—do you remember who made Minerva's impregnable armor?"

"In Vergil's *Aeneid* it was the cyclopes—let's see, Steropes was one, and Pyracmon, and—" She stopped.

"And *Brontes*," finished Charlotte. "The third cyclops was named Brontes! You sought protection of, took the name of—gave *us* the name of!—a pagan monster?"

"I'm afraid I prayed to all three, but yes, I adapted our name to the name of that one. I dropped the S when I signed the registry at the college, and the old Brunty name was dismissed as a transcription error."

"And," asked Charlotte, her voice tight with the effort of maintaining a respectful tone to her father, "have the cyclopes provided you with their armor?"

"No. All I took away was the name."

"They also made thunderbolts," ventured Anne. "And when we were children watching thunderstorms you used to point to where lightning would strike next."

Patrick smiled and shook his head. "Hah. When I was right, it was sheer chance; though I recall it impressed you children."

Emily cocked an eyebrow. She knew the particular kink of that smile—her father's statement had not been entirely honest.

"But you did exorcise the Welsh thing," said Anne, "somehow?"

"Emily's wounded man today didn't seem to think so," said Charlotte, "if Emily didn't dream the whole encounter—a man who could barely crawl one moment hurrying beyond sight in the next!"

Emily knew Charlotte believed her story and was trying to convince herself otherwise. Emily smiled at her.

"I did," said their father. His forehead was dewed with sweat, and Emily thought he would like to unwind the long cravat that hid his throat and supported his chin. "Exorcise it. Finally. Imposed restraints, at least—"

"That winter when Mama was dying," interrupted Charlotte, "you dragged the chairs from her room and sawed them to pieces out in the yard. And you burned her hearth-rug."

"You were three years old," protested Patrick, as if it was unfair that she should remember it. He groped his way back to the table and leaned forward, pressing his palms on it. "I had no reason to believe that—" He straightened and moved away, and Emily saw the faint outlines of his hands in steam on the polished table surface. "Those were precautions, against the remote possibility . . ."

"That something had been in her room and sat in the chairs," finished Anne mournfully, "and stood on the rug."

Their father shook his head, then reluctantly nodded. "I thought I had been doing enough to keep him restrained, but after your mother's death I actually went to the extreme of getting a Catholic priest out here to do a formal Papist exorcism, in the churchyard! And for an instant the priest and I both saw the figure of the boy appear, standing on the wall! It seemed to convulse as the priest intoned his Latin prayers, and then it fell on the other side of the wall, and was gone when we went to look. And, in the years since, there has been no sign of him."

"A Papist!" said Charlotte. "You're an Anglican priest. Why didn't you do it yourself?"

"I did, I did!—with no result. The Papists have had more practice." He turned in Emily's direction. "Your wounded man by Ponden Kirk clearly knew something of our family history, but it's all moot now, you see."

Except perhaps that our sisters Elizabeth and Maria both died of "consumption" four years later, thought Emily, at the ages of eleven and nine; and that several times in the years since, I've seen the figure of the dark boy, which breaks up into a flock of crows; and you don't know about Branwell and Anne and me leaving our blood in the fairy cave at the foot of Ponden Kirk.

And I believe you know something about that double-bladed knife.

She would ask him about that in private. Now she stood up from the couch and said, "And teatime is upon us. Anne, I could use your help in the kitchen."

Anne and Charlotte both stood up, and Patrick started toward the hallway door. "I'll have mine in my study," he said.

As always, thought Emily.

+ + +

Branwell sat on the upholstered bench that ran along the wall adjacent to the fireplace, staring into the low blue flames dancing over the coals. He was for the moment alone in this alcove off the main room of the Black Bull, and he sighed, catching the warm smells of beer and tobacco smoke and lamp oil. Mr. Sugden, the landlord, would not ask him to leave, but neither would he advance Branwell any more credit, and among the few Haworth citizens in the tavern at this early hour there was no one likely to buy him a drink.

Every few minutes there came the creak of the front door opening, followed by a sweep of chilly early-spring air. A few minutes ago he had heard a carriage or wagon stop outside, and when the tavern door had been opened the breeze had carried the distant howl of a dog along with the swampy smell of the mid-street gutter.

Branwell heard one pair of boots enter, then muted conversation from the front room. Now a woman in a tweed coat and a long dark skirt stepped around the corner and crossed to the fire, drawing a woolen scarf from around her narrow shoulders; and he dismissed his vague impression that he recognized her. She was carrying a big brown leather valise like a doctor's bag, and set it on the table against the opposite wall. A scent of mimosa curled in the air around her.

She looked directly at him, and he pushed his spectacles up on his nose to see her more clearly.

Her face was leaner than the half-remembered image in his mind, though her bound-up hair was correspondingly dark, but it wasn't until she walked up to where he sat, and poked his forehead with a finger, that his chest chilled in excited recollection. His right palm sent a tingle through his arm to the shoulder.

She lowered her hand, and Branwell bobbed his head vigorously to show that he remembered.

"You," she said quietly. "I've wondered when we'd see you again. I assume you too are here because of the one-eyed Catholic."

"Yes," said Branwell instantly, not having any idea of what she was talking about; for here seemed to be a chance to retrieve one of his great missed opportunities: his cowardly flight, ten years ago, from this woman and the Reverend Farfleece and ... power, dominance ... personal importance!

He had been a member of the local Masonic lodge for nine years now, and it occurred to him that her enigmatic statement might be the first part of a recognition exchange, in which case his reply couldn't have been the right one—but her expression hadn't changed. Evidently it had been a genuine question. He must bluff, figure out what she meant.

She sat down beside him, and in spite of everything he sat up straighter and stroked his scanty chin-beard and wondered if she found him attractive.

She snapped her fingers. "Northangerland."

"That's *right*." It warmed Branwell to acknowledge the name. He looked at her and raised his eyebrows.

She cleared her throat. "I am Mrs. Flensing." She went on, in an accent Branwell thought was vaguely Continental, "Of course really he had two eyes, like all of them these days. I think he was at Ponden Kirk to die by his own hand and defile the place, but when the regent lord of the tribe attacked him, he changed his mind—defended himself with a dioscuri."

Branwell's mind leaped from *dioscuri*, which he knew was a Greek term for the mythological twins Castor and Pollux, to *twins* to the double-bladed knife Emily had dropped. *Defended himself*—"The knife," he said, trying to sound confident.

"Yes. You knew that the regent—chief among the saints!—was killed in that affray?"

"No," ventured Branwell. Remembering Emily's return to the parsonage a couple of hours ago, he asked, "What became of the, er, dioscuri?"

"The murderer took it away with him, I suppose. Are you so afraid? He must have been sorely wounded himself."

"No no, of course not, it's just—knives like that are uncommon. Worth noting, when you come across one of them."

"True. Only one purpose, conflicted wound response. This man has long been perceived as a possible threat, and I had followed him from London to an estate outside Allerton." She exhaled in evident frustration, "But he killed two people there last night, and eluded me in the ensuing confusion. What do you know about him?"

Branwell felt a drop of sweat roll down his ribs under his shirt. Emily had been evasive—tellingly evasive!—in front of him. She'd

said that she and Keeper walked *west, and east again,* and found the dioscuri knife on a path. This woman had said that the "one-eyed Catholic" meant to "defile the place" with his suicide.

"Just that a man with a knife like that was seen on the moors west of the parsonage here," Branwell said. "Today. Uh, in the area of Ponden Kirk, as you say." His face was hot. "I assume it was the . . . the one-eyed Catholic." He ground his teeth—this was pathetic.

Mrs. Flensing frowned at him and stood up. "I gather you know nothing."

"My sister," Branwell burst out, "went walking on the moors this morning, and came back with a dioscuri, and blood on her shirt. She didn't say where she'd been or what she'd seen."

Mrs. Flensing sat down again. "Was she injured? Bitten?"

"*Bitten?* No. It didn't seem to be her own blood."

Mrs. Flensing gripped his wrist tightly. "You must learn from her what she saw, what she did, how she got the knife. Do you understand me?"

"Yes, certainly," Branwell assured her, though he wondered how much of the old intimacy with any of his sisters still endured.

"I assume she has not been baptized."

"Of course she has. Our—Oh! No, not with a—" He poked his right palm with two fingers. Racking his mind for anything else that might hold Mrs. Flensing's precious attention, he added, "She *was* bitten once, by a—a sort of dog." Though she cauterized the bite, he added mentally.

Mrs. Flensing stiffened. "Ah? Out on these moors . . ." She gave him a fierce look. "Do you mean what you appear to tell me? What sort of dog?"

Emily hadn't described the dog that had bitten her, so Branwell cast his mind back to the day he himself had been bitten by a strangely acting and perhaps mad dog.

He had been about nine years old, and to impress his sisters he had approached the misshapen animal and extended his hand to it; and its blunt head had darted out and cut his wrist with its teeth. The creature had immediately gone loping away over a hill, and Branwell had bound up his wrist himself and told his sisters to say nothing about it. The wound had been slight and had healed within a day, but the invasive fright of the encounter had so interfered with his

sleep for the next month that his father had allowed him to stop attending the local village school.

"Big, bigger than a bullmastiff," he told Mrs. Flensing, suppressing a shiver even now, "with a short, flat black face, and long legs and toes. Coarse sparse hair, like a pig...and," he recalled, "its growl, she said its growl was like a baby crying. An enormous baby, you understand."

Mrs. Flensing was breathing deeply. "I meant to act alone, tonight, but *three* aligned souls will assure success. We must have your sister too. Where does she live?"

"At the—right here in the village."

"Excellent. I imagine there's a room at this establishment for private meetings?" When he nodded, she reached into her coat pocket and handed him half a dozen shillings. "Reserve it for tomorrow night. I'll meet you then, an hour after sunset. You will bring your sister with you. Before anything else, she must be baptized. You must help me persuade her." And she said again, "Do you understand me?"

Suddenly Branwell was afraid that assenting to the woman's questions carried some actual consequence, like signing a contract. But Mrs. Flensing was staring into his eyes, and he did his best to assume the character of Northangerland, the boldly amoral hero of his stories. Northangerland can do this, he told himself.

He managed to pronounce the word "Yes." He cleared his throat. "And what place," he went on more steadily, "is there for me in this company of...ours?"

She gave him a speculative look. "A high one, perhaps. Do you know this village?"

"I live here too," Branwell admitted.

"I see. Well, you can advise me. Attend now, as you value your future, and believe." She stood up and crossed to the table against the opposite wall, and her hand lightly touched the big leather bag. "There is a grave here," she said softly, "and the body under the stone suffered an amputation long ago. It must remain...not fully whole, for now. But the tribe, the shadow they cast, was made weaker by the murder today, and so the body's integrity must be more nearly restored, in order that our...*wellsprings* here in the north may not falter irreparably."

Seeing his blank incomprehension, she went on, "The body under the stone is not precisely dead. When its head is brought near to its body, its identity will to some extent respond, arc across the gap between them, restore the potency that the regent's death compromised."

Branwell wondered why Mrs. Flensing didn't want the thing fully restored; and he remembered Reverend Farfleece's talk of their "biune" god, the two persons of which were presently separated. The young clergyman had said that the goal of his order was the reuniting of them, but he hadn't seemed eager to see it happen any time soon. Could the thing under the stone be one half of their two-person god?

Mrs. Flensing glanced at the doorway to the bar, then unbuckled the bag and spread it open. She beckoned to Branwell, and he stood up unsteadily and crossed to where she stood. He looked down into the bag.

Only after she had closed the bag and he had tottered back to the bench was he able to make sense of what he had seen. The rippled ivory oval was the top of a big misshapen skull, and the wide opening below one end was where a nose or snout might once have been. He had only been able to see the outward curves of long teeth.

Branwell was dizzy and afraid he might vomit, but in this moment he didn't doubt what Mrs. Flensing was saying. This was magic, sorcery, necromancy—forbidden secrets!—and he, negligible onetime railway clerk and tutor, was an initiate!

Mrs. Flensing rejoined him on the bench. "The body," she said, "is under the floor of the church in this village, under a ledger stone marked with certain grooves. You must show me a place, ideally in the church itself, where that bag can bide undiscovered. Do you know the interior of the building?"

"Yes. Thoroughly."

"Good. And your sister's baptized presence and cooperation will be enormously beneficial."

Branwell tried to imagine Emily cooperating in anything she didn't want to do—but Mrs. Flensing bent to peer into his face, and he forced himself not to flinch.

After several seconds she nodded and reached into an inner pocket of her coat, and pulled out a flat leather case. She pressed the catch to open it, and Branwell saw six small glass vials held down by

segments of a black ribbon. She pushed one free and held it out to him.

He took it. It was cold, unsurprisingly; and it seemed to contain some black fluid that had coated the inside of the glass.

"Do you have a spare pair of spectacles?" she asked.

There was the pair he had worn as a boy, long outgrown, its hinges rusted from having once been left out overnight. He was fairly sure he knew where they were in his room.

"Yes."

"Tomorrow," she told him, "when the sun is up, rub a film of this on the lenses; walk around for half an hour wearing them—but stay in the village, don't go out onto the moors. Wear them a bit more every day."

"What, uh—" He hesitated, unsure if he should admit to not knowing what the stuff was.

She cocked an eyebrow. "Dragon's blood, devil's tears, Gehenna mud, what do you care?"

"Uh, not," Branwell admitted.

"And you will be here tomorrow, *with your sister*, an hour after sunset."

"Yes."

Mrs. Flensing stood up in one smooth motion. She draped the scarf around her shoulders, picked up the leather bag, and strode out of the room. He heard the tavern door open and close. A few moments later there was the rattle of a coach getting under way.

Branwell turned to look again into the fire.

And what place is there for me in this company of ours?

A high one, perhaps.

A week ago he had heard that a village girl named Agatha, one of Charlotte's Sunday School students, was being treated for cholera, and on impulse he had decided to visit her. He had stayed with the girl for half an hour, and read to her from the Psalms . . . and when he returned to the parsonage, Charlotte had asked him why he seemed sad.

He had told her about his visit to little Agatha—and Charlotte had given him a look that had hurt him profoundly: the sister who had always been his closest friend and confidant, his onetime collaborator in writing stories of the imaginary land of Angria,

stories which they had often signed WT or UT for "we two" or "us two"—had looked at him with an expression of scornful skepticism. It had been woundingly apparent that she didn't believe he was any longer a person who would bestir himself to comfort a sick child.

He looked away from the fire now and stood up, clenching his fists. What do I owe any of them, anymore? he thought—Northangerland doesn't need any of them.

The tavern's door squeaked open again, and in the entryway he heard the hearty voice of John Brown, his father's sexton. Northangerland or not, Branwell was too frightened of Mrs. Flensing to spend one of her shillings on drink for himself, but John Brown would certainly be willing to buy him a glass of gin. Or two.

CHAPTER FOUR

A visitor had called on their father shortly after Emily and Anne had carried the dishes and cups and teapot back to the kitchen. Emily had heard Tabby open the front door and talk to a man, and then heard her father's voice; the men's voices had withdrawn into her father's study and Tabby clumped back up the hall to the kitchen.

"A gentleman to see your father," she said, settling onto her stool by the black iron range, "talking idolatry, if you ask me. But he must be an acquaintance, as Keeper didn't bark at him."

Now old Patrick's voice sounded from down the hall. "Girls," he called, "I think you'd be interested in this gentleman's errand."

Emily and Anne looked at each other. "Idolatry!" said Anne, suppressing a giggle as they walked out of the kitchen.

Their father was standing in the hall by his study door, and Charlotte stepped into the hall from the parlor. Keeper stood by the front door now, alert but not growling.

At a wave from their father, the three sisters approached and walked past him into his study. A man stood by the window, and Emily, always shy of strangers, first looked only at the visitor's obviously expensive but travel-worn boots.

And a chill swept over her, for she had seen those boots only a few hours ago, stumbling and dragging across grass and mud beside her own.

"Mr. Curzon," came her father's voice, "my daughters: Charlotte the eldest, and Emily and Anne."

The sisters curtsied, and Emily looked up as the stranger bowed and straightened. And she kept her face immobile.

A lamp had been lit on the desk, and by its amber light she could clearly see the black mane and the dark, craggy features of Alcuin, the man she had tried to help this morning. The black eyepatch again covered his left eye, and he was now wearing gray corduroy trousers and a white shirt under a black frock coat.

His single exposed eye had widened for one startled moment, but now his face too was expressionless.

Emily wondered that he was able to stand up, much less walk even the short distance from the village. Did some medicine exist that could have restored him to this extent?

"Ladies," he said. For a moment it seemed that he was about to say more, but his lips closed firmly.

"Mr. Curzon," said their father, "has heard that as curate of Haworth I supported the Catholic Emancipation Act twenty years ago, and consults me now about the feasibility of establishing Catholic parishes in Yorkshire."

Emily had told Charlotte and Anne about her morning's adventure, including the detail of Curzon's superfluous eyepatch; and peripherally she caught Anne's questioning glance, and nodded.

"*Are* there Catholics in Yorkshire?" asked Charlotte drily.

Curzon looked from Emily to Charlotte, and his face creased in a bleak, resigned smile. "Enough to fill a church or two, I suppose." His voice had lost the hoarse, pained rasp Emily recalled, but it was still deep, and still seemed to carry a trace of French accent.

"Possibly in Leeds or Bradford," Patrick went on, blinking at nothing, "but certainly not many out here by the Lancashire border. I'm sorry you should have come all this way, sir, to no avail!"

"I'm traveling," said Curzon, "and I was nearby." He exhaled and scowled at Emily.

And she knew it was high time that she spoke up. "I'm glad to see that you've recovered from your wound this morning, Mr. Curzon," she said. She turned to her father. "Papa, this is the gentleman I told you about."

For several seconds old Patrick Brontë stood motionless. Then he groped for his desk and pulled open a drawer; and when he raised his hand he was holding the twin-bladed knife.

"Emily," he said, "catch." And he tossed it in the direction of her voice.

She caught it by the grip, and with her free hand waved her sisters back toward the door.

"Is our visitor," asked their father carefully, "wearing an eyepatch?"

"Yes—though this morning you said it was only a formality, didn't you, Mr. Curzon?"

Curzon just clenched his fists by his sides.

Their father peered blindly toward Curzon. "My daughter," he said slowly, "tells me there was blood on that knife, when she found you. I think you may be more ally than adversary."

Curzon rolled his head to look at all of them, and his voice was cold. "I'm no ally of fools. Yes, it was the blood of a lycanthrope." Speaking directly toward Patrick, he went on, "And you!—after revitalizing their kind, you have brought your family to live out here where the things thrive!"

A nudge at her thigh let Emily know, without looking down, that Keeper had joined them. She felt the vibration of a growl too low to hear.

"Catholic parishes, was it?" said Patrick scornfully. "Something else, I think!" He raised his head. "My daughter tells me you mentioned Welsh this morning; it's true that I brought him—it—back to England. Inadvertently. But my children are safe from him when they're *here*, with *me*."

"*Here?*" demanded Curzon. "What *protections* do you imagine you provide, Mr. Brunty? Blind, shooting a gun over graves every morning? I heard about that in the village shops. Keeping buckets of holy water around the house? Their weak radiance avails little."

Emily was watching Curzon, but peripherally she saw her father's face redden above the endlessly overlapped silk cravat. Holy water? she thought. Not in an Anglican house! The buckets of water ... in every room and hallway of the house ... are kept filled in case of fire, and have no other value, surely.

Keeper was looking directly at Curzon, and his growl was audible now.

"It's clear," said her father stiffly, his Irish accent more pronounced now, "that your ostensible purpose in this visit was a sham. I certainly don't care to participate, especially through deceit, in any scheme of the Huberti, and—and so I note your opinions and bid you good day."

Curzon bent to pick up a tweed cap from a chair by the window. He hesitated, and Emily wondered how his conversation with her father might have developed if she had not been present.

As it was, Curzon just said, "I pray I may never one day need to kill your children," and walked to the door, pushing rudely between Emily and Charlotte. Keeper snapped at him, and Emily heard cloth tear. Curzon grunted but didn't look back as he strode to the front door and left the house.

Her father sat down heavily in the chair behind the desk.

"A lycanthrope?" said Charlotte breathlessly.

"Holy water?" said Anne.

"A drop," said her father, waving that subject away, "in each bucket. Yes, lycanthropes—call them werewolves if you like, or gytrashes, as the locals do. Emily—would you see which way he goes? Down to the village or out to the moors?"

"Who are the Huberti?" asked Anne, but Emily was already in the hall, with Keeper trotting close at her heels.

When she stepped outside into the cold wind and closed the door behind her, she saw the tall figure of Alcuin Curzon striding down the lane beside the churchyard—not even limping! Clearly he was going to the village, and probably to some transportation away from Haworth.

On an impulse, she began running after him. Keeper trotted easily at her side, not pulling ahead.

She soon caught up with Curzon on the paving stones beside the church. "Mr. Curzon," she called when she was a few yards behind him.

He stopped and turned, frowning, and Emily noticed a rip in the knee of his new trousers. Keeper tensed, and she didn't have to stoop to catch his steel-studded leather collar with her left hand.

"Evidently," she said, "your wound this morning was not as dire as I imagined."

"Restrain your dog," he said. "I'd not hurt him."

Emily realized that she was still holding the peculiar knife in her right hand. "He and I defend each other," she said, not at all out of breath from running. "And he won't ever let you kill me, as you said you might try to do."

"Yes, if you were to change. But"—he bared his teeth in what

might have been a smile—"you helped me today, so I'd try to see that you were shriven first."

"Catholic magnanimity!" She shook her head. "You do know something about this business—"

He didn't move, but just stared down at her with his exposed right eye. Emily wished it were covered too.

She went on in a rush, "Have you seen the dark boy who becomes a flock of crows?"

Curzon's eye widened at that, and he stepped back. "My God, girl—Miss Emily!—are you already marked as his?"

He took another step backward when she extended the hand that held the knife, but she tossed it clattering onto the pavement at his feet.

"Take it—you left it behind this morning. I meant to indicate my hand."

His eye held her gaze for a moment, then looked down. And he nodded. "As I guessed this morning, it's a scar from teeth as well as a burn—you cauterized the bite. If you were quick about it—and I expect you were—then *you* haven't seen Welsh's spirit; someone has told you about that apparition. Your idiot father? One of your luckless sisters?" He raised his eye from her hand to her face. "Someone is lethally marked."

Lethally marked? Emily wished now that she hadn't dropped the knife; but Keeper was with her, quivering under her fingers gripping his collar. She pressed on, "The boy is Welsh's spirit? I *have* seen it a couple of times, far off, out on the moors." She took a deep breath. "Tell me about Ponden Kirk."

He cocked his head, and his eye narrowed now in what might have been pity.

His cold gaze was steady, but she just stared back at him.

It was Curzon who looked away—past her, back toward the parsonage. He rubbed his hand across his mouth. "You're not lost to him, necessarily. Damn! You present a heartily unwelcome interruption and inconvenience, and likely you have no more intelligence than your demented father . . . but I think in all good conscience I must take you with me. Come now, this minute—don't go back to that house of doomed souls."

Emily quickly crouched and straightened, and she was again holding the knife.

"God, not you, will judge their souls," she said, "and whatever their state, I'm one of them."

The wind shook the bare branches of the trees in the churchyard. Emily shivered and wished she'd grabbed her coat, but held the knife steady. For several seconds the only sound was the clinking of new gravestones being chiseled in the stonecutting yard behind her.

"I think you are, at that," Curzon said, almost in a whisper. "Keep the knife, and I pray you find the grace to use it on your own throat one day."

He turned on his heel and strode away.

Emily started to turn back toward he parsonage, but Keeper stood immovable until Curzon had disappeared around the corner of her father's church.

Night had fallen by the time Branwell stumbled out of the Black Bull, though it was much earlier than his usual hour of returning home; but when he clambered over the churchyard wall to take the shortcut among the gravestones, a long, menacing howl from Emily's dog made him stop and look up from watching the cautious placement of his boots in the moonlight that filtered through the tree branches.

And so he stumbled against the base of one of the flat gravestones and, trying to catch his balance, sat down on it. The stone was cold, and he shivered and slid his hands into his pockets. His fingers closed on the vial Mrs. Flensing had given him, and he pulled it out.

The dog was barking furiously now, up by the parsonage door, and though each roar seemed to vibrate in Branwell's bones, he tried to ignore the noise and focus on the vial.

In the darkness, its contents seemed to be faintly luminescent. Several glasses of gin had dispelled the intimidation Mrs. Flensing had imposed on him, and now he laughed softly in embarrassment to recall how he had stammered and stumbled when answering her questions.

"Quiet!" he shouted at the dog, across the scarcely seen gravestones. He looked down at the vial again. "Devil's tears!" he muttered. "Let's see how devils weep."

He thumbed the cork out of the vial, and then hesitated with one finger poised over the narrow rim. But what has Northangerland to

lose? he asked himself with giddy bravado, and dipped his finger into the cold liquid.

It stung, and he quickly recorked the vial and pulled off his spectacles to wipe his finger on the lenses and then on his coat.

He peered irritably in the direction of the jarringly barking dog, but the trees and gravestones around him were just dim, blurred shapes. He tucked the vial into his pocket and fitted his spectacles back over his ears.

He found that his vision through the lenses was clearer than before he had rubbed the oil on them; contrasts between moonlight and shadow were more distinct, and the shapes of the trees and the standing stones were more perceptibly three-dimensional solids.

And now he could see that there were other things visible in the intermittent moonlight.

Shapes like unmoored shadows shifted among the headstones. Their outlines were difficult to distinguish from the tree branches beyond them, but they seemed to move with volition.

Branwell froze, staring at the things.

He could see that they were all moving between the tombstones, out of the churchyard toward the open moors, and when they shivered at each booming call from the dog, Branwell realized that they were fleeing from the sound.

The dog's baying was shaking Branwell too, like blows to his spine, and to escape it he followed the vaguely human figures— over the low west wall and along a path that curved across a moonlit field, away from the parsonage and the churchyard and the village.

Branwell was shivering with both fear and excitement. The upright shapes were more distinct in the open moonlight, and in spite of their blurred outlines he could make out flexing limbs swinging from shoulders and hips, and heads like big mushrooms loosely rolling. When the breeze blew across them he caught a sulfury scent, like marsh gas.

The manlike shapes were aware of him as they hobbled and hopped along. Their bag heads frequently swiveled toward him, and the things moved aside to clear his way. Several of them extended diaphanous arms with smoke-tendril fingers waving at the ends, and, sensing respect and deference, Branwell giddily stretched out his own

arms. His palms felt a faint tingling as the indistinct fingers swept across them.

As the dog's barking faded behind them, Branwell was able to feel a pulse that was not his own, through the earpieces of his spectacles; and when the shapes around him began bobbing to the same rhythm, and opening and closing holes in their heads in counterpoint to it, he realized that they were, after a fashion, singing.

It became clear to Branwell that the things were no longer fleeing the barking of Emily's dog, but taking a deliberate course. The moon was high now in the starry sky, and it seemed to renew the alcohol in his bloodstream and give him boundless energy. When the misshapen figures began spinning as they moved along the path, and awkwardly waving their rippling upper limbs at the sky, Branwell found it fitting to spin too, laughing, and to leap around and among the things.

His increasingly frenzied activity didn't tire him at all, and his breathing was no faster than it would be if he were simply walking rapidly. He was aware of the very cold wind tossing his hair, but he wasn't shivering; and the air was laced with the scents of heather and damp soil and the smell of the figures around him.

Their way led up hillsides where Branwell was able to leap over projecting rocks that slowed his more awkward companions, and they all skirted the bank of Dean Beck for at least a mile to reach an ancient stone bridge, though in many places stepping stones were set only a few feet apart across the rushing water.

After some unconsidered length of time the ungainly company stopped, and when Branwell glanced around at his frail companions he saw that they were all folded and shorter—kneeling—and facing the same direction. They swayed in the wind like tall grass, and it occurred to him that he had not seen them raise dust in their steps and gyrations, nor cast any perceptible moon shadows on the paths.

Branwell's spurious energy had at some point left him. He was panting now, shivering in the cold wind and the sudden awareness of being many dark miles from home.

All he could see ahead was a tall, roughly rectangular escarpment, black against a gray slope in the moonlight, and he sagged in dismay when he recognized it. He seldom ventured out on the moors anymore, even by daylight, and he hadn't been this close to Ponden

Kirk since that day sixteen years ago when he had enticed two of his sisters to join him in leaving blood in the cave at its base.

Now he could see that the body of a big animal lay halfway up the stony slope.

He turned away from it and took a step back—but the wispy figures, the wraiths that had accompanied and led him here, clustered together now to block him. He began to push his way through them, and it was like pushing through twigs and cobwebs ... but the openings in their bag heads gaped like muddy drains, and they were audibly sucking air, though they had nothing like lungs. Branwell felt a corresponding tug at his own breath; he was able to keep his throat closed against it, but he dreaded getting into the middle of them, and he retreated and reluctantly faced Ponden Kirk.

And there was motion at the base of the monument. Out from the shadows now stepped a tall figure, imposingly solid in contrast to the figures behind Branwell.

The figure walked forward, down the slope, and heather crunched under its bare, blocky toes. It was a man—naked except for a belt with a cartridge box attached to it, but so thickly covered with coarse hair that Branwell knew its sex because of the bushy beard and broad shoulders. The man's eyes glittered in the moonlight as they stared into Branwell's.

Branwell was dismayingly sober, and trembling. His legs tensed for a headlong, thrashing flight through the things that swayed behind him, but he made himself call up all the failures of his life, all the opportunities that had frightened him into retreat, and he whispered, "Northangerland" and stood his ground. And when the big man had walked down to where Branwell stood and extended a hand, Branwell didn't let himself flinch at the sight of the short fingers and long, thick nails. He reached out his own hand and clasped it.

For several long moments Branwell's soft palm was pressed against rough pads; then the man released him and waved up the slope, toward the dead animal.

The man rocked his furry head back and opened his mouth, and the high, droning wail that issued from his throat rocked Branwell back on his heels. Out here on the moors at night, at the foot of Ponden Kirk, the piercing sound was nothing at all like the crying of

an infant—it was high-pitched, but expressive of subhuman grief and rage.

Branwell was sure that the very wind halted until the terrible sound stopped. And then the wail was echoed distantly by other such voices, from widely separated points far away in the night.

The man stepped back and waved toward the Kirk. Branwell took a deep, dizzy breath, and picked his way up the uneven slope until he stood a few yards short of where the animal's body lay.

Even in the shadows, with his new vision Branwell was able to see the thing clearly. It was something like a huge dog, with a short snout and long, muscular legs. Its fur was wet, and stood up in long tufts like pine needles, not everywhere covering dark patches on the skin beneath, and he could see a gash in the corded neck. The cold air was sharp with the smell of linseed oil, familiar to him from the days when he had hoped to be a portrait painter.

The tall naked man stepped past Branwell, dwarfing him, and from the cartridge box his blunt fingers extracted a stone and a short steel bar curled at one end; and when he crouched—his head level now with Branwell's—and struck the stone against the steel, a cascade of bright sparks fell onto the dead animal's fur.

A moment later the body was engulfed in glaring flames and the man stepped back. The sudden heat stung Branwell's face and hands, and the air was sharp with the reek of burning oil and fur.

Now someone else was stepping down the slope from the Kirk, a small barefoot figure in tattered clothing—short in stature but throwing a giant firelight-shadow onto the black stone edifice behind it.

Branwell recognized the dark boy who had haunted his dreams, and whom he had once met in the snow-blanketed churchyard, many years ago. In the firelight Branwell saw him smile—

And then, without having moved, Branwell was looking *down* the slope—past the burning body of the animal, at the tall man and a slender young man in a woolen coat, with bushy red hair and crooked spectacles.

He met the gaze of the bespectacled young man, and realized dizzily that it was himself; and he knew that the person staring at him out of his own eyes was a stranger.

Branwell cringed and raised a hand to block the sight, and it was

not his own hand; it was grimy, and *small*—the hand of a child. He tensed, and bare toes curled against gravelly dirt.

His mind convulsed away in shock, and he sat down and fell backward across weeds and stones; but he could feel his own coat tight around his shoulders, and his own boots on his feet.

He completed his involuntary backward somersault and got up in a crouch, facing the fire and the Kirk but not looking at the dark boy; for several seconds he just huddled there, gasping, his hands pressed against the dirt. Then his nerve broke and he was up and heedlessly clawing his way right through the cluster of bag-headed wraiths and past them, running away into darkness. He heard no pursuit, and after a hundred yards he realized that the full moon was lighting the familiar paths and hills brightly enough for him to snatch the polluted spectacles from his face and tuck them into his pocket.

CHAPTER FIVE

Usually at eight o'clock Patrick joined his daughters in the parlor for evening prayers, after which he would bar the front door, advise the girls not to stay up late, and then ascend the stairs to his room, pausing at the landing to wind the clock; and before getting into bed, he would load and prime his pistol for the morning's shot over the churchyard.

And on most nights after prayers, Charlotte, Emily, and Anne retired to the kitchen, where they would propose and elaborate and write down stories, one or another of them sitting down to write while the other two walked in circles around the table. When they'd been younger, the stories had been set in their imaginary lands of Glass Town and Gondal and Angria, and Branwell had been a lively participant. It was different now.

Having paid for the publication of a book of their poems, they had ambitions of an audience beyond just themselves, and Branwell had found broader and coarser companionship at the Black Bull. He seldom made his way home until after his sisters had put out the candles and gone to bed, leaving the kitchen door unlocked for him.

Tonight, though, when the prayers were finished and their father got up from kneeling, he didn't walk into the hall to see to the front door. Instead he sat down at the dining table and swung his head back and forth as if he could see his daughters, who glanced at one another and pulled out chairs for themselves. A wind from the west rattled the curtainless windows, and the flames of the candles on the table wavered. Keeper had come in an hour ago, and now lay under the table, grunting from time to time.

"Anne," Patrick said, "you asked who the Huberti are. I'm afraid I wasn't—"

"I missed your answer entirely," interrupted Emily. "I was out chatting with Mr. Curzon."

"Yes," said Anne, "tell Papa what he said to you."

Their father pursed his lips, then turned toward Emily's voice.

"He was alarmed," said Emily, "to hear that I had seen the dark boy who can become a flock of crows."

Patrick inhaled sharply and opened his mouth, but Emily went on, "And he said that since I helped him this morning, he would see that I'm given the benefit of Catholic absolution, before the day comes when he shall have to kill me." Her tone was resolutely light. "Then he changed his mind and decided I might be saved after all, and insisted that I go away with him—that instant."

Patrick stared in Emily's direction. "You can't have seen the boy, not *seen* him, surely! The exorcism the Catholic priest did—"

"I've seen him a couple of times," Emily said, "out on the moors, far off."

"I have too," said Anne, almost too quietly to be heard.

"A boy can't turn into crows," muttered Charlotte.

"A dead boy can," said their father hollowly, "if he wasn't precisely a boy in the first place. He can gather mass to temporarily show a physical form." He sat back and closed his nearly useless eyes. "O, what a rogue and peasant slave am I!" he said, and Emily mentally supplied phrases from the same monologue of Hamlet's that her father was quoting: *Am I a coward? Who calls me villain?*

Anne had also recognized the quote. "We don't call you villain," she said. "You did what you thought was sufficient."

"Mr. Curzon told me the boy is Welsh's spirit," said Emily. "Meaning ghost?"

Her father nodded unhappily. "It takes the form in which it was banished across the Irish Sea—open wild water—in 1710: the dark little boy in ragged clothes, whom the sailors wished to throw overboard." In a whisper he added, "And may my great-grandfather be cursed, for preventing them."

Anne looked shocked, and Charlotte was frowning, evidently dismayed by the idea that this story might after all be true. And Emily recalled Charlotte's response, sixteen years ago, when Branwell

had proposed that memorable hike out to Ponden Kirk to see their dead sister Maria "made alive again": overcoming evident reluctance, Charlotte had said, *You three go and have your game.*

Charlotte glanced at the darkness outside the windows and stood up to tilt the wick of a new candle into one of the candle flames. She fitted it into a brass candleholder and resumed her seat. The buttery smell of the freshly ignited wick wafted across the table.

Anne caught Emily's eye and, with a questioning look, held up her left forefinger, on which surely no scar remained. Charlotte was looking again toward the window, and Emily shook her head at Anne. Let's not trouble him with that, she thought, yet.

"I should have let Curzon speak," said Patrick. "Though he considers me a fool and I consider him a dangerous charlatan, he might know of some protections. Emily, did he give you any way to reach him?"

"No. I suppose I can ask in the village, in case he left information." She took a deep breath. "So who are the Huberti?"

"A French Catholic cult," said Patrick, "which pretends to date back to a seventh-century Belgian saint, Hubertus. He was bishop of Liege, and this cult claims that he was a great scourge of... werewolves."

Anne spoke up, "Saint Hubert of Liege! He's the one who was hunting a stag, and when it turned to face him he had a vision of the cross, between its antlers."

"That's genuine Papist folklore," agreed her father. "This werewolf business was certainly cooked up somewhat more recently. Half a dozen of the Huberti *approached* me in a tavern in London, in 1807, very excitedly, when I was in town to be ordained. They took me back to a private room. One of them knew me from Cambridge, and knew that I had come over from Ireland five years earlier. They addressed me as Brunty, and I let it stand." He sat back and made a sour face. "Oh, they're a weird crew—they all wear eyepatches! It's only a formality now, they see perfectly well with both eyes, but I gathered that in previous centuries they would actually, each of them, *put out* one of his own eyes!"

Anne shuddered, and Charlotte gave Emily a revolted look; but Emily was thinking of the cyclopes.

Caught up in his memories, Patrick went on, "They wanted to

recruit me—compel me!" He laughed without humor. "I really thought they meant—never mind formalities!—to cut out one of *my* eyes, right there in the tavern! Their goal, they said, was to stop the predations of devils in the north country, which had been increasing in recent years. They knew I had inadvertently brought one there from Ireland, an important one, and they wanted me to work with them. They showed me a knife—double-bladed, like the one the Curzon fellow had—and they said it was efficacious in the killing of werewolves."

"And," said Anne breathlessly, "then?"

Patrick spread his hands. "I kept them talking until a steward looked in on us, and I pushed past him and ran away!" He sighed and rubbed his brow. "I was already a joint curate in Wethersfield then, in Essex. I was engaged to be married to a girl there . . . but the things those mad Huberti had said troubled me. I went back to Ireland for a week—preached at the old church at Ballyroney—and spoke to my father."

The three sisters were listening closely. Their father spoke so seldom of his family, or his life before ordination, that today's scanty revelations on those subjects were as arresting as the fantastic and not-quite-plausible talk of werewolves.

"He told me much of what I told you girls earlier, about Welsh's origin and his—provisional, God help us!—death. And my father directed me to an old peasant woman named Meg, who . . . well, I'm not sure she wasn't an outright pagan witch, to be honest. But in exchange for sweets and tobacco she told me of one way that I might impede Welsh's spirit. It sounds foolish—" He cleared his throat and frowned defensively. "She told me to take rust scrapings from the church bell that was rung at Welsh's funeral in 1771—cast iron, like an inverted Dutch oven—and mix them with lead, and cast bullets from the result."

"You," said Emily, forcing down an incredulous laugh, "must have taken a lot of scrapings."

"I took the whole bell," he admitted. "It's in a bucket of water in a locked closet in the church sacristy. Every few days I scrape rust off of it and dry the powder to stir into the melted lead. The gunshot, the old woman told me, would be a way to 'ring Welsh's funeral bell' again."

"And remind him that he's dead," said Charlotte tonelessly.

Patrick cocked his head, apparently unsure if her remark was sarcastic. "After your mother died," he said slowly, "I got that Catholic priest to do the exorcism." He nodded, retrospectively justifying his action. "That was twenty-five years ago—and until hearing from Emily and Anne just now, I've believed that ritual finally banished the Welsh devil to Hell."

"Though you've still rung his funeral bell every morning," observed Emily.

"Against," said their father softly, "the remote . . ." His voice trailed off.

For several seconds none of them spoke. Wind battered at the window, and Keeper growled from under the table.

"Did you marry the girl?" asked Anne at last.

Patrick raised his head and sighed. "No, child. Her family had money, and they strongly disapproved of her engagement to a penniless Irish clergyman. In any case I had been studying Wesley's accounts of devils in Yorkshire, and I knew I had to come here, to put a stop to the illness I had revived in the land."

They all jumped then, for a loud, shuddering wail sounded from somewhere far out in the dark night—it was joined by another, and then still another, and the sounds wove together in barbaric harmony for many long seconds before fading.

None of the people at the table had moved, but from the corner of her eye Emily saw that Keeper was now standing in the hall, swinging his great head from the front of the house to the rear and back, and he seemed bigger, more solidly real than the wall behind him or the stone floor under his massive paws. His black lips were drawn back, and from one of his breaths to the next she could see all his teeth.

At last, as if it had been proposed and agreed on, Patrick and his daughters all stood up at once and filed out of the parlor and down the hall to the warm kitchen, Keeper crowding so closely beside Emily on one side that her shoulder brushed the wall on the other. Each of the sisters carried one of the candles, and Emily crossed to a lamp on a shelf by the black-iron range and lit it with her candle. Keeper stood by the back door.

"What was—" began Anne, then just shook her head.

Their father had found a chair at the table and sat down. He shook his head, then turned toward Keeper's deep-throated growl. "Never mind, boy," he said, "there are buckets of holy water by every door."

Charlotte clicked her tongue.

Emily realized that she was listening for the awful sound to come again out of the night, and that the others were too.

When perhaps a minute had passed with no repetition of it, Anne and Charlotte pulled out chairs on either side of Patrick and settled into them.

Patrick cleared his throat. "I've heard that sound before—in Ireland, on the evening after a village priest claimed to have killed a *faoladh,* which is the Irish term for a werewolf; no one believed him until that wailing came on the same night. Emily, I think Mr. Curzon killed one today."

And those were the voices of its mourners, thought Emily. Beside her, Anne shivered.

"You came here," Emily prompted, "to cure the illness in the land."

"I didn't know to come directly here," her father said. "For full many a year I was a sort of itinerant curate, at churches all over Yorkshire, searching for indications of Welsh's sort of devil. Anne, my dear, is it possible you could give your poor father a glass of whisky?"

Anne raised her eyebrows but said, "Yes, Papa." She moved a stool and stood on it to reach a high shelf, and when she stepped down she was carrying a heavy jar. She unscrewed the lid and carefully poured amber liquor into a teacup. She screwed the lid back on and got up on the stool again to put the jar away, then resumed her seat.

Her father took a solid sip, exhaled, and went on, "In each parish I took care to talk to the people, and hear their tales of what they called gytrashes, barguests, boggarts—monsters in the night. I was curate in . . . Dewsbury, Hartshead, Liversedge, Thornton . . ."

"Closer and closer to here," observed Emily.

Patrick held up his teacup. "How do you keep this from Branwell?"

"The jar is labeled 'Emetic,' " said Charlotte. "Go on."

"Yes. In Thornton I heard that John Wesley had preached a memorable sermon here in Haworth, and William Grimshaw had

been rector here for twenty years in the last century. I already knew that Wesley was aware of . . . lycanthropy on the moors, and when I read Grimshaw's sermons it was clear to me that he too was concerned about it." He finished the whisky, hesitated, then set the cup down. "And at Ponden Hall the Heatons were kind enough to let me study in their library."

Emily had felt Anne start at the word *Ponden,* and then relax a moment later. Ponden Hall was the two-hundred-year-old estate of the wealthy Heaton family, three miles west of Haworth and well northeast of the desolate Ponden Kirk monument. The Brontë children had been playmates of the Heaton children.

"I found some documents on local history—journals, letters— there was a copy there of *The Wonderfull Discoverie of Witches in the Countie of Lancaster,* published in 1613, which fairly indicated Haworth as the center of the supernatural whirlpool—and a disturbing Gaelic manuscript by one Uilliam Luaith Beannaigh."

No one spoke, and in the moments when the wind paused, Emily could hear the ticking of the clock on the stair landing. Keeper was sitting beside her now, and licked her hand.

"If a good deal of what you've heard and read is true," said Charlotte, "why do we stay here? Why not move back to Thornton?"

Patrick stirred, and went on slowly, "That ledger stone in the floor of the church, a few yards closer to the door than the stone over our family vault."

"The one with the grooves cut in it," said Charlotte with a nod. "You once said that the grooves were to keep people from slipping, if the floor were wet. I asked you why there weren't grooves over the whole floor in that case, and you said it proved to be too costly."

"Did I? I'm afraid I lied to you. The grooves are *ogham*, the ancient Celtic tree-alphabet. In that crude alphabet some of those grooves spell out the name of a creature that lies beneath that ledger stone. It's what I was searching for, through all those years—and, having found it, it's why I've kept my family here. You're . . . not precisely safe, but *safer*, here, where I can keep it down and—and, God willing, keep the Welsh spirit away from it."

"Keep it down?" said Emily. "It's not dead?"

"Not . . . irretrievably, I'm afraid. Frozen halfway there, say, like a stalemated king in a chess game."

"What *is* it?"

"According to the Luaith Beannaigh manuscript, it is Welsh's inhuman twin. Someone at some point killed it, mostly, more than a hundred years ago, and had its ogham name incised in the ledger stone laid over it, along with a negating branch of lines which ... *contradict* the name. The Reverend Grimshaw made sure to keep the grooves cleared of dust and mud, and added a repressive Latin phrase to the Pater Noster in his Sunday service. My fool predecessor here stopped using the Latin entirely—he insisted, reasonably enough anywhere else, that the Pater Noster should be said in the King's good English—and he even proposed filling in the grooves in the stone with mortar." Patrick shook his head. "The congregation knew better. They came near hanging him, and might have done, if I hadn't replaced him."

Emily recalled hearing how the congregation had expressed its displeasure. A donkey had been led into the church in the middle of a service, and on its back, facing the donkey's tail, was a man wearing a stack of twenty hats. It had effectively disrupted the curate's reading of a lesson, and when Emily first heard the story she had thought it was merely a grotesque clown show.

Now she said, "Facing backward on the donkey? Twenty hats?"

"The man on the donkey was not simply ridiculing the ignorant rector," her father said. "After the donkey promenade, the people dragged the poor rector outside and rolled him in a pile of ashes. The people didn't remember what it was, but in fact they were enacting an ancient pagan Celtic ritual of banishment—the man on the donkey facing away, wearing a lot of hats to represent the entire community, and ashes to show a vacated space." Charlotte had huffed as he spoke, and he added, "It's true, my dear. All that world is still not far below the surface, out here."

"*Brachiun enim,*" said Emily softly, quoting the odd Latin phrase that her father inserted into his recital of the Pater Noster, always striking a string-suspended iron triangle as he voiced the enigmatic words. "You mispronounce brachium, but that's 'arm for,' " more or less. What does it signify?"

"In Latin," her father said, "inserted before *voluntas tua*, it's a needless reference to God's arm. But in a dialect of old Celtic, those syllables—*breagh gan ainm*—mean 'Lie nameless.' Spoken while

ringing that triangle, which I chiseled and hammered from the rim of Welsh's funeral bell, it emphasizes the contradiction of the twin's name inscribed on the ledger stone, and—by the grace of God—has kept the twin down."

The clock on the stairs struck nine, and he sighed and got laboriously to his feet. "That's enough," he said, "there's nothing anyone can do tonight. I'm for bed. Don't . . . stay up too late." He yawned, as much from tension as from weariness, and turned toward the hall. "And don't let Branwell get into the emetic," he added over his shoulder.

When their father's slow steps had ascended past the stair landing, Emily told her sisters, "Later. Tomorrow."

Anne and Charlotte nodded with evident relief at postponing discussion of the things their father had said, and the three sisters pushed back their chairs and walked down the hall to fetch their folding wooden writing desks. It was reassuring to resume their usual nightly routine and open the desks on the kitchen table and set out ink bottles, pens, and sheets of paper. Even Keeper, recognizing the familiar homely ritual, consented to lie down at Emily's feet.

Charlotte allowed herself to say, "Celtic tree-alphabet! God help us!" before sighing and bending over a manuscript page.

"Tomorrow," said Emily firmly.

"Amen," agreed Anne, smoothing a page of her own.

Emily uncapped her ink bottle and dipped the nib of her pen.

Soon the kitchen was silent except for the scratching of pens. Anne had already begun writing a novel while working as a governess last year, and it was about the vicissitudes of a governess's life. Charlotte had decided to abandon the old tales of Angria and write a novel herself, drawing on her two years as a student in Brussels. Emily felt ready to begin a novel of her own, but she was resolved not to base it on her own life—her vision was of the wild, windswept moors and the isolated souls to be found in that that wilderness.

CHAPTER SIX

Branwell's room, his "studio," was at the back of the parsonage, with a big window overlooking the moors, and Charlotte and Anne slept in what used to be their aunt's room; but Emily still slept on the narrow camp bed in the small room they had all shared as children. The window overlooked the churchyard and the church steeple beyond, but when she awoke this morning and peered out, dawn was just a red streak in the sky and she saw only deep shadow below.

The room was of course too dark for her to see the pencil sketches that she knew covered the whitewashed walls, but as she lay in bed she called up in memory all those drawings of birds and faces and flowers, and the children who had busily drawn them there. The higher drawings showed more skill, being done as the children had grown taller, but Emily's thoughts were of the lowest, the clumsy rabbits and dogs done by the smallest hands.

In this predawn dimness the big old house seemed timeless, its various tragedies and joys all equally present, but paused. Wondering what had awakened her, she got out of bed and put on a robe and silently descended the stairs. Keeper followed her, and when she heard faint fumbling at the kitchen door, she knew who it must be because the dog didn't even growl.

She opened the door, and Branwell brought a gust of cold clay-scented air with him as he came stumbling into the dark kitchen. "Sit down and be quiet," she said softly as she bolted the door. "Papa hasn't fired his pistol yet. I'll make tea."

By touch she unerringly found matches and glass paper to strike

them on, and soon had a fire going in the big black-iron range and an oil lamp lit on the table. Keeper stood on the other side of the table, near Branwell, and Emily thought the dog's attitude was both protective and cautious.

She put the kettle on the range and sat down across the table from her brother, as a few hours ago she had sat here with her sisters. Branwell looked as if he'd been waylaid and robbed—his face was scratched, his clothes were muddy and disheveled, and he wasn't wearing his spectacles—but he had walked in without limping, and he wasn't obviously injured.

He pulled his spectacles out of his coat pocket, and she could see that they weren't broken.

"Could you," he said, "wash these?"

She took them from him, with a wry smile at the idea that it was his spectacles that particularly needed a wash, but stood up and rinsed them in the pot she had cleaned the teacups in. She dried them on a towel, and noted some sort of brown oil that still clung to the lenses; another dip in the pot, and rubbing with her thumbs, got them clean, and she dried them again and handed them back to him.

He fitted them on over his ears and blinked nervously around the high-ceilinged room, then sighed deeply and looked at her. He cleared his throat and said, hoarsely, "I've been through Hell tonight."

She took the kettle off the range and poured a splash of hot water into their aunt's teapot—with Grimshaw's statement painted on it in gold: *To Me to live is Christ, to Die is Gain*—swirled it around and poured it out, then filled it with hot water.

Ever since coming home after his acrimonious dismissal from his tutorial position, and the end of his claimed affair with Mrs. Robinson, his employer's wife, he had declared every day that he was suffering the tortures of the damned; but Emily respected suffering even when it was deserved, or based on delusion.

She put the teapot on the table and spooned some tea leaves into the pot, then set two cups on the table and sat down. "Tell me."

"I was—" he began. "It has to do with something that happened to me in London. I—" He stopped, clearly reconsidering what he had been about to say. "I walked out to Ponden Kirk tonight. I got lost on the way home—thought I'd die out there." He waved one hand in a gesture that took in the state of his hair and clothing.

Emily nodded. "And," she said, "London?" She wondered if he even still remembered his story of having been waylaid by robbers before getting to London, eleven years ago.

"Well—that was earlier. There was a woman at the Black Bull today, a woman I met when I was in London. She remembered me. She—she has connections, uh, employment—I think you'd—like to—"

Then his mouth twisted and he lowered his head, and he was silently crying. Emily thought of the boy who had done so many of the drawings, down near the floor or higher up, in the room they had once all shared.

She stood up and fetched the bottle labeled Emetic, and poured a liberal splash of whisky into one of the cups, then filled both cups from the teapot. As tea, it would be little more than hot water, but she pushed the fortified one toward him. "That'll cool it off for you. Drink it and go to bed, before people start getting up—tell me about it all tomorrow."

He took a sip of the tea, then looked with surprise at the jar of whisky. "Where do you keep that?"

"On the roof. Go to bed."

"Yes," he said, "bed. Sleep, that knits up the ravel'd sleave of care, and—oh, God help us, Emily."

"God can help us tomorrow."

The whisky must have cooled the tea, for he drained the cup in three big swallows, then pushed his chair back and got to his feet. Keeper watched him shuffle out to the hallway, and didn't sit down beside Emily until Branwell's steps had faded to silence on the stairs.

The north wind had died down during the night, and the whole house was silent. It was too early to sweep the kitchen and begin cooking oatmeal porridge for her father and her sisters, and Emily sat and sipped her watery tea. Keeper was sitting on the floor beside her chair, and the big mastiff's eyes were nearly level with her own.

"I think he did meet a woman," she said softly to the dog, "and go out to Ponden Kirk. But he's ashamed of something, and frightened." Perhaps understanding her, Keeper raised a massive paw and laid it on her thigh. "Of course," she said, "but we're all as God made us, and he's my brother."

The kitchen window gradually brightened, and after a while she heard her father's dawn gunshot. Ringing Welsh's funeral bell, she

thought, reminding him that he's dead. She sighed, got to her feet, and put on her apron.

Patrick usually took all his meals alone in his room upstairs, but this morning he came down and sat in the dining room, where his daughters joined him for breakfast while Tabby was in the kitchen peeling potatoes for dinner. He had brought down from his room a wooden case like a flat toolbox with a leather strap handle, and laid it on the table. He didn't speak as he ate; his blind gaze seemed to be fixed on the far wall.

His daughters exchanged questioning looks over their bowls of porridge. They had talked in whispers in the kitchen; Anne was for getting another Catholic priest out to do an exorcism, while Charlotte sternly advised consulting an Anglican bishop for advice. Emily had no suggestions, wanting to talk further with Branwell before deciding on anything.

Here at the dining room table Emily imagined her sisters felt, as she did, that any remark now would be either presumptuous or unbearably inane.

"Emily," Patrick said at last when he set down his spoon and napkin beside the wooden case, "would you join me in the churchyard?"

"Not soon, I hope," she answered with a smile. "And why in the churchyard, when we've got our own vault in the church?" Her father winced, and she regretted her flippancy. "Certainly Papa," she said.

He pushed back his chair and stood up, lifting the wooden case, which swung heavily in his hand. He walked to the hall and the front door, and Emily stepped past him and drew the bolt; when she swung the door open the morning air was cold, and smelled of dew-damp paving stones.

Today was a Thursday, but Patrick left the house every Sunday for the short walk to the church, and this morning he tapped down the front steps as unerringly as if he could see. He made his way less steadily down the path through Emily and Anne's garden, and set the case on the low churchyard wall and opened it.

Standing beside him, Emily saw that the case contained a long-barreled flintlock pistol with a curved wooden grip, and a couple of small tin boxes.

"We'll get you a pistol of your own," he said as he lifted the gun and slid a rod out of a slot below the barrel. "It's time you learned to shoot." He blinked in the direction of the clustered graves and said, "Sometimes the Greenwoods lay a plank beside their family's markers, so as not to sink in the mud when they lay flowers on them. Is it there?"

Emily stepped up onto the mossy stone wall and peered. "Yes."

"Would you set it upright against a tree or headstone about . . . twenty feet away?"

She hopped down and scuffed through dead leaves to the plank, pried it up and leaned it against one of the standing stones. Back over the wall beside her father, she watched him open the tin boxes and, clearly working by memory and touch, shake black powder from a jar into a little brass cylinder; when it was full he tipped it into the raised barrel of the gun. Next he picked up a two-inch-square patch of cloth and licked it, then laid it over the pistol's muzzle and pressed a lead ball the size of a blueberry into the center of it.

"Now to ram it down," he said, picking up the rod. A little brass cup was mounted on one end of the rod, and he used it to push the ball and the patch down into the barrel. "All the way down to sit on the powder," he said, "with no air gap. Air might blow the whole works up in your hand."

He thumbed up the pan cover and laid a couple of pinches of powder in the pan, nudging them toward the touchhole at the rear of the barrel, then closed the cover. The hammer was a curled piece of steel with a little vise at the top, in which a chip of flint was wedged, and he pulled the hammer back until it clicked and stayed up.

He handed the pistol to Emily, who held it carefully, with her finger away from the trigger.

"Extend it well out," Patrick told her, "and aim along the top of the barrel—and when you've got it pointed at the middle of the plank, pull the trigger."

She did as she was told, and a moment later the familiar *crack* shook the air; peering through the cloud of acrid white smoke, she saw that the plank had flopped forward and was lying across another gravestone.

"I heard it fall," said her father approvingly. He reached out a hand. "Let me load it again, and you watch closely how I do it."

From one of the boxes he lifted a brush, which he screwed onto the other end of the rod. "Scrub it out thoroughly between shots," he said as he thrust the brush down the barrel and twisted it. "You don't want a stray spark still in there when you pour in the fresh powder."

"What am I to shoot?"

"Set up the plank again—if you split it, the Greenwoods can get another."

"I mean . . . the church tower? Planks?"

"Oh." Patrick tugged the brush out of the barrel and paused, holding it. "Charlotte can't see well enough, and Anne's frail . . . you must shoot anything that menaces the family, you understand? Carry it with you during the day, until we get you one of your own."

Emily noted that he hadn't mentioned Branwell.

"Yes," she said. "I'll want a good deal of practice. Here, let me have it—I saw how you did it."

She deftly loaded the gun again, then laid it in the case and vaulted over the wall to set up the plank again.

"A word, Emily," said Branwell quietly, trying to sound casual.

He hadn't come downstairs until after the rest of the family had eaten their noon dinner; Emily had cut up some cheese and cold mutton for him and served him in the kitchen. He only nibbled bits of the food, but drank several cups of tea.

She sat down across the table from him. Her chestnut hair was shining in the sunlight through the window behind her, and Branwell thought she looked almost repulsively healthy and fit and alert.

"So?" she said.

He squinted at her. "So . . . what?"

"You walked out to Ponden Kirk last night," she prompted, "after meeting a woman at the Black Bull." Her tone was simply interested, curious.

"Oh. Yes, that's right."

"Did you do that because of something she said?"

"No, no—well, yes. I wanted to think clearly, in the night air." Guessing at her thoughts, he added, "I wasn't drunk." After a pause, he shrugged. "Very well, not remarkably drunk."

"This morning when you came in, all disheveled, you said you'd been through Hell."

Branwell stared into his empty teacup and forced himself not to think of the ghosts he had marched and danced with under the moon, and the burning body on the slope below the ancient monument, and the furred giant whose hand he had shaken—and the boy who had seemed for a moment to switch identities with him.

Without looking up, he said, "Well yes, I got *lost* out there! Stumbling into marshes, freezing in the wind—! I really thought I was going to die! Hell enough, I'd call it."

"With some kind of grease on your spectacles, too."

He shook his head, wishing she would drop the subject. "Some sort of marsh oil, I suppose. But—"

She cocked her head. "I think something frightened you at Ponden Kirk. You must have *run* home, to get into such a state as you were in last night."

He forced a laugh, hoping she might not recognize it as forced. "Well, all alone by m-moonlight below that terrible stone! You'd have imagined a gytrash or two yourself."

She sat back. "What did this woman say?"

"Well, as I think I mentioned, she has connections—"

"Employment, you said."

Branwell passionately wished he had said nothing at all to her this morning. "I meant income, money." Branwell wondered unhappily what Mrs. Flensing was going to say, in a few hours. He should prepare Emily, smooth the way as much as possible. "She wants us to do her a favor. A trifle—just a matter of reverence, really."

"Reverence?" said Emily, raising her eyebrows.

"It's a . . . I believe it must be a Catholic thing. She has a relic that she wants kept in the church, that being a holy place and all. Nonsense, of course, but her family owns a publishing company . . ."

He knew that his sisters had kept up their silly writing, and surely the idea of an amenable publisher would interest her.

But Emily pursued the wrong topic. "What kind of relic?"

"It's apparently a—what does it matter?"

"These are strange days, and we should watch our thresholds. A hand, a tooth?"

"A—" He considered several lies, but Mrs. Flensing might very well *show* his sister the loathsome thing. "Well, it's a *skull*, actually, but very old, clean—"

"And she's from London?" Emily's smile was skeptical. "Were there no churches in London, that she had to bring this skull to Yorkshire?"

Anne and Charlotte were doing embroidery in the parlor down the hall, and Branwell made a flattening gesture with one hand to get her to talk more quietly.

"It's mostly already here," he said, hoping his face wasn't reddening, "the rest of the body, I mean, the skeleton—it already rests in our church, you see. So it's not as if—"

"In our church?" Emily frowned, doubtless wondering where in that building an undiscovered headless skeleton might be. "Where?"

"It's very old," he repeated, "it's under that ledger stone with the lines cut in it, in the main aisle, but the—this relic of hers could be placed anywhere in the church. And in exchange for doing her this favor—this trivial favor!—she could favorably consider manuscripts—"

Emily's face had lost all expression, and Branwell was afraid that she considered the publishing idea just another of his fantasies.

"I didn't imagine all this." He was hurt, even though the story she apparently doubted was in fact mostly a lie. "I told her about you, and I said I'd introduce you to her at the Black Bull this evening. It could," he added, having to adopt his amoral Northangerland persona to go on, "benefit the whole family, financially."

He knew that his sisters had inherited some money when their aunt died four years earlier—her will had been written when his own prospects had been bright, so that he himself had been left only trinkets—and that Emily had prevailed on Anne and Charlotte to invest it all in shares in the York and North Midland Railway Company; and he had heard Charlotte express doubts about the wisdom of the investment.

The mention of finances seemed to have worked. Emily's jaw was set, and she nodded. "I think I had better meet this woman."

"Good, good," said Branwell, draining his tea and getting up. Leave before she can ask any more *questions*, he told himself.

Branwell couldn't relax for the rest of the day. He spent an hour in his room trying to work on his translation of Horace's *Odes*, but his fingers trembled too much to grip a pen, and his thoughts kept reverting to Emily's imminent meeting with Mrs. Flensing. He could

still call it off—oh yes, and lose, no doubt forever this time, the entrée into a secret, magical world; and be left as he was, to die in shabby obscurity, his talents abandoned.

In the midafternoon he sent a note to John Brown, the stonecutter and church sexton, asking him to bring five pence worth of gin to the lane by the churchyard, and Branwell managed to put on a coat and totter out to take it from him. He carried the mug up to his room without any of his sisters noticing, and after downing the fiery liquor in one gulp, he lay down on his bed and closed his eyes.

But sleep wouldn't come. When he closed his eyes he saw what he had seen for a moment last night, below Ponden Kirk—his own body standing a few yards farther down the slope, staring knowingly into his eyes; and the hand, a child's hand, that Branwell had raised to block the intolerable gaze.

Mrs. Flensing had said that the "regent lord of the tribe" was killed yesterday by the "one-eyed Catholic." Had that spectacle last night had to do with that? How could it *not*? But the dead body that had been ceremonially set afire had been some sort of enormous malformed dog.

Regent lord of the tribe?

And the terrible little boy in tattered clothing—Branwell had seen him in dreams since childhood, and once in the churchyard, barefoot in the snow—and perhaps yesterday in the churchyard, fragmenting into a flock of crows before Branwell could see the figure clearly. Always in the form of a child.

He recalled again the conversation with Mrs. Flensing last night:

What place is there for me in this company of ours?

A high one, perhaps.

A high place . . . in a company of devils.

A secret company that conducted funeral rites at Ponden Kirk, the primordial Ponden Church; among whom was a man who seemed half beast, and a child who never grew old and could switch identities with a man; a company into which he himself had been baptized by a dioscuri knife eleven years ago.

Walking away from this now might conceivably get him killed! But if he cooperated, and if Emily's imagination were such that she could grasp the admittedly dark power and glamor of it all . . .

And even if she should draw back from the opened possibilities,

for his sake she must submit to the—minor!—ordeal of having her palm pricked by the dioscuri. After that, she'd surely be free afterward to dismiss it all as one of his delusions, and go back to her placid life of cleaning and cooking and scribbling inconsequential stories.

He thought back to the lie he had told Emily—that Mrs. Flensing had some connection to a publisher. The woman did have connections in London, at least.

As far as he knew, all three of his sisters were wasting what small literary skills they might have on short melodramatic tales—fragments, really—set in the imaginary lands they'd all dreamed up in childhood.

Branwell, though, had embarked on a real novel, which he had titled *And the Weary Are At Rest*. It was not easy to get much of it written down in the periods when he wasn't too drunk or too depressed—he had found that writing a novel required more work than, as he had once described it to a friend, "the smoking of a cigar and the humming of a tune"—but he had managed to get a fair stack of pages written, and if Mrs. Flensing wouldn't object to him spurning this haunted village and moving to London, he was sure that with her help he actually *could* find a publisher who would gratefully accept his novel.

He got up and pulled his manuscript out of his desk drawer and slumped into the chair. Wearily he shuffled through the manuscript to the last page. The top half of the page was filled with blotted words that he was sure would be legible if he puzzled over them, but he dipped his pen in the inkwell and simply began writing new sentences without thinking.

A cramp in his hand eventually made him stop, and he saw that at some point the pen nib had broken, and scratched through the paper; he estimated that for at least ten minutes he had simply been indecipherably scoring the surface of the desk.

He tried to remember what marvelous scenes, what fanciful worlds, were lost in the scratches in the wood—but they had all drained from his brain through his uselessly scribbling hand, leaving not a wrack behind.

He slowly lowered his head until his forehead rested on the torn paper. "Resurrect me, Mrs. Flensing," he whispered.

CHAPTER SEVEN

Emily was waiting in the parlor for the sound of Branwell's clumping steps on the stairs. She was snapping her fingers and reminding herself to breathe deeply. God only knew when she had last been inside the Black Bull—her uneasiness with anyone besides the family and Tabby was such that she seldom walked the three hundred feet downhill to the village at all, and she didn't even like to meet the postman when he approached the parsonage. When she ventured out from under its roof it was always west, across the lonely open moors, with no company but Anne, often, and Keeper, always.

And this evening she was to go out and meet this damned woman—no doubt literally damned!—who clearly wanted to somehow *augment* the thing under the ledger stone in the church! The thing which her father had said was the halfway-dead twin of the Welsh ghost, which itself was hardly all the way dead.

Branwell hadn't heard their father's story, so he didn't know the significance of the woman's request to have that unholy skull placed in the church. But he had evidently had some uncanny encounter out at Ponden Kirk last night, after his conversation with her; and it had scared him so badly that he was willing to cajole his own sister into getting involved.

I told her about you, and I said I'd introduce you.

At the age of twenty-nine, Branwell was a broken man. But he was broken because he had tested himself against the outside world—as art student, portrait painter, tutor, even railway clerk—and had proved himself to be weak, insufficient. Emily too had tried dealing

79

with the outside world, in short stints as student and teacher, and she too had retreated at last to home. The difference between them, Emily knew, was that Branwell tormented himself with his lost opportunities, while she was entirely content with the life of housework and her writing and the seasonal changes in the infinite countryside.

Of course Branwell couldn't have helped but fall under the woman's spell.

This all seemed to have started yesterday morning, with Alcuin Curzon apparently killing a werewolf out by Ponden Kirk. Emily wished she had never found him out there, and at the same time wished he had not left.

Now she heard Branwell on the stairs. She stood up and pulled her wool coat over her white silk blouse; the blouse's sleeves were snug on her forearms and baggy by her shoulders, and she knew from reading the *Leeds Intelligencer* that it was long out of style, but she liked it. Her long skirt reached down to her boot tops, and the cuffs of the woolen gloves she pulled on overlapped the coat cuffs. She picked up her knitted handbag, and she held the fabric bunched in her fist instead of letting the bag swing by its cord, for it was very heavy.

Branwell came down the stairs at last, and Emily stepped into the hall. Her brother was wearing a frock coat of their father's that was too long in the sleeves, and gray wool trousers and his good pair of black boots. She reflected that in any sophisticated company the two of them would be a laughable spectacle, and she wondered how this skull-toting woman would appraise them.

When she opened the front door, Keeper came padding up to them from the kitchen. His muscular bulk seemed to take up a third of the width of the hall, and Emily knuckled his head affectionately.

Keeper followed them out into the cold evening wind on the front steps, and Branwell said, "Good lord, he can't come along!"

"He goes or I don't," said Emily. "Men bring their dogs into the tavern with them, don't they?"

"Not—so big." When she didn't move, he spread his arms and bobbed his head. "Very well! Just see that he doesn't bite anybody."

"Only if there's a necessity." Emily and Keeper stepped down to the pavement, and after more exasperated gesturing Branwell followed.

On the walk to Main Street, Branwell shivered and glanced anxiously at the dark churchyard, several times pulling off his spectacles to rub them with his scarf, but Emily walked along briskly, taking confidence from the bracing cold air. Her right hand was on Keeper's collar, and the dog growled at the churchyard as they passed it.

Abruptly Branwell asked, "Oh—I meant to ask—how did you get that knife? The one you dropped in the kitchen yesterday."

Emily suspected that the mysterious woman had told him to ask her that question. She kept the sadness out of her voice as she answered, "I found it on a path, as I said."

"But—and there was blood on your shirt sleeve. What happened out there?"

She laughed. "I found an injured hawk. I tried to help it, but it wasn't as badly hurt as it seemed, and flew away." True enough, she thought, after a fashion.

Branwell just shook his head and kept walking.

The Black Bull was a two-story brick building that had been a coaching inn in the sixteenth century. Emily had never before seen it by night; the lanterns that hung by the entryway threw a golden light across the street's paving stones, and when Branwell pulled open the door and held it while she stepped inside, the air was warm, lively with loud conversation and the smells of roast beef and tobacco smoke. The lamplit room was wide, and crowded with men at tables or standing by the bar, and many of them waved and called to Branwell—it was all hopelessly foreign to her, but she found herself sympathizing with Branwell's nightly retreat to this place.

At least one voice was raised in protest against a big dog coming in, but several others called, "Nah, it's just old Keeper," and the objection was overruled.

Branwell's face was red, and he was already sweating. He shrugged out of his coat and hung it on one of the few open hooks along the left-side wall, and Emily stuffed her gloves into her pocket and hung her coat over his.

"I've reserved the snug," Branwell said into her ear, and he pushed her forward into the noisy main room. "All the way at the back."

He stepped ahead, and she and Keeper followed him in a winding course between tables and groups of men. Emily nodded civilly to

several of them whom she recognized from her father's Sunday services; they nodded back, in some evident surprise to see the curate's reclusive daughter here. Branwell greeted nearly everyone they passed, with a joviality that surprised Emily; clearly her brother was a different person here than at home. Keeper stayed by Emily's side as they moved through the room, forcing some patrons to move their chairs, and paid no attention to any of them.

Branwell slid open a door in the far wall and stepped though, and when Emily and Keeper had followed him he slid the door closed, effectively shutting out the racket of conversations.

This chamber was much smaller than the main room, but two oil lamps on the long polished table threw an amber radiance across six comfortably spaced armchairs and a tall, glass-fronted cabinet displaying a variety of bottles and glasses. Emily was peripherally aware of wainscotted walls and framed prints, but her attention was fixed on the woman standing behind one of the chairs.

A coat and scarf and a big brown leather valise on the table clearly belonged to her. She was as tall as Emily, several inches taller than Branwell, and her snuff-colored skirt and blouse emphasized her dark hair. A scent of mimosa prevailed over old smells of cigars and furniture polish.

Her glittering brown eyes were fixed on Emily's. Emily made herself stare back with no expression. Keeper stood rigid by her waist, and she curled her fingers more tightly around his collar.

"Mrs. Flensing," said Branwell with nervous formality, "may I present my sister, Miss Emily Brontë; Emily, Mrs. Flensing."

Emily might have reflexively curtseyed, but Mrs. Flensing's eyes had widened, and Emily hesitated, standing straight.

The woman stared at her for several seconds, then turned to Branwell. *"Brunty?"* she asked.

"Brontë," spoke up Emily, rolling the R slightly. "It's Italian." She didn't glance at Branwell.

"That's right," he said, waving their remarks aside, perhaps not having heard them. "I was telling Emily," he said quickly, "that your family owns a publishing company—Emily writes," he added, turning to his sister, "don't you?" After a moment he added, "Could we all sit?"

Mrs. Flensing hadn't taken her eyes off Emily. "Take," she said, "the dog out of here."

"We're away, then," said Emily. "It was nice meeting you, Mrs. Flensing."

Branwell threw himself down in one of the chairs. He looked at his boots and waved a hand over his head. "I'm sorry! It's both of them or neither!"

Mrs. Flensing nodded slowly, looking from Emily to Keeper and back. "You'll pardon me then," she said, "if I take a precaution which is, I'm sure, unnecessary."

From a pocket in her skirt she drew a knife; Emily recognized it as a duplicate of Curzon's.

"Now," the woman went on, sinking carefully into the chair next to Branwell's, "as your brother says, my family does own a London publishing company, and we would certainly give serious consideration to any production of yours. From what your brother has said, I'm confident that we have a future together."

Emily nodded, doubting it and wondering what the woman's accent was. She hung her handbag on the back of a chair across the table from the other two, and slowly sat down. With her left hand she held Keeper's collar to keep him from standing up with his paws on the table.

"But first of all," said Mrs. Flensing, with a tight smile, "I must note that we regard our writers as members of our publishing family, and we indulge in an old custom, dating back to the days when Swift and Addison were among our clients. No doubt it will strike you as silly." She raised the knife. "A prick to the palm."

"It doesn't hurt," said Branwell.

Emily was sure now that the woman had no connection at all with any publishing company.

"And a relic to be deposited at our church," Emily said, with a wave toward the leather bag on the table.

"Oh," said Mrs. Flensing. "Yes. A small thing. Your brother needn't have mentioned it." From the corner of her eye Emily saw Branwell flinch and open his mouth; but Mrs. Flensing went on, "As you say, it's a relic, and my family would like it deposited in a church."

"May I see it?"

"No, my dear. It's . . . a sacred object, and we prefer—"

"It's the skull of a monster," said Emily.

"Emily!" wailed Branwell. "I never—"

Emily felt Keeper tense under her hand. Mrs. Flensing stared at her blankly for a few seconds, then laughed softly. "Your brother chooses to see what he fears. There are no monsters."

As she spoke she reached into the pocket of her coat on the table, and pulled out a flat case. Branwell stiffened, but when the woman opened it Emily saw that it contained a row of narrow green cigars. Mrs. Flensing lifted one out, sniffed it, and then tucked it between her lips.

She pulled one of the lamps closer. "What you have to consider," she said as she lifted the glass chimney and leaned forward to puff the cigar alight from the lamp flame, "is"—and the syllable was a twist of smoke—"extension of perspective, and vitality. Ah, what can the woman mean, eh?" The glass chimney clinked back into place and she leaned back. "Something frightening? Well, yes, if you choose to be frightened by wider horizons."

She exhaled a plume of smoke, and the aroma was not that of burning tobacco. The smell reminded Emily of heather and clay and wet stone; sharp in her nostrils, even astringent, but as invigorating as a cold spring breeze at dawn.

Mrs. Flensing went on, "But your path is not the path of the herd, narrow and short. Through no fault or virtue of your own, yours is no beaten path at all, for it stretches to the horizon in all directions—yourself everywhere inviolate, untouched—your name kept safe, never pared down to letters chiseled on a stone to erode away to nonentity."

The sharp smoke was making Emily dizzy, and the woman's talk of horizons brought up visions of endless windswept moors under gray skies...hills and unexplored valleys and cold becks, the landscape marked for eternity with the old standing stones...

Mrs. Flensing was speaking again: "Why would a knife need two points? Wouldn't one do?" She exhaled a curling cloud. "No. Not for us. A double-pricking to confuse location, each of us apart."

Branwell clenched his right hand into a fist and then opened it again.

"Encroaching order," said Mrs. Flensing, "encroaching *time*, are pushed back." She lowered her hand and reached out to touch the leather bag on the table. "New freedom always strikes us as wrong, monstrous, at first. But what I propose is simply restoring a relic to

its proper, honorable place." Her smile was welcoming. "You are already set apart, you know. Give me your hand, and never need to take anyone's hand again."

The woman reached again into the pocket of the coat, and this time set on the table a small glass jar that seemed to contain clear oil.

Emily thought of the ways in which she was indeed already set apart. The idea of marriage and children had never held any attraction for her, and conviviality of the sort going on in the bigger room beyond the door at her back was unfathomable: dissipation, in every sense. The people of the village, and of the remote busy world, were ciphers—their motives, if any, only to be guessed at. Her strength and firm identity thrived in solitude.

Emily's right hand crept forward almost involuntarily—but, below the table, her left hand on Keeper's collar was pulled downward as the dog lowered his heavy head. Keeper's jaws closed firmly on her ankle, not puncturing her stocking but pressing hard enough to hurt; and she felt the vibration of his inaudible growl.

And the dog's insistent presence called to her mind the real moors over which the two of them ranged nearly every day; a land that was expansive and wild, but in fact bounded by towns and roads and the cycles of, for her and Keeper, finite numbers of seasons.

Emily and her dog lived and thrived in the uncompromising natural world, snow and wool and springtime and potatoes to be peeled; and what this woman offered was a rejection of that—no doubt to gain something else, but it would be something else. Emily flexed her legs and shifted her feet on the stone floor.

From the corner of her eye she saw Branwell squinting anxiously at her. For all his weakness and delusion, he was inextricably a member of her solitude; as were Anne and Charlotte and their father, and Tabby, and Keeper himself. What good did Branwell imagine this diabolical woman offered *him*?

Emily smiled and withdrew her hand, and reached across to slide it into her handbag. She pushed her chair back from the table, and when she stood up and shook the handbag off to fall on the floor, she was holding her father's pistol.

Mrs. Flensing was on her feet too, facing Emily with her hands at her sides. Her face was rigidly set, and she whispered, "Prove it if you must."

But Emily swung the barrel to the side, toward the leather bag on the table, and pulled the trigger. The gun's pan cover flipped up and powder sizzled in the pan, and even as Mrs. Flensing shouted and vaulted across the table the gun flared and the air in the room shook to the confined bang of the gunshot. Sparks flew in all directions.

Mrs. Flensing howled, and through the churning smoke Emily was able to see the woman slide off this side of the table; she landed crouching, furiously knuckling at her eyes with her free hand, and Emily scrambled back as the woman lunged blindly at her with the knife—

And then the woman was flung backward by the impact of Keeper and, somehow, another big mastiff, and both dogs were snarling loudly and leaping at her.

The knife in the woman's hand flashed toward Keeper's shoulder; but neither mastiff fell back, and the woman was now bent over the table while the dogs tore at her arms and clothing.

The woman howled again, in pain as much as frustrated rage this time, and a moment later she had grabbed the holed leather bag and used it to batter her way past the two lunging dogs. Covering her head with one bloody hand, she wrenched open the sliding door and plunged through the group beyond that had obviously leaped to their feet in alarm at the gunshot and screams.

Keeper moved back beside Emily, who quickly picked up her fallen handbag and shoved the still-smoking gun into it. Blood drops were spattered across the floor, but when she glanced at Keeper she saw only a small cut on his shoulder where the woman's knife had caught him, and it wasn't perceptibly bleeding.

She collapsed back into her chair just as half a dozen men came crowding into the room, blinking in the gunpowder smoke. The second dog was nowhere to be seen; could it have run out through the crowd? Emily had not been able to get a clear look at it in the violent confusion, but it had been darker than Keeper, and not quite as massive.

"What the hell happened?" yelled one big man in an apron, who Emily took to be Mr. Sugden, the landlord.

"The woman who just ran out of here," she said, "fired a gun at my brother. My dog spoiled her aim." Keeper was standing beside her, watchful but no longer tense.

Branwell's face was in his hands, his fingers clutching his curly red hair. "Oh," he almost sobbed, "true, yes, that's what she did. Oh God."

"Damn me!" exclaimed Sugden. He looked over his shoulder toward the front door. "Is she gone? Some of you catch her, or fetch the magistrate or something." He turned back to look around the still-smoky room. "Is Keeper hurt? There's blood there!"

"No," said Emily. "She cut her hand when the gun went off."

"Recoil," muttered one man.

"Can't have been holding it properly," agreed another.

The men in the doorway shuffled back toward the bar, talking loudly among themselves.

"She was in yesterday," Sugden said. "You spoke with her, Branwell. Who is she?"

Branwell lifted his face. "A . . . Catholic agitator."

Emily thought this lie was unfair to Mr. Curzon, who apparently really was a Catholic, but this was no time to muddy the story.

"My brother refused her enticements," she said.

Branwell groaned.

Two men blundered up behind Sugden and breathlessly announced that the woman had run out to the street and disappeared.

"Did you look for her?" Sugden demanded.

"We looked up and down the street from the doorway," one of the men said, adding defensively, "Who's to say she hadn't another gun?"

"I'll fetch a mop," muttered Sugden, turning away.

Emily stood up and stepped to the table. Her pistol ball had dug a splintery groove in the polished wood, and scraps of leather and bone fragments were scattered on the table and the floor.

Branwell stood up at last. His voice was squeaky with shock. "You ruined it," he said. "Emily. My chance—our chance."

Keeper lowered his head and dropped a couple of pale, two-inch long objects at Emily's feet. She caught her breath—but glanced toward the doorway, then quickly crouched, picked them up, and tucked them into her handbag. She was glad Branwell hadn't seen—it would do him no good to know that Keeper had bitten off two of Mrs. Flensing's fingers.

She wiped her hand on her skirt and reached across the table to take Branwell's arm. "Home," she said gently.

Branwell stepped around the table and stood unsteadily beside her. "I . . . need a drink. God, several drinks."

"There's whisky in the kitchen."

He nodded several times, and let her escort him through the main room, moving from a haze of gunsmoke into one of tobacco smoke. People shifted out of their way, and a couple of men called offers to buy drinks for the two of them, but Branwell seemed not to hear, and Emily shook her head. Keeper walked ahead of them, sniffing the tangle of smells in the air.

Branwell's hands were shaking so badly that Emily had to help him into his coat before putting on her own.

She looked around at the street as they stepped outside, but there was no sign of Mrs. Flensing. The men who had looked out the door for her had not mentioned horses or a coach—was the woman crouched in some recessed doorway, out of the moonlight?—still holding the knife? Keeper was pacing vigilantly beside her, and she reached down to touch his head as she tried to hurry Branwell along the pavement.

Branwell took off his spectacles as they approached the churchyard. He was panting deeply and rapidly; clouds of his breath whisked away on the night wind.

"Where in *Hell*," he said, "did that other dog come from?"

"I can't imagine," said Emily. "Could it have been under the table all along?"

Branwell sniffed and shook his head. "There was blood on the floor! My God! How badly did they maul her?"

Emily thought of the two severed fingers in her handbag, but shrugged. "She ran out fleetly enough, even with smoke in her eyes. She poked your palm with that knife, didn't she?"

"What? Oh—yes, years ago, when I was in London. It's done me no harm! Why did you have to ruin . . . it would have been . . ."

"What did I ruin?"

"Besides . . . *everything*?"

The razory wind was much colder now than it had been when they had left the parsonage less than an hour ago, too cold even to carry smells, and it found every gap between Emily's coat buttons. She rubbed Keeper's bristly back.

Branwell faltered to a stop, eyeing the churchyard ahead of them.

"Mrs. Flensing," he went on through clenched teeth, clearly trying hard to speak coherently, "gets a bit *mystical*, it's true. All that talk of ... *paths* and *horizons* and being *set apart* is just a lot of cant about *spiritual awakening* that she got from reading Swedenborg. But she's a member of a ... an old aristocratic family, and their position, their *influence* was crippled yesterday when some kind of *one-eyed Catholic* killed their, er, patriarch."

They resumed walking, past the church belltower that their father shot at every morning, and Emily glanced ahead at the lighted windows of the parsonage. "And that skull?" she asked.

Branwell spread his hands and bared his teeth at the dark sky. "They need assistance in restoring their position—and placing that relic in our church would have gone a long way toward accomplishing that." He gave her a sidelong glance. "Socially, you understand! Politically! And she probably *could* have got your damned stories published! But you had to—" He shoved his hands into his pockets and hunched along more quickly, so that Emily and Keeper had to hurry to keep up. "Oh, what's the use of *anything* anymore."

"Did she let *you* look at it? The skull?"

"No," said Branwell curtly, and Emily knew he was lying. Reviewing his pathetically adapted account—*socially, politically!*—she was disappointed to realize that Branwell *had* in fact known that he was aiding devils, and had tried to get her to do the same; but she was impressed to hear it confirmed that Alcuin Curzon had killed one of the things.

She heard faint noises from the darkness beyond the low churchyard wall—twigs snapping, and a swishing as if someone were sweeping up last year's dead leaves in the dark. Branwell blinked in that direction and looked away, but Keeper kept looking back toward the church. Emily breathed in and out strongly, for the bad air in the churchyard sometimes made breathing difficult.

At last they reached the foot of the steps up to the parsonage front door, and Emily put her hand on her brother's shoulder. "It *was* the skull of a monster, you know," she told him quietly.

"How do you know?" He sniffed and wiped his nose on his coat sleeve. "You didn't even see it, you just blew it up."

"I know what the rest of its body is. It's under that ledger stone in the church, the one with the grooves cut in it."

He stepped away from her, shivering. "Wha—how do you know about this? Can't we go inside? I caught a devilish chill last night, and this wind—"

"What that woman offered was a place in Hell."

Branwell wailed and swept his hand in a wide gesture that took in the parsonage and all of Haworth. "Better to serve in Hell than rot in Purgatory."

A flicker of light behind him, beyond the churchyard, caught Emily's eye. Now it was gone, but she was sure it had been in one of the church windows.

She caught Branwell's arm. "There's someone in the church."

Branwell turned to look in that direction, and after a moment of blinking uselessly he fitted his spectacles back onto his face—and flinched.

"Somebody praying," he said shortly. "Let's get inside."

"It's her. She'll hide what's left of the skull there somewhere—and even a stray tooth might accomplish some part of her purpose." She took his arm again. "Come on."

"I won't. There's things among the graves."

"Nothing that will come near my dog."

She hurried back the way they had come, clutching Keeper's collar to keep him from running ahead, and in fact the dog did seem to sense something in the churchyard to their right. Certainly the trees were creaking. But Emily hurried past it, tugging him along the walk that slanted away from the street toward the church. Branwell's footsteps scuffed close behind her.

She strode up to the church's side entrance; one of the pair of tall ironbound doors was ajar, and she leaned to peer in. The long nave was in complete darkness, and only in her memory was she aware of the rows of pews, and the altar and raised pulpit at the far end to her right. She let Keeper sniff around in the doorway before she stepped through.

The still air inside the church was slightly warmer, but over the usual smells of old wood and candlewax she caught a taint of mimosa; and she heard a thump that seemed to shake the stone floor. After a few seconds she heard it again. She shivered, and felt the muscles of Keeper's massive neck flex under her hand.

Then there was light—up by the altar to her right, a point of yellow light resolved itself into the bullseye lens of a dark lantern

with the shutter now retracted, and by its glow Emily saw Mrs. Flensing bending over what appeared to be a bloody severed head on the altar. The woman hadn't shed her coat, but the sleeves were pulled back to the elbows.

Emily hurried along the side aisle toward the altar, and she thrust her hand into her handbag and fumbled past the pistol to clutch the two severed fingers she had picked up from the floor at the Black Bull. Keeper trotted ahead of her, weaving from side to side to prevent her from passing him.

Mrs. Flensing had set the lantern on the altar and had both hands, one now missing two fingers, on the red-streaked object that sat on the flat surface. Her disordered hair hung in strings over her face, which gleamed with sweat. Emily could now see that the object on the altar was the deformed skull of a big animal, with the rim of one eye socket missing and a gap at the temple. Clearly Mrs. Flensing had reassembled many of the pieces of the skull Emily had shot, apparently using her own blood as glue.

Emily couldn't imagine what species the skull came from. The top of it was a high dome, and its canine teeth extended down past the jawbone.

She caught up with Keeper and again took hold of his collar. In her handbag, the two cold fingers in her hand twitched, and she nearly let go of them.

She heard a grating sound from the central aisle, and then the massive thump sounded again, echoing among the high crossbeams of the church ceiling; and Emily's chest went cold when she realized that they were the sounds of the ledger stone lifting slightly and dropping back into place.

The woman looked up, blinking and squinting at the sound of Emily's footsteps on the stone floor, and she quickly extended her left arm, pointing along the central aisle; and she turned her bloody palm up and raised her maimed hand. There was nothing on her palm, but she grimaced as if her hand were meeting strong resistance.

Again Emily caught the sound of stone grating on stone ... but this time it was not followed by the heavy impact of the stone falling back.

Emily's face tingled in alarm. It seemed Mrs. Flensing had decided to fully revive the thing.

The severed fingers in Emily's hand were bending and straightening more energetically. Gripping them in her fist, she pulled them free of her handbag and held them out in front of her, and she rotated her fist so that the fingers were pointing downward.

The floor shook to a resounding slam.

And Keeper's collar was wrenched out of Emily's hand as the dog bounded forward.

Mrs. Flensing retreated to the back wall, and the double-bladed knife was in her unwounded hand—but Keeper leaped past her, up onto the altar, and closed his jaws in the nasal cavity and the broken eye socket of the big skull. He shook his head violently, as if with revulsion, and pieces of the blood-smeared skull flew in all directions.

For one full second the ledger stone in the aisle chattered in its bed, and Mrs. Flensing fell back against the wall, gasping.

Behind Emily, Branwell had howled in the same second, and when she turned to him he had fallen to his knees, with one hand braced on the floor and the other thumping furiously against his temple; his lungs emptied to wheezing silence, and then he was panting as if he'd just finished running a race.

Emily looked back toward the altar in time to see the sacristy door slam shut. Mrs. Flensing wasn't visible, and Keeper had jumped down from the altar and was peering around in the reflected light of the abandoned lantern.

In four long running strides Emily was up on the raised floor beside the altar, but when she wrenched open the sacristy door she was met with a gust of cold night air, for the exterior door at the far end of the dark room was swinging back and forth in the wind. She dropped the severed fingers into her handbag.

She turned back to the obliquely lit nave and ran down the side aisle to where Branwell was slowly getting to his feet.

Scared by his fit moments ago, she shook him by the shoulders till his eyes focused on her. She said loudly, "Do you know me, Branwell?"

"I—wish I didn't."

"Who am I?"

"Emily." His panting had slowed to normal breathing, and he yawned. "I'm sick."

She let go of him and stepped back. "Be sick later. We've got some cleaning up to do here."

"In the morning—"

"In the morning you'll be even less use than you are now. Take that lantern and walk over the floor, down every pew and looking under it, and *pick up every piece of bone.*"

"I'm sick, I tell you. That cigar of hers reeked of London—factory smokes, unwashed crowds, vomit—"

Emily reached into her handbag. Mrs. Flensing's fingers were inert now, limp. And with a shiver she wondered what the cigar smoke had smelled like to Keeper.

"Find every scrap of bone," she said. Keeper had trotted back to where they stood, and she ran her fingers through the fur on his big shoulder. "Keeper will help you find them, and he'll know if you shirk." She felt a matted tuft at one point among the fur, and pulled the dog forward so that a reflection of the lantern beam lit the spot. Parting his fur carefully she saw that there was only the one small puncture in the dog's skin that she had noticed earlier.

But how could that double-bladed knife have inflicted only one puncture? Suddenly dizzy, she thought: Well, there were two dogs.

She shoved Branwell toward the altar. "Every piece, as you may still value your soul. I'll find a collection basket to hold it all."

"What will you *do* with them?"

Emily just stared at him, and he waved his arms over his head and then shambled toward the altar, peering at the floor. I'll bury them, Emily thought, at widely separated spots far out on the moors. The thing under the ledger stone can go headless for eternity.

Their father had gone upstairs to bed by the time Emily and Branwell and Keeper returned to the parsonage, and Anne opened the kitchen door when Emily knocked. Branwell blundered past Anne and Charlotte without a word and stumbled away up the stairs. Keeper stood by the back door until Anne closed it, then lay down by the big iron range.

Emily pulled a chair out from the table and sat down. She laid her handbag on the table and exhaled, and after a moment looked from Charlotte to Anne.

"I believe," she said, "that the sickness in the land is cured."

Charlotte slid a cup of tea in front of Emily's right hand, and Emily lifted it and took a sip. She was very tired, but her hand was steady. "Or at least," she amended, setting the cup down, "restored to the sort of remission Papa has strived to maintain."

"Oh?" said Charlotte, raising an eyebrow. "When? How?"

"Can he stop shooting his gun at the church every morning?" asked Anne.

"Not quite." To Charlotte, Emily said, "An hour or so ago"—and she reached into her handbag and pulled out their father's heavy gun—"this played a part," she said. "So did poor Branwell, in spite of himself. The real heroes, though—"

Anne sat down beside Emily. "Did you shoot the . . . the Welsh thing?"

"No. I—no." Emily smiled tiredly. "I shot a werewolf's skull."

Anne nodded uncertainly. "That's always a good thing to do, I imagine."

"The real heroes?" prompted Charlotte, taking the chair across the table.

"That Curzon fellow, for one," said Emily. "In spite of his abominable manner. It seems that the werewolf he killed yesterday morning was a sort of king of the species, and with its loss the whole species is severely weakened. The other hero was Keeper."

She reached again into her handbag. "This is unpleasant," she warned Anne, then pulled out Mrs. Flensing's two fingers and laid them on the table. It was the first time Emily had been able to look closely at them, and she shuddered at the ragged blood-clotted ends and the long nails.

Anne had sat back, and she darted an alarmed look at Emily's hands before meeting her eyes. "Keeper did that?" she whispered.

"Are you in some trouble now?" asked Charlotte, fastidiously looking away from the gruesome exhibit. "Bury those things!"

"I think I'll keep them," said Emily, "though I might get rid of this bag. Yes, Keeper did it, God bless him. And I might be in some trouble, but nothing to do with the laws of England."

She stood up, looking around the kitchen. "I don't want them in my room—I'd imagine them crawling around like caterpillars." On a high cupboard shelf stood a row of dusty glass jars containing old iron nails and chisels and brushes; one jar was empty, and she stood

on tiptoe to fetch it down. She dropped Mrs. Flensing's fingers into it and then reached up to slide it back onto the shelf. "They can't get out of that."

She resumed her chair. "Tomorrow if you like you can go to the Black Bull and look at the table in the snug. It all started there, with Branwell and a woman."

Curtains glowed in the houses that closely fronted the steep, narrow main street of Haworth, but no one opened a door to question the solitary figure trudging carefully downhill in the dark. Tonight Mrs. Flensing's hired carriage and driver waited at the bottom of the street.

Yesterday the two horses had labored to pull the carriage up the street to the level area by the inn and the church, in spite of the paving stones laid crossways to give hooves some purchase, and today the driver had refused to try it again. The three-mile trip had been all uphill from the town of Keighley, and he had told her that if the horses slipped on the Haworth street the carriage would probably roll all the way back there.

It had been no use for her to argue that he must frequently be called on to carry passengers from the hotel in Keighley to Haworth, and she suspected that he was familiar with local legends and had at some point yesterday managed to sneak a look into her bag—now lying somewhere on the church floor back there, torn and empty.

Her hand was throbbing under the handkerchief she had wrapped around it, and she wondered bleakly if the fingers would grow back separately or as one ungainly semi-thumb, which sort of thing she had seen happen with others in the tribe.

Alone on the dark, slanted pavement, she bared her teeth in a snarl. She had finally blinked and rubbed the stinging gunpowder dust out of her eyes, and they seemed to be undamaged.

If only Curzon had succeeded in killing himself, as she was fairly sure he'd meant to do. The sanctimonious Huberti were so proud of their abstinence—it must have undone him to learn that rage could provoke the old, vainly renounced change in him.

Mrs. Flensing spat on the street.

But he *would* try to marry outside his clan! Vain folly—as was no

doubt impressed upon him when he saw the broken meat of his precious fiancée on the steps of her family home.

And then he had *not* killed himself; instead at Ponden Kirk he had been confronted by the regent of the moorland kindred—and had managed to kill *him*! And the sustaining supernatural field generated by the wild kindred, whom Reverend Farfleece likened to an electric battery, had suddenly been depleted all across these northern moors.

Even miles away, Mrs. Flensing had felt that death as a blurring of her vision, an ache in her joints—and she knew that the Obliques in London too must be alarmed at finding the early signs of age and infirmity intruding on their artificially maintained youthfulness.

Farfleece's "battery" needed a strong renewal.

But it was more like a whirlpool than a battery, really—a *hyper*-natural distortion of *ordinary* natural possibilities, and the greater the number of conscious entities that participated in its deviant spin like children dancing around a maypole, amplifying the distorting momentum, the deeper and more powerful the "whirlpool" became. The druids had long ago deduced the implicit counter-nature impulse in ordinary reality, and set it in motion by using its initially small potential to cure mild illnesses or blight the crops of rival tribes. Gradually they had deepened and accelerated it until it could encompass effects like shape-changing, earth-rending, the liberation of ghosts . . . and, at a comfortable distance, wealth and extended life and immunity to injury and disease.

But this morning the "whirlpool" had, as it were, become turbulent, and lost much of its depth.

When Mrs. Flensing learned of the killing yesterday, she had hired a horse and ridden far out across the moors to the top of Crow Hill, and had retrieved the twin's skull, hidden away for more than a hundred years.

It had been all she could think of to do. The twin's skull had been kept separate from its body under the church floor because the twin was one half of the Obliques' biune god, the other half being the boy Welsh, who had been exiled across the Irish Sea—and in truth none of the Oblique order were very eager to have the two persons of their god actually revived and reunited. Though they would never say so outright, it was felt to be an apotheosis that was better anticipated

than achieved. Whatever the result, it would be tumultuous, and would certainly upset their reasonably augmented lives.

And getting the skull had not been easy. Originally a cairn had stood at the top of the hill, marking the burial site of the skull, but in 1824 the hill had erupted and sent a massive flood down into the valley. The cairn was gone, but the skull had still been there, above the gullied and already overgrown east face of the hill. Mrs. Flensing had had to cut her hand and leave baptized blood in the dirt even to be able to see the skull, which would otherwise have eluded focus and been securely lost in the overall view of the rocky landscape. And then the ungainly thing had resisted being tugged free of the ground, as if it had grown invisible roots.

When she had finally got it into her bag, she should have ridden straight to the Haworth church and hidden it wherever she could. It had been a mistake to ride back to Keighley to wash her face and hands and change her clothing and hire the carriage. And it had been a disastrous mistake then to delay so that the *poseur* Northangerland could fetch his vandal sister.

Mrs. Flensing didn't want to think of the twin's skull, shot to pieces—and then, after painful and partial reconstruction, flung in fragments all over a church floor by that giant dog...which had seemed to become *two* dogs, when it had attacked her earlier!

Emily Brontë. Emily *Brunty*, without a doubt. Northangerland had said that she had been bitten by what was clearly a kindred animal—the girl would have to be brought into line, baptized, before she could do even further harm.

When Mrs. Flensing reached the bottom of the steep street at last, the moonlight was bright enough for her to see that the carriage was gone. The driver had probably worked himself into a state, imagining boggarts and gytrashes rolling and hopping along the road, and fled.

She looked back up the steep street, but it was impossible to guess what story the Brunty siblings might have told about her.

It would be many more hours before dawn. She began walking north, toward Keighley.

In the dark upstairs hallway, Keeper sat in front of the door to Emily's little bedroom. He was aware of Charlotte and Anne in the

room to his left, Tabby's room the next door past that, and the girls' father in the room to his right. The next door down the hall on that side was Branwell's.

Keeper had lapped up some water from the bucket beside Emily's door, but he remembered the elusive sourness of the woman's blood. It was familiar, but from long ago, calling up just a few seconds of traumatic memory: the man called Welsh attacking the dog's young master, Hugh, and Keeper leaping and driving his teeth into Welsh's face. That blood had had the same bitter taint.

But that had been the other dog, whose name was also Keeper, the dog whose eyes and muzzle he sometimes saw instead of his own in still, sunlit pools; the dog who had joined him in protecting Emily from the woman with the sharp weapon tonight.

Later, in the darker building, the woman had brandished the weapon again, but Keeper had lunged past her and shaken to pieces the bones of... something that was both an animal and a man, which had in the moment seemed to be the greater threat. The woman had fled then, but Keeper hadn't pursued her because that would have meant leaving Emily alone with the one called Branwell.

Branwell was a troubling figure. He was a member of Keeper's family, and Emily loved him, but there was the tendency toward unanticipated rage, even a quality of interloper, in the young man.

As if summoned by Keeper's mental image, the door to Branwell's room now opened and Branwell stepped out into the hall, carrying a lit candle. He was still draped and sheathed in the clothes he'd been wearing earlier.

Keeper stood up, staring at him. Branwell's feet were bare now, and he had padded past Tabby's door before he saw Keeper. For a full ten breaths the man and the dog stood staring at each other. At last Branwell exhaled hoarsely and turned away.

When Branwell had gone back into his room and the door had closed and clicked, Keeper hooked one big paw into the bucket and pulled it over; its rim clanked on the floorboards, and the water spread out silently across the floor all the way to Branwell's door.

Keeper sat down. Emily would scold him for having spilled the bucket, but he would remain by her door, alert, until she woke up in the morning.

PART TWO:
SEPTEMBER 1846

✠

[A] rapid torrent of mud and water issued forth, varying from twenty to thirty yards in width, and from four to five in depth; which, in its course for six or seven miles, entirely threw down or made breaches in several stone and wooden bridges—uprooted trees—laid prostrate walls ...
—Patrick Brontë, *The Phenomenon; or, an Account in Verse, of the Extraordinary Disruption of a Bog, Which took place in the Moors of Haworth, On the 12th day of September, 1824*

CHAPTER EIGHT

Emily unbolted the front door of the parsonage and stepped outside.

Her long walks on the moors had not led her out to the grim monument of Ponden Kirk since the morning she had found Alcuin Curzon there, six months ago, though it often figured in her dreams. The dreams were nearly always just views of the black edifice from far off, but last night she had found herself reliving the day when three children had hiked there and left blood in the fairy cave at its foot.

As she closed the parsonage door behind her and started down the steps toward the lane that led past the narrow cemetery to the church, she took deep breaths of the cold morning air, and shook her head to dispel the clinging fragments of the dream—young Branwell with his pocketknife, her own voice saying *They look like Roman foundations*, and Anne's remark: *This wasn't a game at all, was it? And it never had anything to do with Maria.*

Branwell would certainly sleep till noon today. It was just as well.

Keeper trotted beside Emily on the still-damp paving stones, his massive shoulders rippling under his short tan fur. The right side of Emily's coat swung heavily with the weight of her father's pistol, which she had fired over the churchyard an hour ago.

For these past two weeks Charlotte and their father had been thirty miles away in Manchester, where her father had undergone an operation to remove the cataracts from his eyes and restore his vision. The oculist who had performed the operation had declared it a success, but their father had to remain in bed in a dark room for

101

four weeks afterward, and Charlotte had rented rooms in Manchester for the duration.

And so Emily had taken on some of her father's more obscure duties, and on this Wednesday morning she had a matter to attend to in the church.

The substitute curate that the Vicar of Bradford had sent to the Haworth church had, not surprisingly, recited the Lord's Prayer in English during his Sunday services, and omitted the Latin phrase that the Reverend Grimshaw had begun using in the last century. And of course he had not rung the triangle that Emily's father always struck at the end of the prayer—chiseled from the bell that had rung at Welsh's funeral in 1771.

The villagers understood that her father would be back soon, and at the last two Sunday services several of them had smiled at Emily and nodded, evidently aware that she was doing what she could to maintain the sensible forms. There was no necessity for a donkey in the church with a backward-facing rider wearing twenty hats.

At the side door of the church she turned and looked back at the parsonage, across the flat and standing gravestones. If their father were to die of an infection down there in Manchester, she and her sisters and Branwell would be turned out of the place, for the building belonged to the Leeds Diocese of the Church of England, and would house their father's replacement and his family.

Emily and her sisters had some experience as teachers and governesses, but any such jobs as they might find would hardly be likely to be at all close to one another. And of course Branwell would die in an asylum.

The sisters had completed the novels they had begun in the late winter, and Charlotte's *The Professor*, Anne's *Agnes Grey*, and Emily's *Wuthering Heights* had been submitted—fruitlessly—to several London publishers; and only yesterday Emily had received a letter stating that all three novels had once again been rejected.

The London firm of Aylott & Jones had published their book of poems three months ago. Two copies had sold.

Emily shivered and pulled open the church door. The tall stained glass windows in the north and south walls threw a dim radiance over the empty pews, but she didn't step inside until Keeper had sniffed the cold air and led the way in. She followed the big

bullmastiff along the side aisle to the altar, and from the way Keeper swung his head to look ahead and behind, she guessed that he would always remember shaking the half-human skull to pieces six months ago. And she recalled that the following morning she had gone through the pockets of Branwell's clothes and found a piece of that skull. She had buried it miles away from the church . . . far from the grooved ledger stone in the floor.

She glanced at that section of the main aisle now, and could just discern the outline of that stone in the shadows—only a few yards from the stone that covered the Brontë vault, where lay her mother and her sisters Elizabeth and Maria.

Her footsteps echoed among the side arches as she crossed the wide raised floor and mounted the spiral steps to the high pulpit. The substitute curate had not found the makeshift iron triangle at the back of a shelf below the lectern, and she reached in and pulled it out.

Projecting her voice to reach and ideally shake the ledger stone, she began, *"Pater noster, qui es in caelis, sanctificetur nomen tuum . . ."*

While she was saying the prayer, a streak of daylight split the central aisle as one of the tall front doors of the church opened. From the angle of the pulpit she couldn't see who had opened the door, or if they had entered the church, but she finished the prayer, including Grimshaw's five syllables—*brachiun enim*—and struck the triangle against the pillar to her right. The note rang out over the pews.

For several seconds there was no further sound; then boots were knocking on the stone floor and a deep voice called, "Miss Brontë?"

Emily didn't descend from the pulpit, but waited while the man walked up the aisle. And when he stood in the light from the stained glass window behind her she recognized the forehead and cheekbones under the mane of black hair. The eyepatch again covered the left eye.

On the raised floor below the pulpit, Keeper stood up, watching the newcomer but not growling yet.

"Mr. Curzon," said Emily, concealing her uneasiness. "You should not speak so loudly in a *Christian* church."

"It's Miss *Emily*," he said, stopping below the pulpit and squinting up at her. "Of course it wouldn't be you that fled." He glanced cautiously at Keeper, then added, "That was hardly a Christian

command that you inserted into the Pater Noster." He shrugged and nodded. "But it is a Protestant church."

She laughed in spite of herself. "Did you bring your knife? Are you here to kill me at last?"

"Why haven't you all followed your father and your sister? It was the wisest course."

A breeze from the open doorway behind Curzon tossed the tails of his coat and flicked at Emily's hair.

"They didn't *flee*," Emily snapped. "They'll return in two weeks. My father needed an operation to restore his vision." She slid the triangle back onto its shelf. "And there are things that need regular attention here."

"Shooting at ghosts every morning." Curzon nodded. "If his vision should be *fully* restored, he'd be wise to take the poisonous lot of you to somewhere across the nullifying sea, and leave this war to those who know how to wage it."

Keeper was still not growling, and Emily turned away and walked down the steps to the altar-level floor. Facing Curzon, she said, "You? Where were you six months ago when a woman tried to reunite the skull to the body of Welsh's twin?"

Curzon stepped back, and flipped up the eyepatch to stare at her with both eyes.

"This happened? Where is the skull now?"

She pulled the pistol from her coat pocket and held it up. "I shot a hole in it, and then my dog shook it to pieces." Curzon didn't speak, so she went on, "I buried the pieces, widely separated, far out on the moors. Nowhere near Ponden Kirk."

"Did the woman have a name?"

"She called herself Mrs. Flensing."

Curzon nodded and rubbed his chin. He started to speak, then shook his head. Finally he said, "And the body of the twin? Do you know where that is?"

"You're standing on it."

He stared at her for several more seconds, then slowly lowered his gaze to his boots. He crouched and traced one of the grooves with a finger.

"Ogham," he said quietly, straightening up. "I can't read it. But that phrase you added to the Pater Noster was old Irish—*Lie nameless*."

"The ogham symbols spell out its name," said Emily, and she repeated her father's words: "with a negating branch of lines which contradict the name."

Curzon quickly readjusted the eyepatch over his left eye. Brusquely he said, "You must tell me everything you know."

"I've told you enough. It's good that you killed some kind of... *werewolf king,* back in March, but you have no claim on me."

"Your gun has been fired and not reloaded." He waved at it. "The pan cover is up. But—I respect your dog."

"He'd shake *your* skull to pieces," Emily assured him.

Keeper was in fact staring at Curzon, and Emily saw watchful caution in the dog's tensed ears.

"He's my keeper," she added.

Curzon shook his head in angry bafflement. "You can't accomplish anything," he said. "Fire your gun, ring your bell, pronounce your syllables—while more devils roam Yorkshire every night!"

Emily bit her lip. In the last couple of months, Tabby had told her and Anne stories she'd heard in the village from farmers and sheepherders. Always in a portentously lowered voice, the old housekeeper had relayed accounts of unnatural animals seen loping across the moonlit hills, voices singing out of the deep sinkholes known as pots, and *ignis fatui* lights dancing over bogs on moonless nights. Several children, she'd said, had disappeared from remote farmhouses—no one could say if they'd been kidnapped, killed, or lured away by the creatures known locally as boggarts and gytrashes.

"Any scraps you may know," Curzon went on, "you can't possibly understand. Tell me how you and your dog came to break the skull."

Thinking of Branwell's unadmirable part in that whole episode, Emily said, "I won't."

Curzon bared his teeth. "Ignorant peasant fool!" he burst out; then held up his hands. "Very well. You may rely on it that I know things you'd like to know. We can trade—a fact for a fact. I'll even be the first to push one forward."

Emily took a breath to give him a scornful answer—*ignorant peasant fool* indeed!—but she glanced at the ledger stone at his feet, and hesitated. During these last two weeks she was sure she had heard faint *grating* from it, and on one cold morning when the

flagstone floor had been visibly damp, that stone had been dry, as if it had been warmer. She had not dared to walk over and touch it. And there were Tabby's stories.

Curzon did have knowledge about all this: the two-bladed knife, Welsh, the unknown thing under the stone that lay between Curzon and herself as they spoke.

"Not here," she said. "I've said too much already, here."

"You think it *listens*? With no head?" His tone was light, but he took two steps back, off the stone. "But I'll humor you. Can we speak privately at that inn next door?"

Emily thought of the back room of the Black Bull, and the table that probably still showed the groove of her gunshot; and she shivered at the thought that some powdered bone from the skull might be imbedded in the wood.

"Certainly not," she said, with an air of primness.

"Cling to propriety. The churchyard?"

"Just as bad."

"Really! The middle of the street?"

Emily recalled the buckets of holy water in every room and hall of the parsonage. Papist superstition, but still . . .

"Our kitchen," she said, stepping down to the main floor, closely flanked by Keeper. Anne should be present for this, she thought, and even Tabby might have insights.

Curzon gave her a tired nod, as if to say, *Your accustomed domain*.

Emily scowled, but she and Keeper followed Curzon down the side aisle, past the door through which they had entered, and out through the front door into bright daylight.

A stout, four-foot walking stick leaned against one of the stone columns, and Curzon took it as he walked to the steps. Emily saw now that he was wearing a woolen jacket and worn corduroy trousers, and as he stepped to the walkway he flipped a battered gray cap onto his shaggy head. His boots were scuffed brown leather.

He stepped along briskly, and Emily wondered again at his recovery from what had seemed to be a near-mortal injury in March. As the three of them rounded the corner of the building, and the churchyard and the parsonage swung into view, Emily asked, "Why were you in the church?"

"I'm on a . . . a walking tour, and Haworth is more or less on the

way. At that inn they told me that one of the curate's daughters still fired the old man's gun every morning, and was in the church. I assumed it would be the eldest." He sniffed the air and remarked, "I imagine few children live to adulthood here."

"More than half," said Emily defensively. "And it's not devils taking the ones that die."

"No, I'm sure it's the cholera. Are all the town's pumps downhill from the cemetery?"

Emily lifted her chin. "My father has sent several petitions to the General Board of Health in London, demanding improvements in sanitation."

"Wonders, that'll do. Like shooting a gun over the graves."

Emily glanced past Curzon at the cemetery, and said quietly, "He's not a fool. It's not loaded with an ordinary pistol ball."

"Silver?" Curzon startled Emily by spitting onto the pavement. The man's manners were appalling. "That's fairy-tale stuff. Better he should stop fooling about with things he doesn't understand, and use the money to pipe water in from high ground."

"They're not silver. Be quiet."

The churchyard was behind them now, and Emily hoped Curzon wouldn't ask why there was always the clinking of a chisel from the stonecutter's yard to their right. *It's not devils taking the ones that die,* she thought. She led Curzon and Keeper past the little garden to the south side of the parsonage, past the peat room and around the corner to the kitchen door. She pulled it open, and whatever Curzon might think of her accustomed domain, she was heartened by the warm air and the homely smells of onions and bacon. Curzon leaned his stick against the doorframe.

Old Tabby looked up from a bowl of peeled potatoes when Emily and Keeper entered; and her eyebrows rose when Curzon followed them in, ducking under a string of drying washcloths.

"It's the Papist gentleman, I think?" she said doubtfully as she noted Curzon's common-laborer clothing and the cap he was now holding.

"Yes. Mrs. Ayckroyd, this is Mr. Curzon."

Tabby seemed taken aback by the introduction and the use of her surname; she wiped her hands on her apron and essayed a sort of uncertain curtsy. "Shall I bring tea into the dining room?"

The windows of the dining room overlooked the close churchyard, which was probably why Emily had thought of the kitchen. "We'll have our tea in here, I believe," she said. "And stay and join us, Tabby. You were there too, when Crow Hill exploded twenty years ago."

"Ah?" said the old housekeeper. "Like that, are we? Twenty-two years ago it was. You were only six years old." She filled a pot with cold water and set it on the black-iron range that stood against the wall opposite the hallway door.

Anne stood now in the doorway, looking younger than her twenty-six years in a plain linen dress with her chestnut hair parted in the middle and curling around her cheeks. "I was four," she said, "but I remember the boulders hurtling through the air, and the flood, and the storm."

"And we all ran through the rain to Ponden House," said Tabby.

Seeing Curzon's eyes widen, Emily said, "It's a mile and a half from Ponden Kirk, no connection. 'Ponden' is *pond-dene*, it means a cleft in a marshy pond."

Emily sat down at the table and waved at the other chairs. The other three joined her, Tabby with some hesitation.

"Where is Crow Hill?" Curzon asked, "and what happened there in 1824?" He laid down his cap and spread his hands. "Boulders?"

Anne and Tabby looked to Emily, who shook her head. To Curzon, she said, "You're to push out the first fact."

"For God's sake. Very well—the undead thing under the stone in your father's church was killed, for the most part, in 1771."

Emily nodded. "That's when our great-great-grandfather adopted Welsh, its twin, in Ireland." She cocked an eyebrow at Curzon. "Welsh had a human appearance. The thing whose skull I saw could not have."

Tabby was listening eagerly, and seemed to be repressing questions of her own. Emily reflected that the old woman had always loved spooky stories, especially if they might be true.

Curzon shifted in his chair. "Welsh took after the mother, while the other was much more like the, er, father. Your double-great-grandfather found Welsh on a boat, of course."

"Yes," said Anne. "Why 'of course'?"

Curzon gave her an incurious look, then spoke to Emily. "You

owe me one. My great-grandmother, who was given the task of killing both of the twins, did mostly kill the monstrous one, the one that's in your church, though the thing's head was lost. But the other one—she couldn't bear to kill what seemed to be a small boy. So she hid him on a packet boat in Liverpool, bound for Warrenpoint in County Down, across the Irish Sea. She believed that three hundred miles of open ocean would be enough separation to sever Welsh from his twin, and break the . . . shadow, the quickening *influence* the two of them, paired, would have imposed in northern England."

Emily started to speak, but Curzon went on angrily, "And it *would* have been enough, if your father hadn't *brought Welsh back*."

Emily nodded. "Or if your grandmother had killed the boy, and not shirked her duty."

Anne gave her sister a surprised look.

Curzon sat back and made his face relax. "We can perhaps excuse our forebears their errors. Tell me about Crow Hill."

Emily started to object, but Tabby was already speaking. "It was fair weather," Tabby said, getting up and shuffling to the range, "when we started out for a walk on the moors—Emily, Anne, Branwell and me. But the clouds did gather very dark when we were out as far as the Lad Stone—"

Seeing Curzon's blank scowl, Tabby explained, "That's a marker of the Lancashire border, at the top of Crow Hill. They put it up last century at the spot where there was a cairn before. We were only a hundred yards from the hill when—"

Anne shivered. "It exploded!"

"Did it not!" agreed Tabby. "Flying boulders and mud, and thunder and rain too! The whole hillside to the east just tumbled down into the valley in a great roaring flood of muddy water. We all ran north through the storm to Ponden House, where the Heatons kindly gave us blankets and tea and sent a rider to tell your father that you were all safe."

Curzon rocked his head back and stared past the hanging washcloths at the high ceiling. "You lot just couldn't ever resist raising devils here, could you? A male Brunty descendant approached its cairn—what did you *imagine* its response would be?"

"I didn't know until this moment," Emily protested, "that a cairn was there before the Lad Stone boundary marker! What *is* it?"

"It must have been the head, damn it, the skull you shot! We searched for it, but the tribe must have buried it there."

For several seconds none of them spoke.

"Well," said Anne, "Emily and Keeper destroyed it, so the quickening influence must be damped now, mustn't it?—if not extinguished outright."

Tabby clicked her tongue and muttered, "That's not the word in the hills beyond the village." She had poured hot water into their aunt's teapot, and now, hardly watching what she was doing, stirred in four teaspoons of tea leaves. "Lately the bad night folk are said to be lively as ever—fires by the standing stones on the hills west of the Lad Stone, marsh lights calling to late travelers, two more childer gone missing up toward Cowling."

Clumping footsteps sounded on the stairs then, and Emily raised a hand. In a conversational tone she said to Curzon, "Do you have family in Yorkshire, sir?"

The question had been meant as an innocuous change of topic, but to Emily's surprise Curzon winced and half-raised a hand. "I—waste my time here." He pushed back his chair.

Branwell leaned in the hall doorway, and blinked in surprise at the dark man with the eyepatch who was sitting with the housekeeper and his sisters at the kitchen table. His curly ginger hair stuck out in all directions.

"Bad dream," he muttered. "I beg your pardon—hello, sir—have we met?"

He was wearing the white linen shirt and woolen trousers that he'd been wearing yesterday, and had undoubtedly slept in.

Curzon stood up, and Emily said, wearily, "Mr. Curzon, our brother, Branwell."

Curzon stared at the young man, and though his swarthy face showed no expression, Emily saw his jaw muscles tighten.

He nodded, and Branwell did too, jerkily.

Branwell turned to Tabby and waved at the teapot. "Do you have another cup?"

Curzon gave Emily a look she thought of as smoldering, and said, "I can't stay."

With no further comment he picked up his cap and strode out of the kitchen into the yard, snatching his stick from beside the door as

he went. Emily got up and quickly put on her coat, and Curzon was already on the path that led out onto the moors by the time she and Keeper caught up with him.

Keeper loped ahead of Curzon and turned to look back at him.

As the man glanced at the dog and then stopped, Emily reflected that Keeper's attitude toward Curzon had always been a sort of watchful caution, neither hostility nor full acceptance.

When she had found Curzon below Ponden Kirk six months ago, wounded and temporarily unable to walk, Keeper had growled—at the bloody knife that Curzon dropped; and the dog had growled again, and set his paws on Curzon's chest, when the man had caught Emily's hand as she had tried to examine his wound, but Keeper had stood back when Curzon released her; and when Curzon had rudely pushed Emily aside in walking out of her father's study later that day, all Keeper had done was to tear the man's trousers with his teeth—no more than a reminder of manners, really. If a stranger had treated Emily that way, the dog would have been at the stranger's throat.

Not for the first time, she wished her dog could talk.

Curzon didn't turn around on the path, but Emily saw his shoulder rise and fall in a sigh.

"Miss Emily," he said, and turned to face her. "What, did I short you on the fact exchange?"

"Probably," she said as Keeper trotted back to stand beside her. "I wasn't keeping track. What does this walking tour of yours have to do with the business we were discussing?"

"You assume I have no concerns in life other than the travails of your ill-fated family?"

"Your memory is deficient, sir. We were talking about the ill-fated land."

"Yes," he admitted. He thumped the base of his stick in the dirt. "And yes of course my journey today has to do with that business! Now go home, importunate child! It would do you no good to know more."

"Now that I think of it, you do owe me one more fact." She waved out at the infinity of sunlit green grass and purple heather rippling in the wind that swept across the hills. "What's your destination?"

"A place far from here."

He turned his broad back on her and resumed walking. She and Keeper fell into step beside him.

"It's many miles," Curzon said without looking at her, "and I have a long stride."

Emily didn't reply, but kept walking. His warning didn't impress her—she and Keeper often hiked all day, fording nameless becks, skirting deep ravines, and following remote sheep paths that were probably older than the Roman roads.

Curzon didn't speak, but he soon turned north on a narrow trail that wound between low hills well known to Emily, and the three of them walked for a while in silence. Keeper sometimes rambled ahead or paused to sniff at wayside stones and clumps of grass.

When they came to the narrow River Worth, they walked west along the bank and then crossed it by an old stone bridge.

On the far side of it, Curzon stopped, and with his one exposed eye he stared at Emily in angry exasperation. "Go back. You'll exhaust yourself on these pathless northern moors, and I can't waste the day carrying you to some farmhouse."

Emily thought he probably could carry her quite a distance now—unlike the morning when she had practically carried him away from Ponden Kirk—but she was confident that she and Keeper could outlast him, and she just returned his stare.

"Very well," he said, turning away, "die out there. I won't stop."

He waited several moments, then muttered what was probably a curse and strode forward, away from the river.

Emily and Keeper again fell into step beside him.

"You're the Brontë boy, aren't you?"

Branwell had been standing on the flagstones just past the churchyard wall, halfway between the Black Bull and the sexton John Brown's stonecutting yard, and he had just nerved himself to ignore the ominous chipping of new gravestones and go ask the sexton for a few shillings to be added to his already sizeable debt.

He looked up, squinting in the oppressive daylight, and recognized a sheepherder who sometimes walked to town to attend old Patrick's Sunday services, though his stone house was even farther away than the Sunderlands' Top Withens. Robson? No,

Wright, Adam Wright. The man was walking up the street from the village shops, and stopped in front of Branwell.

"Yes sir," Branwell said diffidently, knowing that he looked pale and sickly in his slept-in clothes. Why had he got up so damned early? He could almost feel himself wilting in Wright's tanned, clean-shaven, hearty proximity.

"We heard your father is gone to Manchester to get the eyes mended," Wright said, "and my daughter was asking if you've taken over conducting the services."

Branwell bobbed his head. "No no, I'm no public speaker—"

"Nonsense, lad! I recall you standing up on the hustings right here in front of the Bull before the General Election in '37, telling the crowd that if they wouldn't let your father speak, you wouldn't let them speak either!"

Branwell found himself nodding, even nearly smiling. He had been nineteen years old, nearly a year past his humiliating trip to London, and politics had begun to interest him. His family had been stoutly Tory in their support for the conservative Robert Peel, while most of the village was Whig, favoring Lord Melbourne. Old Patrick had stood up right here to make an impassioned plea for Peel and the Tory cause, and when the crowd began jeering at him, Branwell had stood up too, and denounced them all just as Wright said.

—And a day later the villagers had carried down the street an effigy of Branwell, a caricature made of burlap and wood, its crude hands gripping a herring and a potato—a disrespectful reference to his family's Irish background.

Branwell shrugged. It was all a long time ago, and he had been a different young man.

Wright nodded. "That capped me, though I'm a Whig myself! Hark now, I've been up since before dawn with the livestock, and I was just going to have a pint and a bite." He waved toward the pub's front door. "Are you free?"

Branwell stood up straighter, ran his fingers through his disordered hair and sparse chin-beard, and pulled his coat more snugly around his narrow shoulders.

Summoning his most distinct tones, he said, "I am, sir, as a matter of fact."

Wright led the way and held open the door, and when he had paid

for two mugs of stout and asked for a couple of mutton pasties, he and Branwell sat down at a table by the street window. The low-ceilinged room smelled familiarly of old beer and tobacco smoke, but Wright seemed to bring in with him a breeze spiced with earth and iron and sun-heated stone.

"Drink up, lad," Wright said. "You look like you had a flaysome night."

Branwell managed a smile, and took a couple of deep swallows of the stout. He wiped his mouth and said, "I suppose I did." In this very room, he thought, remembering a jovial group and a succession of free whiskies.

"Ah." Wright gave Branwell an amused, assessing look. "We've met before, you know."

"Several times," agreed Branwell, "at church."

"Aye, there too. But I was thinking of a latelier time."

Wright paused, and after a few seconds Branwell raised his eyebrows.

"A midnight in early March," Wright said, "below Ponden Kirk, at a funeral pyre. We shook hands, if you recall."

Branwell's face was suddenly cold, and his legs tensed in readiness to run out of the inn.

But Wright caught his forearm in one big browned hand. Branwell tugged, and only managed to splash some stout onto the table. "Easy, fellow!" said Wright with quiet urgency. "You're one of us!"

"I almost *was*!" said Branwell, nearly in tears. "That boy took my body, put me in his!"

"Yes, and you ran off before we could make things clear to you. We dinna chase you, did we?" Branwell relaxed slightly, and Wright released his arm. "I was in a different form than this," Wright said, "wasn't I? You were in another form too, for a moment. Folk like us aren't stuck forever in one sort of body, see. Those die after a while."

Branwell thought of the death of his mother, and then of his sisters Elizabeth and Maria—especially Maria, who until her death at the age of eleven had practically been a replacement mother to him and his sisters. Gone forever.

"Sooner than we'd like," Branwell whispered.

"There's a sturdier family, and you're the prodigal son. Come home."

Branwell tore his gaze away from Wright's. Across the room was the door to the snug, where Emily had put a pistol ball through the malformed skull six month ago. And when Mrs. Flensing had partly reassembled it in the church, Emily's damned dog had wrecked it for good; and then Emily—it must have been—stole the piece of it that he had saved.

"You—" Branwell began, then shivered, remembering Wright's appearance that night. He took a fresh breath and went on, "You poured oil on an animal's body, and burned it. Was that a member of the family? Had someone moved on, from that body?"

Wright sat back and sighed. "No, lad. That great person was killed outright, and a big loss his death was to us all. I hailed you this morning because his murderer has come back into the area, and may well have more such murders in mind."

Something Mrs. Flensing had once said to him now belatedly surfaced in Branwell's mind. "The," he said excitedly, "yes, the one-eyed Catholic!" Wright started to speak, but Branwell interrupted him. "He's in our kitchen! Or was, an hour ago. His name is . . . Curzon."

"In the parsonage?" In one swift movement Wright was on his feet. "Take me there straightaway."

"He's gone, he walked out, angry." And apparently despising me, Branwell thought. "My sister Emily went after him, they're an hour gone. She's—" Branwell paused; Emily was the only member of his family who both understood him and wished him well. But he met Wright's compelling eyes, and remembered his own Northangerland alter ego. "She's the one who destroyed the skull that Mrs. Flensing wanted to hide in the church."

"A bad girl," stated Wright, pulling Branwell up from his chair. "And that Curzon fellow murdered his fiancée a few months back. Which way did they go?"

"West—across the moors."

"Come on, lad, quick! I'll need you to help send a call."

"A call—to whom?"

Wright didn't answer, and a moment later Branwell found that he had been hustled outside, and that Wright was pulling him toward the church and the cemetery.

Look, he told himself—I have no choice.

+ + +

In the wilder country north of the River Worth, Curzon tended to leave the broad heaths and make his way down into stony ravines, out of the cold wind, and when those sooner or later bent away from his evident course and he climbed back up to level or rising ground, he squinted at the clouding sky and the lonely trees and the occasional stone house visible on remote hilltops.

"People live in places like that?" he said finally, pushing back his cap and nodding toward a bleak gray rectangle a couple of miles away.

Emily and Keeper both looked at him curiously as they strode through tall grass beside an ancient waist-high dry-stone wall. "Not much anymore," Emily said. "Most of the time when you hike to one, you find it's just four roofless walls. We took shelter in one like that on the night Crow Hill exploded."

"In a rainstorm? Not much shelter."

"They block the wind. And—"

"And you're out of sight." He nodded. "There's value in that."

"And in walking down in gorges instead of up here on open tracks."

"Yes."

Ragged sheets of gray cloud had crept across the sky during the last hour of their walk, and patches of shadow that had at first darkened individual slopes or hilltops had now merged in an overall gloom. Emily wished she had brought a satchel with food for herself and Keeper.

Soon the old stone wall they had been following ended at a low green field furry with bracken and reeds.

"Catch that froggy smell?" asked Emily. "That's a marsh. I know the way around it."

"Do as you please." Curzon started forward, and after a few paces his boots had sunk to the ankles in black mud.

"Oh for God's sake," said Emily, "what do you think your walking stick is for? Poke the mud to see how deep it is. And step on the clumps of reeds. Look at Keeper."

The big bullmastiff was taking long strides, sometimes leaping from one raised cluster of waving fronds to another; but even as Emily spoke, the dog paused, staring ahead.

A faint spot of colorless light bobbed over the marsh a hundred

feet away, not far from a twisted willow and a cluster of hawthorn bushes. Curzon was staring in another direction, and Emily saw that he had noticed a second dim light. Soon there were three, moving together by the willow. Keeper loped back to stand by Emily.

"*Ignis fatui*," she said, just loudly enough to be heard over the wind. "Hill folk say they trap you in the bogs with hallucinations."

"I know what they are."

"I've never seen them out before dark."

Curzon waved at the now thickly overcast sky. "It *is* dark."

The luminous spots were so faint that it took a moment for Emily to realize it when they disappeared.

"There," said Curzon, moving forward again, "you're right, they're shy in the daytime."

But Keeper growled and Emily hung back. "Wait," she said. "If they come again—"

The lights didn't reappear, but the hawthorn bushes shook, and separated into three hunched shapes; leaves flattened and branches twisted in, and when a wriggling, rocking clump was raised at the top of each, these settled and became recognizable as wizened faces with tangled gray hair streaming on the wind. Now there were three old women hunched beside the willow, in robes made of haphazardly woven twigs.

Emily took an involuntary step back, sinking her boot. She had heard of *ignis fatui* leading lost travelers over cliffs or into bogs or sinkholes at night, but the stories had never hinted that the things might take even this approximately human form.

The three old women out there by the tree swayed together, and ragged mouths opened in the clay-colored faces as they began chanting in birdlike voices. Emily couldn't make out the words, but her hand on Keeper's collar was pulled sideways, away from the things.

Curzon was already moving in that direction, and Emily followed Keeper. She kept looking back over her shoulder, but the figures didn't move away from the willow, and within a minute they had subsided back to ordinary-looking hawthorn bushes.

Emily took a deep breath as she plodded along. "Keeper and I have crossed this marsh before. And we've been out at night often enough to have seen *ignis fatui* aplenty."

"The two of you should turn back," Curzon said without looking at her. "Rain is looking likely."

"They never turned into old women before."

Curzon didn't comment.

The ground rose ahead, and soon the three of them were able to follow a north-slanting path for at least a while. Emily looked at the big figure of Curzon striding steadily along, and asked him, "Your wound is quite healed?"

"Wound? Oh, when we met! Yes, entirely."

"What are you, exactly?"

In this gray light the lines of his face seemed more like weathered stone than flesh, as if he, in common with the *ignis fatui*, wore the aspect of humanity only conditionally.

He didn't answer.

"I would have thought," she went on, "that it was impossible for a person with a wound like that to be up and walking about only an hour or so later."

"Keep silent when you know nothing, girl."

She was wary of pushing this brooding stranger too far. The two-bladed knife that she had picked up below Ponden Kirk six months ago was in a dresser drawer in her room back at the parsonage. She wished she had it now; and she stepped wide of Curzon as she repeated the question she had asked him in the kitchen two hours ago. "Do you have family in Yorkshire?"

Suddenly he stopped and was facing her. His lips were pulled back from his teeth, and his walking stick shook in his right hand. The fingers of his left hand were spread in an apparent effort to keep them from clenching into a fist.

Emily didn't flinch, and Keeper only stood close, and after a few tense seconds Curzon grated, "Go to Hell," and spun away from her. He resumed walking north, lengthening his stride to leave her behind.

Emily and Keeper followed, steadily staying several yards behind him.

Soon the divided trio was climbing another hill, their boots thrashing through tall grass. As they neared the crest, Emily saw the top of a rough, upright column of granite, and when she and Keeper scrambled up to it she saw that another stone column stood behind the one she had seen from below, and that Curzon was standing by

the farther one, panting from the climb and squinting north with his one exposed eye.

"The River Aire is about a mile that way," Emily said, breathing easily.

Ignoring her, Curzon was looking down the steeper slope on the other side. He opened his mouth and, after a moment's hesitation, called a dozen syllables of a language Emily didn't recognize, though there was no sign of anyone else who might hear him.

Keeper turned and looked the other way; and when Emily pushed back her windblown hair and looked in that direction she saw distant black spots against the dark gray sky.

"Crows," she said, "behind us."

Curzon looked over his shoulder at her, and at the sky beyond her. He shrugged irritably. "And hedgehogs in front of us, I daresay. Be quiet." It occurred to Emily that he was frightened by whatever it was he meant to do here.

Keeper stood watching the distant crows, but Emily walked to the north side of the hilltop and stood a few yards to Curzon's left. Below them spread a mile-wide heath between rocky promontories, and a hundred feet from the foot of their hill she could make out lines of stones among the patches of gorse and heather. She looked more carefully: allowing for interruptions, and gaps where a new beck had cut through them, the lines traced a square perhaps fifty feet on a side; and now she could see stones indicating a smaller square that lay in the middle of it.

Keeper barked, and Emily looked back past him at the southern sky. The crows were closer, more distinctly visible; and they were clearly flying toward this hill.

"They'll be here soon," she said.

Curzon turned impatiently, opening his mouth to say something, but he paused when he looked past her pointing finger.

He stared for several seconds, then said, "Get away from here. It's me he's after."

He turned back to the slope and began hastily sliding down it, half squatting and half sitting, his boots digging grooves among the grass and sending pebbles rolling ahead of him.

Emily followed in a hopping crouch, and Keeper went bounding down after them. Curzon snagged on a rock and tumbled to the level

ground, but quickly got to his feet and began running toward the nearest line of stones. Keeper had paused near the foot of the incline and was looking up the slope, past Emily, and as she caught up with him he ran beside her after Curzon.

All three leaped simultaneously across the first line of stones—and abruptly Emily was thrown off her feet as the ground shifted, and when she sat up she was blinking back at the hill in jarringly bright daylight; she squinted against the sudden glare and got up on one knee—and then she was in darkness, though she could still feel crushed grass under her hands.

"Keeper!" she called, and then Keeper's cold nose was reassuringly in her face. Looking up, she saw a crescent moon in a clear night sky. A moment later another dog was shouldering up to Keeper.

Bright daylight sprang up again, and the hill they had just descended, or one very like it, was clearly visible against a stark blue unclouded sky. No crows were visible. Keeper and the other dog, a bullmastiff like him, stood beside where Emily knelt.

"Your dog," came Curzon's strained voice from behind her, "is two dogs."

She turned around, and gasped and instinctively clawed the turf for steadiness when she saw that Curzon was standing in the open doorway of a low stone house with a high, conical thatched roof. Its walls, she was sure, were where the stone lines of the inner square had been.

"You shouldn't be here," said Curzon. "How is it that you are?"

Emily stood up, and didn't have to shift her feet to keep her balance. She tossed her hair back.

"We jumped over the outer line same as you did," she said. The dogs still stood on either side of her, and she touched the stranger's wide head; he was as solidly present as Keeper, and licked her hand.

"Is the curate's daughter some pagan priestess?" asked Curzon.

Emily raised her chin, looking past him. Her heart was thudding in her chest, but she kept her voice level: "Is this place intruding in our time, or are we intruding in its?"

Curzon waved at the wooden lintel-beam over his head. "I don't know. We're not precisely *in any* time, here." He leaned his stick against the irregular stones of the wall, and then Emily was surprised

to see him draw a double-bladed knife from under his coat. He raised it in both hands, laid across his open palms like an offering. He took a deep breath, turned, and stepped across the threshold.

Emily shivered, sure that she could almost hear the distant music she sometimes imagined out on the moors—repetitive and atonal, older than humanity. She hesitated only a moment before following Curzon into the small stone chamber, accompanied by the two dogs.

A foot-wide opening in the far wall provided the only light away from the doorway, and it wasn't until Emily's eyes adjusted to the dimness that she noticed the wicker figure on a stone block below the opening.

She shuffled forward to look at it more closely, though Curzon looked away from his upraised knife and hissed at her to stop. She waved without looking back at him.

The figure on the block was an exaggerated representation of a woman, about four feet tall. It was made of twigs that had clearly been bent into shape when they had still been green and pliable, for the rounded head, breasts, and wide hips almost looked naturally formed. Its arms were less carefully made: simple bundles of straw, spread at the ends to resemble clusters of fingers.

She turned to Curzon. "Who is this?" she asked.

He exhaled and closed one hand on the grip of the knife. With his free hand he took hold of her wrist and pulled her back to the doorway. Keeper followed her, and the other dog was sniffing the wicker figure.

"At the moment," he whispered tersely, "it's not anyone, it's an effigy."

Emily rocked her head. "So I supposed. An effigy of whom?"

"A goddess. This is a temple."

"What—" Emily began.

"Stand here, will you?" Curzon interrupted. "Don't move till I come out."

Emily leaned against the stones of the doorway and Keeper sat down. Curzon hesitated, frowning, then elevated the knife in both hands again and turned and stepped back inside. After a harsh syllable from him the other dog came out and sat beside Keeper.

Emily looked in and saw that Curzon had laid the knife aside and was kneeling on the dirt floor near the image. As she watched, he

tossed a handful of what might have been bird bones out in front of him. He stared at them for a moment, then gathered them up and threw them again.

She watched as he cast the bones, studied them, and scooped them up, over and over again, with evident dissatisfaction—but all at once he reared back with a gasp and sat down. Emily looked past him, and her face went cold when she saw that the wicker figure's straw right arm was moving—bending and lifting.

Curzon had scrambled to his feet and now stood closer to the doorway.

The crude arm straightened.

Curzon looked over his shoulder at Emily. "It's ... pointing at you."

Emily's head was ringing and she was dizzy, and her first impulse was to grab Keeper and run away from this place, back to their home; but she sensed that this place and this effigy were no part of the power represented by Mrs. Flensing, and she knew she would be forever haunted by the memory of this uncanny greeting, if she were to flee.

She stepped forward again, reaching out with her scarred right hand. Her fingers brushed the spread strands of straw at the end of the token arm, and it fell back to hang as it had been.

She had felt nothing distinct in that moment of contact, just a comprehension of this stone temple and the two standing stones on the hilltop—and an impression of balance maintained, equilibrium.

Natural law, she thought. Law of some kind, at any rate.

Curzon was watching her closely, and he spread his empty hands.

Emily waved toward the litter of tiny bones on the dirt; and she was grateful that he understood without her having to try her voice just yet.

He crouched again, gathered the bones and tossed them.

This time Emily could see that their arrangement on the dirt was not random. They formed a shape that might have been a letter or symbol, albeit one she had never seen.

He quickly picked up the bones and flipped them out of his hand, and they took another symbol-like form.

He did it six more times, with similar results, whispering to himself as if to remember each symbol; then he picked up the knife and got to his feet, leaving the last shape as it lay.

He blundered past Emily out into the sunshine, and after tucking the knife away and hastily making the Catholic sign of the cross he leaned forward, bracing his hands on his knees.

Emily looked at the motionless wicker figure, then walked out to stand beside Curzon. "Who," she said carefully, "is she?"

Curzon squinted up at her for several seconds, considering. Finally he said, "She was known to the Celts down around Bath as *Sulis*, and the druids in these northern parts called her *Brigantia*." He straightened up and glanced at the two dogs. "There's the remains of a Roman road up by Skipton, and the Romans used to come down here to consult her. They knew her as Minerva."

Minerva, thought Emily; and she shivered with the same sense of liberating excitement she had felt when her father had described his first action upon arrival in England—*I went directly to Chester . . . there's an ancient shrine to Minerva there. When I should have put my trust in our Lord, in my fright I sought armor from a pagan goddess*.

Curzon walked in a circle, alternately staring at the ground and the blue sky, then faced Emily.

"How is it," he asked hoarsely, "that she knew you?"

Emily thought of several answers, then shrugged. "She and my father go way back."

"*What?* What the Hell *are* you Bruntys? Not *Christians*, it's clear—"

"Says a statue-worshipping Papist!" Emily retorted hotly, "who performs pagan divination with bird bones! What right—"

He was just staring at her.

After several seconds she took a deep breath and let it out. "When my father first arrived in England," she said, "and realized that Welsh's spirit had come back across the Irish Sea with him, he—went to an old Roman shrine to Minerva near Liverpool, and asked the goddess for the protection of her armor. He knew it was wrong, but—"

She was interrupted by the sudden howling of both dogs and a piercing high-pitched voice from behind her that cried, "Bruntys and Curzons, murderers, both!"

Emily had spun around as the voice was cutting the air. Several yards away across the sunlit grass and heather, beyond the outer line of stones, a swarthy, black-haired little boy was smiling at her and Curzon. He was barefoot, draped in a ragged white shirt and

trousers, and Emily found it hard to focus on him, as if the air around him were rippling.

Curzon stared at him for a moment, then glanced back at the stone temple before facing the boy again. "You can follow us?" he asked hoarsely. *"Here?"*

The dogs quickly advanced to the row of boundary stones, and their howls had wailed away now to rumbling snarls.

The boy walked forward and pointed at the mastiff who stood beside Keeper. "That dog and I," he said, "killed each other in the same tick of a clock—we share that death, he can't hide from me." The boy pursed his lips and whistled three descending notes. "And *I'll* choose where *here* is."

The daylight had faded by stages as he whistled, and the sky was once again darkly overcast. Emily glanced behind, and saw that the little temple was gone—only the lines of stones among the grasses showed where it had been.

The boy whistled again, and with a rumbling jolt a six-foot patch of ground in front of Emily imploded and fell away into subterranean darkness. She stepped back from the new sinkhole and looked toward Curzon; a hole had opened in the dirt behind him, and even as she watched, a gaping fissure broke into view between the dogs and the boy.

Curzon was holding the double-bladed knife, and he took several steps across the grass toward the boy, but when two more whistled notes shivered the air he rocked to a halt, for a woman now stood between him and the boy.

Emily crouched with her arms spread, breathing quickly and ready to jump if the turf under her boots should move, and she blinked in surprise at the woman who faced Curzon. The woman was somehow in deeper shadow than Curzon, and her blonde hair hung in ringlets above a long black gown and an embroidered shawl.

The two mastiffs had bounded around the gap in front of them and now leaped at the boy—and landed on the heather behind him, as if he had not been there. They spun around, and the smaller mastiff again jumped uselessly through the apparition— while Keeper's attention was caught by something a few yards to the side.

"Madeline?" croaked Curzon; and then the woman's face opened in a jaw-stretching scream and she raced toward him. Curzon stumbled back two paces—and toppled away out of sight into the sinkhole behind him.

Emily gasped and started toward the hole, but the little boy had leaped over the fissure and was now only a couple of yards in front of her. His ragged garments, and even his small body, rippled in the cold wind, and his eyes were holes in the tight skin of his face. Below the eyes the mouth opened in a frothy spray, and the child's voice said, "For your father's sake, surrender now and be mine."

Emily looked desperately toward Keeper. The dog was advancing on what appeared to be an unoccupied expanse of dirt; but her view of the hill wavered there, as if it were seen through nearly still clear water.

The apparition of the boy was closer to her, and its voice repeated, "Surrender—"

Then Keeper sprang, and for an instant Emily saw the boy over *there*, falling back from the dog's claws and teeth—and in the next instant it wasn't a boy, but just a flock of cawing crows flapping wildly away in all directions. One crow didn't fly away, but dangled bloodily from Keeper's big jaws as the dog turned around.

The apparition of the boy was gone from in front of her, and the woman in the black gown took two more running steps and then simply vanished like a reflection in a swiftly rotated mirror.

Bursts of fog were now billowing out of the new holes and fissures in the ground and fragmenting away in the wind; Emily could see no one at all now besides herself and Keeper—the other mastiff was nowhere to be seen—and she hurried to the wide hole Curzon had fallen into.

She crouched at the edge of it, gripping the grass on the rim, and squinted against the cold vapor blowing into her face. She could see nothing down there.

"Curzon!" she shouted.

From an unguessable distance below, his voice shook the fog: "Leave me, you fool!"

"The boy is gone," Emily called, "the woman is gone. Climb up— I believe the holes are filling."

After a pause, his voice came again from the depths: "I deserve to be buried among these. Go."

Emily frowned, then tried, "Will you leave me out here, lost?" And it occurred to her to add, "On top of everything else?"

Now she heard grunts of effort, and muttered curses, and the thumps of clods of earth tumbling. She peered uselessly in the bursts of rushing fog, and then started back when a grimy right hand suddenly appeared below her.

But she recognized the cuff of Curzon's coat, and she lay flat on the grass and reached down and gripped the wrist strongly; and the fingers of the hand closed on her own wrist.

Her chin was over the edge of the hole. "Climb up me," she said. "I'll pull you in."

The edge of the hole was crumbling, and Emily heard soil cascading below her; but she felt a tug on the back of her coat, and when she turned her head to peer back past her shoulder she saw Keeper standing braced beside her, gripping her coat between his jaws.

"Impossible," she called to Curzon.

"I'm weak," came his voice, but his other hand came lashing up out of the fog and gripped her forearm; his right hand now released hers and she heard his boots scrabbling for some purchase and he lunged upward, reaching—and then his fingers were digging into the dirt of the hole's rim beside Emily's face.

With a muscular effort that wrenched at her shoulder, he swung his left leg up onto the rim, and Emily was able to push herself back. A moment later he had rolled up onto the grass and braced himself on his elbows, panting and blinking around at the lonely landscape. Emily rolled over and sat up.

Fog still blew out of the holes, but there was less of it. Keeper walked up and dropped the dead crow on the grass; he sniffed at the hole, swung his head to look around, and then lay down beside Emily. She flexed her right hand and arm, forcing herself not to wince, while with her left hand she brushed twigs and bits of dirt from the front of her coat. Her face was damp with sweat, and cold in the wind.

The fog abruptly stopped billowing up, and when she looked at the hole she saw that it was filled to the top with freshly turned soil. A glance around showed her that the other holes and fissures had also stopped emitting vapor.

Curzon got stiffly to his feet. His coat and trousers and boots were caked with black mud, and his cap was gone. He waved toward the torn body of the crow. "Your dog actually damaged Welsh."

Emily nodded. She sighed and stood up.

"He's just one dog now," Curzon observed.

Emily nodded again.

"Let's rest at the top of the hill," said Curzon, "between the stones."

They walked to the foot of the hill and slowly made their way back up the slope down which they had slid and tumbled some time before. Keeper climbed along beside Emily.

At the top, Curzon sat down across from one of the tall upright stones and waved toward it so that Emily could sit on its lee side, somewhat out of the wind.

"I should be grateful that you saved my life," he said as she sat with her back against the stone.

"True, you should." Keeper laid his massive head in her lap, and she scratched behind his ears. "When you were down in the pot—" Seeing his raised eyebrows, she explained, "Hole, pit, sinkhole. You said, 'I deserve to be buried among these.' Among what?"

Curzon exhaled through pursed lips. "The old restless dead, lost in their bad dreams. They began to . . . greet me."

"I've disappointed them, then. I'll be sure to apologize when I'm among them myself."

"They won't listen. But then, you won't remember."

As if anticipating Emily's next question, Keeper raised his head and looked at Curzon.

Emily glanced away, out across the moors, and asked, "Who was that woman?" When he didn't immediately answer, she looked at him and added, "In the black gown, down there?"

"That woman." Curzon leaned back on his hands and looked at the top of the stone Emily leaned on. In the gray daylight the lines in his dark face seemed deeper. "That," he said flatly, "was the ghost of Miss Madeline Atha, my onetime fiancée. She—fell to her death from the turret of her family home in Allerton, on the third of March."

Emily recalled that she had found Curzon wounded below Ponden Kirk on the morning of the fourth; and from the defiance in his tone she suspected that he was daring her to remark on the connection.

For a full minute neither of them spoke, and the wind stirred the hilltop grass around their boots.

"So you see," he concluded, "I *might* have had family in Yorkshire."

The words *I'm sorry* formed in Emily's mind, but she didn't voice the phrase. In spite of having saved the man from a living burial—and a welcome among the old restless dead!—saying it would seem to imply some minimal regard between them that didn't exist.

She scanned the leaden sky and saw no birds at all. She stood up and clicked her tongue at Keeper. "A longer walk home," she said, "as it'd be wise to take a different route than the one that led us here. East to Cononley, I think, and then the Keighley Road south."

Curzon got laboriously to his feet, not looking at her. "Oh, you're a cool one, Miss Emily Brunty." He stretched and looked south. "My walking stick went with that druid temple," he said, and his voice was a controlled monotone, "but I think I'll retrace the direct route."

Emily was disconcerted. "There's that marsh."

"And our footprints, still, probably."

"And the . . . the *ignis fatui*—the three old women?"

"I can outrun them, if need be."

She reached for the taut shoulder of his coat, then closed her hand in air and let it fall to her side. "But—there are things you should know!"

"I know your dog carries the ghost of a dog that killed Welsh in 1771. Keep him by you."

Curzon began walking away down the south side of the hill, not looking back.

"But," Emily called after him, "what did the goddess spell out for you?"

"In bird bones?" He stopped and faced her. "She said the dead sister remains dead under stone, but the dead brother is up and taking the pledged host." His deep-set eyes were in shadow. "Thank you for saving my life."

Then all she saw was his windblown black hair and his receding back.

Emily watched him until he reached the foot of the slope and struck out across the heath.

"Wait, you fool!" Emily began running down the south slope of the hill, while Keeper bounded on ahead of her.

Curzon didn't turn or slow down, but Emily and Keeper quickly caught up with him.

"You need a guide who knows these hills and valleys and bogs," Emily said when she was once again striding along beside Curzon.

"I don't want your company," he said.

"You never did."

After ten minutes of walking in silence, he gave her a wary sidelong look. "I don't plan on meeting any more pagan goddesses, you know."

"God only knows what you'll meet. But you'd better have my dog—my dogs—along to save you from it."

They reached a path, but Emily shook her head and led the way out across a grassy heath.

Curzon opened his mouth several times as if to speak, and finally said, "And you, I suppose, to pull me out of any more *pots* that I might fall into."

"That too."

"In all honesty, girl, you'd be wise to leave me in the next one. It was weakness on my part that made me cooperate in my rescue."

"'Girl.'" Emily shrugged. "I'm always rescuing animals in trouble." They strode on through the tall grass. "Even repellent ones."

She felt a tap on her hair, and then several cold drops streaked her face. Within moments rain was falling steadily.

And rain was falling on London. Though it was only early afternoon, warehouse and dockside lanterns shone like dim, flickering stars along the Thames shore by the entrance to the Limehouse Basin and West India Dock, and the veils of rain muffled the boom and clatter of cranes working in the trainyards. The few saloon steamers out on the river had been left behind on the upriver side of London Bridge, and the vessels visible from the little rowboat now were the big flat-bottomed barges moving with the tide.

Mrs. Flensing huddled under a hooded Macintosh cape in the bow. She understood the necessity of what was going to be done next, but wished it weren't to happen so very soon. She had been unhappy when the boatman easily shot London Bridge through one of the new wider arches, for it was on this side, here among the commercial craft in this bend of the river, that they were to meet

the old purl-man's skiff. Under the rubberized fabric, she flexed the two new fingers of her right hand—spider-leg thin, and twice as long as the corresponding fingers of her left hand.

Aside from the laconic boatman at the oars, the only other person on the boat was Evan Saltmeric, a chubby young street magician who embellished his meager sleight-of-hand skills with flickers of genuine supernatural effects; but these had been waning in the last six months, and he was willing to assist in anything that would deepen the reality-distortion that was generated up in Yorkshire.

The man Mrs. Flensing was resolved to meet was known as Napper Tooney, and he plied a skiff up and down the double bend in the river from St. Katharine Docks below the Tower of London to the Millwall Dock on the Isle of Dogs. His primary business was selling purl—hot, gin-fortified beer—to sailors and riggers and ballast-heavers on the mercantile vessels that crowded the waterway.

Mrs. Flensing had been told that he was very old, and that he restocked his wares from various barges along the river but never went ashore. Ghosts lost their frail coherence if they tried to venture across running water, and the story was that many vengeful ghosts haunted the Thames banks waiting for the day when Napper Tooney might incautiously step onto dry land.

Mrs. Flensing peered ahead from under the hood of her cloak, trying to distinguish the skiff that had been described to her. It would be equipped with the necessities of the man's trade, casks and tin jugs and an iron stove, but she had been told that under the rower's thwart was a lidded tub whose use was only possible in Tooney's perpetually unmoored waterborne situation.

From somewhere ahead of the rowboat a bell clanged through the rain, and the boatman relaxed on his oars to cock his head, listening.

"That's Tooney's bell," the boatman growled, "hailing one of the coal boats from the Limehouse Basin." Peering ahead, Mrs. Flensing saw the light of a bobbing lantern against the dim silhouettes of boats and shorefront buildings. The boatman lifted a whistle that hung on a string around his neck and blew three shrill blasts. "That'll bring him here. Your sort of trade is heftier than selling beer."

The bell clanged again, closer, and again the boatman blew his whistle, and soon Mrs. Flensing could see a broad skiff rocking

toward them over the low waves. The boatman lifted the starboard oar out of its lock and laid it along the gunwale so that the skiff could come alongside.

When the two boats were bumping against each other, Mrs. Flensing squinted across at Napper Tooney. All she could see of him under the brim of his leather hat was a hooked nose, prominent cheekbones, and a short clay pipe sticking out of a shaggy white beard.

"Over you go," said Mrs. Flensing's boatman, and she stood up unsteadily and, waving her arms in the rain for balance, stepped over the shifting gunwales into the purl-seller's skiff; she immediately sat down on a thwart, shifting the skiff so that Tooney had to reach across and pull the boats together again. Evan Saltmeric came across more easily but with less dignity on all fours.

The man in the boat they had left used his oar to push away from the purl-seller's skiff, and soon his boat was just a receding shape in the dimness.

Tooney's voice was harsh around the stem of his pipe: "You've brought a part of somebody?" When Mrs. Flensing nodded he went on, "Is it fresh? You're wasting your money otherwise. With a stale bit I can grow a head, but it'll just blink at you for a day or two and then rot."

"This will be fresh."

He tipped back his dripping hat to peer at her from narrowed eyes. "Will be?" He looked speculatively past her at Saltmeric, who was huddled in the stern beside a rack holding the casks and metal jugs. "I don't do murders."

Saltmeric laughed nervously.

Mrs. Flensing pulled her right hand from under the cape, and flexed the two thin, grotesquely extended fingers. "Take another finger."

Tooney nodded slowly. "Your sort is one of the reasons I stay on the water. Hah." He spat over the side. "You want me to cut off one of your normal fingers, and grow a head from it, am I hearing you right?"

"Yes. I was told it would take a week or so for it to be ready to decant."

He nodded toward her two malformed fingers and then looked

at her face. "It might not be exactly like ... the way you look right now ..."

Mrs. Flensing nodded impatiently. "I expect it will take the more primitive form, yes. And it must be big, with a high cranial dome. You can do that, I'm very sure."

Toomey raised his white eyebrows. He slapped the thwart he sat on and said, "I can make it as big as my incubator tub will fit, and I can stretch the brain case molding it by hand as I go, and adding more fish paste to the brew." He rubbed a gnarled hand across his mouth. "This won't be a small expense."

"I should hope not."

"And you pay in advance. Forty gold sovereigns."

Mrs. Flensing had been told that Napper Tooney ordinarily charged ten sovereigns to grow a somewhat living head from a piece of a fresh corpse, but she had expected to pay more for this. She looked over her shoulder and held out her good hand, and Saltmeric dug a purse from his pocket and counted out forty coins.

When she had handed them to Tooney, he hefted them but didn't put them away. "My knife is for cutting ropes. It'll hurt."

"I'll heal, after a fashion."

"You're not dead—it'll just be a head, it won't have a ghost to animate it, keep it from decaying."

"There's a ghost destined for it, one presently under stone. But I'll get a new one quick, to keep it fresh until then."

"Bad news for somebody, sounds like."

Mrs. Flensing sat back, and she managed a smile in spite of the prospect of this man cutting off one of her fingers.

"It's only fair," she said. After all, she added to herself, she's the one who destroyed the original. Her and her dog.

Branwell sat down on another flat, puddled gravestone and pushed his oiled spectacles back up on his nose to watch the ghosts. The wispy figures were still clustered like columns of smoke and thistledown around the last stone he'd been sitting on out here in the rain, and he waited for them to notice that he had moved.

Adam Wright had left hours ago, and by now Emily might be a cooling corpse rolling downstream in the rushing rain-deepened waters of some remote beck.

A bad girl, Wright had pronounced her.

She had walked away across the moors with the Curzon fellow, and Branwell had helped Wright call something or someone to . . . go after the two of them, with some purpose.

When Wright had dragged Branwell from the Black Bull to the parsonage kitchen, he had demanded that Branwell give him something of Emily's, some object that expressed her personality. Branwell had hurried to the parlor and opened her folding writing desk; in it was a stack of handwritten pages and a pencil sketch of her damned dog. The sketch looked very preliminary, with the dog both head-on and in profile at the same time, but he had taken the drawing and hurried back to the kitchen.

He had begun to speak: "I won't stand for any actual harm coming to—"

But Wright had snatched it from him and grabbed him by the arm and pulled him out onto the road that led west to the moors—and Wright had set a strenuous pace. After a mile he had stopped beside the standing stone known as Boggarts Green, and he had twisted Branwell's arm so sharply that he had cried out. And simultaneous with Branwell's cry, the man had whistled one piercing note into the cold wind.

They had stood there for a good five minutes in the shadow of the tall stone, Branwell shivering and Wright turning his head to scan all quarters of the gray sky. Branwell had begun dreading another arm-twist and whistle, when Wright had tensed, staring west—and when Branwell had looked in that direction he'd seen bobbing black dots that he had known were birds. Crows.

The ghosts were drifting among the tombstones in the rain now, waving indistinct arms and rotating their foolish bag heads. Branwell lifted his spectacles, and saw only the flat or vertical stones and the dripping trees and, vaguely through the falling rain, the black bulk of his father's church. He lowered the spectacles, and again the ghosts were visible.

They had located him now, and came curdling up to the stone he sat on. When they surrounded him their funnel mouths gaped open and began sucking air, and breath rushed from Branwell's lungs for a couple of seconds until he stopped the theft by firmly closing his

throat. He stood up, his wet clothes heavy on his shoulders and legs, and plodded through the mud and wet leaves to another flat stone, several yards away. He sat down on it and breathed deeply.

A few weeks ago he had come out here smoking a cigar, and he had touched an insistent ghost with the lit end of it. The thing had disappeared in a flash of flame that had singed Branwell's eyebrows and knocked the cigar out of his hand. But he had no cigar today, and in any case the rain would have put it out.

He thought the things seemed baffled that they were not able to cling to him and steal his breath, and in fact he was baffled too. According to local folklore, ghosts were the actual cause of many deaths that were officially attributed to consumption, but he seemed to have some inherent protection from their lethal ministrations.

He slid his hands over the surface of this flat, puddled gravestone, briefly wondering if the name the sexton had chiseled into it corresponded to one of the wraiths still huddled around the stone he had just vacated.

He shivered, remembering how the crows had winged closer and closer across the gray landscape and had finally flown in a tight, flapping circle around the heads of himself and Wright. Then they had landed in a group on the wet grass—and for a moment the crows disappeared and a middle-aged man in a cloak had seemed to be standing and staring into Branwell's eyes; a moment later the figure was gone and the crows were again hopping in the grass.

Wright had seemed disconcerted. "Never seen *him* before," he'd muttered. "Have you?"

Branwell had just shaken his head, though in fact he *had* seen the brief apparition's face before.

Wright had shrugged and wadded up Emily's drawing and tossed it into the group of crows, who quickly pecked it to shreds and then took wing again, this time flying away to the north.

"Barring interference on her part," Wright had said, finally releasing Branwell, "*she* stands today in no great peril."

Branwell had tried to imagine Emily refraining from interfering in anything she perceived as wrong. It had been too late for him to stop whatever chain of events Wright had set in motion, and to stave off his sudden dismay, he had tried to assume the cynical detachment

of Northangerland—but that imaginary identity eluded him. He was just Emily's brother Branwell, miserable and scared.

The last thing Wright had said before turning away and starting west across the moors was, "I'll be seeing you."

The rain was coming down harder now, thrashing in the bending branches of the churchyard trees, and it was difficult for Branwell to see the ghosts, even through the oiled spectacles. But he did see a solid figure hurrying down the parsonage steps and splashing through Anne and Emily's little garden.

He recognized the figure's height and stride, and he leaped up even before she had clambered over the low wall. Confirming her identity, Keeper leaped over the wall right behind her.

"Emily!" Branwell cried, and stumbled around the graves to meet her. Her wet hair clung in strands across her forehead and her clothes were as soaked as his.

"Thank God!" he said, and his exhalation was a sigh of profound relief, not a theft by the ghosts. "What happened?" He blinked past her at the parsonage, suddenly aware that he was very cold. "Get inside, we're both drenched to the bone." He had an impulse to hug her, but the family never did that, and with all their layers of wet clothing it would almost have been as if another person stood between them.

"We're already as soaked as we can be," she said, "and I'd rather keep this from Anne and Tabby for now."

The ghosts, Branwell saw, had finally followed him to this gravestone, and evidently saw Emily as a more vulnerable target, for they clustered around her, curling their limbs and extending their heads.

And Emily exhaled sharply—but caught her breath with an impatient shake of her head. "The air here is always bad," she said.

Branwell jumped when Keeper bayed, and the ghosts retreated. Emily of course had not seen them, not having Branwell's oiled glasses—but in the moments before Keeper had barked, she too had seemed able to resist their breath-stealing.

Now she looked around suspiciously at the graves. "We'll talk on the steps," she said, and led the way back to the wall. She had to help Branwell over it. Keeper cleared it in one bound.

When they had sat down on the wet parsonage steps, Emily said,

just loudly enough for Branwell to hear her over the drumming of the rain, "You saw that skull, in the church, six months ago."

Branwell was staring down at his boots. "I saw your dog break something up."

"You saw it before Keeper destroyed it, before I shot it. You saw it the day before, when that woman showed it to you in the Black Bull." She smiled at him through the strands of her wet hair. "I know you! I know you did."

He shrugged and looked away, toward the street.

"She told you that bringing it into the church would... have an effect on the thing under the stone. And she asked you to bring me to her." Emily simply sounded curious, and she didn't ask him why he had then done as the woman had asked.

Branwell was glad of the cold rain on his face. He couldn't even meet the dog's gaze.

At last he stood up and waved at the parsonage and the church and the village rooftops beyond it, all dark in the rain. "This doesn't—*contain* me!" he yelled. "I—*shrivel*, here!"

Before she could speak he went on, "I think it doesn't contain you either, Emily! I looked in your writing desk today—you're writing a novel! I'm sure it's wonderful, but it'll wind up in a publisher's fire, unread, you know it will!" He could feel the Northangerland identity creeping up in him. "That's not the way to... power, respect, *dominance*."

She leaned back on her elbows, smiling as she blinked up at him in the rain. "What did you want to see in my desk?"

He sagged, and almost threw himself at her feet and blurted, *Forgive me, I used your drawing to set devils on your track*—but his laggard Northangerland persona finally took over, just in time.

"I wanted to see your work, see if you showed strength." Of course he hadn't read a word of her manuscript, so he went on quickly, "And you do—you can make amends—I know they'll forgive you, if you're with me!"

They might, he thought. His forehead was hot, and he knew that sweat was mingling with the rainwater on his face.

"Amends," she said, and she stood up. "They." Keeper scrambled to his feet too, and shook himself. "When Keeper broke up that werewolf skull—yes, don't gape like a fish, you know that's what it

was—you were only a few yards away, and you had some kind of fit. Are you finding power, respect, dominance?" She wasn't smiling now. "Who is 'they'?"

"I—can't tell you. You refused to let Mrs. Flensing baptize you."

"*Baptize* me?" She cocked her head. "Do you mean poking my hand with that knife? Baptism into what? Not the Anglican Church."

"Into something *real*!" Branwell pushed back his sopping hair to stare up at her. "What if its glamor *is* dark? Can you honestly oppose it, with allies like that one-eyed Catholic, that *Curzon*, who murdered his own fiancée?"

Emily stepped back. "Who says so?"

With a choked, wordless yell, Branwell pushed past her and opened the front door, and he hurried down the hall to the stairs. A few moments later he was upstairs in his room with the door closed, shivering and stripping off his sodden clothes.

He heard Emily pad past his door, and then the door of her own room opening and closing. She would have left Keeper down in the kitchen to keep him from jumping onto her bed.

"'Anglican Church,'" he muttered. "You nearly never go to church anyway—your church is the moors, your priest is your dog, your God is—I don't know what. The wind."

In dry trousers and shirt and stockings, he paused before putting on his shoes, and he stared at a painting that hung framed on the wall.

It was a portrait of himself and his three sisters that he had done when he was seventeen, twelve years ago—ten years after the Crow Hill explosion and nine years after he had been bitten by the thing that had seemed to be a misshapen dog.

He had effectively caught his sisters' likenesses with his brush: Anne shy and watchful, Emily blankly defiant, and Charlotte chubby and distracted. But the figure that was supposed to be a self-portrait, standing between Emily and Charlotte, didn't look like Branwell at all, in spite of much scraping and repainting at the time. He had grown so tired of his sisters pointing this out that he had taken the painting down from the parlor wall and hung it here.

The figure between Emily and Charlotte was a young man, certainly, of about the correct age of seventeen, but the face was detectably too broad, and in spite of the colors he had mixed and

remixed on his palette, the hair had turned out far too dark, and the skin was almost swarthy.

His hands clenched into fists as he stared at the picture, for he realized now that he should not have resisted the remembered impulse to paint the hair coal black.

When the crows had come to Wright's whistle this morning, and landed in a cluster on the grass, both Branwell and Wright had for a moment glimpsed the figure of a middle-aged man; and when it had vanished, leaving only the crows, Wright had asked Branwell if he had ever seen the man before. Branwell had shaken his head—but in fact he had recognized him.

The man had clearly been the adult version of the young man in the painting; who, in turn, Branwell now realized, was the adolescent stage of the dark little boy who had for a few moments possessed his body at Ponden Kirk six months ago.

Branwell shuddered now with a mixture of panic and fascination. *Little boy, adolescent, and grown man—I've now "seen" this person at three stages of his life.*

And he occupies my place in my painting.

Of the painted faces, only the stranger's appeared to be looking directly at the viewer, and after a pause Branwell met the gaze of the painted eyes.

He gasped—

—and took a step to catch his balance—

His feet were icy cold and he was soaked, shaking in frigid wind in gray daylight. He was outdoors, in—he blinked around wildly—in the kitchen yard, standing in cold mud in his stocking feet, and his wet shirt clinging to him was worse than no shirt at all. He clasped his arms across his chest, and nearly cut his face with a knife clutched in his right hand; he let go of it, and when it splashed in the mud he saw that it was one of Tabby's carving knives.

He turned back toward the house. The kitchen door was open, and he stumbled to it and slammed it behind him when he had got inside.

Tabby was standing by the big black-iron range and staring at him in alarm.

"Some villain is out there?" she asked.

"Uh...no."

She sat down at the table. "Nowt but more of your alarms, then, and your feet all mucky? And my knife?"

"I'll," said Branwell through chattering teeth, "get it—later."

"And Keeper?" Seeing his blank look, she went on, "He went out with you."

"Oh—ch-chasing a hare." It occurred to him to ask how long he had been outside, but Tabby was already staring at him as if he were suffering from delirium tremens.

He hurried to the hall and ran up the stairs, glad to see that Emily's door was shut. In his own room with the door closed, he sat down on the bed and clutched his wet hair, breathing in short gasps.

"I didn't even see through *his* eyes, this time," he whispered shrilly. He didn't look at the painting, and he was afraid even to voice the loud question in his head: *Who—what—are you?*

The dark little boy—the adolescent in the painting, the man who had for a moment replaced the crows on the grass—had taken his body again, just as it had done on that night six months ago below Ponden Kirk. It had only been for a moment, that time. How long had the stranger occupied him this time?

He had apparently said something to Tabby about *villains* in the yard and had taken a knife outside; and Keeper had gone out with him. What had been the stranger's purpose, interrupted by Branwell's return to awareness and control?

How long would the stranger occupy his body *next* time?

Adam Wright had told him, *Folk like us aren't stuck forever in one sort of body.* No, not when there were dupes like the Brontë boy ready to hand!

This big, yes, *darkly glamorous* world into which he had stumbled—like the worlds of literary or artistic fame—was clearly going to go on without him. Not without his physical form, it seemed, but without *him*.

How can I ever sleep in this room, he wondered, with that face staring at me from the painting? Perhaps if I'm careful always to be incapacitatedly drunk . . . no, that would probably only clear the way for his intrusion! And even if I sleep in my father's room, away from the painting . . . can I be sure the stranger can't follow me now, having worn this body twice?

Branwell leaped up, still in his wet clothes, and hurried to the

dresser. He pulled open the bottom drawer and tossed aside some heavy winter shirts, and came up with his paint box and a ruler. He set the box on the dresser and opened it, and shuddered at the smell of linseed oil; but he pawed through the jumbled contents and found several glass jars of paints that he had mixed for some unfinished project last year, together with a palette knife and a lot of pencil stubs and variously-sized brushes. He snatched up a pencil and the ruler and turned toward the painting.

With his eyes unfocused and half-closed, he drew two vertical pencil lines on the canvas, extending down from the top edge, one ending at the right side of Emily's face, the other at the left side of Charlotte's—bracketing the figure of the stranger.

He tossed the pencil and ruler aside and returned to his paint box. Some of the jars had leaked and dried out, but he found an intact jar of ochre and one of sienna, and twisted off the lids. He had no idea where his palette might be, so he tapped a blob of each color onto the dresser surface and used the palette knife to mix a dab of the brown sienna into the butterscotch-yellow ochre, then dipped into it one of the still-pliable brushes.

He took a deep breath, then faced the painting again and extended the brush toward the peripherally glimpsed face of the figure between Emily and Charlotte; and the brush stopped an inch from the canvas. He bared his teeth in panic and *pushed*, and the brush jerked forward and smeared paint across the figure's eyes.

There was no further resistance, and in minutes he had covered the pencil-bordered area with fresh paint, obliterating the alien figure, so that now a featureless pillar stood between and behind his two sisters. Beginning to relax, he mixed more of the sienna into the ochre and added some perfunctory shading to the pillar, though in his haste he deprived both sisters of some of their hair.

He dropped the brush. There, he thought, that might—

He jumped in surprise, for suddenly he was in total darkness.

He collided with a waist-high wooden partition, and his quickly groping hands slid across a polished wooden surface. His clothes were wet, again or still, but he was indoors; shoes on his feet knocked against a dry wooden floor. His throat stung, as if he'd just been shouting.

In what felt like a contrastingly low, timorous voice, he called, "Is

anyone there?" The echoes were familiar—he was in his father's church, in fact standing in the elevated pulpit.

A sound like a heavy door slamming shook the church, and he ran down the pulpit steps to the raised altar floor and hurried across it with his hands extended in front of him. Remembering the skull that Keeper had shaken to fragments right on this spot, he moaned as he ran on through the sacristy and pulled open the back door.

The rain had stopped, but the wind from across the churchyard shook his legs and hunched his shoulders, and through tears he saw that the sky behind the parsonage was several shades darker than it had been when he'd been in his room—subjectively only a few moments ago.

Something had closed or dropped heavily in the church nave behind him. Someone must be back there, in the darkness.

His breath came in jolting sobs as he ran up the walk past the churchyard to the parsonage steps, and he knew it was not yet eight o'clock because the front door opened when he turned the knob and tugged at it. But his father was the one who always bolted it, and his father was in Manchester having his eyes treated—would his sisters have remembered?

He might have gone to his father for help, if he had been here, but in any case Branwell had no reason to believe that his father would know what to do in this awful occult predicament.

Without a pause he went pounding up the stairs and knocked loudly on Emily's bedroom door.

CHAPTER NINE

Anne was sitting on the narrow bed, and Emily gave her a wide-eyed look as she stepped to the door and pulled it open. Keeper, his fur still bristly with dampness, lifted his head from the rug and regarded Branwell in the doorway with, Emily thought, a mournful expression.

In the glow of an oil lamp on the table beside the bed, Branwell's face was pale, and it seemed to Emily that his eyes were even more sunken than they had been when she had talked with him on the front steps an hour ago.

"What time is it?" he croaked.

"You just passed the clock," Emily told him, and Anne said, "About a quarter to eight."

"Still Wednesday?"

Emily nodded. "The ninth of September."

Branwell slumped against the doorframe. "You've told Anne everything, I suppose."

"Of course. Change into dry clothes and join us."

He sighed shakily and looked down the hall toward his own door. "I'll try," he said. "Er ... pray that I can." He nodded and walked away.

"Pray that he can change his clothes?" whispered Anne.

Emily shrugged and sat down in a chair by the bedside table. "Might as well."

"And I'll pray for you too. Consulting pagan goddesses!" Anne looked down at her hands.

"I learned it from our father."

In two minutes Branwell was back, in a fresh white shirt and dark trousers and dry shoes, and he looked pitifully relieved to see his sisters still as he had left them.

"What have you done?" asked Emily gently.

"I believe I've damned my soul," he said with, even now, something of his usual staginess, "not to Hell but to helpless oblivion." He sat down on the bed beside Anne. "Don't," he said, looking up at Emily, "let them stick your hand with that two-bladed knife."

"I won't."

He looked past her at the levels of pencil drawings on the wall. "You'll think I'm mad, but—there's an ageless little dark boy—"

"We've seen him," said Anne.

"I saw him today," said Emily, "on the moors west of Cononley. I believe he tried to kill me. By opening pots in the earth! Keeper killed one of the crows that he sometimes becomes."

Branwell peered at both of them. Then he just muttered, "I'm surprised I didn't feel it." He seemed to brace himself, then went on quickly, "Emily, I took a drawing from your writing desk this morning and gave it to a . . . a bad man, who gave it to the crows so that they could track you."

Emily nodded. "Why?"

"Can you forgive me?"

She considered him for several seconds. "Are you repentant? Do you have, as the Catholics say, a firm purpose of amendment?"

"I do, I swear. I'm so sorry! If I can get free—"

"Why did you do it?"

"Because I'm not like you—I ache at anonymity, insignificance! Oh, I'm sorry, but—you're content with the fact that a hundred years after you die, nobody will remember Emily Brontë. Or Anne, or Charlotte . . . But I wanted to live on—I hoped even physically!—for a hundred years, more, and have influence, power, *respect* . . ." He clenched his fists and burst out, "I wanted to be Northangerland!"

Emily cocked her head. "From your stories? He was a villain."

"He was—he is!—above virtue and vice. Sophisticated, cynical, worldly!"

And tall and handsome, Emily recalled, and arrogantly attractive to women. She saw tears in her brother's eyes.

"I almost *was* him," he whispered, "sometimes. But they cheated me. The thing that is that boy, and sometimes an adolescent and a grown man—"

"His name is Welsh," said Anne. "He's the ghost of a man—a creature—that our grandfather killed in Ireland in 1771."

"Wha—are you sure? How could you know?"

"Papa told us," Anne said. "You were . . . indisposed."

Branwell scowled at them. "*Perpetually* indisposed?"

"Yes," Emily said.

After a strained moment Branwell laughed, though not happily. "A ghost—that makes sense, God help me! He wants to possess me. Twice in the last hour!—I've found myself standing somewhere with no awareness of having gone there, as if someone else had *inhabited* me for a while." He looked from Emily to Anne and back. "I was sober!"

"Where did you find yourself, after?" asked Anne.

"The first time, I was standing in the yard outside the kitchen— in my stocking feet!—holding Tabby's carving knife. The second time, just a few minutes ago, I was suddenly in the church, and my throat felt as if I'd been shouting."

"Shouting," repeated Emily. "Were you alone?"

Branwell shivered and clasped his hands between his knees. "I don't know. I heard a loud slam from out in the dark church, and I ran out through the sacristy."

"A slam," said Emily. "Like wood on wood, or—like stone on stone?"

"Like stone." He shrugged. "I suppose it was that stone with the grooves on it. They don't need me," he added, touching his temple. "Not—*me*."

Emily recalled what Curzon claimed the goddess had spelled out in bird bones this afternoon: *The dead sister remains dead under stone, but the dead brother is up and taking the pledged host.*

"Why did you want the crows to track me?" Emily asked once again.

"*I* didn't want it, Mr. Wright wanted it. And he only sent them after you because you were with that Curzon fellow."

"Wright?" said Anne. "Adam Wright, the sheepherder?"

Branwell nodded.

"You were sitting on a grave," said Emily, "in the rain, when I came home. You were surprised to see me unhurt and alive."

Branwell muttered, "I was glad."

"True, you were. Mr. Curzon is alive too—though only because of me, and Keeper."

"Small loss if he weren't. Murderer."

Emily sat back. "We can be sure he killed some sort of werewolf king, six months ago. Whose word do you have that he has killed anyone else? Someone like Mr. Wright, or your Mrs. Flensing?"

After a pause, Branwell nodded again, miserably.

"Mr. Curzon has taken a house in the village," Emily said, "and after a good deal of mutual acrimony he invited me to dine with him there tonight, at eight."

"Emily!" exclaimed Anne. "Just the two of you?"

"I believe he's Continental. I refused." She looked pointedly at Branwell. "But I think I'll go after all, and bring my brother with me."

Branwell shook his head. "I couldn't possibly."

"If it weren't for Keeper, I'd likely have died today. But yes, I forgive you."

He sighed, looked around the narrow room, and sighed again; and at length gave her a twitching smile. "For that, I'll go. If God is merciful, the man will kill me."

"You're family. Keeper wouldn't let him. No, Anne, you stay. Curzon knows me, and Branwell is the lost sheep."

"The sacrificial lamb," Branwell said. He opened his mouth to speak, and Emily knew he was going to phrase some reason why he couldn't go after all.

"I forgive you," she repeated before he could speak. "Get a coat and hat."

The house Curzon had rented was past the church and a hundred yards down the steep incline of Main Street, and Emily couldn't remember the last time she had ventured this far down into the village. The sky was dark behind the rooftops, but the rain had stopped. Golden lights shone in the leaded windows of the street-fronting houses and gleamed on the wet paving stones.

Branwell hung back when Emily stopped at the house and rapped

the door knocker, and Keeper stood behind him as if to prevent him running back to the parsonage or, more likely, the Black Bull.

There was the snap-and-slide of a bolt, and when the door swung open Alcuin Curzon seemed to fill the doorway, a tall, dark silhouette against the glow of a fire behind him. The air that billowed out around him was stingingly warm after the cold walk, and smelled of boiled mutton.

Curzon stepped back, and Emily saw that his eyepatch was casually flipped up on his forehead, and he wore an unbuttoned black silk waistcoat over a shirt with rolled-up sleeves. If he was surprised to see her, the narrowed eyes in his dark, seamed face gave no indication of it.

"Miss Emily," he said; then, looking past her, "and . . . the brother. And Keeper."

"Keeper has already had his dinner," Emily said, stepping past him into a small whitewashed parlor. She took off her coat and hat and hung them on a peg by the door.

A table and three blue-painted chairs sat in the middle of the room on a worn rug, and several short logs lay on the sanded wood floor beside the fireplace hearth. A desk stood against the far wall beside a door that presumably led to a bedroom and perhaps a kitchen.

Emily and Branwell had clearly interrupted Curzon's dinner—on the table was a plate with slices of mutton and a pile of peas on it, flanked by a pewter knife and fork and a bottle and a glass.

"You refused my invitation," Curzon said curtly, "so I told the landlady that I'd be dining alone." To Branwell he added, "Come in, then."

Branwell and Keeper walked in, and Curzon closed and re-bolted the door. Branwell blinked around warily, and Keeper stood at the door.

Curzon sat down by the plate and picked up the knife and fork, then hesitated. "Oh hell," he said, and pushed the plate to the other side of the table. "Sit, eat," he told Emily. "You had an exhausting day."

Emily pulled out one of the remaining chairs and waved Branwell to the other, then sat down and pushed the plate back to the middle of the table. "No, you're right, I refused your invitation."

"I'm not going to eat while you don't."

Branwell had hung up his coat and hat and was eyeing the bottle. Emily said, "Keeper doesn't like peas, but he'll be glad to take the mutton." She laid her hands flat on the table. "We never finished our exchange of facts."

Curzon looked speculatively at Branwell. "Sixpenny facts."

"We need gold sovereign facts," Emily told him. "I'll start—a local sheepherder named Adam Wright sent that demonic flock of crows after us today. He gave them a drawing of mine as a—you might say as a scent."

Curzon gave her a grudging nod. "How did he have a drawing of yours?"

Branwell shifted in his chair, but Emily said, "Your turn. What is the significance of the two-bladed knives?"

"How many have you seen?"

Emily stared at him.

Curzon sighed. "You saved my life today, Miss Emily, you and your dog, and I respect the efforts of both of you. I'd be pleased if you'd eat." When she didn't move or speak, he said, "Why is your brother here?"

Emily turned to Branwell.

He raised his sparsely bearded chin. "I appear to have been chosen, sir," he said, "as the leader of a group, from London, intent on raising an ancient supernatural power in Yorkshire."

"Oh, Branwell," said Emily, "you're being *possessed* by a *ghost*."

"An old potent spirit—"

"Which pushes you aside when it acts."

Branwell reddened, and shoved back his chair and stood up. "So who *is* this man? You're convinced that he killed a *werewolf*, though nobody seems to have witnessed it." He glanced toward Keeper, then turned a bold glare on Curzon, who was frowning at him. "There's just as much evidence, sir, to suggest that you killed your fiancée."

Oddly, Curzon's instant response was to flip the eyepatch down over his left eye; but then his chair flew backward and clattered against the wall and he was on his feet, reaching across the table for Branwell.

"Peasant dog dung, you dare—!"

Emily had leaped from her chair to her coat in the same instant, and now leveled the barrel of her father's pistol at Curzon's face.

"It's loaded this time!" she said loudly. Keeper was standing on Emily's chair, his big paws on the table in front of Curzon and his bared teeth inches from Curzon's face. "You won't recover from this."

But Curzon had stepped back and his one visible eye was staring at Branwell. Emily glanced quickly to the side, and then backed away, the gun now wobbling.

Branwell was hunched over, with his fists to his face, and his gingery hair was shifting, and darkening, as though invisible sooty hands were ruffling it. He spread his arms and raised his face, and Emily gasped—his fingers were shorter, and blunt, and his beard wasn't scanty anymore.

Keeper barked furiously at him, but didn't lunge. Curzon had retreated to the wall and was now holding his two-bladed knife.

"Emily," Curzon shouted, "get behind me!"

But Emily stepped forward and leaned over the table. *"Branwell!"* she said loudly.

Branwell lowered his fists and glared at her with no recognition.

"Branwell!" she cried again.

Her brother suddenly stood up straight, with his eyes clenched shut. As Emily watched, the fingers of his outstretched hands visibly narrowed and lengthened. Blood dripped from the nails. He swiped one hand across his face, leaving a smear of blood even as it brushed some of the coarse new hairs from his cheeks.

Keeper whined at him.

Branwell collapsed into his chair so suddenly that Emily expected to see it break under him. He rubbed furiously at his face until it was streaked with blood and his beard was restored to its ordinary meager state. His hands fell limp, bloody and bristly with black hairs.

Curzon slid the knife away inside his waistcoat and leaned over the table. "Branwell," he said. "Branwell, look at me." When Branwell look up dazedly, Curzon said, "There's a basin with water, and towels, in the next room. Get cleaned up, and then go home." He frowned, then added, "Get the blood and hair off you before you use the towels."

Branwell was panting through his slack mouth and his eyes stared blankly, but he got to his feet. He shambled to the inner door, pulled it open with some effort, and disappeared in shadow.

Emily realized that she had been holding her breath, and now

exhaled. She laid the pistol on the table and hurried through the doorway, and found Branwell in a dim bedroom, hunched over a basin and splashing his face.

"When you've finished there, I'll take you home."

"I'll go home by myself," he wheezed. "I—God!—I told you I didn't want to come here." He lowered his face and rubbed handfuls of water into his hair.

Emily stepped back into the parlor. "What just happened to him?"

"You know what," Curzon snapped. "He wasn't so far into the change that he couldn't hear you, and climb back out. He clearly loves you." He raised his eyebrows. "Not silver, you said."

Emily shook her head. "What?"

He touched the pistol on the table. "The ball in your gun."

"Oh. No. Lead and rust." Emily felt ready to vomit. It can't have been what this man is implying, she thought. And whatever it was, my brother can surely be cured of it. "I have to get him home."

"Come back once he's tucked into bed." Curzon raised a hand. "He wasn't prepared—he'll be exhausted, sleep for twelve hours, and be grossly hungry in the morning."

"No—I don't want to bring Anne back here."

"What? Oh for God's sake, girl, your brother's soul may not be lost beyond retrieval! Nor yours. Are you such a slave to propriety?"

Emily crossed to the door and lifted down her hat and coat. She walked back to the table and said, "No. I'll come back after."

Her hands were shaking, but she got into her coat and tucked the pistol back into the coat pocket.

When she looked up, Branwell stood swaying in the bedroom doorway. "I can get home *unassisted*. Stay here with your *friend*."

Emily carried Branwell's coat to him and fitted his limp arms into the sleeves. She forced a light tone: "I've had to half-carry you home when you've been not as bad as this." She set his hat on his head and unbolted the door.

On the cold walk back up Main Street to the church corner, Branwell said only, "I'm dying, you know. My hair's falling out, did you see? And my fingernails bleed. Since the day I learned that I must never see Mrs. Robinson again, I've prayed for merciful death."

Keeper snorted as he walked beside them, and Emily nodded at him.

It was true that Branwell frequently implored God to take him, but it was always when he knew his sisters or his father were nearby, so that they might pity him and excuse his indolence and dissipation. But Emily had never believed his story of being banished from his employer's house and the whole village of Thorpe Green because of having fallen in love with his employer's wife; and Emily had often wondered what offense had actually led the husband to threaten Branwell with "exposure" if he ever came near their village again.

A Dr. Crosby, evidently the Robinson family physician, even sent Branwell odd sums of money every month or so, contingent on him staying away.

Might Branwell have had a fit at their house, something like the one he had suffered tonight? Could Mr. Robinson have thought Branwell had been ... changing into a *werewolf*?

Emily shivered from more than the cold, and again felt as if she might vomit.

Could that actually have been the case? To whom would Mr. Robinson have *exposed* Branwell? The townspeople, the magistrates, some awful Catholic inquisition?

All she said was, "You nearly got Mr. Curzon to give it to you tonight."

"If I were Northangerland, I'd have—"

"Stop it."

She had to take most of his weight as they made their way past the church and the churchyard wall to the parsonage steps, and it reminded her of the morning six months ago when she had half-carried the wounded Alcuin Curzon away from Ponden Kirk. My unnatural burdens, she thought.

When they had got inside, she waved Anne and Tabby back into the kitchen, and then, not for the first time, laboriously hiked her brother up the stairs to his dark room, where she got him out of his coat and let him fall onto the bed. She pulled off his boots and then stood with her back to the window. She could just make out his form by the diffuse moonlight—he was motionless, but snoring normally.

Downstairs again, she and Keeper simply left the house, and it took them no more than five minutes to hurry back to the corner and down Main Street to Curzon's door.

He pulled it open before she could knock.

"Sit down," he told her as she and Keeper stepped inside. "Why lead and rust?"

Emily resumed her chair without taking off her coat as he closed and bolted the door, and she explained her father's reasoning about rust from the bell that had rung at Welsh's funeral in 1771.

Curzon sat down across from her and picked up the fork. "That's clever," he admitted. He speared a slice of mutton and with raised eyebrows rocked his head toward Keeper. Emily nodded to both of them, and Keeper solemnly took the mutton when Curzon held it out.

"And you love your brother too," Curzon said, sitting back. The eyepatch still covered his left eye. "You'd have shot me, wouldn't you?"

Emily touched the pocket of her coat. "I still might."

His smile was bleak, deepening the grooves in his cheeks. "When was your brother—obviously—bitten by a thing like a big dog?"

Emily pursed her lips, but answered, "He'd have been eight years old. Possibly nine. He's a year short of thirty now."

"That long ago! But what happened recently, then, to trigger it in him after all these years?"

"He—" Emily began, and then stopped. "If you try to kill him, Keeper or I will kill you."

"I understand." He waved for her to continue.

Keeper had laid down beside her, and she reached down to stroke his head. "My goal in this is to save him."

"Of course."

Emily sighed and spoke quickly: "At some time Mrs. Flensing did what she called a baptism, on him: pricked his palm with one of those double-bladed knives. And then—he was very close by when Keeper wrecked the werewolf skull that Mrs. Flensing brought here. He seemed to have some sort of fit when that happened."

"I daresay." Curzon shifted in his chair. "I believe I've told you who this ghost is, that's possessing him."

Emily nodded. "Welsh." She sighed and looked at the low ceiling. "Poor Branwell hoped to become a character from his stories—a Byronic aristocrat he called Northangerland."

"Northangerland," echoed Curzon, shaking his head. "A properly adolescent cognomen." Speaking more quietly, he asked, "Do you recall what the goddess spelled out for me, this afternoon?"

"If an old straw doll knows anything," Emily said. Then,

reluctantly, "According to you, she said the dead sister is still dead, but the dead brother is taking a host."

Curzon just stared at her with his one exposed eye.

"*The* host," she amended; then, "The *pledged* host." It was high time to change the subject. "The knife you carry," she went on quickly, "it's like Mrs. Flensing's. Why do they have two blades?"

"She didn't do that *baptism* on you?"

Emily shook her head.

"Good. I don't know what would follow, in your case."

He picked up the neglected glass of amber liquor and squinted at her over the rim. "There are some among us," he began carefully, then tipped up the glass and took a long sip, "who heal from wounds very quickly. The nerves, tissues, respond to injury instantly, and the damage to the body is entirely repaired within an hour or so. But the two blades inflict *two* wounds, narrow and very close to each other, and so the specifically directed responses interfere with each other—like the overlapping wakes of two boats, they lose their shape, their coherence. Healing is impeded."

Emily let her right hand slide into the pocket of her coat, and she felt Keeper shift against her leg.

"And," Curzon went on, "some measure of the victim's scattered healing energy is held by the knife—like electricity collected in a Leyden jar."

Emily recalled what Mrs. Flensing had said in the back room of the Black Bull: *A prick in the palm with these points—not even enough to draw blood.*

"The baptismal poke," Emily said, "doesn't involve any sort of wound."

"It would nevertheless have an effect on someone who's been bitten or begotten by a—by one of these—"

"By a werewolf."

Curzon raised a hand and let it drop. "As you say. The seeds are in the blood, ready to respond. And it would be a dioscuri that had wounded a . . . a *werewolf,* before, so that the blades are charged with that old misplaced energy. There would be resonance, alignment, discharge. I gather it feels like an electric shock."

"Dioscuri," said Emily. "That was Castor and Pollux, twins but half brothers. A bit grand, but why not."

"You've got your hand on that gun, haven't you? If you choose to use it, you have my forgiveness in advance."

Emily had in fact drawn it from her pocket and was pointing it at him under the table; Keeper stood up and moved to the other side of her. There was one question, or rather one statement, uppermost in her mind, but she put off voicing it.

"You once told me that your eyepatch is just a formality," she said. "But I understand you Huberti used to actually cut out one of your eyes."

He exhaled and shook his head. "We were almost a religious order in those days—penance, 'if thine eye offendeth thee, pluck it out,' as it says in Matthew's gospel." He flipped a finger at the eyepatch that covered his left eye. "Now it's just a salutary reminder of the principle."

"You're very observant of the custom, generally. As now. But sometimes you raise it."

He gave her a warning frown and said distinctly, "To see better."

"'Rather than having two eyes,'" said Emily, completing the quote from Matthew, " 'to be cast into hellfire.' " Her hand was firm on the pistol under the table. "It's not just a custom, and it has something to do with our troubles. And you owe me a fact—for my brother's sake."

He spread both hands and paused, as if about to regretfully push something away. "For *your* sake, say." He sighed and went on, "What it is, child—it involves parallax. Werewolves have two eyes, and it—"

"So does everybody. Dogs, snakes, fish."

"—it's a necessity," he pressed on, "in order for them to undergo the change. According to Paracelsus, in order for a mortal to—presumptuously!—step outside of nature without having been summoned by a god, he must first be standing squarely *in* nature, fully perceiving its dimensions. He needs traction if he's going to jump *out* of it. A one-eyed man sees only two dimensions, like looking at a flat picture, and so isn't able to enact the change." He sat back and rubbed his eyes. "It's true it often happens by the full moon, but that's just because one can *see* clearly then, at night. *Rage* is what causes it."

"The change." Emily took a deep breath. "You're a werewolf yourself."

Curzon dropped his hands. His haggard face twisted, and he spoke hoarsely. "And one of my eyes is covered. You're safe from me. But I'm..." He thumped one fist gently on the table. "I shouldn't be

what I am! We—yes, forcibly!—renounced lycanthropy centuries ago, and the tendency was effectively bred out of us, so that the eyepatches, as you say, became a formality."

The fire wasn't so warm that Emily was uncomfortable in her coat, but beads of sweat stood on Curzon's forehead.

"I discover, though," he said, "that I'm a throwback."

Emily cleared her throat, then asked, "Discover?"

"Goodbye, Miss Emily Brontë! I've sadly come round to owing you all truth. I . . . *did* kill my fiancée, near enough." Curzon's big hands were knobby fists on the table, and pushing each word past his teeth was a visible, painful effort. "Her *brother* wouldn't stand for her marrying a *Catholic*, and one night six months ago—the night before you found me on the moor—I was at a dinner at their family estate near Allerton, and I had dispensed with my eyepatch. Her brother was drunk, and he smashed an oil lamp over my head. The oil all ignited—I was on fire . . . and bleeding, possibly concussed, possibly . . . but my *vision* was unimpaired."

For several seconds he didn't speak.

"I came to my senses," he went on finally, "perhaps five minutes later, standing outside their house, below the turret balcony." He leaned back and stared at Emily, and the naked anguish in his eyes made her look away.

"Madeline was dead on the paving stones at my feet—showing only the injuries from her fall, not—"

Not from teeth or claws, thought Emily. She nodded.

"But obviously I had chased her—she was running from a monster, and leaped to her death—I fled into the night, back to the room I had rented in Allerton a mile away, and at dawn I was above Ponden Kirk, ready to plunge a dioscuri into my heart. And I met . . . another of my kind, didn't I? I had the dioscuri . . ."

He picked up the bottle and filled his glass. "Madeline's brother was found . . . torn to pieces. At the inquest, the servants reported seeing a thing like a wolf bounding down the stairs after the crashing and screaming, and I—I claimed to have been insensibly drunk throughout." He tipped up the glass, and when he put it down it was half empty. "The inquest dragged on, but the servants were sober, respected, and insistent, and the brother's wounds were clearly not caused by knife or axe." He shrugged. "Wolves in West Yorkshire."

This was abominable—incalculably worse than what he had told Emily this afternoon: *Miss Madeline Atha, my onetime fiancée . . . she fell to her death from the turret of her family home*—but now she was able to say what she hadn't said then.

"I'm sorry."

Curzon stood up. "You trouble me, Miss Emily." He paused, then said, "Your brother's condition can be controlled. Prevent parallax—make an eyepatch for him, and when he won't wear it, take his spectacles from him. Try to have him habitually keep one eye closed. Walk him through running water every day."

He crossed to the desk, and she heard a tiny clink and then the scratch of a pen nib on paper. When he straightened and turned around he was waving a small card to dry the ink on it.

"I see no real hope for you or your family, but a letter sent to me at this address will reach me," he said, holding it out.

Emily stood up, now visibly holding the pistol. Keeper padded out from under the table and stood beside her. "You just confessed to a murder," she said. "Two." But the inquest had already been closed—and who would believe an explanation involving lycanthropy?

Curzon didn't move or speak.

With her free hand Emily reached out and took the card.

"Will you kill my brother?" she asked.

"For your sake I will try not to be the one that does it."

"You can't prevent it?"

His silence was a clear answer.

She stepped back, half raising the pistol. "Will you try to kill me?" she asked.

His lips curled down in a bitter smile. "No. I will not."

Emily glanced down at Keeper. The big mastiff was watching Curzon, but only warily, not as if he sensed a threat.

"And so we part, Mr. Curzon," she said. "May God grant we never see each other again."

"Amen," he said.

Emily turned and pulled the door open, and Keeper followed her outside. She closed the door slowly, and didn't let go of the cold latch until several seconds after she had heard it click.

CHAPTER TEN

By the time Branwell woke up, well past noon, the day was bright and clear, and Emily had long since fired her father's pistol over the churchyard and reloaded it. Over breakfast Emily had told Anne everything she had learned—and had told Tabby too, and in fact the old housekeeper had added a couple of cautions: *Carry a new-cut birch stick with one fresh leaf on it, and if the leaf wilts, quick get inside four stone walls*; and, *Put a bright copper penny under your pillow, and if it's gone black in the morning you know your dream was an omen.* They were old Yorkshire superstitions that the two sisters had heard before, but they both nodded soberly.

When Branwell stumbled down the stairs at last, he had of course missed dinner, but Emily had carefully saved him a plate piled with mutton and potatoes, and he fell to hungrily. Emily directed Anne and Tabby to the parlor and sat down across from him at the kitchen table while he ate. The back door was open, and a warm breeze swirled dust across the stone floor.

When he had eaten everything on his plate, Branwell asked for more of the mutton, and when Emily had fetched it for him he made quick work of it too. When he had finished it all and leaned back in his chair with a sigh, Emily sat down again.

"Good morning," she said. "Afternoon, actually."

He looked away from her. "I suppose I disgraced myself again last night." His fingertips were bruised and Emily saw a streak of dried blood by his ear, but his hair was back to its usual carroty color. "Your man was insulting."

157

"Not my man." She frowned at him. "Branwell, listen—do you know what happened to you last night?"

"I insulted him first—" He rolled his eyes. "Very well, I had some sort of fit."

"A fit. Yes." She sat back and stared at him. "Tell me about Adam Wright."

Branwell's eyes widened. "I never saw him before yesterday!"

"Don't be silly, you've seen him a hundred times in the village and in church." Emily cocked her head and smiled. "Tell me."

Branwell blinked, and a tear ran down his sunken cheek into his once-again scanty chin beard. "You have whisky here someplace."

Emily got up and lifted the emetic bottle down from a cupboard shelf, reflecting that they would have to find another place to hide it now. She poured a splash into a glass, hesitated, then filled the glass half full.

She had barely set the glass on the table before he had snatched it up and gulped a third of it.

"I told you they have no place for me," he said on a long exhalation as he set it down. "Not for *me*. Do you remember the time I came home at dawn, from the moors?"

"Of course. You said you had been out by Ponden Kirk."

"I—yes, well I saw a midnight funeral there, a funeral pyre. It was for a dead *animal*, like a big dog."

Emily nodded, recalling the grieving howls that had rung across the hills that night.

"I didn't know it then," Branwell said, "but Adam Wright was the one who set fire to the carcass."

He was staring unseeingly into the glass, clearly reliving that night.

"You didn't know it was him," Emily prompted.

"I washed hair off my face last night, coarse hairs!" When Emily didn't comment, he went on, "Adam Wright was naked, that night, but covered with fur. I shook his hand—his paw. And that dark little boy was there, and for just a moment he occupied my body—"

Branwell was shaking. Emily reached across the table and gripped his hand. "Listen to me, Branwell! It was that boy, Welsh, who bit you, out by the front steps, when you were eight or nine."

"What? He never—I remember that a dog—" He paused, still

staring blankly, and Emily knew he was rapidly correlating memories. He gave Emily an empty look. "When Wright shook my hand, it was recognition of kin, wasn't it?"

Emily glanced at the burn scar on her knuckles. "I'm sure it was. What happened at Thorpe Green last year?"

"Good Lord, I've told you all about that—Mrs. Robinson and I fell in love, and her husband banished me—"

Emily smiled at him. "This is me."

"I think I must have been drunk." He rubbed his free hand across his forehead. "I lost consciousness, I—I must have had a fit, there was broken furniture—and—" He exhaled for several seconds and then looked up at her and spoke quietly. "Obviously it was brief. No one was hurt."

"No one?"

He didn't answer that. "I fled to my room," he went on quickly, "and—yes, my fingers bled and there were new, coarse hairs on my face and hands. I cleaned myself up, but Mr. Robinson drove me out at gunpoint—hah!—that very night. I told myself it couldn't happen again, and it hasn't, until last night."

Emily decided to let her unanswered question go. "I think we can take measures to stave it off until we can free us all from the . . . the illness in the land."

Branwell finally pulled his hand away from hers. "You know how to do that?"

"Not yet. But in the meantime there are some things we can do, if you want to save yourself. Do you?"

"I'm not worth saving. But if you think you can keep *him* from taking me, I'll . . . try."

During the next ten days Emily spent a good deal of time melting nuggets of lead on the kitchen range and adding rust flakes to it to cast more pistol balls, for she was firing the pistol several times a day now: over the churchyard at dawn, at random stones on the moors, and at Ponden Kirk. She carried Curzon's old dioscuri knife with her everywhere these days, in a makeshift pasteboard sheath strapped to the inside of her left shin. And on her walks she generally remembered to break a limb from a birch tree and pluck all but one of the green leaves off of it; and she kept a bright copper penny under her pillow.

Branwell's resolve was half-hearted and short-lived—he gladly let Emily take his old pair of spectacles and the vial of oil Mrs. Flensing had given him, but he complained piteously when Emily took his regular pair too, and only gave them back to him every day after taking him on a short hike out to nearby Sladen Beck, where she made him splash through the running water. He flatly refused to wear the eyepatch she made for him, and after a couple of days he stopped bothering to walk around with one eye closed.

He mostly complied with her instruction to stay away from the Black Bull, but that was because he had exhausted his credit there and his father wasn't at home to give him money to stop his histrionic threats of suicide.

Twice Emily was sure Branwell nearly suffered a relapse.

He generally balked at stepping into the stream of Dean Beck, but one cold morning he recoiled and snarled at her, and his hair stirred more than the wind could account for. Keeper barked in alarm and Emily looked into Branwell's eyes and had to firmly repeat, "*Branwell*" several times before she sensed her brother looking back at her.

And one evening in the kitchen she had noticed him staring through his ordinary spectacles at a teacup, and turning it around and moving it back and forth as if to comprehend its shape and distance; he had been speaking, but his voice sank to a wordless rumble. Emily had stood up and crossed to the nearest pail of holy water and dashed a handful of it across his spectacles. The startled and petulant voice that protested had been Branwell's, and she had taken custody of his spectacles for the night.

Emily very soon located an old pair of her father's eyeglasses and smeared some of the oil from Mrs. Flensing's vial onto the lenses.

Wearing them, she ventured out of the house—and saw ghosts. The blurred forms, bag-headed and branched in approximation of limbs, sometimes hurried toward her as she walked past the churchyard, and her remembered occasions of shortness of breath there were explained now that she could *see* the things crowding up to her and sucking through their gaping mouth holes. But she had always been able to make herself breathe deeply in those moments, and now she could see that the ghosts were repelled when she resisted them.

On a couple of occasions a human face, dimly retained, had been visible on a shapeless head, and once she had recognized the face of a baker who had died in the village during the winter. She had tried to speak to it, and then had had to beat a retreat, panting, when the thing had clung to her and snatched at her breath.

She even walked around the village, lifting the eyeglasses to see normally and lowering them to see the supernatural overlay. A couple of the villagers seemed to glow when seen through the spectacles; others seemed to walk in personal shadow, and she wondered if those people were soon to die. She uncharacteristically attended Sunday church service, and let Anne borrow the spectacles to see several ghosts kneeling in the aisle. Though the things were invisible to everyone else, the swamp-gas smell of them made several parishioners sniff and slide away along the pews.

Often she faintly heard the beat of music through the earpieces, and saw the ghosts ducking and bobbing in clumsy dance steps; and several times she caught vibrations like a scream, and saw a ghost flee down the street from some long-ago peril. Twice she had seen particularly panicked ones spontaneously vanish in a flash of flame; on those occasions even unknowing passersby had blinked and looked around.

Only once, a week after Curzon's departure, did she wear the spectacles on her long trek out to Ponden Kirk. The spectacles showed her trees where there were none, and unfamiliar standing stones on hilltops; a long-ruined farmhouse on a hill had a roof when viewed through the lenses, and vague hunched figures were visible in the doorway and windows, staring at her across half a mile of heather; under a withered cypress in a gorge she had seen the three old women who had metamorphosed out of *ignis fatui* a week before, beckoning and calling after her as she hurried away; and when she was standing on the slope below the towering monument of Ponden Kirk and looking up at it through the smeared lenses, the big black stones of it had seemed to flex, as though it might unfold enormous arms and burst the slope soil to stand up on stone outcrop legs.

Charlotte and his father were due to return home from Manchester in a few days, and Branwell was dreading it. Anne sympathized with his sufferings, though it irked him that she

couldn't seem to really believe that he had actually begun to turn into a werewolf in Curzon's parlor a week and a half ago; Emily, witness to it and aware of all his failings, somehow never swerved in her loyalty to him.

The three of them would certainly not tell his father, at least. But old Patrick would reportedly be able to see now, for the first time in years, and Branwell knew how shocked and saddened his father would be to see his son's wasted appearance.

On a Sunday morning when Tabby and Anne and even Emily had walked down to the church, Branwell sat in the parlor, trying to read the new issue of *Blackwood's* with one eye closed. He had promised Emily not to open the eye until she got back, but it began itching and he blinked both eyes and left them open—and found that the magazine had lost all interest now that he could read it easily. The manuscript of his half-finished novel, *And the Weary Are At Rest,* sat in a drawer in his room, but he couldn't bear the thought of looking at the last shredded page and trying to remember what he had tried to write there.

The parlor, the house, the whole world seemed drained of significance. He knew that he was being kept safe by Emily's incessant shooting, and her daily confiscation of his spectacles, and her rule about keeping one eye shut—though there had apparently been one or two near slips—but he did wonder why Mr. Wright had not come to see him during these ten days since the crows had been sent after Emily. What is going on, Branwell wondered, while I moulder here?

He tossed the magazine aside. Not allowing himself to think about what he was doing, he hurried down the hall and climbed the stairs, and he had pulled open the top drawer of Emily's dresser before he realized what he was looking for.

And tucked between the pages of an almanac he found the old pair of spectacles Emily had taken away from him. The little vial of oil lay on a handkerchief beside the almanac.

He quickly uncapped the vial and dipped a finger into the oil and smeared it onto the lenses of the spectacles. He recapped the vial and slammed the drawer shut, and twenty seconds later he was standing on the front steps of the house with the spectacles perched on his nose.

The bright sunlight seemed harsher, seen through the lenses, and apparently the churchyard ghosts didn't like to venture abroad in it, for he saw only one or two of the spider's-nest forms moving between the gravestones. A couple of boys kicking a ball on the lane were clearly visible through the lenses but weren't there at all when he lifted the spectacles, and a cat on the low wall was three cats when he lowered them.

Branwell actually laughed. He would go to the Black Bull, see the occult sides of its familiar patrons...but one of the ghosts had flowed over the low churchyard wall and was wobbling toward him.

He recalled how easily he had eluded the half-witted things on that rainy afternoon when he had feared that Emily had been killed, and he didn't flinch. And this one was shorter than himself, scarcely three feet tall.

He stood and waited while the bag-headed thing approached him. The marsh-gas smell of it grew stronger in his nostrils.

It was flickering like a frosted glass windchime in a breeze, and for an instant, and then for a moment again, it seemed to be a little girl before reverting to its previous indistinct form.

And his scalp tightened in shock, for he recognized her. This was Agatha, the village girl he had visited last winter—she had been sick with cholera, and he had spent half an hour at her bedside, and read to her from the Psalms...evidently she had not recovered.

But she clearly remembered him! "Agatha!" he exclaimed, stepping toward her with outstretched arms. And she arched into his embrace—and the mouth in her rippling mushroom head opened, and all the breath was sucked out of Branwell's lungs.

She tried to cling to him with twiggy arms, but he easily pushed her away and stepped to the side. His breath was no longer being stolen from him, but it came in hitching gasps because he was sobbing.

He recalled Charlotte's scornful doubt when he had mentioned visiting the sick girl. She hadn't believed he would do such a thing.

He shouldn't have.

Sixteen years ago, at the direction in a dream of what he now knew was the Welsh ghost, he had tricked Anne and Emily into hiking out to Ponden Kirk—and leaving their blood there—by telling them that they would meet their departed sister Maria.

Thank God that had been a lie!

Maria was entombed in the family vault in the church—not many feet from the grooved ledger stone that covered a headless monster—and Branwell hoped that her ghost stayed down there. He didn't want to imagine Maria as one of the mushroom-headed thistledown apparitions trying to suck out his breath.

Suddenly fearful that he *might* recognize her among the few ghosts visible among the gravestones, he snatched off the glasses and hurried back inside, where he forced himself to read, with great care, every article in *Blackwood's*.

Emily was in her room, reloading her father's pistol, when Branwell stepped into the doorway. She looked up warily, but the defensive frown on his face was his own, and he was wearing his ordinary spectacles, and he even had one eye virtuously closed.

He watched as she lowered the hammer onto the empty pan and pocketed the brass cylinder that contained gunpowder. She wouldn't prime the pan and cock the hammer until she was standing below Ponden Kirk.

She had changed into her boots, and her wool coat lay on the bed.

"You always bring the gun on your walks?" Branwell asked.

She stood up, and wondered if his height had diminished during the year—she was at least six inches taller than he was.

"You never know."

"All of us used to go on walks together," he said. "Can I come along?"

She kept any expression from her face, but she was doubtful about his ability to walk three miles and back, these days; and she was uneasy with the idea of bringing him to Ponden Kirk.

"It's a sunny day," he said quickly. "I'll keep one eye shut. I can't go to the Black Bull anymore, and I can't bear to sit indoors another day."

She knew he was anticipating a very uncomfortable time when Charlotte and their father came home in a day or two; and his two near-relapses had happened at dawn and after dark—probably the sun had a dampening effect on the change.

"I've added Ponden Kirk to my daily pistol targets," she cautioned him.

"Well—just don't let it ricochet."

She made up her mind. "You'd be welcome."

And in fact he seemed fit enough as he fetched his coat and tapped down the stairs. Keeper came in from the yard as Branwell was buckling his boots, and soon the three of them were striding along the path that led west, out onto the moors. Anne caught up with them before they had walked a hundred feet, and she too seemed surprised to see Branwell taking exercise.

"Branwell!" she exclaimed breathlessly, holding her hat onto her head against the wind that tossed her fair hair around her face. "You'll be as brown as Emily if you keep this up!"

In fact Emily was uneasy to see Branwell's evident energy as the three of them and the dog climbed gorse-furred hills and picked their way over fallen cromlech stones, but she was reassured to see him step right into the stream of Dean Beck before shaking water from his boots and crossing on the flat stones after her and Anne and Keeper. The sky was a deep cloudless blue and the breeze over the hills lifted the weight of the summer sun, and even the black rectangle of Ponden Kirk, tiny in the distance at first but filling more of the view as they drew closer to it, didn't much dispel Emily's enjoyment of the day.

They paused at the foot of the slope that led up to the massive monument, its top level with the western plateau.

Anne squinted up at the stacked black stones. "We were just children," she breathed. She held up her hands as if to frame the edifice in her vision. "But it looks bigger now than it did then. Do you suppose some atoms of our blood are still in that cave?"

Branwell shifted uncomfortably and took off his spectacles. Emily had known from the state of her dresser drawer that he had handled his proscribed pair today while she'd been at church, but this was his ordinary pair, and his left eye was shut.

"Take your shot," he said gruffly, "and let's go home."

"Yes," said Emily, pulling the pistol from the pocket of her coat. "I've just got to prime the pan."

A child's voice rang then from up the slope: "Your father need not die."

Emily spun in that direction. The swarthy little boy in tattered white shirt and trousers had stepped out from around the base

corner of the monument and now began walking barefoot down the sunlit slope.

"Once more I come to know of thee," he called merrily to Emily, "if thou wilt surrender, before thy most assured overthrow."

Keeper had quickly stood up, the fur bristling on his broad shoulders, but he was sniffing the air and swinging his head from side to side, and Emily quickly dug the brass cylinder of gunpowder from the pocket of her dress and uncapped it.

She recalled that Keeper had been able to sense where the boy's physical form was actually standing, eleven days ago by Minerva's temple, when she had been distracted by a projection of it.

"Where is he this time, boy?" she whispered to the dog.

"The son's destiny is set," said the boy, walking slowly but only half a dozen yards up the slope now, "and in a sense he will be immortal. But the father—he could be spared, and not die and fester in these fields."

"They'll both be spared," said Emily through clenched teeth as she flipped up the pistol's pan-cover and shook powder into the pan. Her hands were steady.

"Branwell's soul has always been immortal," spoke up Anne, "and consecrated to Jesus Christ."

The boy laughed. "Ask him how his immortal soul fares! But no—no Hell for him—he will be beyond all cares, at rest with the weary, forever."

The boy stared directly into Emily's eyes. "Amen I say to you," piped the child's voice, "this hour of this fateful day is your final opportunity to surrender to me and, in merciful exchange, to save your father."

Emily raised the pistol in answer.

Keeper tensed and bounded toward a patch of heather a dozen feet to the left of the Welsh ghost; Emily snapped the pan shut and swung the pistol barrel in that direction. The stones and grass of the slope wavered at a spot there, and she pulled the trigger. The gun fired an instant before Keeper leaped.

A black explosion of eight or ten crows burst away from Keeper in all directions as echoes of the shot rebounded away down the valley.

From the corner of her eye Emily saw Branwell fall to his knees as she raced to where Keeper was shaking something furiously. She slid

to a stop and saw that the mastiff had the bloody ruin of a crow in his mouth. Another crow lay a couple of yards farther away, its head blown off by Emily's pistol ball. The crows that had taken wing were flapping away above the plateau behind the crown of Ponden Kirk.

Anne hurried up and stood beside Emily. "Branwell's fine," she said. "Just weeping. Did you and Keeper kill the Welsh ghost?"

"I think we *shortened* him a bit." Emily stared up at the towering black monument, and noted the position of the sun in the blue sky—it was well past noon. "Let's get Branwell home quickly. I've got that knife, but I only prepared one pistol shot."

The energy Branwell had shown on the hike out to Ponden Kirk was gone. Emily and Anne had to walk on either side of him with his arms around their shoulders, while Keeper walked beside them, looking around and behind. Several times Anne or Branwell called for a five-minute rest, and Emily made sure to drag Branwell's feet through the Sladen Beck as they crossed it. The sun was hovering over the western hills when they finally reached the parsonage.

Branwell was exhausted, muttering about damnation. He didn't pay attention to anything they said, so they pushed and pulled him up the stairs and flopped him onto his bed.

As Emily pulled his boots off his limp feet—for what she thought must have been the thousandth time—he muttered, "I need distraction—a book—"

Anne crossed to his bookcase and fetched a book of Coleridge's poems while Emily found matches and a scrap of glass paper on the bedside table. She folded the gritty paper and pulled the match smartly through it, and when the match flared she lit a candle in a brass holder beside the matchbox. As she blew out the match she pushed the candle several inches farther from the bed.

Branwell held the book in one hand while he flailed about with the other, trying to fold his pillow into a comfortable shape, and Emily was glad she had moved the candle away. At last he was settled, holding the book right-side-up and peering at the pages through his ordinary eyeglasses.

Emily turned to leave, but Anne caught her eye and nodded toward the painting hung on the wall.

Emily had of course seen it many times before, but she paused

and looked at it, and saw that the figure of Branwell was gone now, replaced by a pillar. She just cocked an eyebrow at Anne and led the way back down the stairs.

When they had hung up their hats and coats, Anne lit the oil lamp and Emily set the kettle on the range, and the two sisters sat down at the table.

"I don't think," said Anne, staring at her hands and flexing her fingers, "that I ever quite believed your . . . *accounts* of all this." She turned to face Emily, frowning over a frail smile. "Minerva in a magically appearing temple! Branwell *changing* in the way you said. I've seen that little boy before, from a distance, but today—!" She made a fist and bit her knuckle. "Papa will blame himself."

"He didn't know. Not fully. And he—"

"Merciful God!" Anne had sat back in her chair so suddenly that Keeper stood up from beside the back door. "Emily! Branwell painted out the face in the picture!"

"Yes," said Emily, alarmed at her sister's tone.

"It was never a good likeness of him, was it? Who *did* it resemble?"

"It—" Emily's shoulders hunched involuntarily and her face was suddenly cold. "No, you're just—"

"Think about it! Recall the face in the painting, and the face of that demonic little boy!"

"A child and a young man—"

"Yes yes, but was it the same person?"

"Oh." Emily gave a shaky sigh. "I suppose. Yes."

"I was fourteen when he did that painting of us all."

Twelve years ago, Emily thought. Welsh has been aiming at possessing Branwell for a long time.

"Why all this now?" said Anne.

"I believe Alcuin Curzon forced the issue," Emily said, "when he killed the werewolf patriarch." She found that she had to defend Curzon: "Though obviously it was all going to happen in any case."

Anne took a deep breath and let it out, then nodded sadly. "Yes. All because our great-great-grandfather saved what seemed to be an orphan child from being thrown into the sea." She shivered and went on, "An old pagan demon!" Emily recalled that their father had used that phrase when he had first told his daughters about Welsh.

"That's what we've got," Emily agreed.

Anne glanced at the ceiling and turned a troubled look on her sister. "Do you suppose a person can *choose* damnation? Effectively?"

Emily knew that Anne had, after some struggle, come to the conclusion that all souls would ultimately be saved. Emily herself had no such conviction, and simply tried to be true to her own isolated self and trust in the aspects of God that she derived equally from Scripture and experience.

"Not if we can help it," she said.

They both jumped when the back door creaked open, but it was old Tabby who stepped inside. She closed the door against a gust of heather-scented wind and crossed to the range, rubbing her hands together.

"I'd almost fancy a bit of emetic in the tea," Tabby said. "Emily," she added, "when did you break off that stick?"

Emily looked over her shoulder at a short birch stick beside the door. She had broken it off that morning in the churchyard, and had stripped off all but one of the leaves as she'd walked back to the parsonage.

The leaf now drooped limply.

Anne was looking at it too. "Yesterday, wasn't it? And in the heat of the kitchen . . ."

Emily stood up. "It was this morning."

This hour of this fateful day, the dark boy had said today, *is your final opportunity to surrender to me and, in merciful exchange, to save your father.*

She hurried to her coat and pulled the pistol out of the pocket. "Anne, my loading kit is in my room, under the bed. Could you—"

She was interrupted by something harder than a knuckle rapping fast and loud three times on the back door.

"Miss Emily!" came a shout from outside—and she shivered when she recognized it as the voice of Alcuin Curzon. A moment later he had pulled the door open and lumbered inside. In his boots and long coat, with his mane of disordered black hair, he seemed bigger than ever, and his dark face was tense. In his right hand he held a flintlock pistol and in his left he gripped a dioscuri knife.

Emily quickly lifted her leg and snatched out her own dioscuri, which had once been his. "Who have you come to kill?"

He slammed the door and slid the bolt. "The Flensing woman has

got a new head for your monster, and she and some man are coming to kill you. I came after them from Keighley and just passed them on horseback in that steep street of yours, but they're close." Tabby was staring at him with astonished disapproval, and he added impatiently, "I came to your back door to avoid the delay of being announced, and because I expected to find you in here."

"Anne," began Emily, "hurry—!"

She was interrupted by the boom of a gunshot just outside and the clatter of the door bolt bouncing on the stone floor.

And Emily leaped to snatch a jar from the high cupboard shelf.

Branwell had awakened a minute earlier to find that he was not alone.

The little dark boy had been sitting in a chair against the far wall, just below the painting that until recently had borne his adolescent likeness. His legs weren't long enough for his bare feet to touch the floor.

"Our travails now are ended," the boy had said.

"Not yours," Branwell had said with shaky bravado, avoiding meeting the thing's eyes. He had been tense, not quite sure he wasn't hallucinating, and cautiously confident that Emily would be up soon to check on him. "Emily and Keeper killed your crows."

"You think there's a shortage of crows, boy?" Branwell had shivered to hear a child's voice call him *boy*. "I could gather up *grass* to show a form."

Branwell had noticed then that one of the boy's arms ended in a smooth stump at the wrist. "It cost you."

"Soon to be restored. Today I offered terms, some mercy, but— tonight I call in all the Brunty debts. Your father was always forfeit, and you and your sisters signed promissory notes in your bloods, on stone, sixteen years ago."

From somewhere outside there had come the boom of a gunshot. "I believe," the boy added, hopping down from the chair and walking toward the bed in which Branwell lay, "the ghost of your sister Emily is even now finding a new and unpleasing head to occupy."

A chubby young man in a top hat was the first to shove the door open and leap through the doorway, and as he slid to a stop he whipped

off his hat. With loud buzzing, at least a dozen big wasps came looping up out of it, rocking heavily in the warm air. Then he dropped an apple-sized black ball—when it hit the floor it exploded with a stunning bang and a dazzling flash of light, and he leaped at Curzon.

Blinking against the glare in her retinas, Emily saw Mrs. Flensing stride into the kitchen. A heavy satchel swung at the woman's hip from a shoulder strap, and she was ignoring the wasps—and now Emily could see that she was holding a pistol in each hand, though her right hand looked like a deformed crab with waving antennae. The woman swept the pistol barrels from one side of the kitchen to the other. Tabby climbed hastily onto a stool.

Keeper sprang at Mrs. Flensing—she stepped to the side and her right-hand pistol banged and flared, and the mastiff tumbled sprawling on the floor. Emily tossed aside the glass jar she had grabbed from the shelf.

Emily was looking straight down the bore of the other pistol when Mr. Flensing pulled the trigger, but in the same instant Emily lashed her fist to the side. She was clutching Mrs. Flensing's two dried fingers, and the pistol jerked out of line when it fired. The boom of the shot battered at Emily's ears, and her already-dazzled eyes stung with the burst of smoke in her face.

Another gunshot shook the air an instant later, and Emily was able to see Mrs. Flensing rock backward, blood jetting from between her bared teeth. Curzon dropped his fired pistol and lunged at the woman with his dioscuri knife—but the chubby young man leaped onto his back and clawed at his face, tearing away the eyepatch, and the points of Curzon's knife wavered and fell short.

Tabby had grabbed another of the glass jars from the high cupboard shelf, and she swung it in an arc over the room, scattering iron nails in all directions.

Anne was on her feet and snatched the kettle from the stove; and, wincing, she shook off the lid and flung the boiling water into Mrs. Flensing's face. The woman dropped both pistols and *roared*. The wasps had disappeared in Tabby's hail of cold iron, but now the kitchen was suddenly as cold as the moors in midwinter.

Curzon jerked his knife backward over his shoulder; it thudded to a stop, and the man on his back screamed and slid off of him to the floor—

But Curzon stepped back, staring at Mrs. Flensing. His breath was steam.

Mrs. Flensing's scalded face had turned black—and Emily's ribs tingled in shock as she realized that the blackness was fur, and below the broad nose black lips were pulled back to expose fangs. The satchel fell from the woman's infolding shoulders and her knees bent backward as she crouched, and when she sprang at Curzon there were claws protruding from her blunt, furred hands.

And what met her with a bone-jarring impact in midair was a similar creature—Curzon's ruptured coat flapped around the shoulders and flanks of a mastiff half again as big as Keeper. Loud guttural snarls shook the now-icy air as the two big animals crashed against the wall, tearing at each other with fangs and claws. In the deafening bestial racket Emily and Ann ran back to crouch by the black-iron range, and Tabby hopped down from the stool to stand beside them. The cold air was astringent with a metallic smell.

The fangs of the Curzon creature ripped savagely at the other beast's snout and neck, and the Flensing thing rolled on its back to shred the remains of Curzon's waistcoat and shirt with its hind claws. The rippling dark fur of both creatures was splashed with bright red blood.

The one in the tatters of Mrs. Flensing's coat broke free with a shrill wail of rage and bounded out through the open back doorway into the night, leaving her big satchel on the floor. The young man who had come in with her leaped past the Curzon werewolf as it thrashed on the floor trying to get its legs under itself; he picked up Mrs. Flensing's satchel and Curzon's dropped knife and took one wide-eyed look back, his face a mask of crisscrossed blood streaks, then blundered against the doorframe and fell onto the stones outside.

The thing in the tatters of Curzon's coat hiked itself to its feet and spun toward the three women on the other side of the room. No glint of recognition or humanity showed in its unblinking black eyes. It flung the table aside and rushed directly at Emily with open jaws and red-streaked fangs, and she lunged at it with her dioscuri held in a fencer's thumb-and-two-finger grip.

The creature jerked its head aside, and her knife plowed deeply into its shoulder.

She was braced for the impact of the thing's massive body, but the knife in its shoulder stopped its rush like a pistol ball—though it had

taken worse wounds in the last few moments from the Flensing werewolf—and it recoiled back and tumbled to the floor beside Keeper, who was beginning to twitch and roll his head.

Emily stepped forward cautiously, still holding the knife extended.

The body in the remains of Curzon's coat and trousers was shifting, creaking and popping, changing shape. Groans were wrenched out of the flexing throat.

With a startling clatter of claws on the stone floor, Keeper stood up. A raw graze showed in the fur above his eyebrow ridge, but he was alert as he looked to Emily.

On the floor, her attacker wiped clumps of hair from its shortened face with bloody hands, and then it was recognizably Alcuin Curzon who rocked his head from side to side to look around at the room. He drew his legs up and tried to roll over, but the arm below the shoulder Emily had stabbed just slid limply on the floor.

He coughed, spat blood, then said hoarsely, "They're gone?"

"Yes." Emily still held the knife ready.

"Are you—unhurt?"

"Yes," she told him, "because I stabbed you, in the shoulder. I was aiming for your eye." His suffering gaze was helplessly fixed on hers, and she nodded toward Anne and Tabby and went on, "You were about to kill the three of us."

He sank back, letting his head knock against the stone floor. "Do it now, for the love of God. Through my eye to my beast brain." When she didn't move, he thumped a bloody fist on the floor and managed to yell hoarsely, "Do you care nothing for the lives of your wretched family? *Do it!*"

Emily shifted her grip on the knife. "Two weeks ago I asked if you would try to kill me. You said you would not. I discover what your word is worth." She knew it had not truly been *him* that had attacked Anne and Tabby and herself moments ago, when the change had been on him—but it had been his body, and could be again.

Curzon groaned and closed his eyes. "You're right, it's worth nothing, *I'm* worth nothing, *do it!*"

He's a werewolf, she told herself, and took a tentative step toward him—

—When a full-throated scream from Branwell echoed down the stairs.

CHAPTER ELEVEN

The dark little boy had stood beside Branwell's bed, bending forward and, hardly noticeably at first, inhaling. Branwell hadn't resisted when he'd felt his own breath begin escaping between his slack lips—he had been shaken to hear that Emily was dead, but if she were truly gone there was no reason why he should go on clinging so painfully to his wasted soul—when he had heard crashing and loud animal roars from downstairs.

His immediate thought had been that Emily could not be dead—he couldn't imagine such clamor going on down there without her active participation.

He had blinked—and he had been staring into his own pale face inches away; the eyes had been wide, fierce, and he had known that as the breath left that body it was being replaced there by Welsh's identity.

This was really happening! In a convulsion of unreasoning vertigo he snapped his mouth shut and felt his own jaws click together. He saw the boy's swarthy little face crowding up again, openmouthed and hungry, and Branwell managed to fill his own lungs and empty them in a despairing scream.

Emily forced her aching legs to race up the stairs, past the landing and the clock to the upstairs hall, and she was panting as she lunged to Branwell's bedroom door and wrenched it open. Her pulse thudded rapidly in her temples.

By the light of the candle on the bedside table she saw two figures

standing in the middle of the floor. One was Branwell, disheveled and pale, and the other—she bared her teeth in dismay but flexed her fingers on the grip of the dioscuri—the other, barefoot in tattered shirt and trousers, was the dark little boy, the Welsh ghost, *in the house.*

Keeper stood tense beside her, growling, his great head swinging from one figure to the other.

The little boy clutched his ragged shirt with his right hand and wailed, "Emily! Get him out of me!" She saw that his left arm ended at the wrist, in a smooth stump.

The Branwell body waved toward the boy. "Set your dog on that discarded husk, if you like."

Emily took a deep breath and stepped forward so that her face was close to Branwell's. The curly ginger hair and the receding bearded chin were her brother's, but it wasn't Branwell who looked back at her from the blue eyes.

She slashed her brother's shirt with the edge of one of the paired blades, then leaped back to avoid a swung fist; but the attempted blow had been weak, and wouldn't have hurt her if it had connected. Welsh wasn't yet fully in control of her brother's body.

She caught the loose fist and spoke into the alien eyes: "Branwell! Take my hand!"

Both bodies spoke in unison then: "You can't—"

She racked her memory for a line from one of Branwell's poems, then recited, "'But I forgot to ask for youthful blood...'"

Branwell's mouth opened, and said, haltingly, "'The thrill divine of feeling unsubdued, the nerves that quivered to the sound of fame...'" And the hand she was holding tightened on hers.

But the dark little boy grabbed Branwell's elbow, and Branwell's hand was slack again, and his face tightened.

"You," her brother's mouth said to her now, "were to be dead."

"Do you want me dead?" she asked.

"No," choked the figure of the boy.

She stared into her brother's alien eyes. "Answer me, *Branwell.*"

The dark boy began panting rapidly, and Branwell's hand clutched Emily's. "No," he said. "No." He shook off the small clinging hand and stood up straighter. "I'm . . . Branwell, not Welsh."

And the figure of the boy began to change. At first Emily thought

it was approaching her, but then she realized that it was growing taller. Within seconds it was nearly as tall as she was, and it no longer appeared to be a little boy—what stood there now was the semblance of a swarthy, middle-aged man in a cloak, gasping. The expansion might not have been voluntary, and seemed to pain the thing. It raised its arms, and Emily saw that it was still missing its left hand.

The separation of Branwell and Welsh was, at least for a moment, distinct; and Keeper sprang at the man in the cloak. The big mastiff's jaws closed on an upflung arm, but there were two dogs occupying the same space, and the other one tore at the man's throat.

And the man seemed to explode.

Emily was knocked backward off her feet by heavy bundles of thrashing black feathers and scratching claws, and as she hit the floor on her hip and shoulder she heard the window break in a racket of beating wings.

Crows! she realized, and then the last of them had collided and fluttered away through the empty casement, and a night wind from out over the moors was cold in her sweat-damp hair.

The candle on the bedside table had been knocked over and extinguished, but the glow of a quickly approaching lamp brightened in the hall, and Anne stepped cautiously through the doorway into the room holding an oil lamp. Tabby was peering over her shoulder.

By the lamp's relative glare Emily saw that in fact not all the crows had fled. Keeper was once again just one dog, and again he held a limp black form in his mouth, one wing drooping.

Branwell had collapsed across the bed on his side, with his legs trailing on the floor. His eyes were closed and snores hitched from his slack mouth.

Emily got up from the floor and sat on the bed beside Branwell, panting. She gave Tabby a questioning look.

"The gytrash you stabbed turned all the way back into a man and crawled out of the kitchen," Tabby said sturdily, "and out onto the road." She stepped into the room and pulled the heavy curtains across the broken window. "There's blood and fur, and broken glass and dead wasps, all over the kitchen floor."

Thank God that Papa isn't here, Emily thought. "Don't let Keeper tear that dead crow to bits. I think it's a piece of death for Welsh."

Tabby gave a judicious nod.

Anne walked over to where Keeper stood. The dog still held the crow in his mouth, but relinquished it when Anne tugged gingerly at its dangling wing.

Emily shook Branwell's shoulder until he stirred and blearily opened his eyes. He stared at her for a moment, then thrashed around and sat up to peer into every corner of the room. He flinched when he saw Anne holding the dead crow's wing between her thumb and forefinger.

Emily interrupted him as he started to speak. "You're to keep that by you," she told him. "The ghost dog . . ." She looked up at Anne. "Our grandfather's dog was named Keeper too, remember?"

Anne nodded. "It killed Welsh in 1771, even as Welsh killed it."

"The ghost Keeper," Emily went on, "reenacted it here, tonight. I don't know how badly that might have weakened Welsh's ghost, but"—she turned to Branwell—"if he should come back, that dead crow was expressed in his remembered death—it might repel him."

"I—what, a dead bird?" Branwell touched the volume of Coleridge on the blanket beside him. "Like an albatross? It'll smell . . ."

"We can dry it in the stove," Emily said, "and then steep it in sal volatile or something." She tried to smile. "It would probably fit in a coat pocket."

"That'll smell worse—"

"It'll smell medicinal. You're known to be sickly."

Branwell just shook his head.

Emily looked at the ceiling and ran her fingers through her damp hair. "I'm told," she said, "that restless dead souls—ghosts, vampires—can only enter a house after they've been invited in." She lowered her head and nodded toward his book. "As in Coleridge's 'Christabel.' "

"Did Tabby tell you that? And a horseshoe over the door will catch good luck, and . . ." Branwell felt his shirt with his right hand. "My shirt's torn, and I've got a scratch on my stomach. Did Keeper . . . ?" His voice faltered, and he wasn't looking at Emily.

"When?" she asked.

"You and Anne were there too," Branwell muttered, "on that day at Ponden Kirk when we—signed promissory notes in blood. Why must it have been me?"

Anne inhaled sharply, but Emily just repeated, "When?"

Branwell waved his left hand, but it flopped limply; with the fingers of his right hand he brushed her question aside. "What happened here tonight—" He paused. "I say, what *did* happen? I heard the most frightful row from downstairs."

Emily just looked curiously into his eyes.

"Could I," he said, "talk to you privately?"

"Promissory notes?" burst out Anne.

"To what end?" Emily asked him. "Anne and I—and Tabby!—have no secrets from one another."

Branwell pounded the book on the bed with his right hand. "I was fourteen! It was a year after that day at Ponden Kirk, and Charlotte had gone off to that horrible school at Cowan Bridge, twenty miles away—I couldn't write properly without her, if it wasn't *us two*—on my own I could only write about Northangerland—" Tears were running down his gaunt cheeks. "I saw the dark boy in the churchyard in the snow, and he was barefoot! How could I *not* invite him in?" Emily started to speak, but he went on, "But he didn't come in, then! Why would he wait all these years to"—Emily felt him shudder—"come inside the house, physically?"

Emily wanted nothing so much as a cup of tea and bed, but there was a mess to clean up downstairs. "Oh," she said absently, "there were obstacles, I suppose. Keeper, Papa's banishing gunshots, perhaps even the buckets of holy water." She looked at the dead crow dangling from Anne's fingers, and her attention sharpened. "But the nightfolk lost their . . . their lycanthropic *king* not long ago, and since then their efforts to—to what, restore their power?—have pretty much stumbled."

She stood up. "I believe tonight was the big effort, meant to settle everything at last. Welsh was here to take full possession of you, and Mrs. Flensing—she was part of that row in the kitchen, wasn't she, Tabby?—had a bag that surely held a replacement head for the thing under the ledger stone in the church."

Branwell's eyes were wide. "He—the Welsh ghost—told me you were killed, and that your ghost was finding a . . . 'a new and unpleasing head to occupy.' "

Emily had not flinched during the events of this terrible night, but she recoiled now, remembering the monstrous skull she had seen partly reassembled on the church altar six months ago; they had intended to put her soul into something like *that*? Why? Even as she

asked herself the question, she guessed at the answer: as a placeholder for Welsh's twin, awaiting revival under the ledger stone.

"Promissory notes?" said Anne again. "You told us that day that we'd see Maria."

"Oh . . ." Branwell shifted his feet on the floor but didn't stand up. "You want to see Maria?" he snapped. "Have Emily give you my old spectacles with Gehenna mud smeared on them, and look at the churchyard some evening! You'll see her, or things indistinguishable from her."

"I have," Anne told him. "I've seen them. And Maria would not be one of them. What did we promise when we left our blood on the stone in that cave?"

Branwell looked away. "We—I was thirteen, and simply doing what I'd been told in a dream! But—very well!—we marked ourselves for attention, but also for protection. The ghosts are particularly aware of us—you must have noticed that your breath is sometimes snatched when you walk by the churchyard?—but at the same time we can resist them, they can't *force* themselves on us."

"And," pursued Anne, "what is the debt?"

"Ah, well—ceded control of oneself, I suppose."

"Emily has defaulted on that. So have you, tonight."

"I believe," said Branwell with evident reluctance, "it means control of oneself after one's death."

"We will default on that too," said Anne sternly.

"Yes," Emily agreed. "And I think you've now revoked your old invitation."

Branwell was prodding his left hand with the fingers of his right. Emily noticed that his left hand just rocked limply. And she recalled that the Welsh ghost, in the appearance of a boy and then a man, had been missing its left hand.

Perhaps, she thought with a chill, the invitation hasn't completely been withdrawn; perhaps Welsh still has one hand over the threshold.

Under a hedge a mile away, Mrs. Flensing was rolling back and forth in the dirt, grunting and sweating as her wounds reknit. Evan Saltmeric couldn't see her very well in the deep shadows, but it was clear that most of her dress had been torn away in the fight with the other werewolf, and her silk chemise was dark with blood.

He had tied a strip torn from his shirt around his forehead, and the knife-cut Curzon had given him had apparently stopped bleeding.

The satchel with the big grotesque head in it sat beside him on a flat stone. Mrs. Flensing had not succeeded in killing the Brontë girl, and the head would soon begin to decay if some ghost weren't implanted in it. Saltmeric knew the procedure, and he knew that Mrs. Flensing would not let it rot.

It was a summer night, but the wind from over the infinite quiet hills and valleys was cold, and he ached to be back in smoky, noisy, bright-lit London.

He had made his living as a pantomime street magician for ten of his twenty-five years, and early on he had come to the conclusion that some of the celebrated magic shows made use of real supernatural effects. He had eventually followed one of the popular magicians to the abandoned-looking church in St. Andrew Street, and had met Reverend Farfleece and Mrs. Flensing, and been judged worthy of submitting to the dioscuri baptism.

Dioscuri! He sat back against the hedge and touched the angular bulk that distended the pocket of his coat and had probably shredded the lining. He had still not sufficiently gained their trust to be given one of the double-bladed knives, but half an hour ago he had picked up the one Curzon had dropped when the change overcame him.

Farfleece and the Flensing woman had shown Evan Saltmeric some small ways to tap into the supernatural warping of reality that was generated by these frightful Yorkshire atrocities—genuine magical effects that could be achieved with silver coins and fire and a bit of blood—and his pantomime street performances had gained in wonder and glamor. But there were grander things to accomplish.

His ambition had not moved beyond being a performer, but he dreamed now of abandoning his squares of urban pavement and presenting extravagant magic shows in such venues as the Oxford Music Hall and the London Pavilion, and even the theater that Robert-Houdin had established at the Palais Royale in Paris.

He needed to maintain his alliance with the Oblique order, at all costs. Mrs. Flensing had told him of all sorts of wonders—of remote moonlit fairs where ghosts danced; and Celtic temples where old gods still survived; and a *mundus loci*, a tree in a magical grove in

Yorkshire that was the center of that region's supernatural whirlpool, with arches that opened onto places of power. But for the last couple of weeks she had recruited his aid in less glamorous and sometimes illegal undertakings: robbing graves in Highgate Cemetery, poisoning holy water fonts in Catholic churches, and—weirdest of all—having this *werewolf head* grown in a pot by a madman who lived on a skiff on the Thames!

And now that awful head lay beside him in Mrs. Flensing's satchel. She had meant to put into it the ghost of that Brontë girl, but her gunshot had somehow missed, and then everything had gone to hell. Saltmeric had followed the badly wounded werewolf that was Mrs. Flensing until it had collapsed out here in a field and begun to change back.

The head in the satchel would need a ghost put into it damn quick, and as soon as Mrs. Flensing recovered she would see that it was done. And Saltmeric himself was the only other person within a long dark mile in any direction.

On the turf in front of his boots Mrs. Flensing had stopped writhing. Even in the shadows he could see that her legs had regained human form and shed the bristly pelage, and her face was visible as a pale oval—only patchily darkened with fur now.

Quickly he unbuckled the satchel and tilted the horrible head out onto the grass. The neck had been cinched shut with wire and tarred, and it still had no hair, but it was recognizably the head of something like a very big canine. The open eyes were milky white, and he shuddered at the thought of his own spirit locked behind them.

He tugged the dioscuri knife free of his pocket and looked at the two long blades—conflicted wound response!—and he leaned forward to rest the points against Mrs. Flensing's bloodstained throat.

She opened her eyes, but they didn't yet show alertness, so with one fearful spasmodic thrust he drove the knife in to the hilt.

Immediately he was horrified at what he had done, doubting his memory of what had happened in the Brontë parsonage kitchen and praying that he might be allowed to undo these last few seconds; but Mrs. Flensing's bare feet scuffed in the grass and the hand he could see—her normal one—clenched in a fist; and then her hand opened and her body sagged, limp and clearly dead.

Desperate to counter the dreadfully accusing sight in front of him,

he pictured himself standing on a bright-lit stage in evening clothes, facing an audience that receded into far shadows and filled tiers of galleries on either side ...

Working quickly, as she had meant to do with the lifeless body of the Brontë girl, he picked up the raw, damp werewolf head with both hands and laid it beside Mrs. Flensing's slack face. Her ghost would, he understood, soon relinquish its hold on the killed human-form body and settle in the vacant bestial head.

He sat shivering for several minutes, and when he was sure the transfer must have occurred if it were ever going to, he rocked the knife back and forth until he was able to pull it free of Mrs. Flensing's throat. With distracted care he thoroughly wiped the parallel blades clean on a still-white corner of her ragged chemise, then tucked it into his coat pocket and rolled the heavy head back into the satchel—nervously dismissing his suspicion that it had twitched under his hands.

He fastened the buckles and hoisted the strap over his shoulder. He would blame her death on the Curzon werewolf, and surely in her absence he would be invited to take a higher place in the Oblique order.

He took a quick look up at the stars, then struggled to his feet and set off walking south, toward the Keighley Road.

CHAPTER TWELVE

Branwell simply stayed in bed all the next day, and on the following day Charlotte and their father arrived back home at the parsonage. Old Patrick was clearly delighted with his restored ability to see and read, and pleased to hear that Emily had faithfully fired his pistol over the churchyard every morning; but he was troubled by his son's wasted appearance. It baffled him to hear that Branwell had not spent more than a couple of evenings at the Black Bull in his absence, and he concluded that Branwell must be suffering from consumption, which in fact had taken his eldest daughters Elizabeth and Maria twenty years earlier.

Charlotte was overjoyed to be with her sisters again, and she soon told them that she had written half of another novel while sequestered with their father in Manchester. On her first evening home she read several chapters to Emily and Anne, and though they thought that her main character, "Jane Eyre," ought to be beautiful, Charlotte was adamant that the character should be "as plain and small as myself, and who shall be as interesting as any of yours."

The kitchen had of course been thoroughly cleaned and straightened, and it was evident that, in spite of accounts from Emily and Anne and Tabby, Charlotte couldn't make herself believe that the apparition of the Welsh boy had been a physical presence in the house—much less that two *werewolves* had got into a fight in the kitchen. Her sisters told her that Branwell's left hand was still limp and numb, corresponding to the missing hand of the Welsh apparition, but she didn't want to concern herself with her brother

any more than family routine called for, and she dismissed any disability of his as a consequence of perpetual drunkenness.

And it was clear that she didn't entirely approve of the expensive gift their father had brought back from Manchester for Emily: an Osborn Gunby flintlock pistol and loading kit.

The following morning the village was buzzing with the news that a woman had been found murdered on the moors—the body had reportedly been nearly naked, and stabbed in the neck. A magistrate from Bradford had been called in, and concluded that the woman must have seriously injured her attacker, for the remains of her chemise were stained with much more blood than the wound in her neck could account for—but Charlotte reproached her sisters for speculating that the poor soul might have been one of the werewolves who had fought in the kitchen.

Emily knew that it must have been a dioscuri knife that had killed Mrs. Flensing—and she let herself hope that the woman's plans had died with her. And three days had now passed since Welsh's appearance in Branwell's bedroom, and Branwell gave every indication of being entirely and exclusively himself again. Emily had soaked the talismanic dead crow in aromatic spirits of ammonia and, over Tabby's protests, dried it in the stove and sternly told her brother that he was to keep it near him, and never to leave the house without it.

Living with their brother nevertheless continued to be an ordeal. Charlotte's contempt for him only increased a couple of weeks later, when he set his bed on fire one evening in a drunken stupor. Emily had rushed in and doused the flames with one of the buckets of holy water, and had single-handedly dragged him from the smoldering bedclothes and into the hall.

Their father had fortunately been out that evening, and Emily and Anne and Charlotte had gathered in the kitchen once the scorched blankets and sheets had been disposed of and the bed remade and the still-groggy Branwell helped into it.

"He says he fell asleep," said Emily, "and must have knocked over the candle."

"Did he have the dead crow on the table?" asked Anne.

"In the drawer. He doesn't want to have to explain it to Papa."

Charlotte's face was expressionless.

"He couldn't have done it with that left hand of his, I suppose?" ventured Anne.

"I thought that hand was paralyzed," said Charlotte.

To Anne, Emily said, "I don't think so. He was lying on his back, and the candle was on the bedside table to his right." Emily shrugged. "Welsh wouldn't have wanted to burn him up anyway. Even if Welsh is recovered, and could get in again, he'd want Branwell's body . . . intact."

Anne glanced at Emily and quickly looked away; but Emily knew her thought: Branwell's been bitten—any injury would heal very fast.

Their father had of course smelled the smoke when he came home, and from then on Branwell was made to sleep in Patrick's room, where their elderly father would have to deal with any further crises involving his son.

Emily kept custody of Branwell's ordinary spectacles, and now let him have them only when he wanted to read something, or write. He made a show of his consequent bad vision, bumping into furniture and doorframes when his sisters were nearby.

He was more agitated at night, and the sisters pitied their father having to put up with Branwell's insomniac pacing and moaning and threats of suicide.

He occasionally rallied enough to dress and go to the Black Bull, and when the days grew cooler in the autumn he even, with their father's permission and over Emily's objections, managed to take a couple of overnight trips to visit old friends in Halifax, eight miles away. The only consequence was that he spent the next few days in bed, lamenting his wasted life.

Altogether it seemed to Emily that Branwell had, with the intermittent help of alcohol, managed to forget the night Welsh had been in his room. She even allowed herself, sometimes, to hope that Welsh had been effectively banished on that night.

She saw the sheepherder Adam Wright once in church, and he seemed wary of her—possibly imagining that it was Emily who had killed Mrs. Flensing. He didn't meet Emily's eye, nor presumed to call on Branwell at the parsonage, but Emily noted that he sat in a pew near the grooved ledger stone.

Emily and Anne and Keeper maintained a cautious vigilance.

Throughout the autumn, until an early and especially severe winter made it virtually impossible to leave the house, Emily continued to load and fire her new pistol several times a day, hiking out to fire one shot at Ponden Kirk; Anne and Keeper always accompanied her on that hike, and Charlotte often joined them, outwardly skeptical but attentive. Anne got a friend to send her bottles of Catholic holy water, and she surreptitiously added it to the buckets throughout the house. And Keeper was always with Emily, watching all corners of a room or all points of the compass on a moorland horizon.

Recalling Tabby's advice, Emily continued sleeping with a bright copper penny under her pillow—though in the morning it never proved to have turned black, and in any case her dreams were always obviously her own: of cooking, of loading and firing the pistol, of fording moorland streams or climbing hills with Keeper.

That winter was the coldest anyone could recall, and no one in the family ventured farther than the church once a week, not even to buy paper at Mr. Greenwood's shop twenty steps down the street. Anne suffered from asthma, Charlotte could hardly sleep because of a toothache, and Emily and Keeper were restless at the confinement within close familiar walls. Their father had taken back his pistol and resumed firing it over the churchyard every morning, opening his bedroom window just wide enough for the pistol's barrel to fit through.

The family's celebration of Christmas Day was muted. The village poulterer made the short hike up the street to deliver a goose, and while it was cooking in the range, Tabby and Emily prepared smoked bacon and haddock soup and a pot of mashed potatoes with onions, and Patrick brought out a bottle of brandy he had been hiding from Branwell—but all of them had colds, and the parlor with its fireplace and the kitchen with the big iron range were the only rooms that were really warm.

Emily took comfort from the fact that there had been no supernatural intrusions for more than three months, and to Anne she quoted the lines from Hamlet:

"Some say that ever 'gainst that season comes
Wherein our Saviour's birth is celebrated,
The bird of dawning singeth all night long;

And then, they say, no spirit dare stir abroad,
The nights are wholesome, then no planets strike,
No fairy takes, nor witch hath power to charm,
So hallow'd and so gracious is the time."

"Pray the bird of dawning singeth through the coming year!"
Anne said.

Emily shook her head. "Pray that the dead bird in Branwell's
drawer keeps his nights wholesome. Our brother may still be a
contested property."

In his more convivial days Branwell used to impress his friends
with his ability to simultaneously write in Greek with one hand and
Latin with the other. Emily didn't believe he had done it in quite a
while, and of course he couldn't do the trick now, with his useless
left hand; but one morning in March of the new year Keeper pawed
at Emily until she followed him upstairs—and found Branwell
hunched over an inkwell and a sheet of paper, writing furiously with
his left hand.

Emily tried for a shocked moment to believe that Charlotte had
been right—that the paralysis had been had been some consequence
of his drinking, from which he had now recovered; but when he
looked up in guilty surprise, his hand dropped the pen and began
rapidly crawling across the table toward her like a spider.

With his right hand he seized it and pulled it across his chest,
where its fingers clawed at his shirt.

"Greek?" Emily asked brightly, walking past him to the window.
"Latin?"

With his elbow Branwell slid the sheet of paper into his lap, but
Emily had glanced down as she passed him and had seen that it was
three long lines irregularly crosshatched by short ones. *Ogham*, her
father had called that kind of writing, *the ancient Celtic tree-alphabet*.
It was the language incised on the ledger stone in the church.

"My last will and testament," Branwell said lightly. He was
sweating, but forced a smile. "You're not to sneak a look at it."

With her back to the gray light outside the window so that he
would see only her silhouette, she asked, "Where's your crows?"

He choked and then grunted out two syllables in a harsh voice,
and his left hand pushed free of his right and scuttled down his shirt

to the leg of his trousers; it pulled his arm out nearly straight and paused on his knee, flexing up and down like a panting animal, with two fingers extended stiffly toward Emily.

A moment later his right hand had snatched it up and clutched it again to his chest.

In his own strained voice, Branwell said, "What did you say?"

"I said 'Where's your crow?' I told you to keep it by you."

"I—oh yes, the dead bird. Honestly, it was starting to smell so bad!—that I took it outside and buried it." He nodded, approving his story. "I was afraid Keeper would eat it," he added, "and die of that sal volatile you soaked it in."

Emily pushed away from the window and walked to the door. Over he shoulder she said, bleakly, "I hope I don't have to get you another."

The next morning at dawn she had got out of bed and put on her robe and started toward the door, when she remembered the penny under her pillow. For a week or so after the battle in the kitchen she had checked it every morning, but the coin had always remained bright copper, and she had laid it in place when she made the bed every morning without paying particular attention to it.

This morning she struck a match to the bedside candle and lifted the pillow. The penny was a black spot on the white sheet.

And all at once she remembered her dream.

She had been standing in the churchyard in intermittent moonlight among the flat and standing stones, swaying like a reed in the night wind. Between a couple of leafless trees she could see the two-story bulk of the parsonage—the windows were all so dark that she knew there was no glass in the frames, and she could see the paler gray sky through angular gaps in the roof.

A figure had been standing at the parsonage door, and, palpably aware of her even at this distance, had begun walking down the steps. The dream had ended before she had been able to see the figure's face, if indeed it had had a face.

If the penny's gone black in the morning, Tabby had said, *you know your dream was an omen.*

Emily laid the pillow back down, and a moment later jumped at the familiar boom of her father's dawn gunshot. She looked around her narrow bedroom at the dimly visible drawings on the walls, then thoughtfully descended the stairs to begin making breakfast.

Branwell didn't come down, of course, and conversation over the bowls of hot oatmeal porridge was sparse. Their father, who joined them for breakfast these days, only remarked that for once Branwell had slept through the night.

Charlotte complained of her toothache and went upstairs to her room to lie down. Emily and Anne volunteered to help old Tabby wash the pot and bowls, and in the kitchen Emily told the other two about Branwell's hand and her dream and the black penny.

Tabby was troubled by the dream. She acknowledged that the parsonage must one day be a ruin, but objected to the way Emily had seen it. "You were your ghost, there," she said, "but that shouldn't ever be wandering abroad. Your ghost is to lie quiet in the vault, confined with your mother and sisters."

Emily knew that she had been a ghost in the dream, and remembered Branwell saying that he and Emily and Anne had *ceded control* when they had left their blood at Ponden Kirk so long ago—ceded control even, and especially, after their deaths.

I will die before I permit that, she thought; oh, and I won't permit it afterward, either! But she just said, "I'll go where I please, in the flesh or not."

Anne looked up from the sink and said, "Papa told us the ogham writing cut into the ledger stone is the name of the monster under it—with a branch of lines that contradict the name."

Emily nodded and completed her sister's thought. "Branwell might have been—that is, his hand, which is Welsh's, might have been—composing a contradiction to the contradiction."

"Mrs. Flensing's body was found," said Anne, "but that satchel she carried—the young man who came in with her took it."

Emily shuddered at the mention of the satchel.

"Do you reckon," said Tabby as she set about making tea, "it was that young man who put a knife into her neck?"

"I'm sure of it," said Emily. "And I think if he had not, she'd have put a knife into *his* neck—since she hadn't succeeded in killing *me*." And putting *my* soul into the monster head that had surely been in that satchel, she thought.

That head is out there somewhere, she thought, probably with Mrs. Flensing's ghost in it now. And Welsh—his hand, at any rate—is active in our very house.

"Papa," she said slowly, "has a friend, of sorts, who might tell us how to free our family from these...adhesions."

Anne was frowning doubtfully. "Mr. Brown? I suppose he could cut more marks into the stone..."

"No."

Emily thought of a wicker figure in a timeless stone temple.

"Minerva," she said.

The name clearly meant nothing to Tabby, but Anne looked unhappy. "What, *again*?" she said. "A *pagan goddess*! You'll put your immortal soul in peril! Surely a priest, a *Catholic* priest—"

"—Would not be a pagan," Emily finished, "in spite of what Charlotte would say. But it's pagan forces preying on us. Fight fire with fire."

"Could you even find that temple again?"

Emily looked at the floor, where she was sure some werewolf blood must still lie between the stones. Anne repeated her question.

"No," Emily said. "No, the way to it had to be opened."

She and Keeper had several times hiked out to that remembered hill a mile south of the River Aire, but no temple had been visible on the heath below it, nor manifested itself when they leaped over the inert lines of stones in the grass. The patches where the holes and fissures had opened up and then filled were hard to detect, overgrown now with grass and heather.

She got to her feet and walked down the hall to the parlor. When she came back she was carrying her folding wooden desk, and she sat down at the table and opened the hinged lid.

"I need to send a letter in the next post," she said, pulling a card out from under a sheaf of manuscript pages. On it was scrawled a London address, but no name.

Anne recognized the card. "You," she said flatly, "a curate's daughter, will solicit help from a pagan goddess, through the offices of a werewolf."

Emily thought of a woman who had reportedly leaped to her death from a turret balcony in Allerton in early March of last year, and of herself stabbing an unnatural murderous beast in this very kitchen six months ago; but she said, with affected lightness, "At least he's a Catholic werewolf."

Tabby muttered, "Worse and worse."

Emily slid a blank sheet of paper free, and lifted out the ink bottle and uncapped it.

Tabby leaned on the counter, drying her hands with a towel and shaking her head mournfully. "You do dive awful deep," she said, "to find a way to come up for air."

PART THREE:
APRIL 1847

The starry night shall tidings bring
Go out upon the breezy moor
Watch for a bird with sable wing
And beak and talons dripping gore...
—Emily Brontë

CHAPTER THIRTEEN

Curzon did not reply to the letter Emily sent him, and one midnight in April an echoing boom from inside the church led to the discovery that the ledger stone had cracked from end to end.

Emily had pulled on her boots and a coat, and she and Keeper followed Patrick down the moonlit walk to the church. They entered cautiously, and when the lantern Patrick was carrying showed the inch-wide split in the stone, they hurried across the street and Patrick pounded on John Brown's door.

The alarmed sexton quickly mixed up a wheelbarrow full of mortar in his stoneyard, and when the three of them had made their way back into the church, Emily held the lantern while she and her father and Keeper watched the sexton trowel mortar into the length of the crack. None of them needed to ask if the others heard the muffled shifting and grinding under the stone, and Keeper, possibly sniffing some exhalation from below, growled until the last trowel-full was scraped into place.

Patrick was softly saying the Pater Noster, but he raised his voice so that it rang in the high ceiling beams as he pronounced *breagh gan ainm*—the Old Celtic phrase that meant *Lie nameless*.

When John Brown had smoothed the mortar flush with the broken edges of the stone, Patrick crouched and used his church key to trace lines in the fresh mortar, connecting the old incised lines that were now interrupted by the crack.

"That won't do," Patrick said as he stood up. "John, you've got to cut a fresh stone—duplicate those original lines—before sunset."

John Brown was wiping his hands on a scrap of cloth. "I hope," he said, "it will do to just lay the new stone over the broken one. I don't fancy lifting that one."

"I—don't know," said Emily's father. In the lantern glow he looked very old.

Emily and Keeper walked him back to the parsonage. Charlotte and Anne were peering out from either side of the opened front door, shivering in their nightgowns, and when Emily and their father had got inside and he had carefully re-bolted the door, they all walked back to the kitchen and Charlotte put a pot of water on the range to boil. Tabby called down from upstairs to ask if all was well, and Patrick told her to go back to sleep.

After Emily and their father had described the cracked stone and John Brown sealing it with mortar, Charlotte cocked her head judiciously and began, "It could be that shifts in temperature—"

But Emily interrupted her. "No. We heard the twin moving around underneath."

"What can we *do*?" whispered Anne.

"There've been no overtures from its twin, the Welsh ghost," said Patrick. "In years past you *have* seen the ragged boy manifestation out on the moors, but my gunshots—" He paused and nodded to Emily. "Our gunshots have apparently kept him away from the church and this house since the death of your mother. You children are safe from him. I—"

"He was *in* this house!" Anne burst out. "Last September, when you and Charlotte were in Manchester! And Emily and Branwell and I saw him on the moors that day, *spoke* to him! And long before that we apparently wrote *promissory notes*—"

To Emily's alarm, Patrick rocked back in his chair, gripping the edge of the table and suddenly pale. "In the house! Visible?"

Emily laid her hand over one of his cold hands. "We banished him. Yes, visible—he takes crows to make up the mass of a body. But Keeper injured him, drove him away."

"God help me," said Patrick softly, "I thought the Catholic exorcism in 1821 revoked her invitation."

Anne cocked her head. "*Her* invitation?"

"Whose?" asked Emily.

"Ah—your mother didn't know any better. She saw a barefoot boy

in the snow, in the churchyard—it was natural, humane, to invite him in, across the threshold."

For several seconds none of them spoke.

"The exorcism *may* have worked," Emily said, "at least for keeping the thing out of the house. Branwell too saw the boy in the snow, when he was fourteen. And—" She spread the fingers of her free hand.

"How soon," asked Anne timidly, "do you suppose we could get another Catholic priest out here?"

Charlotte poured tea into four cups and glared at her father. "I really think an Anglican priest—such as yourself!—would be more qualified."

"I'm afraid I *dis*qualified myself, praying to Minerva all those years ago." Patrick picked up his teacup and blew across the top of it. "We should pack for a trip to France."

"What," said Charlotte, "all of us? Can we even afford passage?"

"No," Patrick admitted.

"And you can't abandon your parish," put in Anne.

"I'm not leaving," said Emily. "No devils are going to drive me away from where I live."

Patrick gave her a distracted smile. "You shoot them all, child." He blinked and turned to Anne. "What promissory notes?"

"That was nothing," spoke up a new voice from the hall, and Branwell stepped into the kitchen. The loud boom from the church must have awakened him, and he seemed alert. Keeper stood up beside Emily's chair. Branwell went on, "I'm sure Welsh was only trying to frighten you with that phrase." To his father he said, distinctly, "When we were children—I was thirteen!—I proposed a game. We hiked to Ponden Kirk and cut our fingers to dab a few drops of blood in the fairy cave at its base. It had no significance."

"Good God!" exclaimed their father. "Of all the ... foolhardy ...!" He shook his head unhappily, and Emily noted his thinning white hair and recalled that he was seventy years old. "I really think we need to cross the sea."

"Nothing came of it," Branwell assured him. "Certes the blood is long since washed away."

"That's not what you said in September," ventured Anne.

In the last few seconds Emily's face had gone cold, and now the

backs of her hands tingled. That's not what *Branwell* said, she mentally corrected her sister.

"I expect I was trying to frighten you too," Branwell said with a smile.

Tabby had poured another cup, and Branwell picked up the cup with his right hand. Keeper was staring at him, and when Emily stroked the dog's thick neck she could feel the vibration of an uncertain growl.

Patrick blinked up at his son. "It was a monstrously foolish thing to do."

Branwell shrugged and with his left hand patted his father on the shoulder, his fingers flexing. Emily shuddered at the sight of the touch.

"Nothing came of it," Branwell assured him.

Emily kept her breathing even, and held her own cup with a steady hand. He hasn't asked what the loud noise was, she thought; or, if he somehow didn't hear it, why we're all awake down here.

She met Anne's eye, and when Branwell was looking at their father she shook her head. We must not discuss these things in front of him, she thought. We've said too much here already.

She hoped that Branwell had not heard their father mention having prayed to Minerva.

"It's late," she said.

"Far too early to be getting up, at least," said Charlotte.

"There's nothing more to be done tonight," conceded Patrick, sliding his chair back. "I'd relish another couple of hours' sleep." He gave Branwell a weary look, no doubt thinking of the two of them going back upstairs to his bedroom, where Branwell still slept on a cot. "Will you lie quiet, and not complain about your insomnia?"

"I'll be asleep before you are," said Branwell.

"Papa," said Emily suddenly, "stay up with me. I—" She racked her mind for a plausible reason to keep her father from being alone with the thing in Branwell's body. "I want to pray."

Charlotte gave her a surprised look, but Anne nodded. "It's what we can do," she said.

"Of course," said their father.

Emily thought she saw Branwell repress a shudder. "I'm to my cot," he said, stepping to the hall doorway. "It's likely to be a busy day."

When his son's footsteps had receded away up the stairs, Patrick rubbed both hands over his face, then let them drop to the table. He peered at Emily.

"Was that Branwell?"

"No," she said, setting down her cup.

Anne nodded and, to Emily's surprise, Charlotte said, "I wondered."

Thunder cracked and rolled out over the dark moors, as if a late echo of the splitting stone, and Emily was reminded of her father's account of asking Minerva for the armor of the cyclops. *They also made thunderbolts*, as Anne had recalled then.

"Where," asked Patrick in a voice tight with control, "is my son?"

"He's there," said Emily quickly, "and these moments of dislocation are uncommon—he can usually resist them. Tomorrow he won't remember that he came downstairs just now."

"What . . . *personality* was that which spoke to us? Am I unhappily correct in my guess?"

"You are," Emily admitted. "But Welsh was diminished when both Keepers mauled him in September, and until just now I've only been able to guess at Welsh's presence in Branwell—when he's lost track of a conversation for a few moments." And once or twice, she thought, given me a momentary and instantly forgotten look of fury.

"Or *pretends* to understand something Branwell *does* understand," said Anne sadly. "Like our old Glass Town stories."

"That which I greatly feared hath come upon me," Patrick muttered hollowly. "I hope an exorcism won't kill my boy."

Emily quickly walked to the hall and looked up the stairs, and she exhaled in relief to see that the figure of Branwell was not crouched in the shadows, wide-eyed and listening.

She walked back into the kitchen, and shook her head in answer to the alarmed looks the other three gave her.

"Our brother will be back up in the morning, I'm sure," she said. "I don't believe Welsh suspects that we've seen through his moments of imposture—"

"Or cares," said Charlotte.

"—and," Emily went on, "they're brief. Shorter than they were last year, when Welsh did things like walk in Branwell's body to the church. We dealt him a setback in September."

"He might regain his lost ground," said Anne, "if the twin under the stone gets up. It might *force* full completion of the pair—full possession of Branwell."

"Dig out the fresh mortar," said Charlotte, "pour oil down the crack, and ignite it."

Emily shook her head. "The Flensing woman was going to awaken it by restoring its bare skull. Fire wouldn't destroy its bones."

"Though it would certainly destroy the church," said Patrick. He turned to Emily. "*Both* Keepers?"

"One is a ghost," Emily said. "It attacked Welsh's ghost, as our Keeper attacked the form he had assembled."

"Really!" Patrick's eyebrows were raised. "Yes, that would have to be the ghost of our Keeper's namesake—the mastiff that killed Welsh in 1771. Of course. It's a mercy he followed Welsh's ghost here." He pushed his chair back from the table. "Is the floor too hard to kneel on? I think prayer is our best recourse tonight."

Branwell came stumbling down the stairs just as dinner was being served in the parlor at noon, and he grumpily refused anything more than a cup of tea. Emily and her sisters stole glances at him, and found opportunities to nod reassuringly at one another.

Catching a couple of their looks, he ran the fingers of his right hand through his ginger hair, clearly to find out if it was sticking up in an odd way. "I heard an awful boom in the middle of the night," he said. "Has anyone checked to see if the church tower fell over?"

His tone was uncertain and defensive.

Emily looked at him speculatively. "The ledger stone in the church floor split, from end to end."

"Oh no," he whispered, and by his evident dismay Emily knew this was her brother.

Tabby had been told about it as soon as she had come downstairs, and had grumbled at not being told last night. Now as she bustled in to take their aunt's teapot, she just recited under her breath the second line painted on it: "To die is gain."

"Amen," whispered Anne.

Their father had as usual taken his dinner in his room, and when Charlotte and Anne went out front to look at the sparse garden, Branwell took hold of his left wrist and laid that hand limp on the

table. "Did I come downstairs last night?" he asked Emily; and when she nodded, he said, "That wasn't me."

"I know," Emily said. We all knew, she thought.

"I wasn't drunk, that night I set my bed on fire."

Emily raised her eyebrows.

"I woke up, and I could feel him crowding me out of my self! It was as if a glacier were to push a house off its foundations, but fast. While I still had some flicker of agency, I reached across with the hand I still possess and pulled the candle into the bed."

He sat back and closed his eyes. His wasted face under his disordered hair looked to Emily like the face of a corpse.

"It worked, that night," he said hoarsely. "*I* lost hold of my consciousness, but *he* recoiled from the sudden pain. I'm sorry you got burned pulling me out of the bed."

Emily took his right hand and said fiercely, "Keeper and I will kill him before he can take you."

"How?" He opened his eyes. "Kill the crows he assembles? In September he told me he could gather up grass to show a form."

"We'll *do* it." She thought of the two Keepers, and wondered if Welsh were eavesdropping. "I don't know how, but I'll keep you from him."

"I think if I were to be freed from him now, from his sustenance, I'd die."

"I think that's not unlikely. But you'll enter eternity as yourself."

He laughed softly. "Papa should let you preach a sermon."

She gave him a grudging smile. "I'm half pagan."

"I like that half."

She stood up. "The other half is Christian. Pray to God like a madman while you can."

"How else?" He got to his feet. "I believe my *parasite* must always be terribly tense—I feel as if I walked a mile last night. Can I have my spectacles? I'd like to read in my room. Maybe even write a bit." He caught her wary look and added, "In English."

Word had quickly spread through the village that the ogham-chiseled ledger stone had cracked, and by late afternoon the stone was hardly visible under a drift of wooden and iron crosses and upright lit candles and papers with handwritten prayers on them.

After putting out several small fires, Patrick told his daughters that the church might well burn down even without Charlotte's proposed remedy.

Emily and Keeper set out on their usual hike across the hills and becks and sheep-paths, and she carried the pistol in its case so that she could fire across the haunted landscape and reload several times during the long trek. The two of them walked along the north ridge above the valley where the rain-widened Ponden Clough Beck tumbled along its course, and when the black old monument came in view in the distance, Emily sat down in the heather and reloaded the pistol once again. Before she stood up she automatically tapped the dioscuri knife in its homemade cardboard sheath on her calf.

She and Keeper were level with the plateau, and could have walked around by the north path and stood at the top of Ponden Kirk, but they approached it only to a point from which Emily estimated that the sound of the gunshot would carry to the ancient edifice. She fired the pistol in its direction, then turned back toward home. Heavy clouds were massing on the northern horizon, and she was glad they'd be in before the approaching storm swept over Haworth.

By the time they had walked back to the parsonage the lowering sun was casting vales of shadow between the hills, and as soon as Emily had taken off her coat and exchanged her boots for shoes, Tabby put her to work peeling potatoes for tomorrow's dinner.

When the daylight faded from the windows, Anne and Charlotte walked back from the parlor with a new issue of *Blackwood's*, and Anne noted that Liverpool had lately appointed a Medical Officer of Health for the city.

Emily set a pot of water on the range and said, "I wish the General Board of Health in London would act on Papa's petitions."

"Haworth is probably not a priority," observed Charlotte.

Emily was wondering if this were a night on which Branwell would have succeeded in borrowing a few shillings from their father, and make his way to the Black Bull, when she heard his boots descend the stairs to the hall.

But instead of hurrying down the hall to the front door, Branwell stepped past where Emily sat and pulled open the back door.

"Bad guts," he muttered, and stepped outside.

Emily understood that he was going to the privy in the back yard, and she was again reminded of the unsanitary arrangements in Haworth.

"It can't be healthy," she remarked as she stood up to pour hot water into the teapot, "that our well is level with the churchyard, and the whole village is downhill, *downstream*, from it."

She swirled the hot water in the teapot, poured it back into the kettle, and then filled the teapot and measured several spoonfuls of tea leaves into it.

Keeper came in from the hall and nudged her leg.

"What is it, boy?" she asked him.

Anne said suddenly, "What hand did Branwell open the door with?"

Emily's face went cold even as she replayed it in her mind.

"His left," she said. And then she was on her feet, kicking off her shoes and snatching her boots and coat. A few moments later she was in the moonlit back yard, with Keeper right beside her.

The privy was empty, its door ajar.

She whispered, "Where are you taking him, damn you?" And then she began running down the path west, toward the open fields and hills.

She was scarcely a hundred feet away from the parsonage when the damp wind carried a reverberating howl from no more than a mile in the distance. Keeper growled but loped along close beside Emily.

She could see the flailing figure of Branwell far ahead, but he was running at a headlong pace she didn't dare to match on the intermittently moonlit track. Before long she lost sight of him altogether, but she ran on, panting now.

She glimpsed him again as she crested a low rise, but only for a moment—he had stopped beside the tall, solitary Boggarts Green stone, and he stepped to the far side of it, out of her sight.

She reminded herself that it was Welsh that she was pursuing, and she let her pace slow as she approached the standing stone. She hadn't seen Branwell again since he had disappeared behind it. At last she walked up to the stone and rested one hand against its irregular cold surface. Keeper walked to the far side, then stepped back, cocking his head.

Emily took a deep breath and walked wide around the stone to stand beside him.

And she gasped. She had walked past the Boggarts Green stone countless times over many years, and because it was supposed to be haunted she had always eyed it warily as she passed it—and so she knew as well as she knew anything that it stood in a wide field of low gorse.

But tonight there was a grove of clustered willow trees on this far side of it, and a path that wound out of sight between overhanging branches that did not shake in the night wind that was tossing her hair. The scene seemed to be lit by diffused moonlight.

She was certain that if she stepped back and walked around the other side of the stone, she would see only the ordinary familiar field—but she stared ahead, shivering in fascination.

A moving figure briefly separated itself from the tree silhouettes at the farthest visible extent of the impossible path, and she recognized it as Branwell.

From the corner of her eye she saw Keeper move forward; and at the same time she could see that he remained standing beside her. She looked down and saw that it was the second bullmastiff—the ghost of her Keeper's namesake—that was walking into the grove.

It's a ghost road, she thought. But poor Branwell and I have ghost guides tonight.

She ran her fingers through her damp and windblown hair, and then she and her living Keeper followed the ghost dog.

She stepped carefully, staying in the center of the path, for she heard things chittering and slithering back among the curtains of willow branches, and a smell like stagnant water hung in the still air.

It occurred to her to look back—but behind her the path dwindled away between clustered boughs in the spotty moonlight, with no gap opening onto the moor road they had left. She wiped the back of her hand across her mouth. The way out, she thought, if there is one, is forward.

"I'm coming," she said softly to Keeper, who had paused and now started forward again with Emily following.

Soon reflected firelight glittered on the long willow leaves ahead, and when Emily passed a cluster of trees she was looking through a screen of leaves into a wide, spirally rippled clearing that was

dominated by an enormous oak tree in the center. Flaring torches stuck upright in the ground around the border of the clearing showed her many arched openings in the tree's wide trunk, and expanses where the bark had been cut away to make room for serpentine bas relief carvings, and, on the massive trunk stretching away overhead, balconies shadowed and half-hidden by thick branches.

Branwell stood beside one of the arches at the base of the trunk, beside a man and what appeared to be several children decked in multicolored ribbons, but for a few breaths Emily simply stared in astonishment at the entire scene—the broad clearing in the willow grove, the perimeter torches, the gigantic tree in the center of it all. She didn't see the ghost dog now, and she clung to the fact that her Keeper was still beside her, as reassurance that she had not somehow lost a big segment of time.

Branwell and his companion—she saw now that it was the sheepherder Adam Wright—were arguing. Emily slowly bent down and drew her dioscuri from the sheath on her calf.

Wright said loudly, "The villagers will kill that body you're in, if you do it. They love the old curate—"

"They can try," said Branwell's voice. "But I *will* have honor's due."

Small creatures nipped at Emily's boots and crept silently out of her way as she moved across the marshy ground to her left, circling the clearing behind the overhanging boughs. Her boots in the mud seemed to stir up the sulfurous smell. Keeper padded behind her, and though he shook his paws and snapped at the creatures in the mud, he knew better than to growl.

Pausing to peer through the willow fronds, Emily saw now that the childlike figures standing around the two men were in fact wrinkled and bald, shrunken and hunched as if with unimaginable age.

"*I saw a sturdy oak that spun the gyre,*" piped one of them, and another replied, "*I saw a tower big as the moon and higher.*" Emily believed they were lines from an old nursery rhyme.

"*Without some bones we can't crawl off to bed,*" said a third, and the first speaker added, "*Nothing's been killed! Aren't we to be fed?*"

Emily touched Keeper's collar; those lines had not been from any nursery rhyme. Only now did she notice the knives in knitted sheaths that swung on ribbons around the little people's necks.

Wright ignored the little figures and went on, "Last night the stone broke! And you're here, in a body! It's happening, finally. This morning you sent for the head—it will be here in two days, three at most." Wright waved his hands in the air. "Kill the old preacher *after* you and your twin are restored and reunited! Then you'll rule, extend this leapfrog grove to the Lancashire border, Manchester, Lincolnshire—England entire!"

In the torchlight Branwell's face kinked in an unfamiliar smile. "How our London allies would strive to prevent that! They've flourished this century and a half, warming themselves over our banked fire." He shook his head. "But after my twin and I are united in one will, I won't *care* about honor."

"Aye, because you'll be wiser then! Three days—"

"On this boy," Branwell said, slapping his own chest, "I fulfil honor by taking his body and shackling him powerless in it forever. But his father is the son of the Brunty that killed me."

"Not long ago you wanted to let him live."

"Yes, I hoped to see *him* live on in disgraced blind solitude after his children had been possessed like this one, as they promised to me with their blood, or killed—him withering alone, his line ended in defeat."

"And that's still—" began Wright.

"But his daughters yet live, free! I told his daughter Emily that his life would be spared if she would willingly fulfil her blood-pledge and surrender to me—but she refused me, *diminished* me, with a gunshot, in reply! And now the stone is split, and I can't put off honor's demands. The father must simply be killed."

"*I saw two dogs, a woman hiding too,*" spoke up one of the withered figures, and it pointed a twig-like finger directly at Emily and went on, "*Blood for the roots and bones for us to chew!*"

Branwell's body and Wright had not paid attention to the little man's last singsong declaration, but Emily knew that the creature would momentarily succeed in making her presence known to them.

She dug the toes of her boots into the mud and then sprang forward through the curtain of willow fronds into the clearing, and she had taken two long, running steps toward the tree before Branwell's head turned toward her.

Not wanting to kill her suppressed brother, she feinted with her

knife toward his belly—and at the last moment, as Branwell's hands moved to block the thrust, she swung her arm up and drove the two points of her knife at his forehead.

As the blades rebounded from his skull, she spun to face Wright, and with a lunge she speared his defensively outstretched palm.

Keeper had bounded into the clearing with Emily, and now he shuddered and was again two dogs. The bigger mastiff, Emily's, leaped at Wright and bore him to the ground, while the ghost dog sprang at Branwell. The dwarfish figures hopped and tumbled away.

Bright blood ran down Branwell's face from Emily's strike at his head. He blindly lashed out with a fist that collided hard with Emily's shoulder, sending her rolling to the mossy ground.

A piercing three-note whistle blew a spray of blood from Branwell's mouth, and Emily was thrown onto her back when the ground under her shifted. She clutched at the soil as it rocked and continued to move.

She sat up dizzily when it stopped, and blinked at the figures of Branwell and Wright and the dogs that leaped at them, all now twenty feet away, separated from her by a ragged-edged chasm. An upwelling of very cold air behind her made her look over her shoulder, and she saw that another wide fissure had opened close at her back.

Keeper had stepped away from Wright and now stood at the edge of the first chasm, bracing his legs and lowering his great head, clearly ready to try to jump across to her.

"No!" she screamed at him, and he stood back, obedient but clearly unhappy.

Branwell was sitting with his arms crossed over his head, and the ghost Keeper turned away from him. The ghost dog ran to the edge of the wide hole and jumped—

—just as the ground gave way beneath Emily and she rolled into the chasm at her back. Her clutching hands tore up fistfuls of damp soil, but she was falling. The ghost Keeper's paws touched the edge receding above her, and then he was plunging down into darkness with her.

CHAPTER FOURTEEN

Branwell was on his hands and knees in a cold field at night, moaning with the throbbing pain of his cut forehead. He was aware of having called something only moments ago—several syllables, a name—but it had been involuntary, and he was too immediately miserable to pursue the memory.

He rolled over onto his back and pressed his hands to the two inch-long gouges in his forehead, and lay shivering on the dirt and gorse, postponing all thought until, eventually, the bleeding appeared to have stopped.

For some minutes he had been aware of the unmistakable panting of a dog within a few feet of him, but the animal hadn't moved and the panting never became a growl, and when at last Branwell wiped his eyes with his sleeve he was enormously glad to recognize Emily's dog, Keeper.

The big mastiff nudged Branwell's shoulder with a massive paw, and Branwell carefully got to his feet. With shaky, sticky hands he unfolded a pocketknife and cut a strip from the hem of his shirt and tied it tightly around his head. The moon was in the western half of the dark sky, but there was light enough across the low hills and fields for him to recognize the Boggarts Green stone and the path that led to the parsonage a mile away.

The last thing Branwell remembered before coming to his senses here was sitting at his desk, reading Coleridge's "The Rime of the Ancient Mariner"—no, getting up and stepping into the hall to ask Emily a question about it. Clearly Welsh had taken control of his

body once again, and got him into God-knew-what sort of awful trouble. But in spite of some lost blood, he knew he had the strength to walk home.

He took several stumbling steps in that direction, and Keeper, apparently satisfied that Branwell would be able to get home on his own, turned and went bounding away across the moors.

Drops of rain began pattering on the ground, and within a few moments cold rain was falling steadily. Branwell picked up his pace, and his shoes were soon splashing in puddles.

In the shivering monotony of quickly placing one booted foot in front of the other, he remembered the name he had called in the moment when his consciousness had returned: *Emily.*

Emily's shoulder struck a bulge of damp earth in the darkness, and then she was spinning in free fall for a full second before she plunged into a rushing stream. She fought her way to the surface and gasped, and then reflexively coughed out cold water. There was no light at all, and by echoes she guessed that she was in a small cave.

Her collar was being tugged, and when she spread her arms and legs she felt a slope of muddy gravel under the surface of the water; she pulled herself in the direction of the tugging, and in a few moments her collar was released and she was hunched on a low bank with her legs still in the water. The back of her head was pressed against the close ceiling of what she now judged to be a narrow tunnel.

Her head was ringing, and she seemed to hear voices in the taradiddle of rippling water. Then they *were* voices, shrill and faint but clear: *"Planted now, grow with us—flower we downward, bloom in stone below all roots—mingle with us, find true blindness in us—"*

A thick, cold vapor that smelled of stone and loam was rushing along the tunnel now, and heavy things were splashing into the unseen stream—chunks of earth? The small underground space she was in appeared to be collapsing.

She jumped when the loud barking of a dog echoed from her right—and she remembered that the ghost Keeper had jumped into the chasm as she had fallen into it, and must have been the one who had pulled her out of the stream moments ago. She crawled along the unseen bank in that direction, trusting the ghost dog.

The muddy gravel under her abraded hands and knees shook, and a strong burst of vapor from behind tossed her hair, and she guessed that if she had not moved she would now be buried under tons of damp earth. But chunks of dirt fell onto her back and splashed into the stream beside her, and she crawled along faster, following the echoes of the unseen dog's baying.

The tiny voices still shrilled from every side: "*Tarry, taste our roots and feed us with your bones!*" Emily panted through clenched teeth and kept pulling herself forward.

She was fighting off unconsciousness when the dog's booming bark faded as if quickly receding in the distance, but ahead of her now she saw a patch of lesser darkness. Clods of soil were still tumbling onto her back and head, and it was difficult to breathe in the choking mist, but after a burst of scrambling effort that left her dizzy and gasping she found that she had collapsed on grass beside the stream, and was being pelted by cold rain.

Shivering, she sat up and pushed her sopping hair back to look around. Through the curtains of rain she could make out only a hill behind her and the stream cascading down a slope ahead, and certainly she didn't know where she was.

She tried to recall what had led her here. An impossible willow forest by the Boggarts Green stone, a giant oak tree with arched doorways and balconies, tiny old people reciting nursery rhymes—! She was sure she had cut Branwell's forehead and stabbed the sheepherder, Wright, in the hand...

Wearily she got to her feet. Clouds hid the stars, and all she could do was try to walk in a straight line and hope to find some sort of shelter.

Soon she was dragging her boots through a rain-agitated bog, and she paused when she saw a flickering glow in the darkness ahead. Wary of *ignis fatui*, she wiped rainwater out of her eyes to peer in that direction.

It was an amber spot of light, and though it was tiny in the distance she believed it was rectangular—perhaps a lighted window. After a convulsive shudder at the cold, she began plodding toward it.

As her course continued downhill through tangles of wet weeds, she lost sight of the light, but after sloshing through a deep puddle she found that the streaming ground sloped up again, and the soil

was so loose and muddy that she had to use her hands as well as her feet to climb it; but when she had got to the top of the rise, she saw the silhouette of a house—a one-story structure with a chimney at each end.

The light Emily had seen was indeed glowing in a window, and she drove her legs harder, pushing herself forward over unseen rocks and weeds. After some weary, gasping time she saw that the window was hardly bigger than a coal chute, and set only a foot above the ground.

She hurried across the last few yards of mud and crouched beside the window. She pushed ivy leaves aside and peered through the glass, and saw a lower-level room in which three young women in black dresses, presumably in mourning, sat in chairs beside a peat fire. Behind them was a dresser with a row of pewter plates on it.

She raised a hand to knock on the glass, then hesitated.

The scene was familiar, as if from a fairy tale, and suddenly Emily thought: But there were only two sisters in the story—and all at once she remembered that this was a scene from Charlotte's novel *Jane Eyre*, in which Jane, starving in the rain, finds solace at the house of Diana and Mary and St. John Rivers. And even as she thought it, the glow of the fire began to dim.

A hallucination, she thought in despair.

The house vanished, but the glow didn't fade all the way to darkness, and the three women were now clambering up out of a shallow pool.

And in the dim *ignis fatui* radiance she saw their tangled gray hair, and their eyes glittering in their wrinkled gray faces, and their spidery hands groping for her; a clicking noise like the chipping of marble in John Brown's stoneyard rang out from their slack, swinging jaws.

Emily was up and running as fast as she could over the uneven wet ground, and behind her she heard the dragging-branches sound of the old women's rapid pursuit.

Emily's left foot caught in a root, and with a hissed inhalation she fell to her hands and knees in mud—and in that moment she heard galloping hoofbeats and the unmistakable barking of Keeper.

Then a horse had rushed massively past her and was cracklingly trampling the old women, and Keeper was beside her, growling and facing her pursuers.

The *ignis fatui* glow was extinguished, and she heard the horse stamping and kicking, and then it cantered back to where she crouched.

The rider swung down from the saddle, and boots splashed heavily in the mud. A strong hand gripped her shoulder.

"Can you stand?" came Alcuin Curzon's remembered gritty voice over the thrashing of the rain.

"Yes," she gasped, then, more loudly, "Yes." She hugged Keeper and then got to her feet.

A hat was set firmly on her head and a heavy Mackintosh cape was draped over her shoulders. She forced herself not to flinch, and wished she had not lost her dioscuri knife.

"Up you go." Curzon bent and slid one arm under her arms and the other behind her legs, then straightened and lifted her into the saddle. "Don't fall off."

Pacing alongside the horse, he led it away at a cautious walk across the boggy ground. From up in the saddle Emily peered toward Curzon, reminding herself that this man had transformed into a ravening beast—a werewolf!—and attacked her, last September. She leaned from the saddle and was reassured to make out the shape of Keeper padding beside Curzon.

"Vicious damned things," Curzon said, loudly over the rain. "They roused an illusion in you?"

"A scene from a book." She watched his moving silhouette below her in the darkness and asked, "Shall I fear you?"

"No," he said shortly. "Never again. You may rely on it."

Perhaps, she thought. "How is it that you're here?"

"You wrote me a letter," he said. "I came as quickly as I could, once I received it, but I was in a monastery in France, at Rocamadour in the province of Quercy." After a few more plodding steps he went on, "It's a remote place, with postal delivery by donkey—and there were difficulties before I could leave."

Then his voice was clearer, and she knew he was looking up at her as he went on. "I stopped at the parsonage tonight, and they said you and Keeper had gone haring out after your brother. I rode first to Ponden Kirk, to no avail. Then, considering what you wrote in your letter, I started out toward...the course we walked in September, and after a few miles I heard a dog baying. Hoping it

might be Keeper, I called to him, and kept calling. Eventually he found me, and we were each disappointed to find that you were not with the other!"

The rain had stopped drumming on the hat he had given her, and the clouds were breaking up. Curzon was able to lead the horse at a faster walk, and Emily could now clearly see Keeper trotting alongside. She began to relax, and realized that she trusted Curzon's statement: *No. Never again. You may rely on it.*

"Then not far from here Keeper must have caught your scent," Curzon went on, "for he took off running, and when I saw the *ignis fatui* glow I dared to goad my horse into a gallop."

"The ghost dog knew where I was."

"The—ah, again? Keeper's other?" He shook his head. "How did *you* come to be out here?"

"I—" She shivered and pulled the cape more closely around her shoulders. "*Ultimately* I fell into a hole, like the one you fell into in September." Curzon looked back at her quickly, and she nodded. "Among the restless dead, as you put it then. *Taste our roots and feed us with your bones.*"

"Yes, I remember. But you were able to climb out."

"Not climb. Crawl. The ghost dog had jumped in after me, and led me out along the course of a stream."

For a while they walked along in silence, Keeper and Curzon flanking the horse and Emily rocking in the saddle. Finally Curzon asked, "And your brother? Did you find him?"

"I stabbed him in the face, with your old dioscuri. Where are we?"

"A few miles north of your parsonage, I judge. You . . . stabbed him in the face?"

"So far? North?" She shivered. "I came out far from where I fell in."

Curzon's shoulders lifted and fell in a sigh. "Where was that?"

"It was—a marshy copse of willows, with—but you'll think I was delirious."

"Your senses seem to be admirably clear, as a rule."

Emily described, haltingly, the marshy grove of willows, and the little old men and women and their nursery rhymes, and the gigantic oak tree.

"A *mundus loci*," said Curzon, "as described in the apocryphal *Acts*

of Simon Magus. They're ... localized twists in reality. You and I were briefly in one last year, at that Druidic temple. That one straddled time, but the one you were in tonight clearly straddles space, like ... an unreal spider whose legs touch the earth at various real places. Enter here, come out there."

Emily looked around at the dimly visible hills. What Curzon said must be true, she thought, or else something very like it must be. "I'm glad they're localized."

"Hence *loci*. They're too irrational to extend across much distance." After a few more paces, he asked, "Stabbed your brother in the face?"

"I had to."

"How did—"

Emily interrupted, "He was Welsh, and—" Her teeth were chattering, and she clenched her jaws for a moment, then went on in a rush, "The stone in the church split last night! And they've still got the new head for the thing under the stone, Adam Wright has already sent to London for it! And—Branwell was Welsh, and he means to kill my father, and I had to stab him to drive him out of my brother—" She took a deep breath and let it out. "I cut his forehead. I hope that was enough to drive out Welsh, and that Branwell has found his way home." She sniffed and then scowled down at Curzon. "Here you've been taking your ease in a French monastery while we were left in the soup—the ever hotter soup!"

He had been staring up at her as she spoke, and now he burst out, "What? I heard that you killed the Flensing woman, and I assumed you destroyed the new head while you were at it! And you had apparently got Branwell under control, with the measures I told you. I thought things here had been restored to their previous balance—shaky though it was." He raised a fist and let it fall. "Taking my ease!"

"If I hadn't written to you—"

"Be quiet."

Emily leaned back in the saddle and watched clouds scudding across the full moon, and worried about Branwell. He wouldn't have fallen into one of the holes, at least, probably.

"I did consider," said Curzon finally, "informing the Huberti in Rome about developments in this Yorkshire situation. But when they

218 *Tim Powers*

act at all, they can be too thorough. I thought it possible that they'd kill you, as well as your brother."

"You had no concern for my brother."

"None. I won't lie to you."

Emily was suddenly very tired, and she wondered if she might actually go to sleep and fall off the horse. "I didn't kill Mrs. Flensing," she said. "That companion of hers must have done it, and taken the head away with him. She had some means of putting my ghost into it, as a placeholder till they could rouse the ghost under the stone—I suppose her companion put *hers* into it."

Curzon muttered something that Emily was sure was a curse.

The sky had cleared enough for her to see the stars, and she could see that Curzon was leading the horse south. The parsonage really couldn't be far off.

"Tomorrow," she said, "you and I must—"

"You'll be bedridden for days. Lucky if you don't catch a lethal fever from all this."

"I'm not frail. Tomorrow we must do what I said in my letter. Quickly, since now the stone is broken and they've sent for the head."

"It's true you're not frail." He laughed shortly. "You count on your father's acquaintance with her, again? Seeking a task from a goddess can be costly—and having undertaken to fulfil it, you're generally in mortal peril if you fail. Immortal peril, I should say. I only asked her for ... the local news, last year."

"And without my help you wouldn't have got that. I'm not afraid of whatever the cost is."

"You always were a fool. And you blithely expect me to put myself in that peril too."

"Fools," she said, "plural."

He didn't reply, and they walked on in silence except for the muddy thumps of Curzon's boots and the horse's hooves. Keeper padded along silently, swinging his head from side to side to watch the emerging hills.

Charlotte and Anne and Tabby heard the hoofbeats in the yard, and hurried out the kitchen door. When Emily swung a leg over the horse's back and let herself slide down to the pavement, Anne hurried up to her.

"You're drenched!" Anne said, putting her arm around her taller sister's shoulders. "And freezing! Dry clothes, tea, and a warm bed, right now."

Emily protested, but Anne led her into the kitchen, with Keeper following attentively. Anne freed Emily from the wet hat and Mackintosh cape and walked her away toward the stairs.

Charlotte looked out at the tall figure standing in the yard beside the horse, and she recognized the man with the eyepatch who had called on their father a year ago: the man who had later taken Emily to consult a goddess at a pagan shrine, and who—according to Emily and Anne and Tabby—had transformed into a *werewolf* in this very kitchen!

But Emily had written to him, asking for help, and it seemed that tonight he had saved her life. Charlotte took a deep breath. *Accepter l'aide,* she thought.

Tabby was pulling her backward and tugging anxiously at the door, but Charlotte pushed her away and held the door open. "Come in, sir," she called, and to Tabby she added, "Yes, I know who he is."

"God help us!" wailed the old housekeeper, retreating back toward Emily's dog, who simply lay down. Surely it was a good sign that Keeper wasn't alarmed!

"I'll go," said Curzon, looking away. "I have no right to enter this house again."

"I think," said Charlotte, "my sister would have been found dead on the moors tomorrow, if not for you." Dizzy with bravado, she went on, "I'm inviting you in."

Behind her she heard Tabby gasp.

Curzon stared at Charlotte with his one exposed eye. He shook his head and opened his mouth, but Charlotte spoke first.

"Please," she said.

He shifted uneasily, then said, "Very well, Miss Charlotte. After I've returned this horse to the stable down the street." He bowed. "If you'll excuse me for half an hour."

"Certainly."

Curzon led the horse out of the fan of light from the open kitchen door, and Charlotte heard its hooves splashing in puddles as the two of them rounded the corner of the house.

Charlotte closed the door at last, and crossed to the table and leaned on it.

"If your father wakes up," said Tabby, "and finds that devil in his kitchen...!"

"We'll explain that he saved Emily tonight. She sent for him, remember."

"In a mad hour."

"At least we're all within these walls tonight."

Branwell had come stumbling to the back door an hour ago, as soaked as Emily and with a makeshift bandage around his head. Anne and Tabby had stopped him from rushing straight upstairs and had made him sit down until they had cleaned and dressed two cuts in his forehead and put a proper bandage on. He had tearfully refused to tell them where he'd been or what had happened, and upstairs it had been all they could do to get him out of his boots and wet clothes before he threw himself into the bed and ordered them to leave him in peace.

"What *do* you suppose happened out there tonight?" Charlotte whispered now.

"I'll warrant it's to do with the stone cracking," said Tabby.

Charlotte nodded wearily. "How not?"

"At least John mortared it up."

"Mr. Curzon might know the effectiveness, if any, of that. For now all we can do is pray, Tabby."

Twenty minutes later there was a tentative knock at the door, and when Tabby had got a firm nod from Charlotte she pushed it open. Curzon stepped in past her and pulled it shut behind him.

Charlotte had forgotten how big and swarthy the man was, and his eyepatch gave him the look of a corsair. She fell back on courtesy and said, "Do sit down, sir."

He remained standing, and blinked around at the kitchen in evident unease.

"I neglected to ask," he said. "Has your brother—Branwell—come home?"

"A while ago," said Charlotte, "as wet as Emily, and with terrible cuts in his forehead! Do sit, sir, please! Were they out at Ponden Kirk?"

"I don't know where Branwell was," Curzon said. He crossed to

the table and lowered himself into a chair. "I found Keeper, and then Emily, a few miles north of here. Why Ponden Kirk?"

"That's where . . ." Charlotte began, then hesitated. The so-called *promissory notes* weren't her secret to reveal. "Where Emily found you wounded, last year," she finished lamely.

He stared at her with his one exposed eye.

But who can save us, she thought, if this man can't?

"You're Catholic," she said impulsively. When he nodded, she went on, "I was a student, and then a teacher, at a school in Brussels, four years ago. Emily was there too for a few months, but came home for our aunt's funeral and then just stayed here." She glanced at Tabby, who stood by the knife drawer, and at Keeper, who was resting his head on the floor between his massive paws. "In September of 1843 I was alone in that foreign city—the school was closed for summer, and one evening I found myself in front of St. Gudula church."

"I know it," said Curzon patiently.

"I went in. I stayed through the vespers prayers, and then the priest was hearing penitents' confessions, in the little Confessional booth. I—" She could feel herself blushing, and she was aware of both Curzon's and Tabby's eyes on her. "I took a fancy to change myself into a Catholic! Just to see what it was like. I went into the booth, and knelt there while he dealt with someone on the other side, and when he slid the little door open I had to explain that I was a Protestant, and didn't know the formula for beginning a confession. He hemmed and hawed, and finally decided that his hearing my confession might facilitate my conversion to, as he put it, 'the true church.'"

"God save us!" exclaimed Tabby.

"It didn't," Charlotte assured her. "But after I made my confession, he gave me a penance. That's a task," she explained to Tabby, "to clear the collateral consequences of forgiven sins. He told me *accepter l'aide*—accept help. Not seek—accept, and I've waited." She met Curzon's eye. "But," she went on steadily, "I must admit I'm reluctant to accept help from a Catholic who consults pagan goddesses."

Tabby muttered some additional consideration under her breath.

"This was four years ago?" Curzon gave Charlotte a flinty smile. "I imagine he meant help from tradesmen, servants, physicians."

"My confession," said Charlotte, "wasn't such as to suggest those

sorts of help." She made herself look directly into his eye. "I confessed to having given my brother and sisters permission to...do something, at Ponden Kirk, though I suspected that it was very wrong. I was only fourteen!—but they were younger."

"Did it put you all at lasting risk?"

"I fear that—well, it seems it put *them* at risk."

"It's hardly my place to ask," said Curzon quietly, "but—these four years later—are you ready to do your penance?"

Charlotte spread her hands. "Yes."

Anne spoke from the hall doorway: "It's all our penance." She gave Charlotte a wide-eyed questioning look, and when Charlotte shrugged and nodded she walked into the kitchen and sat down across from Curzon. Her pale blonde hair had been hastily pulled back, and stray curls of it framed her young face.

"Emily's in your bed," she told Charlotte. "Her room's too cold. She wanted to come downstairs again once she'd dried off and was in warm clothes, but she was still shivering and pale, and I insisted that she had to get into bed. She did, finally, but only after making me promise that Papa shall not be allowed to set foot out of the house until she gives him leave."

"I'll bring her some tea," said Tabby.

"She's asleep now. She'll be sore in the morning—she's got bruises and scratches all over her."

Anne stretched and said to Curzon, "She told me she trusts you. I confess I don't see how—I know she wrote to you a month ago, asking you to come, but...I was in this kitchen on a dreadful night in September of last year."

Curzon stared down at his gnarled brown hands on the table for several seconds. "You shame me," he said at last, "justly. If someone you had less cause to despise were able to help you, I would send him here."

"My understanding of it," said Charlotte hastily, "is that it was... involuntary."

"And can't recur," said Curzon. He sat back and faced Anne. "What was it you did?"

Anne met his gaze. "Emily and Branwell and I—we cut our fingers and smeared our blood on a stone in the fairy cave at the base of Ponden Kirk."

Tabby moaned softly, but Charlotte was watching Curzon. His face was as immobile as a copperplate engraving.

Anne went on, "Branwell said a dark boy in a dream had told him that it would bring back our sister Maria, who had died five years earlier. I think Branwell was lying, and knew it would do something else. On that night last September he said that what we had done was sign promissory notes."

After a pause, Curzon said, harshly, "It's certain that Emily did this?"

"I was sitting right next to her," said Anne, "on a rock shelf in that cave. After she did it she tried to stop me. But I went along."

"And she loves Branwell still."

"He's her brother," put in Tabby.

"Do you," said Anne hesitantly, "know what we did? We don't. Branwell once said that we marked ourselves for the attention of ghosts who snatch people's breath, but also for protection against them."

"Breath?" said Curzon. "Yes, and ghosts hunger for what rides on breath, vitality. And once you've been opened to their *attentions,* it's not just the ones who shamble up to you in churchyards and startle you by emptying your lungs in an instant—subtler ones attach to you, and take your breath and vitality by degrees."

"Consumption," said Anne.

"Literally," agreed Curzon.

"Can Branwell and my sisters," asked Charlotte, "cancel the . . . attention, without at the same time canceling the protection?"

Curzon stood up. "What can be done, I'll do."

"At a pagan temple?" said Anne, looking away.

"What can be done," Curzon repeated. "I would like to speak to Emily—and Branwell, if he's willing—tomorrow morning." He took his cloak and hat down from the hook Anne had hung them on when Emily had come in wearing them. "Tonight mix your Protestant prayers with my Catholic ones."

"Thank you," said Charlotte as he turned toward the door and pushed it open, "for letting me complete my four-year-old confession."

He might not have heard her. The door closed behind him and she heard his boots receding around the corner of the house.

CHAPTER FIFTEEN

Through the front window Emily saw Alcuin Curzon walk up past the churchyard in the morning sunlight, and she was sitting on the green leather couch in the parlor when he knocked at the door.

Her father stood by the parlor window, his long scarf wrapped so many times around his throat that it supported his chin. Anne and Charlotte sat in chairs at the table, but when Tabby led Curzon in, Emily stood up and said, "I want to talk to Mr. Curzon alone for a moment." She knew that a couple of scratches on her cheek were visible, but she was careful to give no indication of her bruises and stiff joints.

Her father and her sisters looked at one another, then Anne and Charlotte got to their feet and the three of them followed Tabby away down the hall.

"Do sit," Emily told Curzon.

"After you," he said, waving at the couch behind her. "You had a strenuous night. You'll be seeing a doctor?"

Emily pulled out a chair at the table and sat down, willing herself to do it as if effortlessly, and Curzon took a seat across from her. His shoulders and shaggy head were silhouetted by the bright window behind him.

"I'm grateful," she said, "my whole family is grateful, that you found me last night and brought me home. No, I don't like doctors. I'm in good health."

"I suppose you probably are. From what I've seen of you, you're more at home on the moors in bad weather than within four walls."

"Sit over here," she said, waving at a chair to her right. "I can't see your face there."

He got up and moved to the indicated chair. Now she could see the guarded expression on his rugged dark face, and his one exposed brown eye.

Emily spoke carefully. "When Branwell and Keeper and I visited you at the house you took in the village last year," she said, "you greeted us with your eyepatch flipped up. I believe it was a courtesy. Will you raise it now?"

He set his big hands flat on the table. "No."

She had asked him last night if she should fear him. His answer had been *Never again. You may rely on it.*

She cocked her head. "I'm told you all spoke of penances last night." Quietly she asked, "Was it a penance?"

His eye closed. "I meant my penance to be exile from the world, for the rest of my life, at the monastery at Rocamadour. I thought that would be adequate. And I lived a quiet ascetic life among the old monks for half a year—but when I received your letter I realized that exile was an evasion of the penance I actually owed."

"Owed to God," she said.

"Owed to God, yes. And to you."

"I'm sorry." She looked away. "Irrevocably?"

"Yes, child, with a dioscuri." He touched the eyepatch. "I'm now a traditional member of the Huberti." He sat back and exhaled. "Last night on our long walk, you told me some of what happened to you out there. Tell me again, thoroughly."

Emily shook her head at the thought of what he had done. *Owed to God, yes. And to you.* She made herself meet his eye, and said, "My father and sisters need to hear it all too. We haven't told him about the dealings you and I have had with ... an ancient goddess, so please don't trouble him with that." She stood up and turned to the door, then hesitated, looked back, and bent to touch his nearest fist. "I am genuinely obliged to you."

"Not obliged. It was owed."

"Nevertheless." She walked down the hall to the kitchen, and when she came back she was accompanied by her sisters and her father and Tabby.

When her family had sat down and Tabby stood in the doorway,

Emily began, "Last night Branwell went out, and Anne noticed that he opened the kitchen door with his left hand..." She had to pause to explain to Curzon and her horrified father that since September Branwell's left hand was either lifeless or controlled by Welsh; then went on, "So Keeper and I went in pursuit of him..."

When she described the impossible grove of willow trees that had appeared beside the Boggarts Green stone, and the gargantuan oak tree with its arches and balconies, the faces of her father and sisters were blank with concealed disbelief, but Tabby nodded and spoke up.

"The old hill folk have heard of it," she said. "My great-grandfather said a woman led him there one midsummer night, but she disappeared and when he finally found his way out he was miles from the stone."

When Emily came to recount the conversation between Branwell's possessed body and Adam Wright, Anne took her father's hand and looked uneasily at Curzon.

"What can be done," Curzon said firmly. "I find I owe a debt to this family."

"Adam Wright," said Patrick incredulously, "the sheepherder?"

"Yes," Emily told him. Still hoping to spare her father the whole truth about his son, she said, "He has tempted Branwell, in the past."

"In the most dangerously wrong direction," Anne clarified. Meeting her father's frown, she added, "It was while you were away in Manchester."

Patrick pursed his lips but said nothing.

"To drive Welsh out of Branwell," Emily said, "I cut Branwell's forehead with both points of a dioscuri knife. And then I stabbed Adam Wright in the hand."

Emily went on to describe the fissures that had opened in the earth, and the leap the ghost Keeper had been able to make to join her as she fell into one. Her account of the voices of the unquiet dead, and the collapsing tunnel, drew gasps from her sisters and an exclamation from her father—and a nod from Curzon.

"The ghost Keeper led me out, and then," she said to Charlotte, "I found myself in a scene from *Jane Eyre*." She told them about the *ignis fatui* women inducing her to call up an inviting vision. To Charlotte

she added, "I've always thought that scene is like something from a fairy tale."

"A nasty sort of fairy tale they made of it," said Charlotte.

"So I ran from them, and then Mr. Curzon and Keeper found me, and Mr. Curzon's horse trampled them, and he put me on his horse and brought me back here."

"I knew from the start, sir," said their father in a shaky voice, "that you might be an ally. I could not have imagined how crucial a one."

Anne was looking at Curzon. Emily could see that she was recalling past conversations, and when Curzon was facing their father she turned to Emily and, with raised eyebrows, touched her cheek below her left eye. Emily gave her a slight nod.

"Ahh!" Anne whispered. She looked back at Curzon with new curiosity and, Emily thought, wondering respect.

"Is Branwell available?" Curzon asked.

"He caught a terrible chill last night," said Charlotte doubtfully.

"I daresay he can walk downstairs and up again," said Emily.

"I should be the one to rouse him," said Patrick, pushing back his chair and getting to his feet. "He won't be as contrary with me as he would be with one of you."

When he had left the parlor, Curzon said, "Today I'll visit the place Miss Emily and I found last year. I hope—" He paused, looking at Anne; but she bit her lip and waved at him to go on. "The Romans learned to defeat, at least partly, the sort of creature that threatens you all. I'm hoping that at the shrine they frequented I'll be able to learn it too."

"Pagan magic," said Charlotte.

"Magic of the land," Tabby suggested hesitantly.

"It's what can be done," said Emily, repeating what Curzon had said moments earlier. She turned to him. "What you mean is that you'll be seeking a *task* from her, not just . . . local news. I can ride, if the horse doesn't gallop."

"I'll be walking."

Of course, thought Emily. A man on horseback on the moors is conspicuous—and if spotted, a man afoot can get out of sight more easily.

"And you," Curzon added firmly, "are in no state to accompany me."

"You caught a chill yourself," Anne said to Emily.

"Remember how sick you got at the school in Brussels," added Charlotte.

"I was sick there because I was separated from here. I shake off chills."

Footsteps echoed from the stairs down the hall, and Charlotte said, "We mustn't discuss any of this in front of Branwell."

"Good Lord, no," agreed Emily. "Or Papa either." She shifted unobtrusively in her chair to stretch an aching leg.

Their father appeared in the doorway, and stepped back with a wave toward the table. Branwell came shuffling into the room, without his spectacles and blinking in the morning brightness shining in through the window. He was wearing a fresh shirt and trousers and slippers, and above the bandage on his forehead his ginger hair was in a rare state of disarray. His eyes were red and he was mopping his nose with a handkerchief.

"Emily hasn't given me my eyeglasses yet today," he said thickly. "What's—" He peered at the figure of Curzon and flinched, then stood up straight. "I think we've met before, sir!"

"Yes, lad," said Curzon tiredly.

"Some small rented house down in the village." Branwell looked around at the others as his father walked in and resumed his chair, then back at Curzon. "I'm summoned—did you want a portrait done of yourself?" He coughed and dabbed at his nose with the handkerchief. "There are certain colors I don't customarily keep on hand, which I'd have to purchase."

"Hush," said Emily, embarrassed for him. This man is undertaking a perilous task, she thought, to save you . . . for my sake. "We'd like to hear what happened to you last night."

Branwell squinted at her. "*You* were nowhere to be found when I got home," he said. "In any case I don't care to discuss family affairs in front of a . . . stranger."

"He knows about Welsh," Patrick said.

"He doesn't, you know, actually. None of you do. Last night? I went for a stroll, and was caught in the rain. I got lost, but Keeper found me and got me pointed toward home." He started to turn toward the doorway. "Was that all? I should be in bed."

"How did you cut your forehead?" asked Emily.

"Keeper—when he found me he jumped up—his claws—"

"No," she said gently. "You have no idea how it happened, do you?"

"I want my eyeglasses."

"Not today, I think."

Branwell seemed about to protest angrily, then just turned and stalked away down the hall. Emily got to her feet and caught up with him before he reached the stairs. Keeper was right beside her.

She took her brother's shoulder and turned him around. Quietly she said, "Those aren't the cuts of a dog's claws, Branwell—they're from the two points of a knife I poked you with." Over his surprised, angry sputtering she added, "If I had not done it, you'd be possessed by Welsh even now, and God only knows where you'd be." She let go of his shoulder. "You know it's true."

He shrugged, looking at the floor. "You had to cut my *face*?"

"Your hands were moving targets, and I couldn't be sure of both points striking you if I put them through your clothing." She gave him a crooked smile. "I missed your throat, at least."

From the corner of her eye she saw her father step out from the parlor doorway down the hall. She waved him back.

"Where was I?" Branwell asked.

She blew out a breath. "A very odd place. Marshy, with willows—"

"And," Branwell interrupted, suddenly very excited, "very old little people? And an enormous house made out of a living oak tree? I was there, when he lost his hold on me for just a moment or two. Where is it?"

She was uneasy to hear a tone of eagerness in his question. "It's not anywhere. But I found you in it, and you were Welsh, so I stuck you with the knife."

He touched his bandage. "Yes, one of those damnable double-bladed affairs, or the cuts would have healed by this morning. How did you get into that place?"

"Keeper led me in." The ghost of a dog with that name, at least, she thought.

"But from what mundane place? Where had Welsh taken me, to be able to enter it?"

Emily recalled what Curzon had said about the *mundus loci*: a spider outside of reality, its widely planted legs straddling this Yorkshire locality. "Why? Do you want to go back there?"

Branwell cocked an eyebrow. "I suppose not, on the whole."

Moving on quickly, Emily asked, "What were you doing, when he took you? I gather you were in your room?"

"Yes, I—no, I was reading 'The Rime of the Ancient Mariner,' and I wanted to ask you about the lines *'The many men, so beautiful! / And they all dead did lie; / And a thousand thousand slimy things / Lived on; and so did I.'* " He peered back down the hall, then went on, "And I got up and walked to the top of the stairs to call you . . . and that's the last thing I remember before I found myself sprawled on the wet grass beside Keeper." Then he looked up at her, startled. "And I *did* call you—then!—not even aware, for a moment, that time had passed!"

Emily thought of her brother alone in the rainy night, bleeding, far from home. "I'm sorry I couldn't hear you call for me," she said.

"Keeper did." Branwell ruffled the fur on the dog's head, not having to bend down to do it. Keeper stood still, not wagging his tail. "It was wrong of me to blame him for the cuts on my face. Do explain to the others."

He looked over his shoulder at the stairs. "If you are all quite finished with me, I'm going back to bed."

Emily laid her hand on top of Branwell's on the dog's head. "We'll never be finished with you," she said.

He managed a smile. "You and Keeper, at least."

He turned away and began making his way up the stairs; like an old man, Emily thought.

She and Keeper walked back to the parlor. Her father and sisters still sat at the table, but Curzon was gone.

"Mr. Curzon didn't know how long you'd be with Branwell," said Anne, "and since he has a long trip ahead of him, he asked us to convey his apologies."

"Hah!" said Emily. "He thinks I won't go with him!"

"Go with him?" exclaimed her father. "Where? To Ponden Kirk? Back to this magical grove by Boggarts Green? Certainly not!"

Anne didn't look at their father. "You need to rest," she said. "I can see the effort you're taking to act as if you're not in pain."

"I've got to be the judge of my capabilities," Emily told her, "and they're more than you suppose. He can't get far in the time it will take me to load my pistol."

"Will you obey your father?" Patrick demanded.

"When I can, Papa," said Emily. "And please trust me when I can't."

She hurried away down the hall.

Emily had wondered if she would be able to keep up with Curzon across the miles of uneven terrain to the site of the Druidic temple, but as soon as she was away from the parsonage the cold heather-scented wind cleared her head with its familiar hints of a remote, wild music, and she let the light crunch of her boots on the path's damp earth provide a fleet counterpoint to it until she was nearly dancing. She pushed her straw hat off and let it swing on her back by its drawstring. Keeper trotted at her side, tilting his massive head to sniff at the wind and evidently finding nothing objectionable in it.

Last night's rain had left the sky clear blue between towers of dazzlingly white cumulus clouds, and patches of green and purple shone in the divided sunlight on the hills.

She reflected that hoping to meet a goddess from the remote past, on such an assertively new day as this, should seem incongruous; but the heather and wind and stone were timeless, and the lonely paths traced the same ways they did when it was Roman or Celtic or Pictish feet that had trod them.

She saw the figure of Curzon on the northern path, pacing along with a tall walking stick, and she quickly caught up with him. His coat was unbuttoned, flapping like a cape, and his unruly black hair stuck out from under a tweed cap.

He didn't stop or turn around, but when she and Keeper were a yard behind him he said, "I could order you to go back."

"As you have before." Much of the stiffness in her knees had already vanished with the exercise. The aches in her shoulders could take their time.

"I might threaten you with my stick."

"Keeper would find that exciting."

She was walking beside him now, courteously on his right, and he glanced down at her several times as the three of them variously strode and loped along. Eventually he said, "I note an angular bulk in your coat pocket."

"Lead and church-bell scrapings," she said with a nod.

They crossed the River Worth by the same old stone bridge as before, and now the wider extent of moorland hills and valleys lay ahead of them.

Curzon seemed to be watching to see if she'd tire, or ask for a rest, but Emily was invigorated to be away from the close sights of walls and roofs and chimneys, out here where her vision could embrace distant hills and rocky outcrops across miles of clear air.

She thought of the word Curzon had used last September—parallax—and she wondered if to him the landscape had no depth now, with relative distances a matter of interpretation.

Emily knew the way to the hilltop that overlooked the site of the druidic temple, and she was ready to correct Curzon if he misread the inevident landmarks. As he had done last September, he avoided hilltops and ridges, and whenever possible made his way down slopes to follow new rain-fed becks in ravines and narrow valleys, but the temple was always ahead of them.

When their course did take them over the top of a ridge, Curzon always looked around at the horizon, frowning when he saw an occasional ruined stone farmhouse in the distance, but it was Emily who spied the figure of a man standing beside a juniper tree on a hilltop a mile to the west.

She pointed the figure out to Curzon. "Alan Wright, is my guess," she said. "I think he only means to track us—his right hand won't be of much use to him."

They were following a familiar old dry-stone wall now, and it ended at a flat field of lush reeds bending in the wind—the marsh they had crossed last year. Emily looked across the expanse at the willow tree, and the hawthorn bushes that had turned into old women on that stormy day, but by daylight they were just a tree and bushes, and she found their verdant ordinariness almost mocking. But perhaps Curzon had killed the *ignis fatui* spirits last night, trampling them.

She and Curzon followed Keeper across the marsh, and Curzon knew now to poke at doubtful patches of mud with his stick before setting his boot on them. The stagnant smell that Emily thought of as froggy was hardly detectable on the wind.

"A bit south of here," Curzon remarked, "is where Keeper found you."

"Tabby says those things wander at night."

On the far side of the marsh they were ascending a grassy slope, and there was one of the primordial paths to follow northward. Within another mile they were climbing the hill with the two standing stones at its crown.

The wind was stronger at the top of the hill. Emily crossed to the steep northern slope and looked down at the green heath below, and soon identified the stones that intermittently outlined the remembered square within a square, both transected by a now-wider beck, a hundred feet out from the foot of the hill.

Grass and gorse thickly covered the ground, and she couldn't see where the fissures and holes had opened up on that day last year; but she recalled Curzon falling into one, and she touched her pocket and remembered shooting at the rippling spot of air in which Keeper had recognized Welsh.

She looked at Curzon standing next to her. His eye was narrowed and his brown profile was taut, and she realized that he was afraid of what he was about to do—more afraid than he had been last year. *Seeking a task from a goddess can be costly,* he had told her last night, *and having undertaken to fulfil it, you're generally in mortal peril if you fail. Immortal peril, I should say.*

She wondered what his life at the monastery had been like; the life he had abandoned after cutting out his own left eye, largely for her sake.

"I'll be right beside you," she told him, "like it or not."

"At this moment," he said, "selfishly, I'm glad."

His right hand moved halfway to his face and then dropped, and she guessed that he had been about to make the sign of the cross but had thought better of it. He was, after all, about to attempt the conjuring of a pagan goddess.

He cleared his throat and exhaled through pursed lips; and then, loudly and carefully, called a dozen syllables. Again Emily couldn't identify the language, though she was sure it was a different question or statement than what he had called out here last year. The unknown words sent a shiver down her arms.

Remembering what happened on that day, she turned and looked south; but today there were no crows in the sky. *Welsh is wounded,* she thought—*waiting.*

She walked across the grass to the steep north slope and crouched, then began hopping and sliding down, with one hand catching at stones and tufts of grass. Keeper bounded past her on one side, and on the other side rolled rocks and clumps of dirt loosened by Curzon descending behind her.

At the bottom of the slope she stood up, careful not to wince at the renewed aches in her knees, and brushed out her crumpled dress. Curzon came sliding down a couple of yards to her left, and he got to his feet with some evident effort.

Emily shaded her eyes and looked across the empty heath.

The first line of stones lay a hundred feet ahead, and from ground level the stones were hardly visible in the tall grass. Curzon led the way forward across the uneven ground, and paused when they stood over the intermittently marked outer boundary.

"Across the threshold together," he said, "as before."

Emily caught Keeper's collar, nodded to Curzon, and the three of them stepped over the row of stones.

This time Emily was able to remain standing when the ground shifted, and she only blinked when abruptly she found herself in darkness, with a crescent moon high overhead. Daylight came back so suddenly that it was as if the brief experience of night had been a hood whisked away, and she shifted her boots in the grass as the ground tilted again—and then she was once again standing a few yards in front of the low stone temple with the tall, conical thatched roof. The open doorway below the wooden lintel beam showed only shadows and the narrow opening in the far wall; she couldn't see the effigy of the goddess.

She shivered with the old liberating excitement.

Around the primitive building the grassy heath still stretched wide between distant rocky promontories. The only evident change in the landscape in the last few moments was that the stream bisecting the squares was not here, now.

And two dogs were standing beside her.

She touched their equally solid, furry heads, and remembered her entrance into the *mundus loci* beside the Boggarts Green stone last night. To Curzon she said, "I don't think we could ever have got here without Keeper's companion—in spite of your hilltop incantation."

"We won't be trying it again." He wiped his hand across his mouth and took a step, but Emily caught his shoulder.

"I may have established a rapport," she said, "through my father."

He hesitated, then nodded reluctantly and stepped aside.

Emily and the two dogs started forward, and when she followed them under the lintel beam she was able to make out the remembered wicker figure standing on a stone block in the dimness. When she had first seen it last year it had seemed to be nothing but a primitive basketwork effigy, but today it was palpably a presence.

Emily recalled what Curzon had said then: *She was known to the Celts down around Bath as* Sulis, *and the druids in these northern parts called her* Brigantia... *There's the remains of a Roman road up by Skipton, and the Romans used to come down here to consult her. They knew her as Minerva.*

A prehuman power, she thought—no doubt diminished now, but still existing on levels she could never comprehend.

She heard Curzon scuff in behind her, and then tiny white lights appeared in the effigy's empty eye sockets, and brightened. Emily was suddenly certain that the faint lights of the nocturnal *ignis fatui* were a perverse mimicry of this radiance. It was sentient, and pure— she got no impression of malevolence from it, but also no impression of human qualities like compassion or mercy.

As if from long-dormant instinct, the two dogs crossed the narrow chamber and sat down on either side of the stone block that supported the crude figure of the goddess, like attendant demigods. With an audible creaking, the shapeless straw cylinders of the goddess's arms extended outward and down, and touched the heads of the dogs. Then the arm that had touched her Keeper's head rose and extended out toward Emily. The white glow from the figure's eye sockets was bright enough now that Emily saw the bristly shadow of the straw arm on the stones of the wall to her right.

Recalling that no harm had come to her when she had touched the straw arm last year, Emily reached out and touched it again—

And she almost snatched her hand back, for something had cut her left forefinger, though in the brightening glow she could see nothing but dry straw at the end of the goddess's shapeless arm. But she didn't lower her hand until the arm withdrew. She resisted the

impulse to suck her finger, and drops of blood fell unregarded to the stone floor.

Emily was surprised to see Curzon kneel—then saw that he had pulled a handful of bird bones from his coat pocket. The bones he had left on this floor last year were gone, and he leaned forward to toss this new handful like dice.

As before, the bones fell on the dirt in a distinct, nonrandom figure. He gathered them in and threw them again, and the shadows of the symbol the little bones formed made it seem to stand out in high relief. Emily yawned to correct the pressure in her ears.

Six more times Curzon threw, scanned, and gathered in the bones, as the light from the goddess's eyes intensified; he and Emily were both squinting now to see the symbols the bones formed, though to Emily they meant nothing.

She was watching his hand as he scraped up the bones one more time, and so the glaring flash of light that rocked him over backward only made her hunch her shoulders and close her eyes. But a moment later her knees gave way and thudded into grassy dirt.

Peripherally, around a retinal afterimage of Curzon's closing hand, she saw that she was kneeling on the heath in a cold wind under a clear sky, and she scrambled around to peer behind her and to the sides—the stone temple was gone, Keeper was nuzzling her shoulder, the ghost dog had disappeared, and Alcuin Curzon was standing a couple of yards away, staring expressionlessly at nothing.

"Curzon," Emily said, struggling painfully to her feet. "Alcuin!"

He seemed not to hear her. She walked up to him and shook him by the shoulder; he swayed, but his face didn't change.

She stepped around in front of him, and she stood on her toes to meet the blank gaze of his single eye. "Alcuin!" she shouted into his face.

His eye didn't move. She leaned in close to him and was relieved to feel his steady hot breath on her cheek. She stepped back and then slapped him hard on the cheek without the eyepatch—and his face remained stiff.

She walked away, and noticed that the sun was low over the hills to the west. Hours must have passed, here in reality, during the separate time they had spent in the temple of . . . Sulis, Brigantia, Minerva.

Only now was Emily frightened. Once before, she had left him out on the moors while she went to get help, but even though he had been badly wounded then, she had not doubted that he would recover. And when she had come back, then, with the Sunderlands, he had been gone.

She was afraid now that she could leave him and come back in a week, and find him still standing here like this.

And he had presumably learned here, today, what task the goddess had imposed to save her family from Welsh.

She blinked tears out of her eyes and walked back to where Curzon stood; and she pulled her pistol from her coat pocket and thumbed back the hammer. With her free hand she took hold of his left hand and lifted his arm. Remembering a wounded hawk she had found on the moors and nursed back to health, she impulsively kissed his palm, and then raised his hand and fired the pistol between his palm and his ear.

The blast was loud. His arm was jerked out of her grasp and his head turned sharply away in the burst of white smoke. He shook his burned hand and blinked tears out of his eye.

"What?" he barked hoarsely. "Who's shooting? Damn it—"

"Nobody!" Emily shouted in his face. "Can you hear me?"

"No, I can't hear you." He blinked at the smoking pistol in her hand and then stepped away from her and squinted around at the empty landscape. "What were you shooting at? You've near deafened and blinded me!" He held his burned hand up to his streaming eye. "Did you shoot at *me*?"

"No—I wanted to wake you up!"

"Damn, girl! Wait here, *don't move*." He strode over the outer line of stones and crouched to plunge his hand into the rushing water of the stream that bisected the ancient squares. He splashed water liberally over his head and shook his wet black hair. "I wasn't asleep!" he called over his shoulder.

"What did she *say*?" Emily yelled.

"What? Who?"

Emily glanced around before calling the name. *"Min-er-va!"*

Curzon was shaking his left hand. "What, last year?"

"Just now!" Emily waved at the inner square of stones. "When you threw your bird bones!" He tilted his head back and stared at

her in evident incomprehension, and she added desperately, "Bright light, remember?"

He started to speak, then cast a glance at the setting sun.

"The dogs sat on either side of her plinth!" Emily held up her left hand. "She cut my finger!"

Curzon hurried across the grass to stand beside her a few feet outside the line of the bigger square.

"Step over the wall line now," he said, and as Keeper followed at Emily's knee Curzon took her hand and tugged her forward. A moment later all three of them stood inside the bigger square of low stones, and that was all: the stones all lay inert in their ancient lines among the grass, and no temple appeared.

"We already *did* it," Emily said, yanking her hand free. "And the ghost Keeper is gone now."

"What do you *mean,* we—" Curzon bared his teeth at the darkening sky. "Ach! So late in the day, in an instant?"

"We already did it," Emily repeated distinctly.

For several seconds the wind across the heath was the only sound. Then Curzon spoke, and his voice was urgent: "Did she answer? Did the bones form symbols?"

"Yes!" Emily felt tears welling up in her eyes, and she looked away so that Curzon wouldn't see them. In a resolutely level voice she added, "And don't ask me if I remember what they were!"

Curzon walked past the inner line of stones, onto the patch of dirt where the temple had been. He fell to his knees and clawed at the dirt with his right hand, then struck his fist against the side of his head.

"Damn me," he said. "I believe you." He stood up. "We've got to get you home. When did that Wright fellow send to London for the twin's replacement head?"

"Yesterday, Wright said. Probably at dawn."

"With fast couriers they could have it at Haworth tomorrow night."

Emily sighed and let her shoulders sag. "You remember *nothing* of your meeting with Minerva just now?"

He closed his eye and frowned, then shook his head. "I'm sorry, truly. Nothing."

They began walking away from the empty expanse of grass, back toward the hill slope.

"I'm sorry I wrote to you," Emily said. Curzon nodded, looking to the left at their long shadows, and she added quickly, "Please understand what I mean—I'm sorry I called you away from your monastery, and provoked your penance." And, she thought, you'll no doubt have to pay the cost for failing in whatever task those bones spelled out for you.

"The penance was due in any case, child. Ah, look—Keeper prompts us."

Keeper had started hopping and scrambling back up the hill, and Emily and Curzon climbed up after him, Curzon favoring his scorched left hand. At the crest of the hill, Keeper waited while they leaned on the standing stones to catch their breaths.

"Whatever the outcome," Emily said, "I'm grateful for your strenuous and selfless efforts." She pushed wind-tangled hair back from her forehead. "I expect you'll be returning to your monastery now."

"I expect I will," he said, "if I'm not killed in your church tomorrow night. Your Protestant church."

You don't have to stay to the end with us, she thought, and she nearly reached out for the hand that she had kissed and then burned with the pan-flash of the pistol.

But she just gave him a wistful smile and said, "I should deter you from staying. But—yes—please."

They walked quickly down the shallower slope on the south side of the hill and struck out across the shadowed moors. Curzon shook his head sharply from time to time, and looked back, and several times seemed about to speak, but waved off Emily's questioning looks. She and Keeper led the way along paths that they had traversed many times over the years, and it was Keeper who took the lead in crossing the marsh.

Emily glanced to her left at the willow and the three dimly visible hawthorn bushes, but there were still no *ignis fatui* lights.

"Your horse must have killed all three," she said. When Curzon grunted and turned to her, she pointed at the bushes.

Curzon stopped. "Three deaths," he said.

Emily nodded. "The *ignis fatui.*"

"That was—" And then he would have sunk to his knees in the mud if Emily had not caught his arm and braced her feet.

"Yes," he said, so softly that Emily barely heard him over the wind, "we were there, you and I, in her temple!—Yes, the dogs, I remember now—and I had called her from the hilltop, asked for her full attention, and a task, God help us!"

He straightened, and her hand fell away.

"Emily." He breathed deeply. "In the bright light at the end I *saw* her, to the—tiny extent!—that I was able to comprehend her. And she *saw me,* this time. She dwarfed me, her vast age, her spiritual . . . *enormity!* I felt I was a mayfly being crushed just by her *awareness* of me!" He rubbed one hand over his face. "I fled her, hid from her, inward!—far down in the deepest recesses of my mind—and I might never have come out again if you had not fired your pistol at me."

"Not *at* you. I'm glad it—"

"Wait, wait! Three deaths. The symbols in the bones, I remember them now: there was a figure that described something like a lethal parasite that doesn't belong where or when it is, and then a reversing symbol, which would mean the banishing of it. The souls that it purchased must default, renege—forfeit privilege. They must surrender their lives—three deaths, as . . . penalty payment. And a sacrifice must be made from the harvest they're now relinquishing, borne by the dead to the cancelling fire."

"Ahh," Emily exhaled. Keeper was walking away, and she waved in that direction. "Yes," she said as the two of them resumed walking, "We're to break an old, unsought bargain, and pay the penalties."

For several seconds they plodded on through the marsh in silence.

"I'm sorry," said Curzon finally. "I'm afraid the task the goddess assigned is for you."

"It's only right."

The crests of a few hills in the east still shone pale apricot in the sinking daylight, and Keeper trotted ahead of Emily and Curzon, frequently looking back as if to urge a quicker pace.

Eventually Curzon said, "She cut your finger, this time?"

Emily held up her left forefinger. "Yes." In the dusky light she couldn't see the cut, but when she rubbed her thumb across it, it stung, and she felt the edges of broken skin. "The same finger I cut when I was twelve, to leave my blood in the fairy cave."

Curzon nodded and sighed. "The moon won't be up for a while," he said, "but I imagine you see well at night."

"And Keeper and I both know the way back," she assured him.

He nodded, and she knew that he didn't trust his one remaining eye to recognize features of the land in darkness.

Quickly he went on, "I've paid for three nights at that same house on Main Street. I don't think the Obliques can get the twin's new head to Haworth before dusk tomorrow. When would you have me come?"

"Morning," said Emily. "An hour after dawn, say."

"Prepared for a long walk, I expect."

"Yes. And this time you *might* have to carry me back."

CHAPTER SIXTEEN

Emily's father pushed his chair back from the dining room table and shifted around to look out the window toward the dark churchyard. He had not spoken while Emily told him and her sisters about today's hike with Curzon to the capriciously appearing temple in the north moors—which necessitated telling him about their previous visit last year.

For many seconds after she had finished, he didn't speak. Then, "I told you to stay at home today," he said quietly. "When you disobey me, you do it in . . . epic fashion." Without turning back to face his daughters, he raised a hand. "But it was I who put the idea into your head—I should never have told you what I did in Chester forty-some years ago, after stepping off the boat from Ireland. I hope," he added in a whisper, "I have not damned us both."

"You didn't prompt me," Emily told him. "I didn't even know it was Minerva until after the first visit."

Still looking away from them, Patrick clenched his hand in a fist. "But she *knew* you—marked you today!—because of me."

"And gave me an answer."

Emily had returned to the parsonage a couple of hours after sunset. Curzon had said good night at the kitchen door, saying that he wouldn't intrude on her talk with her family, and her father had insisted that she have a restorative bowl of hot porridge and a cup of tea before joining him and her sisters in the parlor. Branwell had been on his way upstairs to bed, and was irritable when Emily stopped him long enough to look at his left wrist; and he had been surprised, as she had not been, to notice a fresh cut on his old scar.

Anne had a cut on her left forefinger, and had thought she must have cut herself while peeling potatoes that afternoon.

"An answer!" said Charlotte now. "A curse, I call it."

She was sitting beside Anne at the dining table, and Emily reclined on the green leather couch against the far wall, near the fire in the fireplace. In spite of her assurances to everyone, Emily was in fact very tired, and her legs and shoulder ached.

Patrick shook his head and finally turned to face Emily. "It is not an acceptable answer. If I'd known you were—so unwisely!—resolved on consulting *her,* I'd have *insisted* on coming along—yes, despite the grave sin of it. I might have *reasoned* with her."

Thunder rumbled remotely out in the night.

Emily's breath caught, and she blinked to hold back exhaustion-readied tears. In the face of this threat against his children, she thought, he forgets that he's seventy years old, and frail—and he has no conception of the entity Curzon and I encountered. He should have wound the clock and gone to bed an hour ago.

Anne too seemed affected, and she took a deep breath and let it out, as if to level her voice, before she said, "A negating fire, a cleansing fire, you said. In the fairy cave, I imagine, to stop payment on the blood we left there, and even eradicate any atoms of it that might still cling to that stone." She sucked her cut finger.

"And then nobody will have any proprietary claim on us," Emily said, "before or after our deaths."

Charlotte opened her mouth to say something, but Anne lowered her hand and sat back, and Charlotte paused. Anne said, "Forfeit privilege. That's clear enough. But what do you suppose your goddess meant by 'a sacrifice from the harvest they're now relinquishing'?"

Yes, thought Emily, *forfeit privilege* is obvious. In these seventeen years since Anne, Branwell, and I made ourselves conspicuous to hungry ghosts, we've had at the same time our unnatural dispensation from the consequence of it, in return for Welsh having a claim on the three of us. And our aim now, having accepted those seventeen years, is to default on that unwitting bargain. As to the harvest . . .

In these stolen years we've written novels, poems . . .

"Consider Cain and Abel," she said.

Patrick was frowning. "This makes no sense at all. You girls have nothing."

Charlotte had been rapidly switching her gaze among her sisters and her father, and now she burst out, "And *three deaths*? Have you all somehow forgotten *that* part of the . . . *pagan oracle's* message?"

Patrick shook his head, muttering under his breath.

Emily had been waiting for Charlotte or her father to finally address that conspicuous point. She leaned her head back and closed her eyes. "And it must follow, as the night the day," she said. "Our special protection will be gone, and our special vulnerability will remain."

She looked down at her scraped hands to avoid meeting anyone's eye. Anne and Charlotte had told her what Curzon had said to them last night: *Once you've been opened to their* attentions, *it's not just the ones who shamble up to you in churchyards and startle you by emptying your lungs in an instant—subtler ones attach to you, and take your breath and vitality by degrees.*

"Consumption," said Charlotte, nodding angrily, "by subtle ghosts!"

"By degrees," Emily reminded her, "and there'll be ways to stave them off."

"For how long?" demanded Charlotte. "A year?"

"Oh," said Emily with a brittle smile, "longer than that, I should say. Twice that, perhaps."

"I should have tied the three of you to your beds on that terrible day!" Charlotte shifted in her chair. "When are you going out there tomorrow with your friend?"

"Not a friend, precisely. Early morning. We should all get some sleep tonight."

"I should go there with you."

"You and Anne stay here with Papa. And Branwell."

"No," said their father, pushing back his chair. "I can't permit it. None of you will stir from this house until after—"

Emily forced herself to sit up. "Oh, Papa, after what? After Welsh has evicted Branwell out of his whole body, not just his left hand? After Alcuin Curzon has probably killed himself trying to prevent Welsh's other half from rising restored from its broken tomb, and the twin devils merge at last?"

Their father had started to get up out of his chair, but now slumped back into it. "John Brown cut a fresh stone today, with the ogham lines copied, and laid it over the old broken one." His voice

was weak, almost petulant. "The old one kept the monster down for a century and a half..."

Tabby had walked down the hall from the kitchen and now she stepped into the parlor and set the refilled teapot on the table. "It's got a head now, though," she said.

"Ahead of what?" said Patrick.

Then it took half an hour, during which Tabby had to go back to the kitchen twice to refill the teapot, for the sisters to fully explain to their father about the skull Emily had destroyed last year, and the fresh head that Mrs. Flensing had brought and that had been carried away by her accomplice...after the accomplice had killed Mrs. Flensing and probably put her ghost into it as a placeholder.

"The head may be in Haworth by tomorrow evening," Emily said.

Their father had stared into the fire throughout the account, and now looked up. "Placeholder for...?"

"The twin's own spirit," said Anne, "presently trapped headless under the stone."

"It needs a compatible head," said Emily, "and Mrs. Flensing found a fresh one somewhere."

"To hear such sentences in my parlor," said Patrick. shaking his head. "Devils' heads, goddesses in pagan temples!" He stared at each of his daughters in turn. "You never thought to...*trouble* me, with any of this?"

"No," said Emily flatly.

"You were blind," said Charlotte.

"And then in Manchester for a month," said Anne.

"And old." He shrugged, and resumed getting to his feet—in order to kneel. "Tomorrow night will evidently be contentious," he said. "We to our prayers, now, and then to our beds."

The three sisters pushed back their own chairs, and Emily was determined to kneel for as long as Patrick wanted to pray, without giving any sign of the aches in her knees.

"And pray that we'll all be kneeling here again tomorrow night," she said.

Even in her dream, Emily recognized her father's dawn gunshot, and she clung to the sound as she clawed her way up out of the dream to wakefulness.

In the dream she had again found herself in the churchyard at night, swaying in spotty moonlight to the vagaries of the wind and watching a shadowed figure walk slowly toward her from the ruined parsonage. She had implicitly known that in her present ghost form she was immune to injury except by fire, and so she had watched the approaching stranger with just wary curiosity.

A broad hat shaded the approaching face, and she wondered who it could be. One-eyed Curzon, saying goodbye?—regretfully? Herself, resenting her ghost lingering this way?

But when the hat was swept off, it was Branwell's face staring at her no-doubt indistinct form. The mouth opened above the still-sparse chin beard, and a voice that was not Branwell's said, "You are all my herd now."

He looked past her and nodded, and the wind obligingly turned Emily around. Behind her she could make out five rippling forms made of smoke and cobwebs, slowly waving jointless arms like seaweed under water, and she knew they were her mother and her four sisters—Elizabeth, Maria, Charlotte, and Anne—frail ghosts like herself, out here in the night. A tangled thing like a broken dried nettle was huddled against the wall behind them, and she knew it was the ghost of their father, trying to hide from their sight.

She knew then to look up, and a ragged curl of captive smoke fluttering in the branches was Alcuin Curzon.

She looked again at Branwell's face. With both hands, his left as deft as his right, he lifted a dog collar that she recognized as Keeper's, and extended it toward the space below her wobbling head.

Then from one of the gaping windows of the ruined parsonage she heard the muted crack of a gunshot, and knew what it was. She flexed her leg to run, and it was a real leg, not the lint-and-dandelion-seed leg of a ghost; she focused her mind on the memory of that real gunshot and with real hands thrust blankets down, as if climbing out of a hole. She forced away the dream vision, and after a few moments of struggle she was sitting up in her bed in her little room. Muted dawn light let her see the drawings on the walls.

She was panting, and flexed her hands in front of her face to reassure herself that she still had a body. For a while, she thought; long enough, God willing.

She stood up and put on her robe. As she left her room and

started down the hall toward the stairs, she heard quiet sobbing from behind Branwell's door. She paused, then knocked.

"Go away," came his voice, so she opened the door and stepped in.

He had his back to her, standing at the window and looking out over the bleak moors. His room was colder than hers.

He took a deep breath. "Only Emily," he said, "would just come in anyway."

"You'd want me to."

He shrugged. "I think today I disappear into him."

"No," she said. "Today I free us. Stop payment on our blood." She found matches on his bedside table and lit the candle that stood there.

He turned around, and in spite of the misery in his wasted face she was glad to see his own self in his naked eyes. "It can't be done."

"I think it can. I've had expert advice." She cocked her head. "You can be free, escape possession. And when we die we won't be part of his ghost herd."

He shuddered, then crossed to the bed and sat down. "I was dreaming of that, moments ago; Papa's gunshot woke me. I was *in Welsh*, mute, helpless. He walked down the steps from this house, and the ghost of you met him—"

"And the house was in ruins, by moonlight."

He looked up at her, squinting without his spectacles. "You dreamed it too? Just now?" When she nodded, he said in a hollow voice, "It was a prophecy."

"A false one, Branwell. Trust me."

For a moment he just stared at her, clearly considering the idea that her confidence might somehow be justified; then he looked away. "But we'll still die, you know. The little ghosts, the ones that are just smoke and vapor—we unthinkingly cough them away now, but they'll get into us, without *his* conferred immunity. They'll kill us."

"Gradually," she said. "By degrees."

"Sooner than later."

"Probably. So?"

For several seconds neither of them spoke.

Finally Branwell managed a laugh. Quietly he said, "In the dream he was able to work my left hand. I *would* like to get it back again, for myself, if only for a while."

"Your soul too. And not just for a while."

"Well yes, that too."

"You can have it back—but it calls for a sacrifice from each of us that were there, that day."

"What do we have? No money—blood, again?"

"A sacrifice from a harvest we took, but now decline to pay for. Seventeen years of harvests." He gave her a blank, slack-jawed look, and she went on, "My first novel is out of my hands, but my second is half-written. Anne's novel is unavailable too, but she has a lot of poetry." She spread her hands and forced her voice to be level. "We'll burn it."

"Are you—hah!—asking me to burn what I've been writing? Along with your—"

"You stay here. I'll take it all out there. Today."

"Your first novel, your *second* novel—you and Anne—little tales of Glass Town and Gondal? *I'm* writing a *real* novel! It's all very well for you two to burn your . . . your *efforts,* but I can't possibly—"

"Whatever their value, we owe a sacrifice from that harvest."

He glanced toward his desk, then back at his sister. "Who says so?"

Minerva, thought Emily; who received me because our father asked for her cyclopes-made armor when he arrived on these shores at the age of twenty-five. Emily imagined trying to explain this to Branwell, then just said, "I say so."

Branwell wiped his right hand across his mouth. "*Truly,* Emily?"

She nodded. "For your soul."

He stood up quickly and crossed to the desk. "So I must cease to be," he said as he yanked open the top drawer, "and, *with* me, what my pen has gleaned from my teeming brain—no high-piled books to hold their full-ripened grain . . ."

Emily recognized the Keats sonnet that he was mangling, and mentally supplied the last words of it: *love and fame to nothingness do sink.*

"For us all, Branwell," she said.

He lifted out a stack of handwritten pages and divided it in two. He handed her the top half. "There."

She looked at the pages still on the desk. "Just half? This is Cain's sacrifice."

"Do you see that?" he said, touching a spot on the top page that was so densely scribbled that a hole had been scraped right through the paper. "My very best writing is there."

"This won't earn us much mercy, afterward."

He slammed the drawer. "Where's this *first novel* of yours, that it can't be added to the pyre?"

"Submitted to a publisher. I wonder if you believe me when I say that if I had it here, I would sacrifice it, to save us."

"Oh," he said miserably, "I believe you, of course." He walked back to the bed and sat down. "What was its title?"

"Wuthering Heights."

"Huh. Terrible title. Well, you sacrificed it by posting it to a publisher, didn't you?—who will surely burn it himself."

"Not unlikely." She held up the pages he had given her. "Thanks for this."

He looked away and waved his right hand in dismissal.

Emily carried the pages downstairs and set about making breakfast for the family.

An hour after dawn, Emily and Keeper were standing at the top of the steps outside the parsonage front door. The sky was gray, and a gusty cold wind shook the bare branches in the churchyard, and she couldn't help glancing to the side to be sure the house's windows still had glass in them.

She wore boots and a wool skirt and coat and hat. In one coat pocket was the pistol her father had bought for her, and in the other was a bulky, string-tied bundle of manuscript pages.

Anne was staying home with Branwell, Charlotte, Tabby, and their father. Emily hoped to return by noon, but she knew that there was practically no sort of catastrophe that she could rule out; so for lack of any better help, she had given Anne the two dried sticks that were Mrs. Flensing's fingers.

Now a figure in a long coat was striding up the walk from around the corner of the church, and Emily could see the eyepatch under the brim of his hat. Curzon held a stout walking stick, and vertical straps on this shoulders, and his somewhat forward-leaning posture, told her that he was carrying a heavy rucksack.

Emily sighed—then took from her shirt pocket Branwell's old pair

of spectacles, which she had smeared with Mrs. Flensing's "Gehenna mud" oil. She put them on and looked at the churchyard.

Yes, there they were—shapes like diaphanous garments with limbs moved by the wind, and bag heads bobbing as if in imbecilic mutual agreement.

Curzon nodded to her as he got closer, walking past the little garden between the parsonage and the churchyard. He stopped at the foot of the steps and patted one of the shoulder straps.

"I brought four gallon jugs of lamp oil and a bundle of wood-wool," he said, then turned his head to look at her with his one eye. "Suddenly you need spectacles?"

"Yes." She walked carefully down the steps, blinking behind the smeared lenses. "I'll pick up fuel now, before we start out."

"I said I've got a lot of lamp oil."

"I need more."

He shifted and looked around. "What, tree branches? Dead leaves? Everything's damp."

She didn't answer, but walked to the western end of the churchyard wall and leaned over it. After a few seconds the ghosts were aware of her proximity, and began drifting toward her. Keeper growled, but she hushed him and rubbed his furry head.

Curzon walked up to the two of them. "We should get moving," he said, looking away toward the road that led west onto the moors. His expression was bleak.

"In a minute."

The ghosts were closer now, and mouths began opening in the fronts of their heads. Emily leaned forward and opened her own mouth. One of the dim figures slid ahead of the others—could it be the ghost of someone she had known?—and Emily exhaled involuntarily.

Another was crowding up behind the first one, and Emily had no sooner caught her breath than it was snatched from her again. She stepped back, and Keeper tugged her a yard farther away from them.

She was panting. "That'll do for a lure." Through the spectacle earpieces she could detect a faint buzzing, as though the ghosts were singing.

Curzon caught her shoulder. "What the hell? Did you just—those

things take more than your breath, you know! They sustain themselves with scraps of your vitality!"

He and Keeper led her away, but she looked back over her shoulder and saw that many of the ghosts were now eeling over the low wall and out of the churchyard.

"We shouldn't walk too fast," she said.

"You can *see* them?" asked Curzon. "Is it those spectacles?"

Emily nodded. "The lenses are smeared with an oil that Mrs. Flensing gave to Branwell. It lets you see . . . more." Half a dozen of the ghosts—no, a dozen, easily—were following them on the road that led west, but not quickly. Emily reached up and touched the frame of one of the lenses. "Would you like to try it?"

"My one eye is fully occupied as it is. You can be the occult monitor." He peered at her as they trudged along. "Are you deliberately *drawing* them along with us? Why?"

She sighed, reflecting that it was a breath that the ghosts wouldn't get. "Through your bird bones, Minerva told us that there must be a sacrifice borne by the dead. There they are."

"Ah!" Curzon was visibly relieved. "I confess I feared it might work out to be one of us."

And you wouldn't have let it be me, she thought. "And," she added quickly, tapping the pocket of her coat, "the sacrifice is here."

Wind shook the heather on the hillsides, and Emily held onto her hat, but when she looked back she saw that the clustered figures from the churchyard were still following.

With a note of melancholy that surprised her, she said, "They're flammable, poor things."

Keeper wanted to hurry, and though Curzon now knew the reason for their slow pace, he was looking worriedly at the darkening sky: but Emily made sure they didn't get so far ahead of the ghosts that the things might lose their perception of her. Curzon shifted the straps of his rucksack.

It saddened Emily to think of how soon they would arrive at Ponden Kirk, even at this pace, and she gently touched the bulky bundle in her left coat pocket. So many of Anne's best poems, she thought, and half of poor Branwell's novel, which must have cost him dearly, whatever its quality. And my incomplete second novel, which draws so heavily on the terrible events of this past year! I hadn't yet

decided how it would end—perhaps by nightfall I'll know what sort of ending would have been fitting.

Curzon must have seen her touch her pocket, and caught her momentarily unguarded expression.

"I won't ask," he said gently, "what the nature of the sacrifice is."

"Certainly not."

Looking left and right through the spectacles as they walked, Emily could see dim figures making their awkward ways down the nearest hillsides. Keeper saw them too, and growled.

She clicked her tongue, meaning *stay*.

"More of them?" asked Curzon, hefting his stick.

"Yes. A gathering of the clans, it seems."

"Perhaps they sense that you bring a . . . an ending."

She looked up at Curzon's stony dark profile. He could have left Haworth last night, she thought. He stayed, and set out on this journey today believing that his life might be claimed to fulfill the goddess's condtions; to help kill the blight on the land—to save my family—to save me.

"Manuscripts," she said.

"Ah," he said, understanding her. "Ambitious?"

"Yes . . . whatever their quality."

"I'm sorry." He kept his eye on the irregular horizon ahead of them. "It's no use, of course, to say that you can write more."

"None," she agreed.

She couldn't tell whether it was herself or Keeper who led the way in a detour across a stretch of heath to stay well clear of the standing stone that was Boggarts Green. She couldn't help but glance at it, and it seemed taller now than she recalled it being.

For an hour they hiked westward, along ancient sheep-paths and across the slopes of hills, avoiding crests and ridges. Viewed through the oiled lenses, the empty moors on this cloudy day looked not much different than usual, though Emily did see ancient-looking low stone walls crossing a couple of hillsides that she knew had none, and a cluster of rabbits that weren't there when she raised the spectacles, and several bare hilltops where she remembered trees.

She might have called for a rest, but Curzon was marching steadily along, and she estimated that the four gallons of lamp oil he

was carrying must weigh twenty-five or thirty pounds. When their course did take them over the shoulder of a hill, all three of them looked around, but the only variations in the miles of natural landscape were occasional far-off standing stones silhouetted against the low gray sky.

At one such high place Keeper stopped and stiffened, looking north. Curzon and Emily halted to squint in that direction.

"Damn my eye," muttered Curzon. The chilly wind tossed his black hair around his face and he brushed it aside impatiently. "What's out there?"

From where they stood, Emily could see beyond the nearest rise to a ridge a couple of miles farther away; and half a dozen dots were moving down the slope of the ridge at what must have been a good speed. She lifted the spectacles—but the things were still visible.

"Six or so," she said, "maybe two miles away—like big dogs, running."

"Find us a ravine," Curzon said, "deep and narrow. At their hunting pace on this terrain it should take them at least five minutes to get here."

Emily thought quickly. Dean Beck was not far south of where they stood, and she was sure she recalled a cleft overhung with alders just beyond it.

"This way," she said. She pocketed the blurry spectacles and began running down the rock-strewn slope away from the approaching creatures—which, she insisted to herself, were probably, actually, werewolves. Curzon was right behind her, and Keeper was leaping over rocks at her left, and she didn't look back to see what her ghosts were doing.

She ignored the mounting aches in her knees, and even leaped right over a low dry-stone wall alongside Keeper, while Curzon had to pause to swing his legs over it. Of course he was burdened by his heavy rucksack, but on this cold overcast day Emily could once again almost hear the wild atonal music of the moors, high-pitched now with mortal peril, and she was nearly dancing as she ran.

They splashed across the six feet of rushing water that was Dean Beck, and she called, "Running water—will it stop them?"

"Just—a leap, to them," Curzon panted. He glanced back. "Where's this damned ravine?"

"There," she said, pointing to the cluster of alders that marked the cleft she remembered.

Half a minute later they had thrashed between the branches and were sliding down the sloping wall of the ravine; it was about fifteen feet wide, and when they were standing among the rocks at the bottom, the top edge was a foot higher than Cruzon's head.

He quickly led the way along the ravine's stony floor for ten yards, then shouldered out of his rucksack and lifted out two heavy glass jugs and shoved them into Emily's hands. He took out two more, along with a bundle of straw-colored wood-wool; he uncorked one of the jugs and splashed aromatic lamp oil onto one end of the wood-wool bundle, then recorked the jug and began crawling back up the slope with both the jugs, to the exposed tree roots at the top edge.

Over his shoulder he called, "Get those up here!"

Emily sat down with her back to the slope and pushed her way up with the heels of her boots. Keeper, unburdened, was already at the crest.

Curzon had wedged his two jugs into spaces between arching roots and the soil. He quickly reached down and took the two Emily was holding and worked them too in under more of the finger-like roots.

He slid back to the floor of the defile and carried his rucksack and the bundle of wood-wool several yards farther along the ravine, and Emily and Keeper were soon beside him.

Curzon crouched and dug into his rucksack. He laid beside the wood-wool a flint stone and a short steel bar curled at one end, and finally he pulled out two flintlock pistols.

Emily tugged her own pistol from her coat pocket.

Curzon gave her a tense grin and pulled aside his coat to show two hilts standing up from sheaths on his belt. He glanced at her pistol. "Lead and church-bell rust?"

She nodded and waved toward the pair of pistols he had laid on the rucksack. "Silver?"

"Plain lead. It can slow them down. Here," he added, drawing one of the double-bladed knives from its sheath and handing it to her. He raised his head. "They'll call when they're upon us."

You know them, Emily thought. She looked back down the defile

to the scraped area where they had descended the slope. That's where they'll appear, she told herself.

With Keeper and Curzon standing strong on either side of her, and a knife in one hand and a pistol in the other, her rapid heartbeat seemed to strike in time to the nearly audible wild music of the moors.

Then, also seeming to be in time with it, came the sudden close ululation of the werewolves—they must have been nearly at the edge of the ravine. Curzon dropped to his knees and struck a spray of sparks onto the wood-wool.

Emily heard claws drumming on dirt, and then two of the things slid heavily down into the defile.

For a frozen moment their panting bulks seemed to fill the space between the slanting ravine walls—canine forms like big bullmastiffs, with glittering black eyes set wide above blunt snouts, black lips drawn back to expose long fangs, muscles rippling under patchy fur, and a harsh metallic smell that even on the cold wind was stronger here than it had been in the parsonage kitchen last year.

The werewolves wailed and sprang forward across the loose stones.

Still on his knees, Curzon snatched up his pistols and fired both of them into the wide, bristling faces; then he had dropped the pistols and was on his feet with a dioscuri knife in one hand and the smoldering bundle of wood-wool in the other.

The two werewolves were momentarily slowed, shaking strings of blood from their ripped faces, and Emily saw several more leap down into the defile behind them in a cascade of dirt and gravel, but Curzon pushed her raised pistol aside.

"Up the slope!" he shouted. "Shoot the oil jugs!"

She didn't pause to nod, but turned and scrambled up the ravine slope, holding her pistol high and digging the points of the dioscuri into the soil to pull herself up. When she was crouched just below the edge of the ravine, she couldn't help but glance back and down.

In the narrow defile below, the werewolves were only able to advance two at a time, and Curzon had evidently killed one with his double-bladed knife and blinded another, and for the moment the ones who might leap over their toppled fellows were recoiling from

the lunges and sweeps of Curzon's paired blades. Keeper was beside Curzon, furiously snapping at thrusting heads and paws.

Emily quickly scanned the glass jugs wedged under roots along the ravine edge, then hiked herself a foot farther up the slope so that they were lined up one behind the other in her view. She raised her pistol, aimed at the closest jug, and pulled the trigger.

A moment later the crack of the gunshot shook the air, and a spray of glass and oil rained down into the defile. Curzon tossed the burning wood-wool bundle at the clustered werewolves, grabbed Keeper's collar, and scrambled back.

With a loud *whoosh* a burst of heat swept up over Emily, and she slid back down the slope. Her hat was gone, and she let go of the spent pistol to beat at her smoldering hair.

The werewolves were on fire. A couple that were fully engulfed in flames tried to climb the slope but fell back, and another ran toward Keeper but dropped and slid inert on the stones when Emily lunged at it from the side and drove her dioscuri into its neck. She burned her hand as she bent to tug the hilt free of the thing's flaming hide.

Keeper leaped past her to fasten his teeth in the throat of a burning werewolf that had got Curzon's arm in its jaws, and when the thing released him to turn on Keeper, Curzon stabbed it in the chest. All three collapsed, but Curzon and Keeper scrambled to their feet.

Curzon hurried to one of the blazing werewolves that was rolling on the gravel, and he crouched beside it, holding one hand in front of his face; when the rolling torch that was its head presented its throat, he stabbed it deeply and then hopped back, slapping his burning sleeve against his thigh.

He glanced at the other one, then shook his head and bent to pick up a melon-sized rock, which he raised and then flung down onto the thing's grimacing head. The head imploded.

"It can't heal from that," he muttered breathlessly, turning away from the gory, flaming mess.

The one he had blinded with a slash of the dioscuri had loped partway back along the ravine and collapsed, now entirely on fire. Curzon stepped over several burning or furred and bloodied bodies and plodded to where the thing lay clawing the gravel. He dispatched

it with another big stone and made his way back to where Emily and Keeper stood.

Emily pointed at his arm, where the coat had been torn away and his shirt was blotted with blood.

"I heal fast, remember?" he said.

"But you've been bitten—"

He closed his eye for a moment, then stared at her. "Emily. I'm one already."

"Oh. Yes."

"Well done, here."

She nodded. Her hand stung and the smell of burning fur and flesh had her panting through her open mouth. These dead things, she thought, were men; one was probably Adam Wright, whom I've seen any number of times in church. He might be the one I killed to save Keeper. And Wright had a daughter, a stout girl who briefly attended the church school—might she be among these?

All Emily felt . . . as when the Minerva effigy had touched her hand last year . . . was a bleak sense of rightness, balance.

A flash of lightning was followed a second later by the rolling boom of thunder, and immediately rain began pattering on her head and the rocks and the smoldering corpses.

She slid the dioscuri carefully into her coat pocket, then looked at the slope on the north side. "We've got to recross Dean Beck and find my poor strayed ghosts."

Two horses were placing their hooves carefully on the crosswise cobblestones of Main Street's steep ascent, and the carriage's lowered drag-staff clicked like a slow metronome as it slid into place on the uphill side of each rain-wet stone. The roof of the clarence carriage had begun to leak, and Evan Saltmeric slid lower in the rear-facing seat to put on his top hat. Across from him sat Reverend Farfleece, with his chin resting on the abominable leather valise in his lap; the clergyman was unshaven, and his straw-colored hair hung in limp strands on his forehead. Seated next to each of them was a junior member of the Oblique order, men chosen for this expedition because of their rough-and-tumble appearances rather than for any piety.

Saltmeric was wearing a pair of spectacles, the lenses of which

were flat glass smeared with the illuminating oil. When he glanced out the rain-streaked carriage window he saw a few hurrying cloaked figures, far too solid to be ghosts.

"Relevant activity?" asked Farfleece.

Saltmeric shrugged. "Just the living, as far as I can tell."

"There should be a good contingent of the departed. Keep your eyes peeled."

Saltmeric shuddered. He had heard the expression before, but today it made him think of the head in the valise. He recalled that its eyes looked like peeled hard-boiled eggs.

He wished he were anywhere else on Earth than here.

This was the fourth carriage they had engaged in the eighteen hours since they had left London, and it too now reeked of sweat and damp clothing and the sweet-pork smell from the leather valise.

The valise creaked, and when Saltmeric looked at it he saw it flex between Farfleece's pale hands. The two lay members of the faith glanced at it and then at each other.

"Do you think she's . . . aware?" Saltmeric asked. Aware of me, he thought, here?

Farfleece shook his head. "Unattached to a sustaining body, I shouldn't imagine so."

Saltmeric looked away, remembering the night he had rolled the horrible head out of the valise after the fight in the curate's kitchen last year, and then rolling it back into the valise after killing Mrs. Flensing and catching her ghost in it. If she were sentient in the thing now, was she aware that it was Evan Saltmeric who was responsible for her lamentable present state? Did she guess that she was shortly to be evicted from even this grotesque object into bodiless wandering ghosthood?

All this effort so that the two persons of the Obliques' biune god could be united at last, after having been separated and killed in the last century—the female god confined headless under the stone in the Haworth church, the male half only recently able to possess a living body.

And Reverend Farfleece didn't seem pleased by the prospect of the imminent apotheosis. It was one thing to look forward to the advent of a god who would change the world, but quite another to face the prospect of that upheaval happening today, within the hour.

Saltmeric looked down at his own right hand, and once again remembered pushing the double-bladed knife into Mrs. Flensing's throat. He wished he were Catholic, so that he could go to Confession; or Jewish, to have his sins forgiven at Yom Kippur.

"Where is the church?" Farfleece asked.

"Just at the top of this street," said Saltmeric, "where it levels out."

"I suppose," said Farfleece a bit shamefacedly, "the report of the stone cracking two days ago is reliable?"

"Our local man Wright swears to it."

"Not just a crack from . . . shifting temperature?"

"Split right down the center, he wrote."

"Ah. Then," Farfleece said hollowly, sitting back, "the glorious day does appear to be upon us."

Evan Saltmeric sat back too, as water dripped on the brim of his hat and the drag-staff on the rear axle clicked like a tightening ratchet on the paving stones.

CHAPTER SEVENTEEN

Anne and Charlotte stood in the open front doorway of the parsonage, looking across the gravestones to the church. Rain splashed on the walkway at the bottom of the steps, raising waves of mist that swept across the pavement. Their father had told them to stay in the house and keep an eye on Branwell, but they had both put on coats and boots.

"He's got his pistol," said Charlotte, "and Emily and Mr. Curzon will be back before dusk."

"But there's nothing he can *do*," said Anne. "Why must he wait in the church rather than here?" She looked up at the dark sky, then said, "I'm getting an umbrella."

"He won't be pleased if you disobey him."

"I don't care. He'll freeze in that drafty church. I'm going to bring him a pot of tea, at least."

"Well—I'll do it. You can stay here and—"

Anne caught her sister's arm, for a carriage had rolled into sight from the direction of Main Street, and through the waving curtains of rain she could see two men, no, four, climbing out of it and hurrying to the church.

"You saw that?" Anne said. "One of them had a bag or case. It's the head for the monster!"

Not pausing to hear what Charlotte might say, Anne turned and ran back down the hall to the kitchen, where she hurriedly snatched up two makeshift dioscuris Tabby had made by tying pairs of knives together with twine.

Back at the front door, she shoved one of the bound double-hilts into Charlotte's hands, and patted her coat pocket to be sure she still had the dried fingers Emily had given her this morning.

A moment later she was tapping down the steps to the walkway, with Charlotte close behind. They were both drenched by the time they had splashed through puddles to the side door of the church, and Anne pushed her sopping hair back from her forehead and yanked open the door.

She heard her father's shout—"Anne! Charlotte! Go back to the house!"—before her eyes had adjusted to the dimness; the sisters didn't move, and a few seconds later she could see their father on the raised altar floor to the right, facing the four men she had seen get out of the carriage. Then she noticed that her father held his pistol raised, pointing it at the men.

She flexed her hand on the twined-together hilts of the two knives and took a step into the church—and then was shoved forward and fell into one of the pews. She heard Charlotte tumble into the next pew, and the clatter of Charlotte's paired knives falling to the stone floor.

Anne rolled over and sat up, and glimpsed Branwell's back as he hurried up the side aisle in the direction of the altar.

"Branwell," she gasped, "wait, we've got—"

But the words stopped in her throat when he cast a glance back at her; by his expression, and his gait as he hurried away toward the altar, she knew that it wasn't her brother, though it was his body. The bandage on his head was more darkly blotted than it had been last night, and he had at some point changed from his pajamas into boots and woolen trousers and a heavy coat.

A stony *boom* shook the floor.

Anne stood up and sidled quickly between the pews toward the four intruders in the center aisle, holding her paired blades out in front of her. Charlotte was right beside her in the next pew.

The four strangers had scuffed around at the sisters' entrance, and Anne could see them clearly now in the gray light from the open door behind her. One of them, carrying a big leather satchel, was about thirty years old, with fair hair, and wore a clergyman's collar on a black shirt; two appeared to be hired laborers; but it was the fourth, a chubby young man wearing spectacles and a top hat, that made

Anne gasp. Six months ago he had burst into the parsonage kitchen with Mrs. Flensing; and he was almost certainly the one who had killed the woman later that night.

He drew a pistol from under his coat and pointed it at the two sisters standing in the narrow gaps between the pews.

The young clergyman flapped his hands, then turned toward the altar and called, "Brontë! Drop your weapon or Mr. Saltmeric will be compelled to shoot these women!"

"They're his daughters," said Saltmeric. His hand holding the pistol was shaking.

"Your daughters," amplified the clergyman.

Anne looked toward the altar. Her father was lowering his own pistol. Branwell, his body at any rate, had climbed up into the pulpit, and now looked down from a good six feet above everyone else.

Branwell spread his arms and began calling out syllables in a language Anne didn't recognize.

Again something heavy seemed to strike the floor, and the four intruders scrambled toward the altar, looking back over their shoulders in obvious alarm.

Branwell was pronouncing the alien words louder now, drawing echoes from the beams that spanned the high ceiling vault, and Anne heard a prolonged sliding sound, as if the heavy baptismal font were being steadily moved across the floor—and she knew it must be the new stone John Brown had cut, shifting off of the old, cracked stone where it had been laid two days ago.

Then with a loud grinding an uneven gray rectangular shape rose up from the central aisle a few yards in front of Anne, leaning away from her at first but moving toward vertical; and she saw on its surface the grooves that were ogham writing.

It was half of the split ledger stone, exposed again and being lifted aside by a force beneath it.

Anne reeled back as a gust of cold air, reeking of tar and stagnant water, stung her eyes and tossed her wet hair.

The near half of the stone fell outward, cracking the pew ends in front of her—and she gasped as a big dirt-caked animal climbed out of the hole where the stone had lain for more than a hundred and fifty years.

Muscles flexed under tight expanses of matted gray pelt; she saw

forelegs like oak limbs, claws breaking the stone blocks at the edge of the hole—and, as the thing rose into view, bristling fur along the ridge of the spine, and ribs as thick as her wrists pressing out against mottled hide—but from where she stood she could see no head above the wide shoulders that swung from side to side.

Beyond it, on the altar floor, Anne's father raised his pistol and fired it at the creature; the shot had no effect, and the fair-haired clergyman turned and punched her father in the face. He fell away toward the back wall, and Anne lost sight of him.

At a shouted command from Branwell, the young clergyman unstrapped the leather satchel and reached into it with both shaking hands; and what he was holding when the satchel fell away was a big animal's hairless head, bigger than his own, with a bulging cranium, blinking white eyes, and a short snout over a slack mouth studded with fangs.

It was shaking violently in his hands. "She's resisting!" he cried. "She doesn't want to leave it!"

"Force it!" shouted Branwell.

The beast from under the stone stood with its forelegs on the church floor; it rocked its torso back, and a booming cry rang out of its open throat.

Anne made herself look away from the monster and the clergyman to Saltmeric. He was shuffling backward, staring wide-eyed at the thing standing in the hole in the center aisle, until his heels hit the raised altar floor and he sat down. The two common-looking men who had accompanied the intruders were now on their knees beside the altar, apparently praying.

The gun dropped from Saltmeric's limp fingers, and Anne began nimbly leaping over the pews toward the altar.

Evan Saltmeric stared in horror at the thing that was half of his two-person god. Reverend Farfleece, holding the awful head, turned to look back at him and croaked, "Help me, damn you!"—but Saltmeric frantically pushed himself backward across the altar floor, for seen through the oiled spectacles Farfleece's face was sunken and withered, scored with unthinkable old sins.

Farfleece spat and turned back to face the monster. He was raising the naked, twitching head up toward the beast, and the beast's

forelegs lifted to take it; the big paws ended in blunt fingers, which closed around the head. The head's mouth was opening and closing rapidly now—clearly the ghost of the woman whom Saltmeric had murdered was experiencing as much terror as it was capable of.

The beast's clutching fingers lifted the head, and its thick forelegs bent out to the sides as the handlike paws turned it to face forward and set it on its shoulders. The jaws still opened and closed spasmodically, though more slowly.

Saltmeric saw that one of the Brontë sisters had scrambled over the pews and now stood on a wooden bench only a few yards from the now-intact wolf thing. In her left hand she held up what appeared to be two black sticks—and then she jerked her hand down.

And the monster pitched heavily forward onto Reverend Farfleece, crushing him beneath its chest. Its newly attached head lifted on its corded bull neck—the eyes had turned glittering black, and through the spectacles Saltmeric saw Mrs. Flensing's ghost vomited out of its mouth. The thistledown ghost rolled across the floor and then scuttled away toward the door to the sacristy, its bag head bobbing. Saltmeric stepped to the side, horrified at the idea of catching its imbecilic attention.

The Brontë girl leaped over the last pew—Saltmeric saw that in her right hand she held some sort of dioscuri—and she hurried to where her father lay against the wall. The other Brontë sister, carrying a similar knife, was running up the side aisle.

The Brontë lad, clearly possessed now by the other half of the god, had come clattering down the pulpit steps, and he ran to the creature that still stood in the pit. It flexed its shoulders and lifted its torso off of the limp, shrunken form of Farfleece; and it extended a big paw to touch the young man's bandaged head.

The Brontë girl beside her father wailed and threw her knife, and Saltmeric couldn't tell which figure she meant to hit. As it happened, the spinning blades glanced off her brother's shoulder, and in a moment Saltmeric could see blood on the slashed shirt.

The young man gave his sister a cold, contemptuous glance, then stepped to the flank of the beast and swung a leg over its spine. He hiked himself up until he was straddling the big werewolf god and clutching its coarse fur. The creature crouched—and then sprang entirely out of the hole and right over the pews to the side aisle,

slamming into the wall and knocking the other Brontë sister sprawling. In two bounds it and its rider had reached the open side door; the rider ducked, and then they had disappeared outside.

The two acolytes Farfleece had brought along from London, who had proved useless in the big reality of this event, cast stricken glances at Saltmeric and the Brontë girl on the altar, then ran away down the side aisle. They edged cautiously around the other Brontë girl and, after peering fearfully around the doorframe, ran off toward Main Street.

Saltmeric stood up and hurried to where old Reverend Brontë was propped against the back wall. Saltmeric had lost his hat at some point, and he pushed the oiled spectacles up into his hair.

"Anne," the old man said, "where's Charlotte?"

"Here," said the other Brontë sister, limping up onto the altar floor. She scowled uncertainly at Saltmeric. "What do you intend? You were going to shoot us."

Saltmeric didn't trust himself to speak, and could only shake his head.

The one called Charlotte was still holding what seemed to be a makeshift dioscuri, its blades pointed in his direction. She panted, "Do you mean us further harm?"

"No, I never—" Saltmeric shook his head and turned to Anne. "That horrible creature—I believe you made it fall, onto Farfleece! How—"

"Welsh has Branwell's body," interrupted old Patrick Brontë hastily. "He's gone to redeem your promissory notes, and—ahh!— unite completely with his restored sister at that"—he paused to cough, then went on breathlessly—"at that primordial pagan church." He managed to stand up, and even in the dim light through the stained glass windows Saltmeric could see that the skin around one of the old man's eyes was discolored and swelling.

Saltmeric spoke quickly. "This wasn't something I ever wanted." His coat hung heavily on his shoulders, but he shivered at Charlotte's stare as if he were naked. "Knowingly sought. God help me."

Charlotte didn't lower her bound-together knives.

"Can we—" said Brontë. He coughed and went on, "I heard a carriage outside—it's no use on the moors, but we can free the horses. I can ride to Ponden Kirk—and stop them."

Saltmeric struggled to keep incredulity and pity from showing in his strained face.

"Papa," said Charlotte, at last looking away from Saltmeric, "there won't be saddles, and—"

"There'll be the saddle strap of the harness. I can hang on."

"And," said Anne, panting and clearly struggling to keep her voice level, "even in this weather over bad terrain, that demon—did you see it?—can surely cover the three miles to Ponden Kirk in the time it would take you to ride a mile. You should be in bed, you're hurt."

Saltmeric recalled a magical grove, a *mundus loci,* that Mrs. Flensing had once described to him, with arches that opened onto places of power.

"I—" he began.

His throat closed against what he was about to say. The action he was about to propose horrified him.

The old man and his daughters looked at him warily.

"I was told," Saltmeric said, forcing out the words, "that there's a druidic standing stone very near here, called Boggarts Green . . . ?"

"A mile west," said old Brontë, with obvious disapproval.

"West—of course. Then I . . . *believe* . . . I know a way to get to Ponden Kirk more quickly."

The younger daughter, Anne, stepped up to him and stared into his face; he looked away and she slapped him.

"Look at me," she said. Her voice was steady. When he met her eyes, she went on, "What's your name?"

"Evan Saltmeric, Miss," he answered humbly.

"Evan Saltmeric, do you renounce Satan and all his works?"

"I—What? That's what they say in baptism, isn't it?" She raised her hand again and he went on quickly, "I don't know about Satan, ma'am. But I renounce," he said with a wave out toward Farfleece's body and the hole in the floor, "I really do, all *this* damnable business."

"And your part in it? I pulled the monster down onto your *Farfleece* by waving two severed fingers of the woman you murdered last year."

Saltmeric forced himself not to look away from her eyes, though his face was hot. "I do renounce it," he said huskily.

"You'll doubtless find your own penance," she said, stepping back.

I fear I will, thought Saltmeric. Abruptly he recalled something Mrs. Flensing had told him about entry into the *mundus loci*: it required a certain sort of escort. "Er—I'll need those fingers."

Charlotte whispered some objection, but Anne said, "I dropped them over there," and hurried down to the nave floor; she looked around, and peered for a moment into the big hole in the central aisle, then bent and picked up the two black sticks Saltmeric had seen her holding earlier.

In a moment she was beside him again; she handed him the dried fingers and stepped back, wiping her hand on her coat. "You can get me to Ponden Kirk quickly?"

"It has to be me," said her father as Saltmeric nodded. "I brought Welsh to England," her father went on, "and it's me, if anyone, who can dispatch him."

"Hurry, then," said Saltmeric, tucking the fingers into his shirt pocket and walking quickly away toward the open side door. He could hear old Brontë shuffling along right behind him.

"Papa!" cried both of his daughters in unison, starting after the two of them. In moments they were all outside in the cold rainy wind.

The carriage and two horses still stood in the lane beside the church, and old Brontë hobbled toward it. "I can unbuckle the harnesses," he said.

But Saltmeric held out a hand toward Charlotte, and after a brief hesitation she gave him her twined-together knives.

Saltmeric hurried past Patrick and simply sawed through all the straps that held the traces onto the horses. He tucked the knives carefully into his coat pocket.

Brontë's white hair clung in wet strands to his forehead. "Get me up," he said, and Saltmeric bent and wove his fingers together to give the old man a stirrup. As Anne and Charlotte both protested, Brontë set a boot in Saltmeric's hands, and Saltmeric heaved him up onto the horse's back. The old man quickly took hold of the saddle strap.

Saltmeric crossed to the other horse and gripped the saddle-strap and the curved wooden hames at the top of the harness, and jumped, pulling himself up. He managed to get one leg over the horse's rump, and then he was straddling the horse, clinging to the wet saddle strap and wondering how long he could ride this way without falling off.

He looked down at Anne. "Pray for me," he said. He slid the oiled speactacles back down onto his nose and pulled the two dried black fingers from his shirt pocket. He took a deep breath, then held them up and beckoned with them. "Mrs. Flensing," he called through the rain. "You know me. Come."

Brontë and his daughters blinked at him in surprise, then quickly looked around at the paved walk and the churchyard; but they weren't wearing spectacles smeared with illuminating oil, and so they didn't see the indistinct form that appeared from around the far corner of the church and hobbled clumsily but quickly to his horse.

He squinted through the spectacles at the horse's head; the ghost was now tangled in the bit and harness. He put the fingers back in his shirt pocket.

A hand like a cluster of withered ferns rose from in front of the horse's head, followed by a frail membranous bag that rippled under the impacts of raindrops. Another feathery hand appeared, and on this hand two grotesquely long fingers trembled in the wind. In the front of the bag a hole opened and closed several times, and he realized that Mrs. Flensing's ghost was trying to speak.

What could she be trying to say to him, her murderer?

You'll doubtless find your own penance, Anne had said.

"Wait," he groaned to the ghost.

He pulled the long reins out from under his leg, and wished he had thought to cut them short. Forcing himself to look away from the ghost, he blinked through the rain at the old man mounted beside him.

"Lead the way," he said to Patrick, and flapped the clumsy reins.

The two horses trotted away from the church, past the low wall beyond which stood the clustered gravestones of the churchyard. Saltmeric glanced that way, and was surprised to see no ghosts bobbing among the trees; though the hands of Mrs. Flensing's recently freed ghost still clung to the horse's bridle, and the wobbly head was still visble between the unsuspecting horse's ears.

They passed the parsonage, and Saltmeric cursed and released the saddle strap with one hand to snatch the oiled and water-beaded spectacles off his face; he shoved them into his shirt pocket beside the dried fingers, and again gripped the strap with both hands. Unable

to see Mrs. Flensing's ghost now, he squinted at the landscape ahead. After a hundred yards the path they were on was an agitated serpentine pond that spread out over flattened grass on either side. Landmarks had to be difficult to make out, and one of old Brontë's eyes was swollen shut.

He called to Brontë, who was riding ahead, "You know the way?"

Brontë just dug his heels into his horse's flank, and soon both horses were galloping through the puddles, and Saltmeric gritted his teeth and hung on as water and mud splashed up in his face from the tossing hooves of the horse ahead.

After about a mile Brontë reined in his horse. He swung a leg over the horse's shoulders and dropped to the mud, then turned impatiently to Saltmeric. An ancient stone stood tall in a little lake on the north side of the road.

Saltmeric slid off his own horse. He raised a hand toward Brontë, who was gesturing impatiently at the stone, and walked around to the horse's head. He pulled the spectacles out of his pocket and fitted them on his face.

Viewed through the wet, oiled lenses, Mrs. Flensing's ghost looked like a crushed wasp's nest tangled in a handful of bracken; but it was flexing as if with rapid breath, and tendrils of it curled and uncurled in the rain.

"Screw your courage to the sticking point!" shouted Brontë.

Find your own penance, Saltmeric thought, and reached out with both hands, took hold of the thing, and tugged.

And it *sprang* free, and attached itself like a clinging spiderweb to his face. The spectacles weren't being pressed against his nose, but the wrinkled mushroom head was blocking his view, and he exhaled as if he'd been punched in the stomach—and he couldn't draw in another breath.

He clawed the head down so that he could see the tall stone, though his lungs were jerking uselessly; and he blundered around the far side of the stone, hoping he accurately recalled Mrs. Flensing's long-ago description of this *mundus loci*.

He took two running steps—

—and it was as if he had crossed through an unseen gate into a big enclosed arboretum. His boots were scuffing on the willow-bordered path Mrs. Flensing had told him about. He clawed the ghost off his

face and threw it into the shadows between the hanging fronds beside the path, and then for several seconds he just stood bent forward with his hands on his knees, gasping and blinking around at his impossible surroundings.

The air was warmer, and the rain and its constant drumming were gone. The path was dry, and dimly lit by such moonlight as made its way through leafy boughs far overhead. He had successfully found the *mundus loci*, but the unnatural stillness of the place only increased his anxiety. He took off the distorting eyeglasses and tucked them back into his pocket, half-hoping that he might be facing the stormy moor again, but the willows and the path were still visible in front of him.

And Patrick Brontë was right behind him. The old man sniffed at the stagnant water reek, and his unswollen eye was narrowed disapprovingly. "This is a devils' place," he said.

"And you pursue devils," Saltmeric panted. He looked back, past Brontë, and his face chilled to see the path and the willows extending many yards behind them, with no gap. "I think we need to hurry."

He led the way along the curving path, eyeing the deeply shadowed areas behind the willows, where unimaginable inhabitants of this region shifted and rattled. He looked back—Brontë was following him, hastily unwinding the long scarf from around his neck. After several more paces the old man pulled it free, and dropped it on the path.

"I think I can no longer clutch my shroud," he muttered.

Soon Saltmeric saw firelight reflected on the willow leaves ahead of them, and he ran forward in the brightening glow until he stepped around a cluster of trees and stood at the edge of the broad clearing Mrs. Flensing had described. Brontë stepped up beside him, and gasped.

The clearing was roughly forty yards wide, lit by flaring upright torches around the perimeter. The sky was now entirely hidden by the spreading leafy branches of the enormous oak tree whose massive trunk filled the center of the clearing and hid the far side of it. In fact the trunk gave the impression of an arboreal castle, with its many open arches, its panels of carving, and the tiers of balconies that receded out of sight overhead.

Clusters of shrunken old men and women sat against the trunk

between the arches, apparently asleep, the colored ribbons on their wrists and ankles trailing across the packed dirt; but they leaped to their feet when Saltmeric and Brontë stepped out into the clearing.

"I saw a parson twelve feet high!" said one of them shrilly. *"A juggler who can dent the sky!"* added another.

Saltmeric noted that the little people, even the ones in tattered dresses and bonnets, all seemed to have knives in knitted sheaths hung on ribbons around their scrawny necks. He nodded to them cautiously as he led Brontë across the rippled dirt of the clearing, and halted a couple of yards short of the curved rough wall of the tree's trunk. The little people scuttled away to either side.

From where Saltmeric was standing he could see three broad arches in the trunk, one directly ahead and two at oblique angles. The one in front of them was the opening of a tunnel that appeared to extend much farther than the diameter of the tree, or the clearing, and Saltmeric believed the spot of light at the far end of it was bright daylight; curls of aromatic smoke drifted from the arch to his left, and the one on his right echoed with distant laughter.

He turned to the nearest of the diminutive dwellers in this *mundus loci* and asked, "Which arch leads to Ponden Kirk?"

The little man goggled at him without speaking, and Brontë said, "The big black stone church with the fairy cave at its base."

"Ah, that's between God's windward and His lee," the little man said as he scuttled away in a flurry of ribbons. Another piped up, *"And what might you have brought us for a fee?"*

From the cluster of little people came a cry, *"The stolen children pine for bones to chew,"* followed by, *"And surely these could spare us one or two."*

Several of them were touching the knives that hung around their necks.

Saltmeric was sweating—Mrs. Flensing hadn't mentioned paying these creatures a fee for passage, much less that it would involve surrendering one's bones!

He stared at the wrinkled little people, and for just a moment they seemed indeed to be children; sunken-eyed and hollow-cheeked, but not one of them more than ten years old. He blinked, and they were again all hunched and old.

It was clear that Brontë too had seen the momentary vision, for he

stepped back, his fist pressed against his mouth. "The children who disappear at night," he whispered. "We never find bodies!"

Saltmeric's ears seemed to ring, and he peered more closely at the once-again aged little figures. These, he thought, at the center of Mrs. Flensing and Farfleece's whirlpool!

He pulled Mrs. Flensing's fingers from his shirt pocket—and as his fingers brushed the spectacles he felt the lens frames vibrate, as if to an unheard scream. But he held out the two blackened sticks on his palm.

"A werewolf's fingers," he said gruffly.

"Ah!" breathed several of the little people, and one of them, wearing a tattered frock, stepped up and gingerly poked the fingers. *"Two of them!"* she said wonderingly. *"The roots will get no blood tonight, alas—but for these holy bones we'll let you pass."*

Many of them were still touching their knives.

"Here," said Saltmeric, tossing one of the fingers to the last speaker. "I'll give you the other when you've shown us the Ponden Kirk arch."

The little people excitedly led Saltmeric and Brontë around the trunk of the tree. The fouled air was beginning to make Saltmeric dizzy, and for several moments it seemed as if he and the old curate were simply lifting and dropping their feet in place while the vast tree itself rotated.

At last their diminutive escorts paused before an arch on the other side of the trunk. Peering around the edge, Saltmeric could see a bundle of straw on a stone block, and a crude stone wall a couple of yards beyond it with a doorway opening on a gray sky. A cold wind buffeted his face when he stepped into the arch.

He tossed the second finger to his escorts, who fell to squabbling over it.

Patrick Brontë had already stepped through the arch and was hurrying to the open doorway. Saltmeric hesitated; it looked as if he had fulfilled his promise to the old man. But he was sure that retracing his steps would not lead him to any way back to the Boggarts Green stone . . . though he might find Mrs. Flensing's ghost along the dim path, waiting for him.

And he found that he couldn't leave old Brontë alone to face whatever waited beyond that doorway.

He swore and stepped forward into the cold wind.

He was standing in a low, stone-walled room with a dripping thatched roof. The bundle of straw moved, doubtless because of the wind; but out through the doorway he saw Brontë hurrying through rain toward the weedy edge of a precipice.

"Wait!" called Saltmeric, and he hurried out through the doorway onto an uneven surface of mud and rocks under a charcoal sky. Brontë had paused, and Saltmeric looked back—the two of them had emerged from some pre-Roman stone structure, possibly a Celtic temple. The back wall had a narrow opening in it, but there was no sign of the arch or the remembered clearing.

He shrugged, and plodded through the mud to stand beside Brontë in the rainy wind at the edge of the precipice.

CHAPTER EIGHTEEN

Emily had fitted on the oiled spectacles several times during the long stormy trek to Ponden Kirk, and though she hadn't wiped off the rainwater for fear of losing the oil on the lenses, she had been able to see that her crowd of following ghosts had lingered on the north side of Dean Beck; and as she and Curzon had moved on and covered the last mile—along flooded paths and over rock-studded hills—flashes of lightning had let her glimpse the frail, flailing shapes of ghosts coming through the rain from all directions.

And at last Ponden Kirk had loomed black against the dark gray sky, standing upright on the slope below the western plateau, its flat top level with the plateau. From this angle Emily couldn't see the entrance to the fairy cave at the base of it, but even after seventeen years she remembered the way up to it.

She paused, staring up through the veils of rain, and only when Keeper barked a warning and she exhaled involuntarily did she think to pull the spectacles from her pocket again and look around through the blurred lenses.

The bag-headed things were clustered closely around her, and she consciously took a deep breath against their ineffective resistance, forcing herself not to gag at the rotten-egg smell of their open mouth holes. She believed she could sense frustration in the ghosts, and she hurriedly batted her way out of the crowd to take several breaths of air that smelled only of wet stone and soil.

The ghosts drifted after her, and she and Keeper stepped rapidly up the slope to where Curzon stood.

Under the brim of his dripping hat, Curzon narrowed his eye. "They're still right with us, I gather," he said.

"Yes." She took off the spectacles. "Give me your flint and steel."

He handed them to her, and she slid them into a pocket of her coat along with the spectacles. Then she crouched beside Keeper. "You," she told him sternly, "*stay*. For now."

The big mastiff understood her, and though he gave her a mourful look, he sat down beside Curzon's boots.

Emily turned to look down the slope. Without the specactles she couldn't see her insubstantial pursuers, but the wind was turbulent around the towering black edifice. She exhaled in the direction of the ghosts—then faced the plateau and begain scrambling up the slope.

When she had pulled and scuffed her way to the bottom blocks of Ponden Kirk, she hurried around the corner of it and hiked herself up into the narrow opening. Water sluiced noisily through channels between the stones. The cave was in darkness, but she found that she remembered where the ledge was on which she and Anne and Branwell had perched, seventeen years ago.

She didn't have to put on the spectacles again to know that the ghosts had followed her up the slope—when she paused, her breath was abruptly sucked out of her lungs. She inhaled forcefully in response.

She crawled into the little cave and felt her way across the wet, tilted stone surfaces to the narrow opening at the far end—the gap, she recalled, through which superstitious girls would crawl in hopes of marrying within the year.

From her pocket she tugged the rain-soaked bundle of manuscripts—hers, Anne's, and Branwell's—and laid it on the stone where the three of them had sat, so long ago. She shook her head and crawled to the gap between the stones at the far end of the little cave.

Bracing one hand on a stone surface close above her head, she unfolded her legs out through the opening into the wind; then rolled over and let herself slide out until her boots touched the mud of the slope outside. She blew strongly back into the cave, and felt spiderweb touches against her face. Clearly a number of the ghosts had followed her into the fairy cave—perhaps all of them, since they occupied no appreciable volume.

"Goodbye, poor—" she began, but she was interrupted by an echoing howl from the valley. She looked to her right and saw Curzon and Keeper ten yards away down the slope, facing an enormous mastiff—and sitting astride the beast's shoulders was a figure that even at this distance she recognized as Branwell.

Quickly she fumbled the flint and the curved steel rod from her pocket, and she struck the steel with the flint.

Sparks flared in the darkness of the cave, and she ducked; and a gout of flame shot out of the narrow opening over her head, lighting the blocks of Ponden Kirk's south face.

Emily slid down the hill, able to see projecting rocks in her way by the radiance of new fire behind her. She ran down the last few yards to the roughly level ground.

Curzon had clearly engaged the monstrous wolf-creature, for his coat was in tatters and the blades of the dioscuri he held glittered red in the glare from Ponden Kirk behind him; and the beast now reared back, baring its fangs and flexing its hind legs for a lunge—when, mounted on its back, Branwell screamed and convulsed, bending so far backward that Emily thought he must snap his spine.

He sagged and rolled off into the mud, and the creature lowered its forelegs and wailed as it turned its massive head to look down at him.

Blinking rainwater out of her eyes, Emily thought at first that her brother had immediately sprung to his feet. Peering more closely, she saw that his body still lay in the mud, and the figure that had leaped up was a piebald thing made of bubbling mud and wriggling clumps of grass.

It turned to face the radiance of the fire up in the fairy cave. A mouth opened in its featureless head, and a windy voice issued from it, haltingly, apparently attempting to form words.

Emily thought Keeper leaped at the man-shaped thing and tore out its fibrous throat, but Keeper nudged her thigh and she realized that it was the ghost Keeper that was attacking the thing.

And she knew then that the mud-and-grass figure was the fully exorcised ghost of Welsh, cut off at last from Branwell by the cleansing fire in the fairy cave, and that it had managed to draw up substance from the ground to form this last crude approximation of a body.

The ghost Keeper evaded the big werewolf's thrusting jaws and leaped again, and tore the Welsh figure's head free of its body; it collapsed, now just a pile of soggy dirt in the rain. The ghost dog vanished.

The beast pawed at the sodden remains of its twin and lifted its head to wail again into the low sky. Keeper loped to the sprawled figure of Branwell, set his teeth firmly in the back of Branwell's coat, and began dragging him away from the monstrous creature that stood above them on four massive legs.

The big werewolf lowered its head and lunged toward Emily, but Keeper let go of Branwell's coat and leaped at the thing's face, clawing its eyes before springing clear and landing poised to attack again; and Curzon darted in and drove his dioscuri at one of the thing's eyes.

It jerked its head to the side, knocking Curzon onto his back, and for two seconds its fangs tore at him as he repeatedly stabbed up at its eyes and nose; then it fell back, howling, and he rolled free. With one more double-edged slash at the thing's face, Curzon retreated up the slope, hunched and clutching his stomach with his free hand.

Branwell had sat up, and for a moment gaped at the monstrous creature as it dug its claws into the ground, and then he was crawling rapidly away from it; after a few yards he got to his feet and ran blindly up the slope.

He rushed past Emily with no sign of recognition and went clawing his way up the rising ground on the north side of Ponden Kirk.

Keeper had feinted at the werewolf and then hurried back to where Emily stood, and as he turned and bared his teeth at it, she raised her dioscuri; and a moment later Curzon was beside her with his own. His wet face was gaunt and haggard, his coat was gone, and his flayed shirt was drenched in blood. His free hand still clutched his abdomen, but his extended hand was steady, and the four blades, his dioscuri and Emily's, gleamed in the shifting orange light from behind them.

The creature gathered its hindquarters for another leap, but a simultaneous white glare and crash of thunder shook the ground— a bolt of lightning had struck a tree some dozen yards behind the werewolf, and the creature convulsed; Keeper sprang back and Emily felt an electric tingle in her legs.

Then, over the ringing in her ears and the constant thrash of the rain, she heard her father's voice—

"Emily!" her father bellowed. "Make distance!"

Branwell had scrambled up the shallower slope on the north side of Ponden Kirk, and in his disoriented panic he hadn't spared a glance at the flames billowing out of the fairy cave to his left. Within a minute the ground under his grasping hands and thrusting boots had leveled out, and he was standing on the plateau.

Scarcely visible through the rain, a little stone building he'd never seen before raised its thatched roof against the low sky to his right, while ahead of him two figures stood gesturing on the level top of Ponden Kirk. The cold wind blew streamers of smoke around them, and their faces were underlit by the inexplicable blaze below.

One of them—Branwell rubbed his eyes and peered again—one of them was, impossibly, his father!

A third figure was rapidly approaching the two from the direction of the low stone building—a short upright column with waving arms but no distinct head. Achingly aware that his father was standing on the edge of a long drop, Branwell ran across the intervening mud and out onto the flat wet stones that were the top of Ponden Kirk.

The man standing beside his father turned around and visibly flinched, either at the sight of Branwell so close or the moving thing that had come out of the stone house; and he raised a knife.

With a last exhausted sprint, Branwell shoved the man away from his father, though the two blades of the descending knife slashed the back of his own wrist.

The man stepped back, and overbalanced; and in the startled moment when it was clear that he would not be able to right himself, he tossed the knife toward Branwell's father. Then he had toppled silently away out of sight below.

Branwell's father had caught the knife by its grip, and he turned toward Branwell. Branwell stared at the weapon in alarm, and saw that it was actually two knives, tied together. And Branwell noted the detail that for once his father was not wearing his scarf.

Branwell held his hands out to the sides. "It's me, Papa!"

One of Patrick's eyes was bruised and swollen shut, but he peered

at Branwell with the other, then exhaled and dropped the makeshift dioscuri. The old man turned back to face the valley.

Patrick raised his arms, and the crude figure from the stone house moved up beside him. Now that it was only a few feet away, Branwell could see that it was a bundle of straw, with two smaller bundles like arms, one of which now extended to touch his father's back.

Branwell reached out to stop it. A moment later he found himself sitting in wet grass several yards behind the two figures who stood at the edge of the drop.

His father flung his arms down, and a simuntaneous flare of lightning and bellow of thunder shook the midair raindrops and rocked Branwell back.

"Emily!" his father roared. "Make distance!"

Branwell was never able, afterward, to fully describe what he saw in the ensuing seconds.

Where his father had stood was now a taller figure, in metal armor that mimicked a bare torso; but when it turned its helmeted head toward him he recognized his father's face. Beside that figure now stood a woman radiating blue light—she too was very tall, and Branwell was profoundly glad that he was seeing only her back, for he was sure that this was a goddess, and that his soul would be crushed if she were to turn and look him in the eye.

Patrick's one open eye blazed in her blue radiance.

The giant that was his father turned back to look down at the valley below Ponden Kirk, and he raised both arms again and then flung them down by his armored sides.

In the same instant a second bolt of lightning lanced down out of the sky with a crash that shook the ground under Branwell.

Branwell could see nothing but the afterimage of the jagged fracture the lightning had made in the sky, but he could feel hot blood on his wrist, and in spite of the fire below, the wind up here was mercilessly cold. He stood up and blundered forward carefully until his groping hand met a frail cold hand that he was sure was his father's.

From the undazzled corner of his eye Branwell was able to see the recognizable silhouette of his father against the fire glow from below, and he pulled the old man away from the edge and off the stone onto grassy dirt. His father looked over his shoulder, and

Branwell hastily looked back too; but the figure that had been a bundle of straw in one moment and a goddess in the next was gone, and there was only familiar flat ground where the stone building had briefly stood.

They both sat down. "Papa," Branwell gasped, "what happened? Who *were* you, there?"

"I was . . . Brontes. Do hush, boy."

After taking several deep breaths, his father shook himself and began laboriously getting to his feet.

"That man who fell," Patrick said. "He's probably hurt. We should attend to his injuries."

Branwell thought of asking whether the man had in fact been threatening his father; then decided that he didn't want to know, yet.

He stood up too. "The slope is shallower on this side," he said, leading his father away from the top of Ponden Kirk toward the way he had come.

Emily, Curzon, and Keeper had retreated halfway up the slope toward the flaring oven that was Ponden Kirk when the second lightning bolt struck, and all three of them were knocked down by an electric shock as the air shivered to the hard blast of thunder.

Emily had made herself roll over to look down the hill, and she quickly glanced right and left before she realized that the exploded smoldering wreckage on the level ground down there was the remains of the big werewolf—Welsh's twin, now as thoroughly banished as Welsh.

Beside her, Keeper thrashed his legs and then stood up, fur bristling, looking around and growling. Curzon had rolled down the slope, and Emily crawled to him on her hands and knees.

He was lying facedown, and she braced one boot against a stone and rolled him over. His one eye was open but his arm flopped loosely; his coat and shirt had been ripped away by the werewolf's fangs, and as rain diluted the welling blood she could see great rents in the flesh of his chest and abdomen. She leaned down over his face, and felt fast, hot breath against her cheek.

"Alcuin!" she said clearly. "Alcuin!"

His lips parted. "Go back," he whispered, "to your sheep, girl."

Footsteps crunched on the slope to her left, and she groped

around until she found her dropped dioscuri—but it was Branwell and, incredibly, her father who were making their way across the uneven incline, their wet faces lit in coppery chiaroscuro by the flames that still billowed out from the sides of Ponden Kirk.

"The man who fell is dead," called her father through the downpour. Emily hadn't known that anybody had fallen. He peered past her. "Has Mr. Curzon . . . left us as well?"

Branwell shambled up, just staring at Curzon's wounds and shivering. His left hand was streaked with blood, but he was able to brush wet hair from his forehead with it.

"He heals," Emily said, "but help me drag him up closer to the fire." Curzon's dioscuri was lying next to his right hand, and she picked it up and slid it and her own into the pocket of her coat.

"We should all be closer to the fire," said her father, clearly trying to address immediate concerns in order to hide vast bewiderment. He looked up the slope. "But it won't last till morning."

"I don't know," said Emily. "Ghosts must have a lot of memories to burn." She got to her feet and peered through the rain down the dark valley. "Afterward I should check on your horse."

Her father waved dismissively, and Emily guessed that the horse he must have ridden here had been tethered too close to the first lightning strike—which he himself had surely summoned.

Emily! she recalled his shout. *Make distance!*

One of her father's eyes was closed and the skin around it was bruised and swollen. She would have questions for him soon.

Keeper and Emily did most of the work of dragging Curzon's heavy body up to within a few yards of the base of Ponden Kirk. The air was hot—on both sides of Ponden Kirk flames gushed from the two openings of the fairy cave, and the gaps between the big facing stones glowed. Emily sat down beside Curzon, and she noticed the body of a man lying in the weeds nearby. Keeper sniffed at it and came back to her.

She rubbed the big mastiff's head and ran her fingers through the wet fur along his shoulders and flanks and legs, and was reassured to find only superficial cuts. She patted her own arms and legs and ribs, but bruises seemed to be the only injuries she had suffered.

Curzon was lying on his back, and she saw that his ravaged chest was still rising and falling. She lay back on the grass and let the rain

drum on her face as she tried to get her aching muscles to relax. "Who was he?" she finally asked her father.

Patrick was sitting closest to the fire, warming his spread hands. "Evan Saltmeric," he said over his shoulder. "An enemy who became an ally in the end. He brought me here."

Emily rolled her head to look again at the body, though all she could see from where she lay was one boot. Who were you? she wondered; then reached up to pat Keeper's shoulder.

Branwell was hugging himself and alternately looking at the dead man and up at the top of Ponden Kirk. Once he gave his father a searching glance, then quickly looked away.

Her father shifted on the wet grass and stones. "We must find shelter. Do you know of any cave, old farmhouse, nearby?"

Emily sat up and turned to face the furnace that was the fairy cave. "We couldn't move Mr. Curzon," she said, "and I won't leave him." She turned the other way and looked out into the dark rainy night. "Mr. Saltmeric's horse may have survived. One of us might ride back and get help."

Her father shook his head. "Saltmeric and I didn't come on horseback."

Emily raised an eyebrow. "You certainly didn't walk."

Curzon was suddenly breathing in harsh gasps. His eye was now tightly shut, and his fingers clawed at the grass.

Emily bent forward to gently pat his shoulder. To the others she said, "He's healing."

"Before our eyes?" said her father, eyeing Curzon with alarm. "Is he himself—one of the—"

"He was," said Emily. "He . . . made himself unable to change, just as the Huberti used to do."

It clearly meant nothing to Branwell, but old Patrick raised his eyebrows and sat back. "Ah, God!" he whispered, touching his own cheek.

For a while none of them spoke, and the rain did not abate.

Emily shifted to get the heat of the fire on her back. "How did you and"—she waved toward the dead man—"Mr. Saltmeric get here, then?"

Her father had been facing the fire, but now turned toward her. "What? Oh—I doubted you yesterday, you know, when you told us your story about the magical grove of willows accessible by Boggarts

Green. But Mr. Saltmeric knew of it, and he and I rode to that stone and entered that—hub place, that—"

"*Mundus loci,*" Emily supplied.

"Yes—yes, that's what it was. The willows, the giant tree, the lost children—"

"Those dwarves?"

Patrick closed his unswollen eye and nodded. "I believe those are the children that have been stolen by the gytrashes and boggarts, over the years."

Emily shuddered, recalling the stunted, wizened creatures. Beyond rescue now, she thought.

"To be remembered in our prayers." Patrick opened his eye and went on, wearily: "And Mr. Saltmeric gave them—a werewolf's fingers!—in exchange for—"

"I gave those to Anne!" interrupted Emily, suddenly anxious. "How did he get them?"

"She's come to no harm!" Patrick assured her. "After the twin," he went on, with a wave toward the still-smoldering ribs and scattered bones at the bottom of the slope, "broke out from under the ledger stone and started for here with . . . well, she gave the fingers to him. After she all but baptized him."

Curzon rolled away from the others and raised his knees to his chest. "Go," he said hoarsely. "Leave me."

"I never do," Emily told him.

"I'll be," he grated, "fine, in an hour or so. You people—in this rain—will not."

"There's a fire, too costly to waste." Emily turned to her father.

"In exchange for the werewolf's fingers," he resumed, raising his hands, "the children showed us an archway in the trunk of that axis tree. I went through—and it led directly to a primitive stone temple up there on the plateau, at the top of Ponden Kirk!"

Branwell moaned and looked at his father with something like fear.

"It was Minerva's temple," said Emily in a voice that she forced to be level. "She gave you what you asked for, forty years ago: the armor—and weapon!—of the cyclops."

Patrick let his hands drop. "Yes. For a moment I was one of them, wielding the lightning."

"Brontes," said Branwell. "I saw it, and I saw *her*, for a moment, from the back—"

"From the back? You're fortunate," said Emily, recalling that Curzon had nearly been driven out of his senses by facing Minerva.

Branwell was clawing his sopping hair with the fingers of both hands. "I'm alone now, I have no one but me." He let his hands slide down to clasp his chest. "But the armor of the cyclopes? The lightning! Truly?"

"I've kept things from you," Emily told him. "We all have. But I've never lied to you."

"But how could I know none of this?"

His father spoke slowly. "It's a shameful story that I hoped to take to my grave . . . but last year I had to inform your sisters. You were—"

Branwell nodded miserably. "Possessed. And now I'm left empty. Even Northangerland has abandoned me."

"You're still God's possession," Emily told him, "even if He's left you out in the weather a bit."

Branwell shivered in the rain and didn't reply.

The rain had already begun to lessen, and within half an hour it had stopped. The fire in the fairy cave was still burning at dawn, though in the early sunlight the flames that had been glaring through the night were just gold-tinted heat ripples in the air. Branwell and Patrick had moved closer to it several times during the night, and Branwell was now in a light, restless sleep. Emily and Keeper reclined against a rock a few feet away from them. Curzon had got to his feet during the last hour; when Emily twice tried to speak quietly to him he waved her to silence. Clothing was still damp, but not cold, and when Emily rubbed Keeper's fur she found it entirely dry.

By the time the sun had risen high enough in a cleared blue sky to light the valley, Branwell had snapped and blinked awake, and stood shivering beside his father. Emily and Keeper had already climbed the slope on the north side and found only the old familiar cracked pavements on the plateau, and slid back down to rejoin the others. Curzon had discarded his ruined shirt and taken the dead man's wool scarf and coat; the coat was tight across his shoulders and chest, but he was able to fasten all the buttons.

Emily gave him back his dioscuri, and he slid it into the pocket of Saltmeric's coat.

He caught her disapproving look and said, "Should I leave a couple of coins for him in payment?" He squinted down the valley. "I can walk."

"Slowly," said Emily's father as he stretched and rubbed a shoulder, "for all our sakes." He took a few steps down the hill and looked back. "We can send a party to retrieve Mr. Saltmeric's body."

None of them metioned the conspicuous other body, the charred and exploded carcass of the werewolf god whose fragments were scattered across a wide patch of blackened heather. Branwell looked away as they shuffled past it, but Emily looked closely at the ruin, and was pleased to see that the big skull was shattered even more thoroughly than the one she had shot last year.

And the four of them began the long, slow trek back across the windswept moors to the Haworth parsonage, with Keeper loping watchfully ahead.

CHAPTER NINETEEN

By common unspoken assent, all of them hiked across a muddy field and over a low dry-stone wall rather than stay on the path when it passed close by Boggarts Green. After a couple of hundred feet they made their way back to the path, and when they were within a mile of the parsonage and could see the steeple of the church, John Brown rode up on horseback. Because they had stopped frequently to rest, it was nearly noon.

Brown immediately dismounted, and after a quick look at the bedraggled wayfarers he boosted old Patrick up into the saddle. "You're secure up there, sir?" When the old man assured him that he was fine, Brown turned to Emily. "You found some shelter in the storm, I gather. I'll hurry your father home, running alongside." He glanced at the grim figure of Curzon, and went on, "Somebody pinched a couple of horses from a carriage yesterday, and they wandered back to the church. I'll saddle one of them and bring it along for you."

"For Branwell," Emily told him.

"Oh?" He peered at her brother. "Oh. Yes. Why don't you all rest here with him till I get back?"

Branwell stood up straight, for the moment hardly swaying at all. "I'll walk, sir," he said.

"As you please." Brown gave him a dubious look, then turned to Emily. "For you, Miss Emily?"

She was dizzy and hungry, but she knew she could walk much farther than the remaining distance to the parsonage. She patted Keeper's shoulder and shook her head.

"I'll walk too," growled Curzon.

Brown nodded, started to speak, and closed his mouth. At last he said, uncertainly, "There's questions to be settled. The church floor is a blown-up mess and there's a very old dead clergyman been found there."

"We'll tell you what happened," said Emily, "after we restore ourselves." She pushed back her hair and managed to smile at Brown. "The thing that was under the stone is destroyed."

"Ah?" He peered again at the battered foursome, more carefully. "Like that, is it? Out there last night?" He looked around as if for reassurance at the wet fields in the bright sunlight. "Yes, I will want to hear it."

Brown turned and began jogging away energetically, leading the horse. Emily was relieved to see that her father was relaxed and steady in the saddle.

When the weary party came in sight of the parsonage, Anne and Charlotte and Tabby were already on the path, hurrying toward them.

"Papa's having oatmeal porridge and a cup of tea," said Anne breathlessly when she was still several yards off. She ran to Emily and took her arm. "Mr. Brown told us you were following. You took good care of her?" she added to Keeper, ruffling his massive head. He licked her hand.

Charlotte and Tabby came puffing up in her wake. "Papa's going to bed directly after he's finished his breakfast," said Charlotte. "Where on earth did you all find shelter last night? At Top Withens? Papa won't say."

"Nobody fired a pistol over the churchyard this dawn," said Tabby, "and I don't want to trouble the maister. Will you do it now?"

"It," said Emily, looking at all three of them, "doesn't need to be done anymore."

"Ah?" said Tabby. She turned to Curzon and said, "Thank you, sir."

He looked startled, and tilted his head to blink at her with his one eye. "Thank Miss Emily," he said.

"Both twins ... *gone*?" asked Charlotte.

"Yes," grated Branwell, not sounding entirely pleased.

"And the ..." Charlotte hesitated, then went on, "... the three, er, deaths?"

Emily gave her a tired smile. "In escrow, for now."

"I see. Well, perhaps something can be done about that."

Emily let her suppose it.

"Mr. Curzon," Charlotte continued, "will you—but you'll want to return to your rooms to refresh yourself and lie down for a bit, I expect—will you join us for supper?"

Curzon sighed heavily and shook his head. "Thank you, Miss Brontë, but I must be off to London, and this evening is for your family." He included Tabby in his accompanying wave.

Anne took Branwell's hand and led him toward the house. "Porridge and bed for you too," she told him. Looking back, she called, "Our family is eternally grateful to you, Mr. Curzon, no matter what you say!"

Branwell stopped and turned around. "Yes," he said. "Thank you. For my soul."

Anne smiled at Curzon and resumed pulling her brother away.

Curzon shifted his weight and pulled Saltmeric's damp coat more firmly across his shoulders. Looking up at his dark, craggy profile, Emily believed she saw stoic resignation.

He bowed. "I must go. A—a good day to you all!"

And a moment later he was striding away toward the church and the main street.

"Strange fellow!" exclaimed Tabby. "Are we ever to see him again, do you think?"

Emily saw that neither Tabby nor Charlotte would be sorry if the answer were no.

"Excuse me," she said, and then she and Keeper were hurrying after Curzon, who, to judge by his pace, had indeed recovered from the wounds he had suffered last night.

"Alcuin!" she called.

He stopped by the churchyard wall and turned around. His one eye stared at her uneasily.

She caught up to where he stood, and after a moment she sat down on the wall. Her hat had been lost sometime during yesterday's strenuous activities, and she shook back her hair, which still carried a scorched smell from the immolation of the werewolves in the ravine.

"London?" she said.

He hesitated, then sat on the wall a foot away from her. "En route."

"To the monastery in Rocamadour."

"Emily—yes. Probably." He tilted his head to see her. "And what will you do?"

"Oh—cook, sew, write with Anne, listen to Charlotte's money worries, humor poor Branwell. Go for daylong walks on the moors with Keeper." She shrugged. "The routines that make me happy."

"Ah." He looked over his shoulder at the gravestones. "Are there any left?"

Emily dug in her pocket. When she pulled the spectacles out, she saw that one lens was gone; but she fitted them on and turned to look out across the graves.

"None," she said after peering through the remaining blurred lens for a few moments. She took them off and put them back in her pocket. "More will arrive."

"I daresay." He patted Keeper's head and looked toward the village. "Will the two of you venture back to Ponden Kirk?"

Emily yawned, and remembered only afterward that she should have covered her mouth. "Oh—probably. Not into the fairy cave, but I'd like to see where Minerva's temple was, this time."

Curzon yawned too, and shifted on the wet stone wall. "We all need sleep. You crawled right through the cave yesterday," he went on. "Out through the gap at the far end of it."

"With all the ghosts of Yorkshire at my heels. Yes."

"I gather there's some . . . local folklore, about that. A girl crawling through that gap."

"Yes." She yawned again, this time with her hand over her mouth. "I think I'll sleep for twelve hours! Yes, it's said that a girl who climbs through that opening in the Kirk will marry within the year."

"That was it."

"Nonsense, of course. And a twenty-eight-year-old woman intent on setting fire to ghosts would hardly qualify in any case."

"I suppose not."

"I'm quite content with the life I described just now."

Keeper yawned too, and laid down between their boots.

"As I will be," Curzon said stolidly, "tending the grapevines at the monastery." He stood up and held out his hand.

"Miss Emily Brontë," he said, "it's been . . . an enrichment to know you."

She shook his hand. "I'm glad I found you on the moor last year."

He gave her a crooked smile, nodded to Keeper, and turned away to resume walking toward the main street, though not as rapidly.

Emily watched his back, and his black hair tossing in the wind, until he had disappeared around the corner of the church.

At last she stood up. "Come on, Keeper," she said, and started back toward where Charlotte and Anne waited on the steps of the parsonage.

EPILOGUE–DECEMBER 1848

Blow, west-wind, by the lonely mound,
And murmur, summer streams—
There is no need of other sound
To soothe my lady's dreams.
—Emily Brontë

After only a week away from it, Alcuin Curzon found that he already very much missed the Benedictine monastery at Rocamadour. The monastery stood among several centuries-old churches and shrines on a cliff terrace above the village of Rocamadour and the Alzou River, and beyond the river the green forests of the Causses du Quercy stretched to the limits of sight. Alcuin Curzon had spent these past twenty months working in the monastery as a lay brother of the Benedictine Order, and the two summers in the south of France had left him ill-prepared for a visit to northern England in December.

In the course of this last week he had taken a packet boat from Calais to Dover, then the new South Eastern Railway to London, where he had boarded the first of two carriages that took him to Keighley; and this morning he had hired a carriage to take him the last three miles to Haworth. The rooms he had rented in town in April of last year were no longer available, and he had taken a room at the Black Bull. Immediately after dropping off his luggage and sending a note to Anne Brontë at the parsonage, he had walked up the icy and snow-bordered Main Street to the old church.

The two big front doors had not been locked, and he had pulled one open and slowly walked up the center aisle between the rows of shadowed pews. He paused a few yards short of the raised altar floor.

Did—you bring your knife? she had asked him, the last time he had stood here, more than two years ago. *Are you here to kill me at last?*

But the elevated pulpit where she had stood on that morning was empty now. Curzon looked down at his snow-crusted boots, which stood on a newly cut stone, with no ogham grooves in it.

He turned to look impatiently at the side door, through which Anne should appear . . . if she cared to reply to his note. Her letter to him had been sent in October, but the February Revolution in France, and the ensuing social disorder that had culminated in the establishment of the French Second Republic, had made postal delivery to the monastery even slower than usual. He had finally received her letter only a week ago.

Emily is dying, Anne had written. *She won't see anyone, but I think she would ask to see you, if she thought it were possible, and permitted herself.*

After leaving Haworth last year, Curzon had employed a solicitor in London to keep him apprised of events in the Brontë family, and a month ago Curzon had learned that Branwell had died in September. The solicitor had, in fact, been very thorough.

The church's side door creaked open, and when he turned away from the altar Curzon saw a figure in a hat and overcoat step in and pull the door closed against the gray daylight outside.

"Mr. Curzon," said Anne Brontë, hurrying up the side aisle. "You arrive very near the end, I'm afraid."

"Miss Anne," said Curzon, bowing and stepping forward to meet her, "I set out as soon as I received your letter, but things are disorganized in France at present."

"All over Europe." In the glow from the stained glass window at his back, her face was still youthful, but thinner, and there were new lines at the corners of her eyes. "Branwell—"

He presumed to take her elbow and turn her back toward the side door. "I got news of it. I'm sorry."

"It—went well, actually." She shook her head as she hurried along beside him. "On his last day his delusions left him—he was calm and remorseful, and he prayed and repented his sins. My father was holding him when he died." Curzon pushed the door open and she paused to look up at him. "You and Emily saved him from the devil

that possessed him." As they stepped out onto the snow-covered pavement in front of the churchyard, she added, "I know *you* didn't do it for him, entirely."

"Not entirely," Curzon agreed.

"At the end, he and Charlotte even composed a bit of doggerel, and when he wrote the letter *U* at the end of it, she gave in and wrote a *T* after it." When Curzon gave her a puzzled glance, she went on, "Sorry—that stands for 'Us Two.' "

Curzon gathered that Branwell and Charlotte had not got along, which was hardly surprising. But his concern had never been with them. "Good, good," he muttered.

As they hurried along beside the churchyard wall, he recalled Emily stopping him here, as he had stormed away from the parsonage on the day they had first met; he had told her that she presented an unwelcome inconvenience, but that to save her soul she should leave Haworth with him, and not return to "that house of doomed souls." Her dog, Keeper, had been with her. *He and I defend each other,* she had said.

And in fact, he thought as the parsonage loomed closer and the steam of his breath and Anne's whirled away on the wind, Emily Brontë *has* been an enormous inconvenience, over these past two years and nine months . . . and thank God for it.

He cast his mind back to their very first meeting, when he had lain wounded at the foot of Ponden Kirk. He had originally intended to kill himself that morning, and might still have done it, if Emily Brontë had not found him.

"She saved me too," he said as they hurried up the steps to the front door of the parsonage. "Body and soul."

Anne pulled open the door and closed it quickly after he had followed her into the hall, in which the air was nearly as cold as it was outside.

Anne whispered, "She's in the parlor with Charlotte and our father." She laid a restraining hand on the arm of his coat. "Wait—I think she'd want me to call them away. And you must understand that she is very weak, and—much changed."

Anne walked around the corner into the parlor, and Curzon heard her speaking quietly. A few moments later Charlotte and their father shuffled out into the hall.

Patrick frowned at Curzon with perhaps no recognition, but Charlotte's eyes widened in surprise.

"You!" she whispered. "Did Emily send for you?"

"I did," Anne told her.

Charlotte stared at Curzon for several seconds, then nodded. "Good," she whispered, and led her father away toward the kitchen.

Anne took several steps after them, then looked back. Seeing that Curzon stood without moving, she nodded toward the parlor doorway, then turned to follow her father and sister.

Curzon took off his hat and gloves and ran his fingers through his now-short hair, then made the sign of the cross and stepped into the parlor. Logs blazed in the fireplace and the air was warmer, but he caught the fresh-bread smell of starvation.

Emily was reclining on the green leather couch to his right, on the other side of the room from the windows, and Keeper lay beside it. Curzon didn't let his expression change—but Emily's face was pale and haggard, the bones of her skull prominent under her skin, her right hand dangling loose over the arm of the couch to touch Keeper's head. She shifted slightly and turned toward him.

Her eyes widened, and in that moment he was able to recognize the young woman who had held a gun on him, pulled him up out of a deadly sinkhole, and twice accompanied him on visits to the temple of a pagan goddess.

"Alcuin," she said, and her voice was faint but clear. "Anne," she added with certainty, and he nodded. "Branwell died," she went on, "did you know?"

"Yes."

"The old debt," she said, and had to catch her breath to go on, "is being paid off. The subtler ghosts."

After a few seconds Curzon opened his mouth to speak, but she waved her fingers and he waited.

"Already," she said, "this is dreadfully hard on Anne. Branwell—" She paused to cough.

Again Curzon waited her out; he was sweating, and took off his coat and laid it with his hat and gloves on a chair. "Branwell," she went on at last, "died well—he renounced his—Northangerland— and on his last day . . ." She paused to take several shallow breaths. "In his last hour, in the final delirium"—she caught her breath and

smiled—"he believed Maria appeared to him, at last—to lead his soul—to its reward."

"That was merciful," allowed Curzon. He added, "You managed to save him after all."

"I was always my brother's keeper."

Curzon realized that it was a tiring effort for her to hold her head turned toward him, and he stepped farther into the room.

She laid her head back, watching him. "You still," she said, "owe me a fact."

He spread his hands.

She made a visible effort to inhale. "I didn't lead you to Minerva."

"No," Curzon said. "I didn't know your family was on such *close terms* with her. She was the adversary of my kind—of inbalance, perversion—long before the Romans came to England. I knew she would see what I was, but I hoped my eyepatch, and the fact that I came to her for help, would serve as . . ."

"An olive branch."

"Yes—though it turned out not to matter, since you were with me." He pulled out a chair from beside the table and sat down. "The second time, last year, was easier—by then I had cut out my eye, in penance."

"Penance," she whispered. "How have you reconciled"—she said, and went on after taking a shallow breath—"being a Catholic—a Christian of sorts . . ." She waved her hand impatiently, then said, "'Thou shalt have no other gods before Me'?"

"I didn't worship her!"

Again she managed to coax a smile to her wasted face. "You knelt."

"To throw the bones! In any case, I've confessed it since."

"I envy you," she said, "two things." Her pinched nostrils flared as she took a breath. "That sacrament of yours—Confession. The assurance that your . . . sins are indeed forgiven."

Her wrinkled eyelids closed, and after nearly a minute he concluded that she had fallen asleep, and he began to get to his feet to go to the kitchen and talk to Anne.

But Emily opened her eyes, and she was clearly still alert.

"The second thing you envy me for?" Curzon asked.

"Your face-to-face look . . . at the goddess Minerva."

"It nearly killed me."

She flipped her fingers dismissively. "Of course. How could it not, if—genuine?" She rolled her eyes to look toward the window behind him. "Do you repent," she whispered, "of having consulted her?"

Curzon stared at the pale, hollow-cheeked face in front of him, and thought of the tanned, vigorous young woman who had walked so many miles on the moors with him. "I don't know," he said at last. "Do you?"

"It led to Branwell's exorcism—redemption." She started to lift her hand, then let it drop and just impatiently blinked away tears. "I don't know either! Did we—declare allegiance? To her? Our eternal lot—serving a straw effigy—in a *mundus loci*?"

"No, Emily." He reached out and took her cold, bony fingers in his hand. "You incinerated your blood promissory note in the fairy cave, and sacrificed your second novel. You completed the task she set you. Your connection with Minerva is concluded, with these in-effect 'backward mutters of dissevering prayer.'"

"You quote Milton, a Protestant!" She closed her eyes again, then paraphrased the next line of Milton's *Comus*: "To free the lady that sits here . . . in stony fetters . . . fixed and motionless."

Curzon didn't let go of her fingers.

"It cured the illness," she went on, "in more lands than this—I think."

"True. The Obliques in England, the Schrags in Germany, the Ferdes in Hungary—all impotent now and disbanded. Revolutions all over Europe, as the old powers are tumbling one after another."

She pulled her hand free of his and raised one eyebrow. "My . . . second novel?"

Curzon felt his face reddening. "I, er, employed a solicitor to keep track of your family's welfare. I hadn't meant for him to intrude on . . . secrets and pseudonyms."

"Ah?"

"But—I confess I've read *Wuthering Heights*, and found it as strong and unrelenting as its author. I saw Welsh in the character of Heathcliff. I hope there was nothing of me, as well, in that character."

"Oh—perhaps appearance, and manner." She began coughing, and it was nearly a minute before she gasped and was able to speak. "I didn't like you much at first."

She lifted her fingers from Keeper's head for a moment. "Do you," she asked, "still travel with . . . a dioscuri?"

He cocked his head. "Yes. It's still useful against plain robbers."

"New?"

"No. It's the one you gave back to me, the one I used when we fought off the werewolves in the ravine."

"Can I have it?"

He was puzzled, and wondered if she had fallen into delirium and imagined that there were still werewolves to defend against. But, "Of course," he said, and stepped to the other chair to fumble in his coat pocket.

He straightened and returned to his chair, and after a moment's hesitation laid the sheathed knife on the couch beside her.

She moved her hand to touch the leather-bound grip. "I want to be buried with it," she said. "Show which side I'm on."

The breath caught in his throat, but he said clearly, "There'll be no doubt on that score."

She closed her eyes. "Go now. I wouldn't have you see me die."

Curzon stood up and lifted his coat and hat and gloves from the table. "Goodbye, Emily. You've—"

When he could go no further, she managed a nod. "I know, Alcuin. You too. Go."

Keeper stood up from beside the couch and walked over to Curzon, and lifted one big paw to touch the man's hand. Curzon ruffled the dog's head, and it walked back to lie down beside the couch. Curzon nodded and stepped out of the room into the cold hall.

Anne was standing by the kitchen doorway, and he walked to her. "I'm staying at the Black Bull," he told her quietly. She nodded, and he turned to face the long hall and the front door, but he paused. "*The Tenant of Wildfell Hall*," he said over his shoulder, "and *Jane Eyre*, are noble books."

He walked to the front door without looking back, and opened it and stepped outside. Slowly he put on his coat and hat and gloves, then walked down the steps and away from the Brontë parsonage for the last time.

Emily insisted on climbing the stairs to her room without aid, though it took her nearly ten minutes, and Charlotte had to help her

put on her nightgown and lift her thin legs into the bed. The next morning Emily made her slow, careful way downstairs, stopping at the landing for a while to catch her breath. At the kitchen table, while her father and Anne and Charlotte ate their oatmeal porridge, Emily managed to drink a cup of weak tea. She could see that they were already grieving at the imminent loss of her, and she especially pitied her father and Charlotte, for she knew Anne was soon to follow her.

Three deaths, as penalty payment.

Branwell had already paid.

For weeks Charlotte had been pleading with Emily to allow a doctor to see her, and Emily had been adamant in refusing it. Curzon had long ago explained it to Charlotte—*Subtler ones attach to you, and take your breath and vitality by degrees.* What a waste of everyone's time, Emily thought, and what vainly raised hopes, to ask a doctor to diagnose that!

But Charlotte had never truly believed it. She had not, after all, left blood in the fairy cave.

Emily set down her cup, then braced one hand on Keeper's shoulder to get up out of her chair.

She mustered her breath and said, "I believe I'll...do some sewing in the...parlor."

She was bleakly pleased to see that her father and sisters had learned not to offer to help her. She traversed the hall and rounded the parlor doorway, and after two stumbling steps slumped onto the couch, panting rapidly. Charlotte joined her a few minutes later and sat at the table; she busied herself with writing a letter, but often cast furtive, anxious glances at Emily.

Emily soon dropped her sewing and slept, fitfully. She dreamed that she was lost and dying among uncaring strangers, but when she awoke some hours later she found that Charlotte had ventured out into the wind and snow and found a sprig of heather to bring to her; it was now thawed after having been frozen, but its purple color was still visible. Emily thanked her sincerely and lay back on the couch, grateful to be dying in her own home, with her father and sisters close by.

"Say I may send for the doctor!" Charlotte pleaded.

Emily smiled at her. "Yes," she whispered, for it was far, far too late now. "Only wait a few minutes."

Even speaking that much had made her dizzy, and she wasn't sure if she were lying down or sitting propped against the arm of the couch.

She reached down to touch Keeper's head, and as she stroked his ears she felt a warm canine tongue lick her hand. Puzzled, she tilted her head to look down, and saw two bullmastiffs beside the couch— standing beside Keeper, entirely solid, she recognized the ghost Keeper.

She looked up and saw that a young woman was standing in the doorway—she was slim and dark-haired and smiling, wearing an unseasonably light linen dress. Though Emily had last seen the woman as an eleven-year-old girl, she recognized her.

Emily whispered, "Maria!" and stood up, her exhaustion and illness forgotten. She walked quickly to the doorway and took Maria's warm outstretched hand. Beyond Maria the front door was open, and through it Emily saw green trees and grass bending in a breeze.

Branwell, Elizabeth? Their mother?

She took a step forward beside her eldest sister, but paused and looked back. Her father and Anne and Charlotte didn't look toward her. The wasted body that had been her own was slumped on the couch, with Keeper standing alongside, pawing at the limply dangling hand.

"Keeper," she whispered, and her dog turned his great head and looked directly at her. "Stay," she said, "for now."

Keeper's mournful gaze shifted from her to Maria and their grandfather's dog, and back, and for a moment his tail wagged hesitantly before he turned again to the body on the couch.

Still holding Maria's hand, with the dog trotting alongside, Emily Brontë walked gladly forward through the open doorway.